Play Games With Me

Recipes for Romance: Book Two

by

Suzie Peters

GWL PUBLISHING

GWL Publishing
Forum House
Sterling Road
Chichester PO19 7DN

www.gwlpublishing.co.uk

Dedication

For S.

Chapter One

Petra

I check my watch. It's five-thirty. I'm due at Rosa's in fifteen minutes and I really don't want to be late. I close the front door and pull my camera bag firmly onto my shoulder, setting off down the street. The walk should only take ten minutes, so I'm sure I'll be fine.

I clench and unclench my fists a few times as I walk. I'm excited and nervous at the same time. I'm excited because I love this kind of work. I love taking candid pictures, catching an atmosphere, creating something a little different. I'm nervous because I've never met the three owners of the restaurant, and I'm not great with strangers. I never have been. Still, I know at least one person who's gonna be there: Ali.

She's the one who commissioned me to take these photographs. She might not own the place, but she's been refurbishing it for the owners and, when I met up with her a couple of weeks ago to discuss her requirements, we got along really well. We were meant to just have a brief discussion over coffee at her hotel, but that turned into dinner and drinks. She's lovely – really lovely. She was upset, partly because she was feeling homesick for London, and also because she was having a hard time with one of the owners… a guy called Sam, who's the head chef, and who was being a bit of a jerk, from what she told me. That made me kinda nervous about meeting him, but when we spoke on the phone last week to finalize our arrangements, she sounded a lot more cheerful. She was a little coy about what was going on, but it wouldn't surprise me in the least if they've fallen for each other. I've got no idea what he's like, but she's beautiful. Any guy would be mad not to want her.

I'm sure I'll find out all about it later – assuming we get the chance to talk. Or maybe I'll just get to watch them together and work it out for myself, while I'm busy blending into the background. It's what I do best, usually in the hope that no-one will notice me. Not that many people do these days. Adrian saw to that. *Damn*… I haven't thought about him for ages and there he is, just when I need him the least – invading my head, making me feel insecure and self-conscious. Great.

I suppose it was inevitable I'd think about him tonight. He used to take me to Rosa's quite a lot – at least twice a week. That was years ago though, when it was run by a husband and wife – the parents of the current owners, so Ali informs me. They've evidently retired to Florida and left the restaurant to their sons, who've now renovated it, with Ali's expert guidance, and are re-opening tonight – an event for which I've been commissioned to take promotional photographs. I remember I used to talk to Rosa Moreno most times we went there. She ran the restaurant itself, while her husband worked in the kitchen. I was aware she had sons, because she always talked about them with such pride, but I thought there were only two – who were training to be chefs with their father.

Adrian loved this place – and so did I. The decor might have been dated but the food was always great. That's one of the reasons we ate there so often; until Adrian's accusations got too much. There are only so many times you can take being accused of sleeping with a guy, just because he's glanced up from his veal parmigiana and happens to have looked in your direction.

I'd thought at the time that, if we ate out less, I might lose some of the weight I'd been piling on, but Adrian insisted on doing the shopping, and the cooking… and my weight kept creeping up. In the end I worked out what he was doing. He was fattening me up. He was making me less attractive to other men. The problem was, that still didn't stop him from accusing me of sleeping with every man who came into my life: clients, models – especially models – repairmen, even the pizza delivery guy. His jealousy was oppressive. It was too oppressive.

The restaurant's just up ahead now and I slow down to catch my breath. I try and walk as much as I can these days, just to get some exercise. I don't like going to the gym, and I'm really not good with routine, but I know I need to do something to keep fit – well, to get fit in the first place, to be honest. I've managed to lose some of the weight in the four years since Adrian left, but I'm still not the size six I used to be before I met him. I'm stuck at a size ten.

I'm starting to regret my high-heeled boots now, and how I'm going to get through the next few hours in them is another matter, but as I stand and look at the exterior of the restaurant, I forget all about the discomfort. It's beautiful. Before, it was all dark wood and slightly garish lettering. Now, the paintwork is dark gray, the windows are plain glass – so you can see inside to the subtly lit interior – and there are two trimmed bay trees either side of the door. It's understated and refined. I like it a lot.

I take a deep breath, and reach inside my open-necked blouse for the necklace I wear every single day, clutching the silver letter 'A' between my thumb and forefinger and pressing it against my lips. "Wish me luck, baby," I whisper, then let it drop back down and check I'm not showing too much cleavage before I push on the door and let myself in.

I stand just inside and take in the changes. It looks so different. All the dark wood has gone. The tables are covered with white linen cloths and surrounded by gray leather high-backed chairs. The walls are painted white and dotted with beautiful framed pictures. From here, I can't tell exactly what they're all of, but the ones I can see are really lovely. The back wall is the most noticeable feature: a large photograph of a magical-looking cliff-side town at night covers the entire expanse, but it's been broken up by white vertical lines. It's a truly stunning effect.

"Petra?" Ali appears from a corridor at the back of the restaurant. "I'm so sorry. I should have been here to meet you." She comes toward me, making her way between the tables. She's as beautiful as her surroundings. She's got very light blonde hair, which I know is long and curly, but tonight she's wearing it in a loose up-do, and rather than the jeans that she wore at our meeting, she's got on a really stylish deep red dress, which shows off her slim figure. Ordinarily, she'd be the kind of woman I'd love to hate – because she's just so perfect – except I think it's impossible to hate Ali. She's way too nice.

"It's fine." I step forward and she hugs me. "I've just been admiring your handiwork. It's remarkable."

She blushes. "Oh… thank you."

"I can't believe how different it looks."

"Of course. I forgot, you used to come here, didn't you?"

"In a previous life, yes. It's so much better now."

Her blush deepens and she checks her watch – either because she's embarrassed by my compliments, and is looking for a distraction, or because she's genuinely concerned that time's moving on and the first guests are probably due to arrive soon.

"I could do with getting some light readings," I say to her. "Do you mind if I dump my bag behind the bar and just wander a little?"

"Feel free." She steps out of the way so I can move further into the restaurant. "I really need to get on anyway. I've got to find Rob. He's in the office, giving the waiting staff a last-minute pep-talk, but he should be out here by now…"

"You carry on," I say. "Just ignore me."

"I'd never do that," she says, moving toward the corridor again.

"Ah, but that's the whole point," I remark. "If I'm visible, I'm not doing my job properly."

"If you need anything, just let me know," she calls over her shoulder, before disappearing again.

I can hear voices coming from the back of the restaurant – the kitchens I guess, and I wonder, just for a moment, how nervous they all are. Still, I've got my own nerves to deal with. I go over to the bar, the front of which is covered by what appears to be a huge sheet of perspex, with a soft white light behind it. It's another nice feature that Ali's added. I open my camera bag, retrieve my Canon, put on the zoom lens and stow the bag in the corner – out of the way, hopefully – and I take a look around. The lighting is quite subtle in here and it's gonna be a challenge to get the kind of shots I know they want, but I'm always ready for a challenge – at least professionally.

Under the bar are some matches and I grab a box and go to one of the tables in the back corner of the restaurant and light the candle in the centre, stowing the matches in my jacket pocket. I want to take a few micro images of the table setting. They'll be useful for Ali anyway, but they'll also help me to get the camera settings right.

I'm staring through the view finder when I hear the sound of murmuring voices and am aware of a group of people coming into the restaurant from the corridor. They head straight for the bar, seemingly unaware of me, and I ignore them and carry on with what I'm doing.

"I don't know what you mean. I'd never do such a thing." I hear a deep male, kinda sexy-sounding voice, coming from the corridor, but continue taking my shots. I've gotta try and get this right before the guests arrive.

"Yes you would – and we both know it," Ali replies, laughing. "Just try and behave, for one night. Please?"

"Okay. I'll try."

I'm currently crouched on the floor, a few feet from the table, focusing on trying to get the depth of field right. I check the image I've just taken on the screen at the back of the camera. It's not quite right and I make a couple of adjustments and try again, conscious now that someone is standing right beside me.

"Two seconds," I say, assuming I must be in their way.

"No problem." That's Ali's voice, so I take the shot and look up at her. "I was just going to introduce you to Rob," she adds, and moves to one side, just as I'm getting to my feet to be faced by a pair of dark, smoldering eyes. At this precise moment, I'm grateful that I always wear my camera strapped around my neck, because I've just dropped it, and I'm fairly sure my mouth's fallen open as well… and my tongue's probably hanging out too. God, I hope not. That would be so embarrassing. Oh Lord… He's gorgeous. Utterly and completely gorgeous. He's tall – very tall – with short, dark hair that's spiked on top, light stubble, a square jaw and full lips. He's wearing a black shirt that shows he's got very broad shoulders, muscular arms, and a perfectly formed chest.

I don't know how long we've been standing here while I study him, but I really should say something. I'm saved the trouble by him taking a slight step forward.

"Hi," he says and I recognize the deep sexy voice I heard a few moments ago. Dear God. He's the complete package. Tall, dark, handsome, sexy… total fantasy material. Except this isn't a fantasy. He's real, and he's standing right in front of me.

"Hello." I whisper and manage to hold out my hand. He takes it and, not taking his eyes from mine, he raises it to his lips, kissing my fingers. My legs turn to jelly, my stomach flips, and I grab hold of the nearest chair to steady myself. Did he really just do that?

"Rob, this is Petra Miller," Ali says, and I'm grateful to her for saying something, being as my vocal chords seem to have temporarily malfunctioned.

"Petra," he murmurs, still holding my hand. My name on his lips sounds like stardust falling from the sky. He focuses for a moment on my mouth, then my eyes and then my hair, before smiling. "You look like an angel," he says.

I stare at him. An angel… me? Oh. I get it now. He's flirting, and I can't help but smirk. "An angel in torn jeans and a leather jacket?" I counter.

"Yeah," he says, looking a little quizzical.

"Well," I reply, pulling my hand away, "I hope you like your angels with attitude."

He smirks himself and his eyes light up, and maybe widen, just a fraction, before he moves a little closer. "Oh, yeah. That's my favorite kind of angel," he whispers.

Rob

"Has everyone got it?" I ask, looking around the collected faces before me in my office. They all nod, but I wish they'd look a little more convinced. "Sure?" I say. Again they nod. "If you have any problems, come find me or Ali. I'd rather you asked than kept quiet." We've been retraining the restaurant staff for the last few days, and I'm fairly sure they know what they're doing, but they seem nervous. I guess that's understandable. They know my brothers and I have a lot riding on this. We've spent a lot of money on the refurbishment, and now the opening is here, we're all feeling pretty anxious – although I'm trying real hard not to let it show.

There's a quiet knock on the door, it opens and Ali steps inside.

"Rob?" she says quietly. Everyone turns to look at her. "Have you seen the time?"

I check my watch. "Shit." Where did that last half hour go? "Okay, everyone. Let's get out there."

Ali stands to one side and lets the others pass, waiting for me.

"Okay?" she asks, stopping me by the doorway.

"Yeah," I whisper. "I didn't realize time had run away with me quite that much, but we're about as ready as we're ever gonna be."

"Calm down," she says, encouragingly. "Everything will be just fine. I promise."

She must sense my nerves.

"Yeah. I know. You've done all this before, haven't you?"

"Just once or twice. But I do understand that it's harder for you. It's your restaurant. Well, yours, and Sam's and Ed's."

"How are they?" I ask, nodding toward the kitchen doors opposite.

"I've got no idea. I haven't been in there."

"Probably for the best," I reply, smiling.

We start down the corridor toward the restaurant. The six wait staff are all gathered by the bar, chatting among themselves. I deliberately chose our most experienced employees for tonight. We can't afford to get this wrong.

Ali stops me just as we get to the end of the corridor.

"Do you think there's any chance you could avoid flirting too much tonight?" she asks, a smile lighting up her face. It's at times like this I really understand why my big brother Sam is so in love with her. He may not have done very much about it yet, but I completely understand his feelings. She's beautiful... really beautiful. And if he ever does get around to getting it right with her, and she even half returns his feelings, he's gonna be one lucky son-of-a-bitch.

"I don't know what you mean," I reply, grinning back at her. "I'd never do such a thing." We both know I flirted like mad with her when she first came here all those weeks ago, before we employed her to refurbish the place and she wanted to see us without us putting on a show for her. Man did I put on a show… and lived to regret it when she revealed her true identity. She took it well though, and we've become friends.

"Yes you would – and we both know it," Ali replies, laughing at me now. "Just try and behave, for one night. Please?"

"Okay. I'll try." I fake a pout and we go out into the restaurant.

She grabs my arm and lowers her voice. "We've just got time for me to introduce you to Petra," she whispers. This is the photographer she told us all about, the one who's gonna be taking some publicity shots for us tonight. "She looks busy, but…" Ali leads me over to the back corner of the restaurant between the tables. Crouched down on the floor I can see someone with a thick mane of dark hair, her shoulders encased in a black leather jacket. She's got a camera held to her face, so that's pretty much all I can see. Ali stops a couple of feet away from her and waits.

"Two seconds." I can just about hear Petra's voice and I'm reminded of how sexy she sounded on the phone when she called a while back to speak to Ali.

"No problem," Ali replies. "I was just going to introduce you to Rob."

Petra finishes up and, moving the camera away from her face, she gets to her feet. My mouth dries and my chest feels like someone dropped a lead weight onto it. How the fuck am I supposed to breathe now? She's perfect. She's completely perfect. Okay, so she's maybe a little tall, but who cares? Other than that, she's perfect. I guess she's around five foot eleven, but I'm six-two, so that's fine. And she's curvy, which his great because I'm really not that keen on skinny women. She's also perfectly proportioned. Her full, large breasts are straining slightly against her white blouse, making it gape slightly between the buttons. I can see a tantalizing hint of white lace beneath just before her camera drops from her hands and covers the view. Letting my eyes roam downwards, I take in her rounded hips and the ripped jeans that encase her shapely thighs, as well as the sexy high heeled black boots. I guess I can revise my earlier perspective. Take the heels off – although I'd really rather not – and she'd be around five foot seven – which makes her exactly what I thought she was already: perfect.

I manage to raise my eyes back to her face again. She's got light olive, absolutely flawless skin, and sparkling gray eyes, and her lips are full, slightly pouting, and really kissable.

I'm suddenly aware that I've been standing here staring at her and that I really should say something before I stumble over my own tongue.

"Hi." I mutter, moving slightly closer to her. Is that really the best I can do?

"Hello," she whispers and the sound of her voice reverberates straight to my cock. She holds out her hand but I don't want to just shake with her, and I remember something my dad used to do to my mom, which always used to make her smile. I take her hand in mine and, while keeping my eyes fixed on hers, I raise it to my lips and very gently kiss her fingers. The contact is electrifying – like nothing else I've ever felt before. Weirdly, she grabs hold of the back of the chair beside her, staring at me, but unlike my mom, she doesn't smile. I'm not sure that was the reaction I was looking for.

"Rob, this is Petra Miller," Ali says, bringing me back to my senses – well kind of.

"Petra," I murmur, still holding her hand. Her name suits her. It's exotic and erotic – and there's something about her that exudes both of those qualities.

I gaze at her lips, wishing I could lean forward and kiss them, then move my attention to her sparkling eyes, and then her hair, which flows in shiny black ringlets over and around her shoulders. It's wild, untamed and long enough to hang below her breasts. She's standing right beneath one of the down lighters and it gives her a kind of glow – a kind of angelic aura. "You look like an angel," I say quietly, voicing my thoughts.

She stares at me for a moment, looking a little confused, and then a slight smirk appears on her face. "An angel in torn jeans and a leather jacket?" she replies. I wonder if she thinks I'm flirting. I'm not. I'm being serious. Sappy, yeah… but serious.

"Yeah," I say. I hope she gets it. I hope she understands that, to me, she's an angel. A perfect angel.

Her smirk becomes a smile, but she pulls her hand away from mine. "Well, I hope you like your angels with attitude."

My cock hardens to steel, and I can't help but smirk myself, before I move just a fraction closer to her. "Oh, yeah," I whisper. "That's my favorite kind of angel."

Her smile widens, her mouth opens and I catch sight of her tongue. Fuck, she's hot.

"Rob," Ali says, interrupting the steamy direction my thoughts having been traveling since the moment I first set eyes on Petra.

I reluctantly turn toward her. "Yeah?"

"Customers."

Fuck.

"Go do your job," she urges, pushing me toward the front of the restaurant.

"I'm going." I quickly turn back to Petra. "See you later?" I say to her. She nods, just once, and that's all I need… for now.

I always knew tonight was gonna be busy, but it's surpassed even my expectations. We're about three hours in, and it's been crazy. I've already taken bookings for the next six weeks or so, and I've had to set up a cancellation list, which is a first for us. I've hardly had two seconds to look at Petra, let alone talk to her, but I'm aware of her all the time. And that's weird, because she's kind of invisible. She real unobtrusive, melting into the background, like she belongs here, and I really like that idea.

At around nine-thirty, I realize she hasn't had anything to drink all evening and, while I'm behind the bar, covering for Greg so he can take a quick break, I manage to attract her attention and call her over.

"Red or white?" I say simply.

"Sorry?" she replies.

"Wine… red or white. You haven't had anything to drink all night."

"Oh. Um… just water, thanks. I need a completely clear head."

"Okay. Water it is." I grab a highball, fill it with ice, add a couple of slices of lime, and a few sprigs of fresh mint, and pour over the San Pellegrino, handing it across to her.

"Thank you," she says, giving me a beautiful smile.

"You're welcome."

"It's going well," she says, taking a small sip.

"Yeah, it is."

All of a sudden, a guy near the back of the restaurant starts clapping and I glance over Petra's shoulder to see what's going on, a smile spreading across my lips. Sam and Ed are standing by the entrance to the corridor that leads to the kitchen, looking – frankly – embarrassed, as the whole restaurant explodes into spontaneous applause.

"What's going on?" Petra says, leaning forward.

I look back at her, glimpsing her sublime cleavage, and it's all I can do not to groan – loudly.

"My brothers," I reply, nodding toward them. She turns, then looks back at me again.

"They're the chefs, right?"

"Yeah. They never normally come out here, but I guess Ali talked them into it. I know she was gonna try." She told me about this earlier today. I warned her she probably wouldn't get them to agree, but I guess she's more persuasive than I thought… especially with Sam.

Slowly, everyone starts to settle down again, resuming their seats, although I notice a couple of people go over and shake Sam and Ed by the hand. It's a nice touch and I'm pleased for them. I always make sure to pass on the praise we get from customers, but it's good for them to see the appreciation for their efforts first hand.

Sam and Ed return to the kitchen just as Greg comes back from his break and I go around the other side of the bar.

"I'd better get back to work," Petra says. She looks a little flushed, but I guess it's warm in here.

"Oh… okay." I'd been hoping we'd have a few minutes to talk, but that's alright… it can wait until the end of the evening.

"Thanks for the drink."

"Just let Greg know if you want anything else," I tell her. "Or find me."

"Okay."

She gives me another smile and moves further back into the restaurant. I lean against the bar and watch her as she passes between the tables, her hips swaying gently. Looking at that perfect ass in those tight jeans, I think I'd give away my share in this place for one night with her. Except I already know one night won't be enough. One lifetime won't be enough. I'm still staring at her, thinking about what that means to a guy who's always specialized in one night stands, when the sound of the front door opening brings me back to reality. I can think that through later. Right now, it's time to work…

I turn and switch on the smile, to be faced by four women.

"Good evening, ladies," I say.

One of them steps forward – well, to be more precise, she elbows her way forward, flashing her teeth and cleavage in my direction. "We've booked a table," she simpers. She's pretty, tall, blonde, stacked. Apart from the hair color, I'd say she'd normally be my type… until about three hours ago, that is.

"Okay. What name?" I ask.

"Barnes. Alexa Barnes."

I scan my iPad, find their reservation and look up again. "Great. If you'd like to follow me?"

As I turn, I notice Ali standing at the entrance to the corridor. She raises an eyebrow, a slight smirk on her face and I smile back at her before she disappears again. I know what she's thinking. I don't blame her, but I've got no intention of flirting… not with anyone but Petra, anyway. Since meeting her. I'm just not interested in anyone else; it's like every other woman has just faded into insignificance.

I guide the four women through to table eleven, which is at the rear of the restaurant, help them to their seats, and hand out their menus.

"Ria will be looking after you this evening," I tell them and go to move away.

The one called Alexa reaches out and grabs my arm. "You mean we won't be getting your personal attention," she says.

"Of course you will." What else can I say? "If you need anything, just let me know." I pull my arm away as gently as I can.

"Anything at all?" She looks up at me through her thick eyelashes.

I don't reply this time. Instead, I just give her a smile. Ordinarily, I would have probably told her she could have anything she wanted – and I'd have meant it. Now I just want to tell her I'm not interested and I'm not available. I can't do that politely, so the smile seems like a good compromise.

We're officially closed now, but the table of four women are taking their time over coffee, as are a couple of other diners. Petra's been busy all evening and we haven't had any further chance to talk. As it's gotten quieter in here, I've noticed her taking a few shots of the pictures on the wall… the ones of Positano. She keeps stopping and looking at them, like she's intrigued. I'd like to go over and explain what they are – that our parents are from there and that Ali went out of her way to source the images – but I can't, not until I'm officially off duty anyway. Right now, she's sitting at the bar, talking to Ali, while the rest of us are clearing down tables, although I'm slowly letting the wait staff go, as the place gets quieter. Eventually, there's just me, Ria, Ali and Petra left.

Finally, Alexa Barnes asks for their check and, trying not to noticeably heave a sigh of relief, I take it over myself. Ria's dealing with the other couple, who are just paying themselves. When Alexa Barnes hands me her credit card, she slips a piece of paper into my hand at the same time. I don't react. I just slide it into my pocket and process her payment, returning her card to her. I show them to the door and, as we pass the bar, she puts her hand on my arm again, pulling me back slightly. "Call me," she whispers. Again, I don't make any response.

"I hope you all had a great evening," I say, loud enough for her friends to hear.

"We did," one of the others replies, turning around. "It's really lovely in here now."

"Thank you," I reply, ushering them out the door, more than relieved to see the back of them.

I go back inside, looking forward to having a few minutes to talk to Petra, and maybe taking the chance to persuade her to stay and share a drink with us.

"Rob?" Ria calls me from the back of the restaurant.

"Yeah."

"I've got a problem."

So much for a few minutes with Petra… I go over and Ria explains that her iPad hasn't recorded any of the drinks that were ordered by the couple she's attending to. They've been honest enough to point out that their check is wrong, and they're quite right – there are no drinks charged. I take Ria's iPad and go back through the order and, sure enough, there's nothing showing. The couple assure me they both had a cocktail before eating, then shared a bottle of Pinot Grigio, and the guy had a Jack Daniels with his coffee. I hope to God neither of them is driving…

"It's fine," I tell them. "It's on the house. It's our mistake."

"Seriously?" the guy says, clearly surprised.

"Of course." I smile at him.

"But that's gotta be seventy bucks," he replies.

"Like I say… it's on the house." It hasn't actually cost us seventy bucks, but he's about right with what we would have charged him.

"Well, thanks," he says, holding out his hand to me as he gets to his feet.

I shake his hand and give Ria back her iPad at the same time.

"Our pleasure, sir." I hold his wife's chair while she gets up. "Would you like me to get you a cab?" It seems wise to offer, in the circumstances.

"No, it's fine. We only live a block away. We're gonna walk."

Thank fuck for that…

Ria shows them out while I finish clearing their table.

"Is that coming out of my salary?" she asks, walking back to me. She sounds really worried.

"No." I turn to face her. "You know that's not how we operate, Ria. It was a mistake, that's all."

"I'm sure I recorded it," she adds, although she doesn't sound that convinced.

"Is there a problem?" Ali comes over.

"I'm not sure." I hand her Ria's iPad and explain what's happened.

"Did anyone else have a problem tonight?" Ali asks.

"No," I reply.

"Okay. Well, we'll see if it happens again and, if not we'll just have to assume it's a glitch."

What she means is we'll just have to assume Ria got it wrong, but she's too kind to say that.

"I'm sorry," Ria says.

"It's fine." I put my hand on her shoulder. "It's a few drinks. Nobody died. Besides, they're gonna tell all their friends what nice guys we are. It'll probably do us good in the long run."

She smiles, just lightly, although I know she'll feel bad about it.

"Go on… you get off home," I say. "You've done really well tonight."

"Are you sure?"

She'd dead on her feet. "Yeah. I'm sure. I'll see you on Monday."

I think we're all real glad that tomorrow's Sunday and we've got a policy of closing on Sundays. It's something our dad started when he first opened the restaurant thirty years ago. He was always real strict about the hours he was prepared to work. He decided to open for lunch, then close again at three and have a couple of hours off, before the evening session. And on Sundays, he chose to remain closed all day.

Even when all our competitors started to stay open all day, seven days a week, he resisted. Dad wanted to have at least one day he could spend with his family, and although we don't always do much family stuff anymore, it's nice to have one day to ourselves.

Ria pulls off her black apron and makes her way toward the corridor, to go out through the back door in the kitchen, just as I turn and find that the rest of the place is empty, other than Ali, who's still standing right in front of me. Petra has gone already.

Chapter Two

Petra

So far, the evening has been going really well. I've got some amazing pictures of the diners, the staff, and the restaurant itself. I think I've managed to capture the atmosphere, which is the hardest part really.

Rob's been present the whole time. He's kinda hard to miss. Well, being as tall as he is, it's difficult to ignore him, but it's a bit like I can feel his presence, as well as being able to see him. It's an odd sensation and not one I'm familiar with.

Half way through the evening, he made a point of calling me over to the bar and offering me a glass of wine. As much as I'd have liked to say yes, I declined and had water instead. I really need a clear head for this job, especially when it's so warm in here. Well, I think it is anyway… although I've noticed that my temperature goes up by several degrees whenever Rob's close. He has that effect.

I got my first glimpse of his brothers then too. One of them looks almost identical to Rob, but with longer hair. The other one is taller, maybe a little darker. They came out into the restaurant for a few minutes, and the whole place erupted into applause. It was quite something. Rob smiled over at his brothers when that happened. He seemed… proud, I guess. It was nice.

When he came around the bar he seemed to want to talk and, while I'd have liked to sit with him, I'd have preferred it to be somewhere quieter. Somewhere we could have a real conversation. Oh, who am

I kidding? Yeah, I wanna be somewhere quiet with him, but I don't want to talk. I'm not great at talking, and in any case, who needs words, when you've got a body like his? I want to find out what his lips feel like on mine. I want to rip the shirt from his back see if his chest is really as toned and hard as I imagine it's gonna be. I want feel his touch, and I know I'm wet just thinking about it. I don't want to talk at all. I want to moan, scream and cry out his name as he makes me come, over and over…

I knew I was blushing and made my excuses to get away before he realized what was going through my mind.

Besides, he needed to get back to work, being as a group of women had just arrived. They were a bit loud and one of them was really flirty with Rob. I noticed he was smiling at her and I felt the stab of disappointment deep inside, right before I realized what an idiot I'd nearly made of myself. Rob's a flirt. I worked that out when he came over at the beginning of the evening and gave me that bullshit line about me looking like an angel; and him offering me a drink was just him being polite. There was nothing more to it than that. Just because I think he's a walking god doesn't mean he's gonna feel the same way about me… why the hell would he?

"You okay?" Ali's standing right beside me as I look up at the wall of pictures.

"I'm fine," I lie. I'm anything but fine. Ideally, I'd really like to leave, rather than have to watch another half hour or so of those damn women flirting with Rob, but I'm booked to stay here until eleven thirty.

"Sure?" she asks.

"Hmm." I nod. It's the best I can manage at the moment.

"They'll be gone soon," she says, indicating the diners at the back of the restaurant. "Then we can relax."

"It's been a long evening." I find my voice again.

"How are your feet?" she asks.

"Killing me?" I smile. "I wish I'd gone for flat shoes now."

"Me too."

We lean into each other in sisterly empathy.

"Come over to the bar," she says. "You can sit for a minute."

"You've still got customers though…"

"Don't worry about it."

I follow her over and we both take a seat at the bar. The barman, Greg, I think his name was, is about to leave, but Ali gets him to pour us both a glass of white wine first. We clink glasses and I take a long sip.

"God, that's good," I whisper.

Ali laughs. "There's nothing quite like that first drink at the end of a long shift."

"Actually, there's just nothing quite like that first drink," I joke.

"You have a point." She takes another sip. "How's it gone?" she asks.

"Good." I don't want to say any more. "But I'm not showing you any of the pictures," I tell her. "I'll send them through after I've edited them."

"Okay." She smiles at me. "I guess I'll just have to wait then."

"Yeah… you will." She turns and I notice her give a slight sigh.

"Thank God for that," she whispers.

"What?"

"They're going," she mutters.

"Who?"

"Both tables. The couple asked for their bill a few minutes ago, and Rob's just taking the group on table eleven theirs now." She sits up a little, as though gathering her strength. "Just a few more minutes… and we can collapse."

"And take our shoes off?"

She laughs. "That too."

I can't help myself… I glance around to where Rob's dealing with the table of four women. The tallest of them – the blonde who's been touching him all evening – hands over her credit card and I notice him slip something into his pocket. Dear God… she's just given him her number. I can't believe it. Do women actually do that? I guess so. What's worse is, he took it. He really took it.

I feel like even more of an idiot now for thinking about wanting a loser like him.

They get up and start toward the front of the restaurant, with Rob accompanying them. Well, God forbid he should leave them alone for five minutes…

As they're passing, blondie grabs hold of him, pulls him back and whispers something in his ear. He doesn't seem to respond, but asks them all if they've enjoyed their evening, before showing them to the door.

He's on his way back and now I'm dreading him coming over and wanting to talk again. Yeah, he's attractive. Well, he's gorgeous, actually, but a guy like that is the last thing I need in my life.

"Rob?" The waitress at the back of the restaurant calls him over and, as he walks back past us and goes over to her, I seize my chance.

"I'd better be going," I say to Ali.

"Oh. Okay. You could stay for another drink, if you like?"

"No, thanks. I'd really just like to get home, take these boots off and go to bed."

"I know the feeling." She smiles.

I jump down from the bar stool, go around behind the bar and grab my camera bag, stowing everything away again, before slinging it over my shoulder. Rob's engrossed with the waitress, and the last remaining couple at the back of the restaurant.

"I'll call you," Ali says, walking with me to the front door.

"Okay."

"We need to finalize the arrangements for next Sunday."

Shit. I'd forgotten about that. I'm gonna have to come back here again. Still, it's just the two chefs she wants me to photograph, so hopefully Rob won't even be here. "Yeah. Fine."

"Thanks for everything, Petra," she says, leaning forward and kissing my cheek.

"You're welcome, Ali." I really like her.

"You're not walking, are you?" she asks, concerned.

"Yeah. I only live a few minutes away. I'll be fine."

"Wait. I'll get someone to go with you. Rob won't be long…"

"No, it's really okay," I say, maybe just a little too quickly.

"You're sure?"

"Positive."

I'm more than positive.

Rob

"Where's Petra?" I ask Ali.

"She left, while you were dealing with Ria's problem," she says.

Damn. I'd really wanted to spend some more time with her, persuade her to stay for a drink with us, and then, try and talk her into maybe having dinner with me tomorrow. *Fuck it.*

I'm just wondering how I'm gonna go about contacting Petra again, when Sam and Ed appear from the kitchens. They've both taken off their chef's whites and are just in jeans and t-shirts, looking exhausted, if I'm honest.

"I'm gonna get a bottle of champagne," I say, putting my thoughts about Petra to one side for now at least and heading for the bar. "I think we need to celebrate."

"It was a good night," Sam replies.

The three of them go over to one of the tables in the middle of the restaurant and sit down, and I join them, bringing a bottle of chilled Veuve Cliquot and four glasses with me. I open it and pour out the foamy liquid, and we all raise our glasses.

"To Ali," I say, and she blushes, just like I knew she would.

"Hmm…" Sam replies. "To Ali, who wouldn't take any credit." He leans into her a little and I struggle to hide my smile. He's so in love it's pitiful. Endearing, but pitiful. I'm pleased for him. He needs this, and I think life owes the guy a break. He's had a fairly horrendous time for the last few years, thanks to his wife – well, ex-wife – Amber. Their marriage was doomed right from the start. Ed and I knew that, but Sam wasn't gonna listen to anything we had to say, so he married her anyway. I think he realized she was bad news within a few months, but he found out she was toxic when she started cheating on him. He threw her out about two years ago, and filed the divorce papers the next day. That's the kind of guy Sam is. Decisive. That's a good word for him. Domineering is another one… but that's a whole other story.

Looking at him now, there's no doubt about it, whatever he's got going with Ali, he deserves it. He deserves to be happy.

"Of course I wasn't going to take the credit," Ali replies and takes a sip of her champagne before putting her glass back on the table again.

"Why not?" Sam asks her. "You did all the work." He waves his arm around the restaurant. "You made this happen."

He's right. Without Ali, we'd never have achieved this transformation. Our restaurant was worn and out-dated, and now it's chic, stylish and modern.

"No." Ali shakes her head, looking at Sam. "I helped *you* make it happen." She sips her drink again, but keeps hold of her glass this time. "Besides, my work here is almost done. I'll be gone soon and you'll need to carry on without me." She looks up at all of us. "So you'd better get used to it." She's smiling, but the smile is a little half-hearted. I guess at least a part of her will be sorry to go home to England and I know we'll all miss her when she does. As for how Sam feels about that prospect, I can only hazard a guess.

"Rob," Ali continues, focusing on me, "I'll need to sit down with you on Monday and go through the advertising campaign."

"Okay."

"And I've arranged for Petra to come in next Sunday."

"*Next* Sunday." If she's gotta come back on a Sunday, I wonder why she's not coming in tomorrow. I wish she was…

"Yes. I figured you'd all be too tired to have your photographs taken tomorrow, but we're going to need some publicity shots of the three of you. I'll speak to her before next weekend and make sure she's up to speed."

It makes sense, I guess. I'd rather not have to wait a whole week to see her, but it's better than nothing. A few minutes ago, I wasn't entirely sure how I was gonna see her again, and now, I've got a chance.

"You'll be here though, right?" Sam asks her.

"Yes, I'll be here," she replies, "but I only allowed for her taking pictures of you and Ed. I just need to be sure she's okay with Rob being included, in terms of her schedule for the day."

Even if she isn't, and she's not expecting me, I'm gonna find a reason to be here.

"So, you're not going home yet? You're staying?" Jeez, Sam needs to cool it and stop sounding so desperate.

Ali looks up at him. "For a little while, yes. Didn't you read the contract at all?"

Sam shrugs his shoulders. "No. I think at the time I was probably too busy being an asshole to bother."

Ali smiles at that. I don't blame her. Sam was horrible to her for the first few weeks she was here. I'm amazed she put up with him. I wouldn't have done, and he's my brother. "Hmm…" She shakes her head. "Well, in the contract it says that I'll be here for two to three weeks after opening night, just to make sure everything runs smoothly, and to deal with things like this photography shoot. I know how difficult you chefs can be." I love that she makes fun of him like this. He needs it.

"Yeah. I'm glad you learned that one. At least you're not bringing that photographer in while we're trying to work. She'd get in the way."

"She can get in my way anytime she likes," I joke. I can think of all kinds of things she can do to get under my feet… well, just under me in general, really.

Ali laughs. "Ah, but Sam's different," she says, turning back to him. "I'd never bring someone into your kitchen who didn't belong there. I learned very early on that you don't appreciate outsiders."

"Only certain outsiders," Sam murmurs and leans into her again.

I think that's mine and Ed's cue to get the fuck out of here. I've already interrupted them a couple of times, most recently in the office when I'm fairly sure Sam was gonna kiss Ali. I spoke to Ali afterwards and she let me know I'd gotten in the way. So, I had a word with Sam, to apologize. He dropped a fairly large hint that my timing was unhelpful, to put it mildly.

"We'll be going," I say, giving Ed a nudge.

I'm not sure whether he understands why we're leaving, but he's so tired, he's not about to argue.

"You haven't finished your drinks." Ali nods toward our half-empty glasses.

"We're tired," Ed replies truthfully. "It's been a busy day."

"It certainly has," Ali says.

I get up and go around to the other side of the table and lean down, giving Ali a quick kiss on the cheek. "Thank you – for everything," I say quietly.

She blushes. "You're welcome," she replies, sweetly.

Ed does the same and we head for the door, giving Sam a wave.

"See you on Monday," I call out to Sam, although I'm damn sure he didn't hear a word I said. I don't blame him either.

"Wanna tell me what that was about?" Ed asks as I open the door to our apartment.

We've walked home in silence, but that's not unusual for us. I know he's been processing the night's events. He goes quiet when he needs to think. He's always done that. I've gotten used to his ways – but it's like that with twins. Sometimes we don't even have to speak to understand what the other one is thinking.

"Sam's in love with Ali."

"I know," he replies, going into the kitchen, opening the refrigerator and grabbing a couple of beers. He throws one at me and I open it, flopping down onto the couch.

"Then why are you asking?"

"Because I wasn't aware Sam had worked it out yet. I thought he was still fighting the attraction."

"Well, I don't know that he has completely worked it out, but I'm fairly sure he's been trying to find the right opportunity to kiss her for a few days now."

"Oh." He sits at the other end of the couch and takes a long drink of his beer. "And you think tonight might be that chance?"

"I fucking hope so."

He laughs. "I think it'll be good for him to have a woman in his life again. It's been too long."

"Yeah, it has."

Ed shrugs. "I guess he needed to get Amber out of his system."

I look over at him. "She's been out of his system since the day she left," I tell him. "I'm not sure she was ever *in* his system. Not really… The problem was that she did more damage than he'd like to let on."

He raises an eyebrow. "How do you mean?"

I shake my head. "You can't tell him you know about this," I warn, and he nods, so I continue, "when Amber left, she told him that the guy she'd been fooling around with was better in bed than Sam."

"Ouch." He winces.

"Yeah. That night, I stayed with him…"

"I remember. Your hangovers were legendary."

"All in the line of duty." I smile over at him. "He was really bothered by what she'd said. It was pretty much all he talked about."

"It was just her being spiteful. He had to realize that."

I sigh. "I don't think he did. You know Sam… Sex matters to him. A lot."

He smiles. "More than it does for you?"

"Maybe, maybe not. " I smirk. " The thing is, I think Amber's comment cut a bit too deep for him. To my knowledge, he hasn't been with anyone since."

Ed frowns thoughtfully. "No, he hasn't, has he?"

I shake my head and take a long sip of beer.

"I'm not really in the mood for this," I say, putting the can down on the table in front of us. "I'm gonna go to bed." I get up, although he stays where he is. "You okay?" I ask him.

He looks up. "Yeah. I'm just gonna sit for a while."

"It went well tonight," I reassure him. Thanks to our dad, Ed's not the most confident guy in the world, especially when it comes to his work. He's good at what he does though – really good.

He looks up. "You and that photographer seemed to be getting along well." He's got a mischievous smile on his face. *Asshole.*

"Yeah."

"That's all you've got to say? 'Yeah'?"

I grin down at him. "For now… yeah." He laughs. "See you in the morning," I add and leave him to himself.

I go through to my bedroom, close the door and switch on the lamp beside the bed, before undoing my belt, then the button and zipper on my pants. I feel something in my pocket and reach inside to find the piece of paper that woman gave me earlier. Her name's written on it. 'Alexa Barnes', with her number underneath. I sit down on the edge of the bed and study it for a moment. Normally, I'd have called her – not now, obviously; it's gone one in the morning – but tomorrow, or the next day. Then I'd have arranged to take her out somewhere and then, without a doubt, we'd have gone back to her place – or mine, but usually hers – and I'd have fucked her brains out for the night. It would just be one night though, because that's what I do. And that's what they do too. All of them. That's what they want from me, when they give me their numbers. One night. No more. And until now, that's been just fine with me. But meeting Petra, has changed everything. I know I want more than one night with her. I want a lot more.

I want a lifetime of nights.

I want forever.

For the first time in my life, I throw the piece of paper into the waste basket.

It took me a while to get to sleep last night, mainly because, even after I'd undressed and had a quick shower, I still couldn't get Petra out of my head. Thinking about her meant I had a raging, aching hard-on as well, which wasn't helping. Obviously, I could've dealt with that, but I didn't want to. So, I lay awake for a couple of hours, remembering those perfect curves, those sparkling eyes and those kissable lips. It was torture.

I'm real grateful we don't have to work today. Ed's making us breakfast and I'm sitting at our kitchen table, with my laptop open, drinking coffee.

"I guess I ought to see if we got any reviews," I say to him, putting down my cup. He turns around, looking a little scared. "Don't look so worried."

"What if they're bad?" he replies.

"We've never had a bad review. Ever. Why would we start now?"

"Because we changed pretty much everything about the restaurant. People don't like change."

"We changed it for the better," I tell him, going onto one of the more popular restaurant review sites. I type 'Rosa's, Hartford' into the search bar and wait while the page refreshes.

"Holy fucking shit."

Ed turns. "What?" He moves the pancakes off the heat and comes over, standing behind me. "What is it?"

"I don't think you needed to worry," I reply, looking up at him. "See?"

Over my shoulder, he reads the twenty or so glowing reviews of the restaurant; people describing the food, the ambience, the setting, the decor. We may never have had a bad review, but we've never had ones quite this good either.

"Look at that." I point at the screen, to one in which the writer particularly praises the desserts he and his wife ate. "I told you not to worry." He blushes and goes back to the pancakes.

"I wonder if Ali's seen them," he says over his shoulder.

"I don't know. I'll call her."

I pick up my phone from the table and go to her details, connecting the call. Ali's so efficient, she's probably already seen them and started copying them over to our new website, but just in case…

"She's not answering," I say to Ed, not bothering to leave a message.

"She may be taking the day off," he replies.

"This is Ali we're talking about." I'm not sure she knows the meaning of the words. She hasn't stopped since she got here. I try and connect the call again, with the same result.

"She might be in the shower," he suggests. "Or she may have gone for a walk, or something."

"And not taken her phone with her? You know she keeps it with her all the time, in case her sister calls."

"Oh yeah…" He brings plates stacked with pancakes over to the table. "Eat those and try again later," he says.

He's probably right. I expect that, like us, she'll have slept in late and is in the shower or something. I'll try again in a little while.

Ed's pancakes are great, but then they always are. Afterwards, he makes more coffee and we sit together at the table.

"Are you gonna try Ali again?" he suggests.

"Yeah."

Ali always answers her phone real quickly and the fact that she's not picking up has got me a little concerned. She was quite subdued at the end of the evening… And we left her with Sam. I'm not saying he'd have hurt her, but discovering what he's like, and what he's into, it might have scared her…

I try her number and yet again, it rings out and goes to her voicemail.

"Still no answer?" Ed says as I hang up.

"No."

"Why don't you try Sam?"

"Sam?"

"Yeah… He might know where she is. If she had plans for today, she might have told him."

I shrug my shoulders and connect a call to Sam. Yet again, it rings out. I try twice more before he finally picks up, sounding just a little out of breath.

"Hi," he says.

"Where the hell have you been? I've called you three times already. I was just about to come over there." I wasn't, but he doesn't need to know that.

I hear him sigh. "What's wrong?" he asks.

"I've been trying to get hold of Ali, but she's not picking up." I pause and look over at Ed. "Do you think she's okay?"

"Yeah," Sam says simply, and I wonder how badly it can have gone last night. Can he have fucked up that much? I hope she's okay…

"Only she normally picks up really quickly," I continue.

"Why did you need to get in touch with her?" he asks. Now I'm really getting worried. He doesn't seem at all concerned about where she is – just about my reason for wanting to talk to her. I thought he cared about her, but now I'm starting to worry about what he's done.

"Because we've had some amazing reviews online. I wondered if she'd seen them."

The line goes quiet for a moment and I start to think we've lost the connection.

"She hasn't seen them," he says eventually. His voice sounds a little weird, kinda strangled.

How the hell does he know that? "How do you know?" I ask him.

"Because she's here with me," he admits.

I can't disguise my surprise. "Seriously? And you're not fighting?" I say. Maybe it didn't go so badly last night, after all.

"No, we're not fighting," he replies. Well, that's a relief. They're still talking at least.

"She's there?" Ed whispers.

I nod, and the penny finally drops. Judging from the look on his face, Ed's got it too… I can have some fun with this. "What? So she came over for breakfast?" I tease Sam.

"No."

"She came for coffee?" Ed stifles a laugh and I kick him under the table.

"No, Rob." Sam sounds kinda irritated. It's easily done with him.

Ed gets up and goes over to the window, unable to stop himself from laughing any longer.

"You mean… she's been there all night?" I try to put a suitable amount of shock into my voice.

"Yes."

I try real hard, but I can't stop myself from chuckling. "You're a lucky son-of-a-bitch, Samuel Moreno. Don't fuck it up."

"I won't," he replies. "If you'll just get off the fucking phone and let me get on with it."

I laugh out loud, but I'm fairly certain he's hung up before he even hears me.

Ed comes back over.

"She stayed the night?"

"Yeah."

He sits back down, a smile on his face. "I take it she hadn't seen the reviews then?" he smirks.

We stare at each other for a moment and then Ed pours us both another coffee.

Ed and I get into work early on Monday. I've got a few things to do in the office anyway, but we want to try and catch Sam before work to find out what's going on between him and Ali. We can't help it. We're his brothers. It's our duty to be annoying.

I hear footsteps on the stairs down from the apartment and dash up from my desk, racing to the open office door, and position myself against the wall outside, just as Ed joins me, trying desperately to look nonchalant, and stands by the doors into the kitchen.

We both manage to keep a straight face as Sam appears... accompanied by Ali. We weren't expecting that. Okay, so we knew she stayed over on Saturday night. But two nights in a row? This is Sam we're talking about...

He looks from me to Ed and then back to me again.

"Anything you want to tell us?" I say to him, trying so hard not to laugh.

Ali looks up at him. I can't decide whether she's amused or embarrassed. A little of each, I think.

"No," Sam replies and puts his arm around her. It's kinda cute, I have to admit.

"Sure?" I ask. I'm not letting him off that lightly.

He gives me one of his more threatening glares. "No," he repeats.

Ali shifts slightly. I think she just put her arm around him too, but from this angle, it's hard to tell. Ed and I stay where we are, waiting...

"Okay," Sam says, finally giving in – because he knows he won't win this one. "Ali and I are... together." He looks at us both. "Happy?" he adds.

I can't help but grin. "Delirious, if it means you'll stop being a pain in the ass."

Ali lets out a chuckle. I knew she wouldn't be offended by us fooling around. She's way too much fun to take us seriously.

"Oh, I'll still be a pain in the ass to you," Sam says gruffly. "But I'll treat Ali a helluva lot better from now on."

Well, thank fuck for that. We'll all have a more peaceful time.

Ali leans into him a little and rests her head on his shoulder, and I move closer to them, at the same time as Ed, giving Sam a quick pat on his shoulder, before kissing Ali on both cheeks.

"Welcome to the family," I say to her.

"I think that's a bit premature," she replies. "We've only been together for two days."

"Yeah, but I know how fast this guy moves." I glance over at Sam and he looks as though he'd really quite like to skewer me. My comment was a little below the belt, I guess. I know he screwed Amber within minutes of meeting her, and married her within a couple of months, but even so, I probably shouldn't have made the comparison. Still… he can take it.

Ali looks up at him, maybe a little bewildered, and I regret the comment. "Some things are worth going after," Sam says, looking down at her. The smile she gives him is enough to melt a guy's heart, but before I have time to comment on that, Ed nudges me out of the way.

"I'm really pleased for both of you," he says. He's a lot kinder and more sensitive than I am.

"Thank you," Ali replies, blushing.

"Just so you know," Sam says to him, "Ali's gonna be working in the kitchen tonight."

Ed's as surprised as I am. The last time Ali was in there for any length of time, Sam yelled at her. "Oh… okay," he says.

Just then, Ali's phone rings and she excuses herself to take the call, briefly kissing Sam on the cheek before going into the restaurant.

Ed turns to Sam as soon as she's out of earshot. "In the kitchen?" he says. "You're gonna have Ali working in the kitchen? Is that wise? You yelled at her the last time she was in there." I couldn't have put it better myself.

"Yeah… well, things change," Sam replies.

I move to my right and stand in front of Sam, staring up into his face. He looks kinda nervous. "Man, you've got it bad," I say. He has. It's so obvious.

He glares at me for just a moment and I wonder if he's gonna hit me, or swear at me, but he doesn't do either. He shrugs. "So what if I have?"

I didn't expect that. "Have you told Ali yet?"

"Told her what?"

Do I have to spell it out for him? "That you're in love with her?" What else?

"No," he says quietly. "And I'd rather do that myself, thanks. If you could just keep quiet about it. I really don't need her hearing that from you…"

Well… fuck me. He actually admitted it. He may not have told her, but he's obviously going to. For a moment – and it is just a moment – I'm stunned into silence.

Chapter Three

Petra

I've got an office set up in what used to be a guest bedroom, which is next door to my room. It's convenient for when I lose track of time and end up working late.

I like it in my office; it's calm and peaceful and, in common with a lot of the house, it's filled with photographs. They're not mine – well, most of them aren't. They're my dad's, and just being surrounded by them reminds me of what an inspiration he was. My dad was always my hero. As a child I would spend pretty much all of my free time with him, learning the art of photography, the old fashioned way, the way it was before everything became digital. He was patient, encouraging and honest. He never gave me undue praise; if I got something wrong, he told me, and then showed me how to get it right. The lessons I learned from him have stuck with me through my career… well, through my life, really, and he remains the greatest influence in everything I do. Unfortunately, by the time he died, I was already with Adrian and I'd discovered the hard way, that not all men have the same qualities as my dad…

I've spent most of my evenings this week editing the images from the restaurant shoot, and I have to say, they've come out really well. I'm pleased with them.

Every so often, I stumble over a picture of Rob. Sometimes he's just in the background, out of focus, and others I've clearly concentrated the shot on him – albeit unintentionally. In most of them he's talking to customers, laughing, sometimes with his hand resting on a man's shoulder, or helping someone with the menu. He's friendly. And from what I saw on Saturday night, he can clearly get too friendly.

Several times I've caught myself staring at the screen for ages, just looking at him, studying his beautiful lips, his dark brown eyes, his square, slightly stubbled jaw… The camera loves him. But then so did every female in the restaurant.

I can't forget the blonde who handed him her phone number, or the fact that he put it in his pocket. A couple of times, I've wondered whether he's met up with her since, but it's none of my business, is it?

I just wish it hadn't been like that. I wish he hadn't been such a flirt. I wish he'd been a genuine guy… the kind of guy I could maybe take a chance on and let into my life. I also wish he hadn't been the first guy in years to make me actually feel anything.

My only consolation is that I didn't say or do anything to give away how I was feeling about him. I left with my dignity intact, if nothing else.

The problem is, my dignity doesn't do a great job of keeping me warm at night.

I've made it through the week and, being as it's a Saturday and I don't have a wedding to photograph, I'm looking forward to changing the bedding and catching up with the laundry – well, 'looking forward' might be overstating it, but it'll hopefully take my mind of the impending doom of going back to Rosa's tomorrow to photograph Rob's brothers. I just have to keep telling myself that at least he won't be there.

Speaking of which, I'm surprised I haven't heard from Ali. She said she'd call this week to run through her requirements, and she hasn't. I'll give her until lunchtime and if I don't hear from her, I'll give her a call.

I'm transferring the sheets from the washer to the dryer when my phone rings. I check the display and see that it's Ali. *At last.*

"Hi," I say, connecting the call and dumping the sheets on the floor at the same time. I go through to the kitchen and sit at the table.

"Hello," she says. "I'm so sorry. I know I was supposed to call you during the week, but it's been a little bit crazy here."

"I can imagine." I know they were fully booked after the re-opening, and if Saturday was anything to go by, I imagine they've been rushed off their feet. "How are you?" I ask her.

"Exhausted." I can hear her smiling though, so I guess that's not a bad thing.

"Are we still okay for tomorrow?"

"Definitely," she says.

"So, I'll get there around eleven, shall I?" It's what we arranged and I can't imagine the plans will have changed. I'm sure she'd have let me know before now if that was the case.

"That should be fine. I don't think it'll take more than a couple of hours."

Ideally, I'd like to confirm that Rob won't be there, but I don't know how to do that without her asking why I want to know… and I really don't want to get into explaining that.

"And you just want some photographs of the two chefs?" I ask. It's the best I can come up with.

There's a slight hesitation before she speaks again. "Well… I need to talk to you about that," she says, "Can you take some of Rob as well?" *Shit.* What did I do to deserve this? I'm really not a bad person… "I know you got some of him at the opening," she continues, "but I'd like to have some where he's not…"

"Flirting," I interject, instinctively.

She laughs and I'm relieved I seem to have managed to cover my embarrassment with fake humor. "I was going to say working," she replies, "but yes, flirting covers it too."

Yeah, I bet it does.

"I can't believe he called me an angel when you introduced us at the opening," I say, trying to make conversation, like I don't care, even though I do.

"Why not?" she asks. "I'm certain he meant it as a compliment." I know she means well, but hearing that doesn't help one bit.

"Yeah, and I'm equally convinced he says that to pretty much every woman he meets." I blurt out the words and wish I could bite them back.

"Don't be so sure about that… and don't put yourself down." I feel tears pricking my eyes. She's so lovely, so kind. She has no idea how much I wish Rob really had meant it, or how much of the last few years have been spent trying to rebuild myself after Adrian did his best to destroy me.

I cough to dislodge the lump in my throat. I need to get us back onto the topic of work. Now. "Okay," I whisper, struggling to control my voice. "So you need some shots done in the kitchen, and the remainder…" I pause, thinking about what's going to be involved in photographing Rob. "Around the restaurant?" I suggest.

"Mainly behind the bar, I think," she says. Thank goodness she took the hint, although the prospect of being in such a confined space with Rob is daunting…

"That sounds fine," I manage to say. "A couple of hours should still be plenty of time." I'm just gonna do my job and get out of there as fast as I can.

"Thanks for this, Petra," Ali says, and I know she means it.

"You're welcome. I'll see you tomorrow."

We hang up the call and I cling on to my one saving grace: Ali will be there. I can keep it friendly, but professional.

It'll be fine…

Rob

It's been a busy week. We knew it would be from the number of bookings we'd taken and I've gotta say, having Ali working in the kitchen in the evenings has been useful. Ed says she's really good. She knows what she's doing and she gets on with it. She's worked with Ed most of the time, although Sam keeps finding excuses to come over and see her. He's evidently really protective of her, but they don't kiss, or touch in the kitchen. I'm not surprised. Sam's way too private to show his feelings in front of other people.

We're about a half hour from opening for Saturday lunch. Ali's working in the office, Sam and Ed are busy in the kitchen and I'm in the restaurant, although I've gotta be honest, I'm not really concentrating. For the last few days, pretty much all I've been able to think about is that on Sunday I'm gonna see Petra again… and Sunday is tomorrow.

I know, I know… I've got it bad too.

The guys are fooling around, making paper aeroplanes out of the serviettes and I join in. We've been set up for a while now and I think we're all a bit bored.

I catch sight of Ali coming out of the office, just as the laughter hits a peak and, right at that moment, I hear a crashing noise from the kitchen and then a second's silence before Sam really yells. And I mean *really* yells. Everyone stops, standing still like statues. Christ, he's loud. I'm glad we're not open yet; it'd look pretty bad if customers heard him shouting and swearing like that. Someone needs to talk to him about it… although I'm not gonna volunteer myself. It'll only start an argument if I do it.

Still, I'll worry about that later. For now, it's time to open up and get on with the day…

"If you'd like to take a seat, Jackson will be your waiter for today. But if you need anything, just let me know." The woman smiles at me, looks into my eyes, and leans forward a little too much as she sits down and, for a moment, I feel kinda sorry for the guy she's with. At a rough guess, I'd say this is probably their second date, but I doubt they'll make it to a third, not if she's gonna flirt with me like that…

I turn and notice Ali coming toward me, carrying a suitcase, and I take a couple of paces to meet her.

"I'm really sorry," she says in a whisper and guides me toward the rear of the restaurant. It's still empty down here and much quieter. "I've got to go," she adds.

"Go where?" I don't understand what she's saying and move closer, in case I misheard. I'm sure she just said she had to go, but…

"Home," she says.

What the fuck? "Home?" I glance at the suitcase again. She didn't have to go back to the hotel to pack, so I guess that means she must've moved in upstairs at some point during the week. Things between her and Sam have obviously been progressing much quicker than I thought. "Home, as in England?" She nods. What the hell's happened? "Is everything okay?" I ask.

"I've had a call from my sister and there are some problems I need to get back and deal with," she says.

"Your sister's not ill, or hurt, or anything?" She shakes her head, and I notice tears forming in her eyes. What's wrong with her?

"No, she's fine," Ali replies. "I'm going to try and catch the early evening flight from Logan."

"You're going that soon?" Her sister's okay, so what's the urgency?

"Yes. Tess needs me and I'm pretty much finished here. There's just the photography shoot tomorrow, and I'm sure Petra can handle that."

I can't help but smile at the mention of Petra's name, or the thought of seeing her again tomorrow. Still, that's tomorrow, and right now, I need to deal with this.

"Is Sam taking you to the airport?" I ask her.

"No."

That seems odd. I know he's busy, but I'm sure Ed could handle one lunchtime shift by himself. I get the feeling there's more to this than she's telling me and, although it's none of my business really, I don't want her to go, especially not like this, so I've gotta ask… "Um… Is everything okay between the two of you?"

She shrugs her shoulders. "If I'm being honest, I don't know. He just yelled at me… badly. Probably the worst ever."

Oh… fuck. I know my idiot brother has said and done some awful things to Ali in the past, but I thought he was beyond that now. And this is the worst ever? He must've had a reason… surely.

"Why?" I ask her.

"Because I walked into the kitchen at the wrong moment… I think. We were fine this morning before work. Actually, we were better than fine."

I don't want to know what that means. When it comes to Sam's sex life, even my imagination isn't up to the task.

"Then what happened?"

"I don't know. I only went in there to tell him I'm going home, but I never got the chance."

"You mean… he doesn't know?"

"No," she says. God, she looks so sad. "I thought all that was in the past, Rob… but I guess I was wrong."

"That's just Sam…" I try to make excuses for my useless brother.

"Yes, but the thing is, we've been talking about the future, and I don't know if I want a future like that… where I'm always treading on eggshells, waiting for the next explosion."

What's she saying? "Are… are you breaking up with him?" He'll be devastated.

"I don't know what I'm doing, other than going home."

"Why don't you let me get him? You can talk it through before you go."

"I can't talk to him right now." Jeez. She's forgiven him everything so far. Whatever he did or said has gotta be bad.

"I'll stay with you. I won't let him hurt you," I suggest, in case she's feeling scared.

"I can't," I says again, and it looks to me like she's about to cry.

Then it dawns on me that, if he doesn't know and she's about to leave, at some point, he's bound to come looking for her.

"Then what am I supposed to tell him?" I ask.

She shrugs her shoulders again. "Tell him whatever you want, Rob… Only do me a favor and wait until the end of service before you say anything?"

She can't mean that. "Are you kidding? He'll kill me." And that'll just be his starting gambit.

She sighs deeply. "Okay. Tell him, if you must."

She's so down, I can't just leave it like that. "I'll only tell him if he asks. How's that?" I offer.

"Thanks."

I take a step toward her. "Don't write him off, Ali." I've got no idea why I'm supporting him, other than that he's my brother and I know he'll be broken by her leaving. "You're good for him… and he needs you."

"Maybe I don't need to be treated like that though."

I don't have an answer to that and I shake my head, then pull her into my arms just briefly. "He's a fucking idiot," I whisper in her ear, and then I let her go. "How are you getting to the airport?" I ask her.

"I booked a taxi," she replies.

"I'd have taken you," I tell her. I would've done too. It would have given Sam another reason to skin me, but I don't like the thought of her going by herself. She's obviously upset, not only by Sam's actions, but by whatever's wrong at home.

"I know you would," she says. "But you're working, and this is my problem, Rob."

Right at that moment, a cab driver comes in and calls out her name. She grabs her bag, but the driver comes over and takes it from her. She says goodbye, and in an instant, she's gone.

It feels so wrong that she's not here, and I know Sam will be devastated when I tell him.

"That was a good service," Jasmine says as the last customers leave. She's right, it was… apart from the fact that Ali left at the beginning of it, it was fucking amazing.

"Yeah," I reply. I'm not feeling very talkative right now.

"You okay?" she asks.

"Yeah, I'm fine."

At that moment, Sam appears from the corridor. He's taken off his whites and is wearing jeans and a t-shirt.

"Rob, have you seen Ali?" he calls out, looking around.

I don't want to shout across the restaurant, even though I feel like yelling at him, so I go around the other side of the bar and walk over to him.

"She's gone," I say bluntly.

His eyes widen and his mouth drops open.

"G—Gone where?" he asks.

"Home." I try really hard not to raise my voice.

"Home," he repeats. "You mean England?"

"Yeah."

To my surprise, he stumbles backward and has to grab the back of one of the chairs to stay upright. Sam's the strongest person I know, in every way, so I certainly didn't expect that reaction and I wait until he's steadied himself. Once he has, he glares at me. "And you knew about this?"

"She told me she was leaving, yeah, just before the cab came to take her to the airport."

"And you didn't fucking well come and get me?" he yells at me. I expected that.

"No I didn't… and you've just demonstrated why." I'm calmer now, but there's no getting away from the fact that he's brought this upon himself, if he'd just open his eyes and see what he's doing.

"What are you talking about?" he shouts, then he reaches into his back pocket and pulls out his phone. I can't think of anything worse than for him to call Ali at this point. He's in no mood to be civil, and she's not up to being yelled at. So, I grab his phone from him. "What the fuck?"

"Just wait," I urge him.

"Rob… give me back my fucking phone. Or, so help me God… I'm gonna hit you so damn hard." It wouldn't be the first time.

"This is why she left," I tell him, keeping my voice calm and quiet.

"You're not making any damn sense." He puts his hand out. "Just give me the fucking phone."

"No. Not until you calm down."

"How the hell am I supposed to calm down when the woman I love has just walked out on me… and I don't know why?"

"Don't you?" I stare at him. "Are you sure about that? She told me you yelled at her. Again."

He closes his eyes, just for a second and I wonder if he's managed to work it out.

"She… she left because I yelled at her?" he whispers.

That's not the whole reason she left, and I guess he needs to know that. "Kinda…" I tell him. "Sit down a minute and I'll explain."

"What's going on?" Ed appears at the back of the restaurant. "I heard shouting."

"Ali's left," I explain to him as he approaches.

"Left? As in gone home?"

"Yeah."

"Is this because Sam yelled at her?" Ed asks.

We pull out the chairs at one of the empty tables and sit down together. "Not entirely," I reply, "but at least you got that bit quicker than our brother."

"Why else did she go?" Sam asks. He looks a little desperate.

"She had a call from her sister," I tell him. I put his phone down on the table in front of me, but I keep an eye on him, making sure he doesn't grab it. He's still not calm enough yet to talk to Ali and I'm not gonna let him screw this up any more than he already has done. "Evidently something's happened and Ali needed to go home."

"She didn't tell me," he murmurs, his eyes fixed on me.

"No. She tried, evidently, but you yelled at her."

His head drops down into his hands. "Shit…" he mumbles. "I should've listened to her. She… she told me she had something to say, but I was impatient… rude." He looks up again. "She changed her mind and said she wasn't going to bother telling me." He rocks his head back and stares up at the ceiling. "She's really left me." God, he sounds so desolate.

I reach over and place my hand on his arm. "I'm not sure she has," I say softly. He leans forward, his eyes fixed on me.

"What makes you say that?" he asks.

"Because I asked her if she was leaving you, and she said she didn't know what she was doing except going home."

"She said that?" The optimism in his voice is touching.

"Yeah. She also said she didn't much appreciate the way you'd spoken to her, and she didn't really want to face a future spent treading on eggshells… so don't get your hopes up." I shrug my shoulders. I had to be honest with him.

"Can I have my phone now?" he asks.

"Are you gonna be polite?" I need to know.

"Yeah. I'm gonna be polite."

I push his phone across the table and he picks it up, presses the screen a couple of times and holds it to his ear. After a few moments, he disconnects.

"She's not answering?" Ed asks. Sam shakes his head and presses another button on his phone. I guess he's going to try messaging her.

For the next few minutes, Ed and I sit and watch, while he types furiously on his phone, and every so often it beeps in response.

"Fucking hell," he whispers, then takes a deep breath and starts typing again.

Then, he stops and holds his phone, looking at it. Nothing happens, so he presses the screen a couple more times and holds it to his ear.

"She's turned her damn phone off," he says eventually, and he looks up at the two of us. "Sorry," he says, raising his voice just a little. "I know you don't need this, but I've gotta go after her."

He can't… He just can't.

"Now?" Surely not.

"Yeah. Right now."

I know he loves her, but… "Whoa, hold on a second. You can't just take off. We've only just reopened. All the recipes are new. You created them. In case you've forgotten, you're the head chef around here. Why can't you call her later, when she gets home, apologize, talk it over and then go and see her in a couple of weeks when everything here is more settled?"

"Because we've got things we need to talk through, and none of what we need to say can be said over the fucking phone," he replies, raising his voice.

"We'll cope," Ed says, putting his hands out on the table. "Go. We'll manage. You've written down all the recipes, and the sous-chefs know them pretty well by now. I—I guess we can take the specials off the menu while you're away, and tomorrow's Sunday, so I've got all day to get some practice in."

How can he have forgotten that today's Saturday? We've got a fully booked restaurant tonight, and Sam's not gonna be here, on top of which, Petra's booked to come in tomorrow.

"We've got the photographer coming in tomorrow," I say. I know I'm making excuses, but if I'm being completely honest, I'm really worried about whether Ed and I can manage without Sam.

"So? She can photograph me cooking, can't she?" Ed replies. Why does he have to choose this moment to suddenly become so assertive?

"And what about Sam?" I'm clutching at straws now.

"I'm sure she won't mind coming back to take his pictures another time." Fuck it, Ed… shut up.

"I'll be on the end of the phone, if you need me," Sam says, turning to Ed. "Even if it's the middle of the night over there. You can just call me. And I won't be gone for long… probably a few days at most. If I can't work it out with Ali by then, I'll be back."

They both look at me. The ball's in my court. I still want to say 'no', because I really am worried about this. It's not just about the kitchens, it's about having Sam there to back us up. He's always been there… all our lives. And he's real important to Ed. He's the one who gives Ed the reassurance he can do all the things we both know he can. I'm no good at that. Ed believes Sam because Sam can cook. Hearing it from me doesn't carry the same weight. The thing is, if I say 'no', I think he'll just go anyway. And he'll resent the fuck out of me for standing in his way. "Okay," I say, reluctantly. "I guess I'm outvoted." And I suppose the best thing I can do now is to bury my misgivings and be useful… I reach under the bar for my laptop. I've been keeping it there while Ali's been using the office. It's easier.

"What are you doing?" Sam asks as I open it.

"Two things…" I go to a browser. "First I'm gonna book you on the next flight…"

"And?" he says.

"And then I'm gonna look up Ali's address in London. I've got it on her emails. I'm guessing you don't want to wander the streets looking for her."

He gives me a smile. "Thanks," he says.

"And then I guess I'd better drive you to the airport. I'll ask Jasmine if she can cover for me until I get back... but Ed's gonna be needed in the kitchen."

Ed pales, realizing finally that he's got to do tonight's service by himself. "Oh... God, yeah. It's Saturday night..."

"You'll be fine." Sam turns back to him and puts a reassuring hand on his shoulder. "Just stay calm, think through the orders and work methodically. You've spent years watching dad and me. You can do this. And call me if you need me."

"You'll ace it," I add, trying to sound supportive. Ed doesn't look entirely convinced.

Sam looks from Ed to me and back again. "Thanks, guys," he whispers. "And I'm sorry to do this to you."

"Just make it up with her," Ed replies. "She's good for you." That's true.

"Yeah... she is," Sam admits. "I'd better pack... fast." He moves toward the back of the restaurant.

He's back in less than half an hour, packed and ready to go.

"Ready?" I ask him.

"Yeah," he replies, although he's really looking at Ed, who's standing beside me. I know Sam feels bad about abandoning him.

Ed takes a step forward. "Try and bring Ali back home," he says. "You're a much nicer person when you're with her."

I laugh, but then try to hide it. I'm not sure Ed meant it to come out like that. "Thanks," Sam replies.

Ed realizes his mistake. "No," he says. "I mean..."

"I get what you mean." Sam takes pity on him. "And I agree with you. Ali makes me a better person. I know that. I can't guarantee I can bring her back though. England is her home, and she has to think about her sister too. I can't just uproot her from her life."

"Try," Ed persists. "Bring the sister back as well, if you have to."

Sam laughs. "What do you want me to do? Kidnap them?"

"If necessary, yes." Ed chuckles. "Ali didn't just make you a better person. She helped all of us." He's not wrong there. "Look at this place," he adds, glancing around the restaurant. "We'd never have done this without her."

"I know," Sam says.

"We need to go," I interrupt, jingling my car keys. "Have you got everything you need?"

"Yeah, I think so," Sam replies.

"Passport?" I ask him.

"Yeah."

"Cuffs? Restraints?" Ed stifles a laugh, but I try real hard to keep a straight face as Sam turns around to face me. He looks worried. "Well… you were talking about kidnapping her… so…"

"Ha fucking ha," he says, shaking his head. "Just take me to the airport and stop being a smart-ass."

He goes over to Ed and gives him a hug, telling him to call anytime, but reiterating that he knows Ed'll be okay. Then I pick up his bag and we head out the door.

I wait until we're on the freeway before saying anything, but I feel it has to be said.

"Why are you always such a fucking idiot?" I ask him.

"It's genetic," he replies and I turn and glare at him.

He's kidding, right? "I'd never have done what you've done, if that's what you're suggesting."

"I'm not suggesting anything. But one day, you're gonna fall in love, and then you'll work out it's not as easy as you think."

This has nothing to do with falling in love. It's to do with being a fucking idiot, and Sam's cornered the market on that. "Yeah, I get that, but why couldn't you just be grateful for what you had? Why did you have to fuck it up?"

"I was grateful. I will be grateful… if she'll forgive me and let me have another chance," he murmurs.

"So why did you yell at her?"

"Because I was having a shitty morning, that's all." That's all?

"And that's a good enough reason to hurt the woman you love, is it?"

"No," he says. "But like I say, one day, you'll find out that love isn't as easy as you seem to think it is."

"I'm not saying it's easy," I reply, trying to sound reasonable. I don't wanna fight with him. I want him to understand. "I'm just saying you've gotta stop hurting her, or one day you'll push her too far, and she won't come back, Sam, that's all. Is that a risk you're willing to take?"

He doesn't say a word. And I guess that's all the reply I need.

Chapter Four

Petra

I knock on the front door of the restaurant at eleven on the dot, and wait.

After a few moments, the chef who looks just like Rob comes through from the back and opens the door for me.

"I'm sorry," he says, standing to one side. "Rob's on the phone."

"It's okay." I'm relieved Rob didn't answer the door. At least it saved me being on my own with him.

"I don't think we were introduced." He holds out his hand and I take it. "I'm Ed. I'm Rob's twin."

That explains it. "Petra Miller." I say.

"Nice to meet you." He smiles. The similarity between them is uncanny, except his eyes don't shine in quite the same playful way as his brother's, and his hair is longer. Apart from that, I think I'd have trouble telling them apart. "Come on through."

I follow him to the back of the restaurant and into the kitchen, which I have to say is beautiful. It's all stainless steel and copper, and immaculately clean… and empty. I dump my camera bag on the surface beside me, wondering where Ali is… and Sam, for that matter.

"We owe you an apology," he says, leaning back against the countertop on the far side. "Sam's not gonna be here today."

"Oh?"

"Yeah. It's a long story…"

From the look on his face, I assume it's also a private one. "Do you want to cancel?" I ask.

"No. Not unless you do. Rob and I are still here, and we'll re-arrange something for Sam when he gets back."

"Okay." I open up my bag and start getting out my kit. "Is it okay if we turn on all the lights?" I ask him.

"Sure." He comes over and reaches behind me, flicking several switches.

"I didn't bring my lights, because I thought Ali wanted me to take some photographs of you working – well, pretending to – so it's not really practical," I explain.

"Oh… okay."

"As far as I know, she didn't want anything too staged, but we can check that with Ali, if you like."

He looks at his watch. "Well… I guess it'd be around four over there, if you want to call her."

I look up at him. "I'm sorry? Over where?"

"England."

I nearly drop my camera. "Ali's in England?"

"Yeah. She went back yesterday."

"Really? But I only spoke to her yesterday." I'm confused now. "She didn't mention going home. In fact, she said she'd see me today…"

"She didn't know she was going." The voice behind me makes me jump out of my skin and I turn to see Rob, dressed in his usual black shirt and pants, and looking even better than he did on the opening night. He stares down at me. "Hello," he says, his voice gently teasing my skin.

"Hi." I'm staring into his eyes, drawn to him like a moth to a flame.

"Yeah, it was all very sudden," Ed adds and I manage to turn back to him.

"What happened?" I ask. I hope nothing's gone wrong at home to make her rush back.

"Sam happened," Rob replies, coming further into the room.

"Oh, I thought… well, I guess I assumed they were getting on a little better. What did he do now?" I know he's their brother, but…

They both look at me, surprise etched on their faces.

"You knew about them?" Ed asks.

"I knew Sam was being pretty horrible to Ali."

A smile twitches on Rob's lips. "Oh. So you didn't know they'd got together, then?" he says.

"No." It's my turn to be surprised. "I mean, Ali had told me Sam had changed, and that he wasn't being quite such a jerk…" My voice fades. "Sorry." I look up at them, but they're both smiling.

"That's perfectly okay," Rob says. "Sam *was* being a jerk."

"She was real upset by what he was doing," I explain. "We talked." Rob nods, his smile softening. "But then she told me he'd gotten better."

"Yeah, he did. He worked out he was in love with her. And he stopped fighting the attraction and went with it instead."

"So, if they got together, what happened? Why has she gone home?"

A frown crosses Rob's face, but it's Ed who speaks first. "Sam forgot to stop being a jerk," he says.

"Sorry?" I look from him to Rob. "What does that mean?"

"It means Sam yelled at Ali, really horribly," Rob explains. "She'd just come in here to tell him she was going home—"

"I'm so confused," I interrupt.

He grins. "Yeah. We're not telling the story very well."

"You mean *you're* not," Ed replies. "What my brother is trying to say is that Ali got a call from her sister, to say there was a problem at home. She – Ali, that is – decided to fly back to London to deal with it, and came in here to tell Sam…"

"And Sam chewed her out," Rob says, completing the story.

"So Ali left?" I ask.

"Yep, Ali left," Rob says.

"Just like that?"

He nods.

"And Sam?"

"He's gone after her…"

"To London? Really?" I'm surprised… again.

"Yeah. With any luck he'll have caught up with her by now."

"Well…" I don't know what else to say. From what Ali had said, I wouldn't have thought Sam would be that… romantic. "I hope they can work it out."

Rob smiles. "Yeah. So do we." He glances at Ed. "Sam's a pain in the ass without her."

Ed grins. "Yeah. He seriously needs to work it out and bring her home," he says.

I can see how attached they are to her, and I don't blame them, but they seem to be missing the obvious.

"This isn't her home, though, is it?" I say, voicing my thoughts. "And you just said she's got a sister, didn't you?"

They both look up at me, like I'm the one not making sense around here.

"Yeah." Rob smiles and I feel myself melt a little on the inside. I wish he couldn't do that to me so easily.

"It'll be fine. I'm sure Sam will persuade her to come back," Ed says with confidence.

He can't be serious.

"He can't ride roughshod over her life," I say, trying to be the voice of reason.

Rob laughs. "He wouldn't do that." He moves closer, staring into my eyes. "But Sam can be real persuasive… it's a family trait."

I swallow hard, wondering what he means by that.

"Even so," I manage to say, trying really hard to fix that image of him flirting with the tall blonde in my head.

"He'll work it out," Rob says softly. "He won't give her up."

"And if she doesn't want to come back here? If she doesn't want to leave her sister?"

"I imagine Sam will persuade her sister to come too," Ed says, smiling.

"What?" That's ludicrous. "Why can't he move there?" It seems a lot simpler to me.

They both stare at me.

"Sam? Move to England?" Ed whispers, then averts his gaze to Rob. "He wouldn't, would he?"

Rob shrugs. "Who knows?" He moves a little closer to me. "It's hard to tell what a guy will do when he's in love."

His eyes pierce mine and I can feel the the heat from his body spreading into me.

I have to stop this.

"I guess we'd better get on," I say, tearing my gaze from his.

"Yeah," Ed says, his voice much quieter now. "Where do you want to start?"

I finish with Ed in about forty-five minutes, and we leave him to get on with cooking for real. He and Rob have explained to me during the shoot that Ed's going to be taking over the main kitchen in Sam's absence and he's spending the rest of the day practicing the dishes he's less familiar with.

Rob and I move into the restaurant and I can feel my nerves spike once we're alone, as he walks through ahead of me.

"Where do you want me?" he asks, smiling as he leans back against the bar.

I decide to ignore the obvious innuendo, and the sparkle in his eyes, and be completely professional.

"Ali wanted me to take some shots behind the bar," I tell him. "So, I guess we'll start there." I keep the camera around my neck, but because I know the space behind the bar is limited, and I'm going to need to move around a fair bit, I remove my jacket and leave it over the back of one of the chairs, placing my camera bag on the table beside it. As I turn, I'm aware of his eyes raking up and down my body and I feel myself flush at the attention. Without my jacket, I feel more exposed. He'll be able to see much more clearly that I'm not exactly thin.

"Okay." He smiles down at me and, pushing himself off the bar, he moves around behind it. I follow into the confined space. It's even tighter than I'd thought it would be back here when there are two people, especially when I'm trying not to get too close to him. "What do you want me to do?" he asks.

"Just be yourself," I say, checking the camera to try and hide the fact my hands are shaking. "Act like you're preparing drinks, and I'll take some shots."

He grabs a couple of glasses and a bottle of wine and I set to work, taking shots from different angles, which include me clambering up on the bar to get a little more height. Throughout this, he mixes cocktails and pours various drinks, clearly very comfortable and confident with himself.

"Do you need any help?" he asks, as I climb down from the bar.

"No, I'm fine. Just pretend I'm not here," I say to him.

"Now, that would be impossible," he replies, smiling at me.

"And stop flirting," I add, without thinking and raise the camera to my face to hide my embarrassment.

He stops pouring, puts the bottle down, and looks straight at me. "I'm not," he says, seriously.

I lower the camera again, and our eyes meet just as he takes a step and grabs my arms, pulling me close to him and kissing me. His lips are hard and soft at the same time, his tongue demanding entrance. I open to him and he delves inside, claiming me. He groans into my mouth and changes the angle of his head, going deeper and I respond in kind. My breathing becomes erratic and desperate… like me. Finally, he pulls back and stares down into my eyes.

"I'm sorry," he whispers, his lips still just an inch from mine.

"It's okay," I reply. "You don't have to apologize." *Everyone makes mistakes…*

"I couldn't help myself," he says and I can feel him studying my face. "I've wanted to do that since I first saw you."

Really? How can he say that? I pull away a little. "Don't," I say. "Don't say things like that."

"Why not?" He looks confused.

"Because it's not true."

He steps back, gazing down at me. "What do you mean?" he asks.

"It's bullshit, Rob," I say, raising my voice a little. "You don't have to pretend with me. I've seen you in action. I saw you take that woman's number the other night…" I focus on his chest, to avoid looking at his face.

He steps closer again. "But what you didn't see was me throwing it away later on, when I got home."

"If you were planning on throwing it away, why did you put it in your pocket?" I ask, looking up at him again.

"What was I supposed to do? Throw it back in her face? Make a scene in my own restaurant?" He stares at me. "She was a customer, Petra. I had to be polite."

"You call that being polite?" I can't disguise my sarcasm.

"Yeah, I do." He moves closer still and takes my camera, lifting it over my head and placing it carefully on the bar. "Listen. I took her number because she gave it to me. I put it in my pocket, because I had no choice. But I didn't keep it, and I haven't called her. And I won't, because it's not her I want." His lips are poised above mine once more, and again, he covers my mouth with his. His touch is gentle and tentative to start with, testing the waters, I guess. Now the camera isn't between us, he's able to move closer, then he turns and pushes me back against the bar, placing his feet either side of mine and, in the blink of an eye, everything changes. He brings his hands up, cupping my face and running his tongue along my lips. I open yet again, our tongues meeting. He grinds his hips into me and I feel his long, thick erection against my hip. I gasp into him and he repeats the motion, moving his hands down to my waist and yanking my t-shirt from my jeans. I feel his hands on my skin and moan into him, reaching out myself to pull his shirt from the waistband of his pants. I want to feel him. His skin is smooth and soft and he groans as I run my hands up his bare back, over his hard muscles. He leans back just a fraction, moving his hands between us and raising them to cup my breasts. My nipples harden in an instant, pebbling into his palms through the thin lace of my bra.

"I want you so much," he murmurs into my mouth.

"Yes… yes." It's all I can say.

He breaks the kiss and lifts my t-shirt, then pulls down the lace cups of my bra, exposing my breasts.

"Fuck…" he whispers and holding one, he gently runs his tongue over the nipple of the other. It's all I can do not to come on the spot and I let my head rock back, savoring the sensations. It feels so good… I've never done anything like this before, but I need him more than I've ever needed anyone. *Oh God…*

The loud ringing of his phone makes us both jump. "Shit," he mutters, releasing me. The noise is intrusive and he straightens, and reaches into his back pocket, pulling out his phone and checking the screen. "She can wait," he says, cutting the call, and I wonder who 'she' is. He dumps his phone on the bar, leaning down to me again.

The moment's gone though. I can't carry on now. I can't actually believe I did that in the first place. I duck away from him and, turning around, I move my bra back into place, pulling my t-shirt down again. I'm blushing… I'm humiliated. I need to get out of here.

I turn and pick up my camera.

"Where are you going?" he asks.

"Home." I glance up at him and wish I hadn't. His eyes are focused on mine and are darker and more enticing than ever. "I'm sorry, Rob. I shouldn't have let that happen. It was great, but… I'm sorry." I'm rambling, but that's because I'm dying of embarrassment. I go around the bar, grab my jacket and camera bag, and, without looking back, I run.

Rob

What the hell just happened? We were kissing. Okay, we were doing a lot more than kissing, but I thought she liked it. I think she said it was great; I know she did actually, right before she ran out of here. I rest my hands on the bar and lean forward, to catch my breath. I've kissed a lot of women, but I've never felt anything like that in my life. The moment our lips touched, it was as though my stomach flipped, kinda like when an aircraft goes through turbulence, but nicer. A lot nicer. And as for the feeling of her skin, her hands on me, and her perfect breasts… And yet she ran. What did I do? Oh God. Did I go too far? I didn't, did I? *Fuck…*

I grab my keys and run out the door, locking it behind me. Ed's on his own and busy in the kitchen. I can't leave the place open. I pocket the keys and move out to the middle of the sidewalk, looking up and down the street. Which way did she go? I'm frantic, and panicking… and then a guy in a denim shirt moves to one side and I see her in the distance. She's not running anymore, but she's walking fast, so I take off after her.

It doesn't take me long to catch up to her and I grab a hold of her wrist and pull her to a stop, turning her toward me.

"I'm sorry," I blurt out, and then I look down at her properly.

She's crying, tears tumbling down her cheeks.

"Shit," I say. "I'm so sorry, Petra." It hurts to see her like this. I mean, it really hurts, like someone just tore a hole in my chest. I pull her close and hold her. She lets me, although she doesn't hug me back and after a few moments, I release her again. "I apologize for what I did," I whisper. "If I went too far… Can you forgive me?"

She looks up at me, her eyes brimming with more tears. "It's fine," she murmurs.

"No, it's not."

"It's nothing, really." She pulls away.

"Come back with me. We can just talk." I really don't want her to leave like this. I don't want her to leave at all.

"No, Rob." I can hear the emotion in her voice and it cuts through me like the sharpest knife. "I don't want you to think you did anything wrong, because you didn't. But we can't do this."

What? "Why not?"

"Because…"

"That's not really an answer, Petra." I step closer to her, lean down and whisper, "You liked what we were doing, didn't you? I—I mean, I thought you did…"

She nods her head. "Yes, of course I did."

This is really fucking confusing. "Then why did you run? And why are you saying we can't do this?"

She moves back again, pauses and looks up into my eyes. "Who was on the phone, Rob?" she asks.

For a minute, my mind goes blank. "When?"

"Just now, when we were… your phone rang."

"Oh. That was my mom."

"Oh… really?" She doesn't believe me.

"Yeah, really." I pull out my phone and go to my missed calls. My mom's cell number is programmed in and I turn the phone around and show Petra the display. She glances down at the screen and a flush spreads up her cheeks.

"I'm sorry," she mutters.

"It's okay." I can see how it probably looked to her. Aside from the inconvenient timing of the call, I remember saying 'She can wait' before I rejected it. She probably thought it was another woman. "Come back with me. I'll make us a coffee."

She shakes her head. "No. Nothing's changed, Rob."

"Why?"

She steps back, putting some space between us. "Because nothing can come of this."

"Why not?" What's wrong with me? There's nothing wrong with her; she's perfect. So, it's gotta be me.

She swallows and blinks quickly, like she's trying not to cry again. "I understand that the call was from your mom and I apologize for jumping to conclusions. I also accept that you threw away that woman's phone number the other night, but that doesn't alter who you are." She sighs and I wait. "I watched you at the opening, Rob," she continues. "I saw all those women throwing themselves at you, and I can't be with someone like that. It doesn't matter how much I want you, I can't do this. I'm sorry." Two tears fall down onto her cheeks and she turns and runs again.

I stare after her, feeling a little shocked. She's just admitted she was wrong about me; she even said she wanted me – I definitely heard that right – and yet she still walking away. Well, she's running again, actually. That hole in my chest just got bigger and a lot more painful. I gaze at her retreating back and wonder if this is what it feels like to love someone? If it is, love sucks. It fucking hurts too. I cover my face with my hands. Can I really be in love, when I've only known her for a matter of hours? Is that possible? I let out a sigh and drop my hands back down by my sides. There's only one way to find out, and that's to spend some more time with her, to get to know her and let her get to know me. I take a step forward to follow her, looking up, and I swear my heart stops. She's disappeared. Why did I take my eyes off of her? "Idiot," I mutter under my breath and I run down the street after her.

I run for two blocks, but there's no sign of her. I wonder for a minute if she maybe went into one of the houses, but it seems unlikely. They're big townhouses and I can't imagine a single woman would live in one of them, not unless she's very wealthy. There's one side street and I double back and stand on the corner. There are maybe ten apartment blocks down there. How would I even know where to start?

Of course… I'm being stupid. I pull my phone from my pocket. She's a photographer. She must have a website. I go onto the Internet and search for Petra Miller Photographer, but all I get are results for a guy called Peter Miller, who I vaguely remember was a famous photo journalist from the late seventies and eighties, who was renowned for going to the world's most dangerous places and reporting back on what he saw, and taking incredible and beautiful photographs to prove it. I don't remember him myself; I'm not old enough, but his reputation as a world-class photographer still holds. I scroll down the page, but there's nothing relating to Petra.

I crouch down on the sidewalk, oblivious to the passing pedestrians.

She's gone, and right now, I can't think of a single way to get her back.

"Where the hell have you been?" Ed asks as I walk back into the kitchen. He looks me up and down and I realize my shirt is still hanging out. I liked the fact that Petra pulled it out of my pants the way she did, but I liked the feeling of her skin, and her breasts, and her kisses even more.

"Walking." I glance at my watch. It's nearly three-thirty. I've been out for hours.

"What's wrong?" he says, coming over to me.

"Petra." I only seem to be able to speak in single words at the moment.

"Care to elaborate?"

I lean up against the countertop and take a deep breath, before explaining to him what happened.

"So you've just been wandering around for the last couple of hours?" he says.

"Yeah. I couldn't think what else to do."

"You could've come back here."

I look up at him. "Back to the scene of the crime?"

"What crime? What did you do wrong?"

I've been asking myself that, over and over, ever since Petra ran away.

"I don't know. It doesn't make sense. She said she wanted me... and yet she doesn't."

"But you want her?"

"Yes."

"You're not messing with her?" he asks, his voice serious all of a sudden.

"No." I'm back to single words again.

He stares at me and folds his arms across his chest. "Okay," he says. "Tell me this... Can you imagine your life without her?"

"What?"

"Answer the question."

I think for a moment. "Yes, I guess I can. But I don't want to." It's a really bleak, empty prospect.

He nods. "If she asked you to, what would you be willing to give up for her?"

"Everything." I don't even need to think about that.

He smiles at me. "You're being an idiot," he says.

"Fuck off, Ed," I explode. "You're not helping at all. I know you've never been in love, but can't you at least show a bit of sensitivity?"

Ed takes a step forward and puts his hand on my shoulder. "Calm down. I didn't mean it like that. I just meant you're being an idiot." I open my mouth but he raises his hand to stop me from speaking. "In the past, when I've had girlfriends who've wanted me to give up my job because they didn't like my hours, or the lack of freedom, I've always gone to Sam for advice."

"I know." What I don't know is where the fuck he's going with this. I just wish he'd hurry up and get there. "And Sam's always talked you out of it," I add to try and speed things along.

"No," he replies. "Sam's never done that. He's always asked me those two questions. And every time I've replied that I could see my life very easily without them in it, and that I wouldn't really be willing to give up anything for them. And Sam's just sat and looked and me. He's never told me what to do; he's just made me see things clearly, and think about how I feel and then he's let me work it out for myself." He sighs. "I was just being Sam for a minute… because he's not here."

"And how exactly does that help?" I ask him.

"Because now we both know how you feel about Petra, I understand that you're serious about her and that you're not fooling around…"

"And?" I interrupt.

"And I can hopefully stop you being quite such an idiot."

"Ed… you're really trying my patience."

"You need to contact her."

"I can't. I told you, I tried looking her up on the Internet."

"That's what I mean about you being an idiot. How do you think Ali got hold of her?"

"I've got no idea."

"Well, neither have I actually."

I clench my fists. I haven't hit him since we were kids, but I'm gonna punch him in a minute. "Ed…" I warn.

"It doesn't really matter how Ali did it," he says calmly, "the point is, she's got Petra's contact details."

I still for a moment. He's right. He's absolutely right. I place my hands on his cheeks and kiss his forehead. "Eduardo, you're a genius," I say, grinning, then letting him go and pulling my phone from my pocket.

"Yeah, yeah." He smirks. He checks his watch. "It'll be getting late over there," he says. "Maybe you should leave it until tomorrow."

"It'll be fine," I tell him. "She doesn't have to reply tonight but at least I'll know I've done something."

I turn to go back out into the restaurant, but he calls me back.

"Do you really think Sam might stay in England?" he asks. I wonder how much he's been worrying about that since Petra brought it up earlier.

"I don't know," I reply, honestly, going back over to him. "I guess, if Sam asked himself whether he could picture his life without Ali in it, he'd have replied 'no', because he's just flown three thousand miles to work things out with her. And I imagine, if she really can't come back here for some reason, and he has to ask himself what he'd sacrifice to be with her…"

"He'd sacrifice this…" Ed finishes my sentence, looking around the kitchen.

"He might, yeah."

"And if he does, what will we do?" he asks. "What will I do?"

"We'll learn to live with it." I put a hand on his shoulder. "And you'll be okay, Ed."

He gives me a smile, but I know he's worried. He really relies on Sam, and he thinks of the three of us as inseparable, which I guess we always have been.

"Don't think about it yet," I say. "Wait until we hear from him."

"Okay," he replies. "Go send your message, before it gets any later."

I sit down at one of the tables in the restaurant, and type out a quick message to Ali. I keep it brief, just asking her if she can give me Petra's contact details, but not telling her why. I don't really want to explain, but also I imagine she's tired… or if Sam's caught up with her, maybe busy.

I wait a couple of minutes, staring at my phone, but she doesn't reply. I'm not that surprised and I go over to the bar and get myself a glass of water. I'm just on my way back to the table when my phone beeps.

I sit down before opening it, but then sigh out my frustration. It's not from Ali, it's from Sam. Call it coincidence, but I guess he's just letting us know he's got to the UK alright. *Damn.*

As I read his message though, I start to smile.

— *Ali can't ask you this, but are you fooling around with Petra, or are you actually serious for once? S*

This means they're together. He's been there for a good eight hours, and they're still together. They're obviously talking too – well, they've discussed my message, anyway.

My reply to him is really simple and honest.

— *I'm serious this time. She's different. R*

I press 'send' and I wait again.

My phone beeps after another couple of minutes. This time it's Ali. She's forwarded me Petra's details from her contacts list and I notice that her company's called 'PM Photography', which explains why my search drew a blank. There's an email address, a postal address and a phone number. I owe Ali. I just hope I get to repay her. But that's gonna be down to Sam.

I type him out a reply:

— *Thanks for persuading your girlfriend to help me out. And sorry I tried to stop you from going after Ali. Why didn't you tell me it was like this? R*

I don't know what he'll make of that, or what he'll think about me calling Ali his girlfriend. With any luck, he'll just regard it as accurate.

Then I type one to Ali…

— *Thanks Ali. You're obviously with Sam, and I'm glad the two of you caught up, and presumably made up. I'm sure he's told you about his disastrous first marriage… I'm absolutely certain his second one will be better ;) Take care of each other, and see you soon. Rob x*

I press send and lean back in the chair. Now all I've gotta do is work out how and when to contact Petra.

Chapter Five

Petra

I let myself into the house, close the door and lean back against it, breathing hard, dragging air into my lungs. I haven't run like that in years and, while I've been trying to get a little more exercise recently, that was definitely overdoing it. I lean down, resting my hands on my knees, hoping that'll help. It doesn't. My lungs scream for oxygen… God, I'm so unfit.

My only solace right now is that I'm at least alone. Rob stood and watched me run away the second time. He didn't follow – thank God. And there's no-one here to witness my humiliation either. And I'm not referring to the fact that running a couple of blocks has gotten me completely breathless. I really don't want to talk, or have to explain what just happened. As if it wasn't bad enough that I humiliated myself in the restaurant, getting carried away like that with Rob, letting him touch me like he did, and so clearly enjoying it… I then compounded the whole thing by showing him how jealous I am. I practically accused him of having another woman waiting for him on the phone, when it was just his mom calling; and I told him outright that I thought he was a flirt. Well, he is, but that doesn't mean I don't want to be with him. I suck in a deep breath and cover my face with my hands. Oh God… I think I might have actually said that to him.

I wasn't lying either. I do want to be with him. I can't, but that doesn't make me want him any less. I can't take a risk on someone like him. He's got too many women chasing after him and I know I couldn't handle it. I can't have a man like that in my life.

If only I didn't want him so much...

If only he hadn't come after me. No-one's ever done that before. I'm pretty sure, if I'd ever run out on Adrian, he'd have waved me goodbye, slammed the door, popped a beer and had a party. But Rob came after me. And he apologized... But what was he apologizing for? Was it because he got carried away? Was it because he felt guilty for what had happened and wanted to make sure I wasn't gonna go running straight to the cops? I'm not sure, but I don't think it was either of those things, and now I come to think about it, I'm almost certain he said he wanted me. He did, didn't he? Or was that wishful thinking? Was it all wishful thinking? I cover my face with my hands, hoping that the shame will diminish... I think I just implied that there could be something between us, if it wasn't for the fact that he's a serial flirt, and that I can't be with someone like that. If he wanted anything from me, it was nothing more than a kiss, a fumble, and maybe a quickie, behind the bar, and I started talking about us having a relationship... a future of some kind. I read too much into it, didn't I?

I'm not surprised now that he watched me run the second time. He was probably relieved to see the back of me.

This is beyond humiliating. It's degrading.

Could today get any worse?

It took me a while to calm down but, after a coffee and quiet sit down in the kitchen, I've moved upstairs to my office. I need to get on with editing the photographs from today. I also need to do something to erase the memory of what happened...

The problem is, I'm editing photographs of Rob. And that's not helping. It reminds me of how good his lips felt on mine, the urgency of his tongue in my mouth, the feeling of his hands on my bare skin, his fingers pinching my nipples. I've had sex before – obviously – but I've never felt anything like that. I'm not even going to consider making comparisons between what I just did with Rob and how it used to be with Adrian. The two things couldn't be any more different. Nothing

I've ever done before has felt as intense as those few minutes with Rob… and we didn't even get around to the sex part. He was aroused though. His erection was pressing into my hip. It felt very long, and very thick, and very hard. And I wanted it… everywhere.

I know I should be blushing; I should feel embarrassed at the way my thoughts are going, but I can't help myself. The idea of being naked with him, being underneath him and feeling him deep inside me has me so turned on, I can't even see what I'm doing, let alone think about it.

I lean back in my chair.

It's no good. I need the release.

I get up and go through to my bedroom, closing the door behind me and walking over to the bed. I undo my jeans and lower them to the floor, together with my panties, and step out of them. I contemplate leaving my t-shirt on, but I might as well get the full experience… I pull it over my head and take off my bra, running my hands over my breasts, remembering how Rob's touch felt. I close my eyes and let my head rock back, recalling the sensations.

I go to the nightstand and open the middle drawer, pulling out my one and only toy – my trusted friend for the last four years – and I lie down on the bed and spread my legs wide, switching it on and feeling the deep vibrations. As I apply the bulbous head to my already wet, swollen clit, I suck in a breath and lose myself to pleasure… and thoughts of what might have been.

Rob

I've spent the whole night trying to work out whether I should call Petra, or text her, or just go around and see her. I've decided on going round there, purely on the basis that she can ignore calls and texts – especially as my number will come up as 'unknown', and most people ignore those. But she can't ignore six foot two of Italian standing on her doorstep.

We're due to open at twelve and, as usual, Ed and I are at work a few hours before that. Jasmine arrives at eleven. She works the lunchtime shift, covering for me while I do the paperwork, have meetings and handle the 'business' side of things. I come out and help if we get busy, but she's good and normally copes by herself – with the other wait staff, of course.

As soon as she arrives, I tell her I've gotta go out. This isn't unheard of. I do sometimes have meetings to go to, so she doesn't query it. I slip back into the kitchen and let Ed know that I'm going and he wishes me luck. Unlike Jasmine, he knows where I'm going – and why.

Out on the sidewalk, I check the address again. I'm almost sure this is one of those big town houses I walked past yesterday, which surprises me. Petra doesn't come across as having that much money… but I guess it can be difficult to judge things like that. She's misjudged me. She accused me of flirting, with her, and those women last night. But that's not true. Last night was just about doing my job, and everything I've said to Petra is completely sincere.

I'm gonna need to explain that to her – and prove to her that I'm serious about us.

Of course, I have no idea how I'm gonna do that, or even convince her that there can be an 'us', but I'll work it out.

It takes me about ten minutes to reach her house and I stand back and look up. Sure enough, it's one of the big town houses, taking up three floors, plus a basement. I know in other parts of the city, these old houses have been converted into apartments, but this particular row of about ten houses are still in their original state – and they're beautiful.

I walk up the four steps to the front door and ring the bell.

Weirdly, I'm not nervous at all. I'm excited. I'm gonna see Petra again. What's there not to be excited about?

The door opens and she's standing in front of me. She looks amazing, and beautiful, in jeans and a tight t-shirt. Her mouth drops open at the sight of me, and her eyes widen, and I think my heart just stopped beating. I'm struggling to breathe, that's for sure.

I open my mouth to speak, just as she goes to slam the door, and I stick my foot out and stop it. *What the fuck?*

"Please, Rob," she says, tears forming in her eyes. "Wasn't yesterday humiliating enough? I told you already. I can't do this…"

"Humiliating? I thought you liked what we did yesterday."

She stares at me for a moment. "I did."

"Then I don't understand. Why are you dismissing me? And why are you upset?" I ask her. "Why are you about to cry? Why were you crying yesterday? If you don't care, and you *really* don't want this, why don't you just yell at me to fuck off out of your life and be done with it?" I pause. "Why does it upset you so much, Petra?"

She tilts her head to one side, like she doesn't have a clue what I'm talking about, then swallows hard, and blinks back her tears.

"It doesn't matter how I feel about you," she whispers. "We can't be together. I already told you that. You need to go, Rob."

"No. Not until you explain to me why it can't work between us, when it's what we both so clearly want."

"Why can't you accept that it was just a kiss – a passionate, intense kiss? Nothing more."

"Because it wasn't just a kiss to me," I reply, taking a step closer, so I'm on the threshold of her house. "And I think if you're being honest with yourself, it was more than that to you too." *Please don't let me be wrong about that…* "Why are you so determined not to at least try being with me?"

"Because I can't." What does that mean?

I reach out to touch her, but she steps back.

"I know I can make you happy," I say to her, not bothering to hide the desperation in my voice.

"I know you can't."

Ouch. That hurt. "You don't even know me," I reply. "Not really. Why are you being so hurtful? You're not even giving me a chance."

"I don't mean to be hurtful, but I can't be with you. I can't take a chance on someone like you. How can I even consider it? I'd be insane to—"

"For someone who doesn't mean to be hurtful, you're doing a great job." I've never been judged like this before and I don't like it. I guess she's probably aware of that right about now

She tilts her head to one side again. How can she not understand that her words are hurting me…?

"What?" I say, maybe a little harshly. "You think you've got the monopoly on being hurt? You think you can just keep insulting me, and that it won't hurt, because I'm a guy? Guys hurt too, you know…"

"I—I'm sorry," she stammers and her tears start to fall, and I know that there is nothing she could ever say to me that would hurt me as much as the sight of her crying.

"Don't," I whisper. "Don't cry." I step closer and pull her into my arms. "And don't apologize."

She brings her arms around my waist, then rests her head on my chest and I stroke her hair. I've never done this before and it feels good. Above all, it feels good that she's letting me.

After a couple of minutes, she leans back and looks up at me, all tear-stained and beautiful, her lips swollen and perfect.

Without saying a word, I lean closer. Her eyes are telling me she wants me to kiss her, and she moves in, her face lifted to mine, her lips parting…

"Mommy?"

I still, and for a moment, everything goes into suspension.

Petra's eyes widen, she chokes and then turns away, moving back into the house a little.

"Yes, baby?" she says.

I've never needed to take a cold shower before, but if I ever did, I imagine this is how it would feel.

I look down. Standing just a couple of paces behind Petra is the most adorable little girl I've ever seen in my life. She's like a micro version of her mom. Her long curly black hair is held back with an Alice band, and she has dark brown eyes, whereas Petra's are gray, but apart from that…

She looks from Petra to me, and then back again.

"Sorry to intrup," she says, struggling over the word. *Christ, that's cute.* "But, can I have some juice, please?"

"Sure. I'll be there in just a minute," Petra replies, smiling down at her.

The little girl goes over and sits on the bottom of the stairs, waiting patiently, while Petra turns slowly back to me.

Right now, I want to yell at her. I want to ask her who the hell she thinks she is, judging me, when she's got a daughter… a daughter who I'm guessing has a dad. Well, it sure makes sense of her saying she can't get involved – even if I'm fairly certain she would have let me take her over the bar yesterday, if my phone hadn't interrupted us… It also makes sense of her living in a place like this, which would take more than one income to afford. I quickly check her left hand. She's not wearing a ring, but that doesn't mean she's not married, or at least in a serious relationship with the guy… and she had the nerve to question *my* standards?

I can feel my anger boiling, just beneath the surface, but even I know better than to lose it in front of her kid.

"I'd better go," I say.

She doesn't reply. She just stares at me, and I turn and walk away.

I take my time going back to the restaurant.

How dare she criticize me? How dare she judge me, and then let me do all those things to her yesterday, knowing she had another man waiting for her at home? The poor guy was probably minding their daughter, playing with her, making her lunch, taking her to the park, maybe… while her mom was practically topless in my hands, and would've done more if it hadn't been for *my* mom.

I might flirt, I might sometimes act on that flirting, but I always, *always*, make sure the woman's single first. I won't be part of anything adulterous. I don't agree with, or approve of, cheating. I never have.

And I don't intend changing now.

The thing is, despite the really cute evidence to the contrary, Petra didn't seem the type to cheat either. She really didn't…

Chapter Six

Petra

I hand April her juice and sit down at the kitchen table with her, watching her drink.

Did Rob really just take one look at my daughter and walk away?

Of course he did. I don't even know why I'm surprised.

Why would he wait for an explanation? Why would he wait to find out about me and my beautiful baby girl, who's gonna be four at the weekend? Why would he be interested in finding out that her father left me before April was even born; that we live here with my mom, because I can't afford to live anywhere else, and that my life's been a lonely hell for the last four years… and without April and my mom I don't know where I'd be.

Why would he bother, when he was only ever interested in having sex with me?

In reality, I'm not even sure he was terribly interested in that. I was just available. Well, desperate, really. I made it too easy for him…

Letting a man into my life is a big thing for me. It's not something I've done since Adrian left, because it's not just me anymore. I have to think about April. I can't let her get close to someone, and then have him leave her. She wouldn't understand. Why should she? She's four – well, nearly.

But when Rob stood there, telling me that guys hurt too, and that I'd hurt him, I actually wondered, just for moment, whether he cared, and if I could take that chance with him, and let him into our lives…

How wrong was I?

April finishes her juice and jumps down from the chair. I get up from mine and push them both under the table again, and I take her hand.

"C'mon then," I say to her. "Mommy's just got another hour or so's work to do, and then we'll have some lunch."

"Okay, Mommy."

She's such a good girl. I know I'm blessed. I'm truly blessed to have her.

We go upstairs and she settles in the corner of my office, like she always does when my mom's not here to mind her, surrounded by her toys and dolls. She mutters to herself, playing, but I find the noise comforting, not disturbing, and I get on with editing the last of the photographs from yesterday's shoot.

I did get back to work yesterday afternoon, once I'd had a couple of orgasms, thanks to my trusted toy, and then laid back on the bed and enjoyed the afterglow for a while.

Mom and April came in shortly after I got dressed and I worked while my mom made our evening meal. That's a regular Sunday routine for us – apart from the orgasms, that is. Mom always takes April to visit her sister, Stephanie on Sunday afternoons, from two until five. It gives me a chance to catch up with work – or housework, if absolutely necessary – gets them both out of the house, gives my mom the opportunity to chatter away with Stephanie in Greek for a few hours, and April plays with Stephanie's grandchildren, Matthew and Emily, who also go round on Sundays. Matthew's a year older, but Emily's the same age as April and they're great friends. Unfortunately, although I get on well with their dad – Stephanie's son, Mateo – I've never really hit it off with his wife, Courtney. I always feel like she's judging me, unfavorably. When Adrian and I split up, she made a few snide remarks about me having 'let myself go', which hurt at the time. Mateo is a fairly well-paid veterinarian and it seems to me that his salary enables Courtney a certain lifestyle, lunching and playing tennis with her friends, not to mention several cosmetic surgery procedures, including a breast enhancement last year. She's just always struck me as one of those women who 'take' all the time, and don't really seem to give anything back. Still, they seem happy enough, so who am I to judge?

I fire up my computer and open the first file. Great… a photograph of Rob smiling straight at the camera, his eyes sparkling, his lips full and perfectly kissable. Damn him.

I swallow down my tears, square my shoulders and try to ignore the fact that yesterday afternoon, when I was lying naked on my bed, just thinking about him and his body, and what it would feel like to have him inside me, made me come harder than I've ever done before. Instead, I get on and edit the remaining photographs and, within an hour, I'm finished.

I still need to email them all through though. I sent the last batch to Ali, but as she's gone home, I guess these will have to go to Rob. I look up the contact details on the restaurant's website and type them into my mail app, keeping the message brief and businesslike. I add a link to the pictures, because they're too large to send as an attachment. And then it dawns on me that I've still got Sam's photographs to take. I can't do it though. I can't go back there and see Rob again. I give him the name of a couple of other local photographers who I know will do a good job, telling him they can take Sam's photographs, being as it might be awkward for us. I'm sure he'll agree. Then I attach my invoice for the two shoots, and sign off with just my name. I press send and rest my head in my hands.

It's done. It's over.

Rob

I have absolutely no idea how I got through the evening session. It's a blur. I don't actually remember getting back to the restaurant. I know it was near the end of the lunch service by the time I got there, but where I'd been in between, I couldn't tell you.

Ed switches off the lights and, working on automatic pilot, like I have been all evening, I grab my keys and we head for the door.

We walk home in silence, and he lets us into our apartment, which is about ten minutes away from the restaurant, but in the opposite direction to Petra's house. Our place is nowhere near as grand either, although we like it. We've got a two bed apartment, with a large living-dining room and a spectacular kitchen. Ed's the cook in our household, but I can turn my hand to pretty much anything as well. Learning to cook wasn't really an option in our home. Our mom taught us to make home-style foods, like pasta, pizza and roasts; our dad taught us the refinements, and although I gave up the kitchen work and went to college after a couple of years, you don't really forget.

It might be just after midnight, but neither of us is tired yet, so Ed gets us both a beer and switches on the TV, settling back in the recliner. I sit on the couch and pull my laptop from my bag. I haven't had a chance to check my emails yet, and I guess I should, just in case anything important has come in. I wait for the app to load, watching a few minutes of the game Ed's put on. It's a replay of the Yankees playing the Red Sox and, although we both prefer football, it's a good enough game to keep his attention and stop me from thinking about Petra… until I look at my messages, that is, and see that I've received one from her. What the fuck can she have to say to me now?

Part of me thinks about deleting it, but then I notice the subject is 'Photographs', so I guess it's related to work, which means I'd better check it out.

I open it and read quickly. Jesus, could she be any more businesslike? We kissed, hard. Did it mean nothing to her? I get to the second paragraph… She's sent me a couple of other photographers we can use for Sam's pictures, because she thinks it might be 'awkward' for us to see each other. Is she fucking serious? Awkward? I slam my laptop shut and throw it onto the couch beside me.

Ed sits up. "Wanna tell me about it?" he says.

"What?" I turn to look at him.

"Whatever it is that's been eating at you since you got back from Petra's." He pauses. "I take it things didn't go well."

I'm almost tempted to laugh – except it's not funny. "That would be a massive understatement."

"What happened?"

"She's got a kid."

He stares at me, waiting. "And?" he says.

"And?" Is that all he can say?

"Well, there's gotta be something else…"

I guess it doesn't make sense to just say that. Not really. "I kissed her yesterday, Ed. Actually, I did quite a lot more than kiss her. But she ran out on me. She said we couldn't be together and let me believe it was because of me – because she'd seen some of the women who were here last Saturday night flirting with me. She said she couldn't be with someone like me. She was really judgmental. It hurt."

"Okay…"

"And then, just as I was gonna kiss her again at her house, her little girl appeared out of nowhere."

"And what did you do?" he asks.

"I left." He stares at me for a moment, then shakes his head. "What?"

"You didn't talk to her?" He seems surprised.

"Of course I didn't talk to her. I wasn't capable of being polite at the time. And I wasn't gonna yell at her in front of her daughter. I'm not that insensitive."

"Glad to hear it," he says quietly. "Even if you are being an idiot… again."

I sit forward, leaning toward him. "Excuse me?"

He pulls the chair into its upright position and leans forward himself, facing me. "You're being an idiot, Rob."

"No I'm not. She's got a daughter. That means there has to be a dad."

"Yeah. But that's just biology. There's nothing to say she's still with the dad. Hell, there's nothing to say she ever was – not in the way you mean, anyway. Accidents happen, and sometimes guys walk away from their responsibilities. But even if she was with him once upon a time, that doesn't mean she's with him now." He sighs and shakes his head again. "Not everyone stays together forever. Just because we come from an old-fashioned Italian family, doesn't mean everyone does. Marriage is a lifetime commitment for us, but that's just how things are in our family. I mean, it might be okay for us to fool around while we're single, but we all know Mama would kill us if we even looked at another woman once we were married, don't we?"

I nod my head absently. He's not wrong. That's how it works in our family.

"Look at Sam's situation," he says calmly. "Look at how Mom and Dad reacted to him getting divorced – even after he explained over and over that Amber had cheated. They still don't talk – not properly."

"They have such a ludicrously unrealistic, idealized image of relationships." He glares at me for a moment, but nods his head, obviously thinking that the term 'ludicrously unrealistic' shouldn't be limited just to our parents. "I mean, why did they expect Sam to forgive and forget when she was banging her boss, and probably a few other guys besides, if the truth's told?"

"Yeah, but I've often wondered if they'd change their views if they knew what she'd done before the wedding,"

"I doubt it," I reply, temporarily putting Petra to one side in my own head and recalling what happened a week or so before Sam's wedding. It's not something we often talk about, and sometimes I have to struggle to remember it myself... We were between shifts, and Ed and Sam were still at work. I was here, at our apartment. We hadn't long moved in and I'd come back to do some unpacking. When the doorbell rang, I assumed it was Ed. No-one else really knew we were living here and he'd said he might come back and help out if he had time. I just assumed he'd forgotten his keys, so I buzzed him up without checking, and left the door open, returning to my bedroom. It was the cough – the very female cough – that alerted me to her presence. Until then I'd been completely unaware there was anyone in the apartment. She was quiet, I'll give her that. Quiet and stealthy. I turned to find Amber standing in the doorway to my bedroom, completely naked, apart from a pair of

red fuck-me heels and a smile. I didn't really know what to do, or say…
well, it's not something that happens every day is it? I mean how often
does a guy find himself in a situation like that? She didn't take her eyes
from mine, but walked slowly into the room and, without saying a
word, she lay down on the unmade bed and spread her legs wide,
moving her hand down between them, across her shaved pussy. She
rubbed her clit for a moment before running her fingers downward to
her entrance and dipping two of them inside. Then she raised them
them to her lips and sucked – hard. Sounds erotic, doesn't it? Not when
it's your brother's fiancée, it isn't, I can assure you. I asked her what the
fuck she thought she was doing, and she giggled and told me she'd often
wondered what I'd be like. The feeling wasn't mutual, so, I grabbed her
hand – the one that wasn't hovering near her mouth at the time – and
hauled her off of my bed and out into the corridor. Her clothes were in
a pile by the door and I handed them to her and threw her out. I told
Ed about it when he got home, and then spent the following Sunday
trying real hard to talk Sam out of marrying her. I never told him why.
I just hoped he'd believe in me and call it off, or at least postpone the
wedding so I'd have a chance to show him what she was really like. He
didn't. He married her. And then he divorced her once he realized for
himself what she was really like.

"No, you're probably right," Ed says, bringing me back to the
present. "Mom and Dad have never really understood about Amber."
He pauses for a moment, still looking at me. "But then you're not being
very realistic or understanding either, are you?"

"How can you say that?" I jump to my feet and stand in front of him.
"She blamed me for the fact that we couldn't get together; she kept her
daughter a secret from me…"

"Hold on a second," he interrupts. "You hadn't even got together
with her. You'd kissed a couple of times, that's pretty much all… but
you expected her to tell you everything about her life? Why should she?
She knows nothing about you."

"Exactly, but that didn't stop her judging me, did it?" I yell at him.

"Jesus," he huffs out. "Has it occurred to you that maybe she wasn't
judging you? Maybe she likes you – has that dawned on you? And

maybe she didn't really like watching you being fawned over by other women… Maybe she was jealous. I mean, how would you have liked it, if it was the other way around, and a bunch of guys were pawing her?" I think about that for a moment and can feel the anger rising inside me, even at the hypothetical thought. "And it's a possibility that she'd be wary of letting a guy like you into her life," Ed continues.

"A guy like me?"

"Yeah, Rob. Hell, she hasn't even seen you at your worst."

I look at the wooden floor and, for the first time in my life, I feel uncomfortable about my lifestyle – well, my former lifestyle, because I know I can't do that again, even if I'm never gonna be with Petra. Seeing it all through someone else's eyes – her eyes – makes it all very different, and very sordid.

Ed's still talking… "You've gotta bear in mind, she's got a daughter to consider. It's not just her, Rob. She's gotta think about that."

"But she didn't tell me." Even to me, that argument is starting to sound pathetic.

"Well I don't blame her," he says, raising his voice and getting up to face me. "She didn't seem the type to kiss you if she's got a husband, or a boyfriend, or whatever at home," he continues, and I can't disagree because I've been thinking the same thing all day. "But maybe she's got trust issues with men. Maybe her daughter's father left her. Maybe that's why she's nervous about getting involved with you – because she thinks you'll do the same thing…"

"But I wouldn't," I murmur.

"I know that," he says, calming down. "The thing is, you need to stop being an idiot, and let her get to know you." He switches off the TV and the silence rings loud. "But first, you're gonna have to find a way to get her to listen to you." He puts his hand on my shoulder. "And I suggest you start that off with an apology – because whatever you think, you're the one who was judging, not her."

He walks around me and goes down the hallway to his bedroom, closing the door quietly behind him, and I stand staring out the window for a few minutes.

He's absolutely right – about everything.

I sit back down again and open up my laptop, going to her message and reading it through once more. There's a link to the photographs, and her invoice is attached. She uses PayPal, so I pull out my wallet and use my credit card to pay her straight away.

Then I hit the reply button and, without even thinking, I start typing...

'Dear Petra,

I'm sorry. I'm sorry for everything. I shouldn't have walked away from you like I did. I should've stayed and talked to you. I made assumptions about you and your life and I had no right to do that. I thought you were judging me and my lifestyle, but it was me that was doing the judging, and that was wrong of me.

It was a surprise to discover you've got a daughter – a very beautiful daughter – but that's not why I left. I left because I jumped to conclusions about you and her father, I shouldn't have done that, and I apologize.

Having said all of that, I'm gonna make one more assumption. I'm gonna assume you're free, because you let me do things with you yesterday that I don't think you would've done if you'd been with someone. If I'm right, and if you can forgive me, I'd like to see you again. I'd like to spend some time with you, to find out more about you. I'd like to get to know you better and, I'd like you to get to know me and see that I'm not the guy you maybe think I am.

If you can't forgive me, or you don't want to know, I guess I'll understand. I'll be real sorry, but I'll understand.

Either way, thank you for the photographs, and for spending some time with me yesterday. It was magical, and memorable. Like you.

Rob x'

I click on the send icon real fast, before I can read it back and change any of it. It's the most sentimental thing I've ever written – or said, for that matter, but it was all true and it was from the heart. I just hope she can see that.

Chapter Seven

∽

Petra

I cried myself to sleep last night.

I know why… It was disappointment. I was disappointed that Rob walked away, that he wasn't really interested in me as a person, or in my life, when I'd stupidly thought he might be different…

Still, I suppose today's another day. And it's going to be a busy one. Well, this morning is, anyway. My mom's minding April for me, because I've got an early meeting with a couple who are getting married in the autumn and want to hire me to take their photographs. We've arranged to meet at the hotel where they're holding the ceremony, which is a short cab ride away, and then I've gotta get back to the toy store around the corner to pick up April's present.

I'm glad I'm going to be occupied this morning. It means I haven't got time to dwell on Rob…

The engaged couple – Andy and Christina – are really nice. They know what they want, which is good, but they're open to suggestions. I've handled a wedding at this venue before and, before I leave them, I agree to send them through some samples of the images I took, so they can see what I've done there before.

I get to the toy store at ten-thirty and go to the collections counter. Unfortunately, when I ordered April's present, I did it online, without really thinking it through, and now I've realized that I've got no means of getting it into the house and nowhere to store it. And as the guy brings it out to me, I can also see that it's a lot bigger than I'd thought.

I've bought her a play kitchen, because – unlike me – she loves to cook. I don't have a culinary bone in my body, but my mom's a great cook, so I imagine that's where April gets it from.

Right now though, I've got a problem… namely, what the hell am I going to do with this thing?

The box has a carry handle, so I can at least maneuver it, and I lug it from the store, evidently to the amusement of the guy behind the counter. *Jerk.*

It's a warm day and I'd planned on walking home. Now, I'm not so sure, but I at least start the journey on foot – if only to give myself time to try and work out where exactly I'm gonna be able to hide this enormous box between now and Sunday.

My route takes me past Rosa's, but I know they won't be open yet and I don't even glance up as I pass, because I'm focused on trying not to fall over the box I'm now almost dragging along beside me.

"Petra…?" Rob's voice makes me stop in my tracks.

I turn and see him standing by the door, leaning against it, dressed all in black as usual, his arms folded across his broad chest. I'd be tempted to run again, if it wasn't for the fact that April's present is weighing me down.

"Hi," I say, my cheeks flushing. I guess there's no need to be rude.

He steps out onto the sidewalk, coming toward me. "Did you get my email?" he asks.

"Um… no. I haven't checked my messages yet. I had an early meeting. Why? Is there something wrong with the photographs?" I let go of the box.

"No," he says, moving closer still. "My message was nothing to do with work."

My mouth dries. "Oh?"

"It was about us."

"Us?" Is there an 'us'?

He sighs and puts his hands in his pockets, looking at the narrow space between us. "I'm sorry," he says quietly. "I know I reacted badly yesterday, but I wasn't expecting you to have a daughter."

"Clearly." I don't bother to hide my sarcasm.

He ignores it and continues, "It wasn't something that had even crossed my mind. But I jumped to the conclusion that having a daughter meant you'd also have a husband – or at least be in a long-term relationship with someone. And I know it was wrong of me to make assumptions like that and then just walk away from you, without giving you the chance to even speak."

"Yes, it was," I say. "April's my life. She's the reason I'm so careful about who I date. Well, I haven't actually dated anyone since her father left me, but…" Shit! Did I really just say that out loud. Judging from the expression on his face, I think I must've done. I avert my gaze, staring at the ground instead. "Still, none of that matters," I add, before he can say anything. "You've got the photographs and my invoice, so our business is concluded." Without looking up at him again, I turn to leave, but he grabs my arm and spins me back.

"No, it isn't," he growls, and placing his hands on my cheeks, he raises my face to his and kisses me – hard. His lips touch mine and, within a blink I'm his again. I open to him and his tongue clashes with mine, his groan echoing through me and meeting my reverberant moan. He takes a half step nearer so our bodies meet, my breasts crushed hard against his chest and, as his hips grind into me, I bring my hands up to his neck, letting them rest there, my thumbs caressing his stubbled jaw. He breaks the kiss, biting gently on my bottom lip, before releasing me.

"I'm not apologizing. Not this time," he says. "That was the right thing to do, for both of us. We both needed it. Every fucking second of it."

I'm not going to correct him, or deny that he's right.

He's still holding me and I'm speechless, gazing into his eyes.

"Come inside," he says, and only now am I aware of the fact that we're still on the sidewalk and that people are walking past us, some of them staring.

"Why?" I ask him, my voice croaking.

"Because we need to talk." His voice is low and sexy.

"We do?"

"Yeah. We do." He lets me go and reaches around to pick up the box, which he does with ease. Then he holds out his hand to me. "C'mon," he says and before I know it, I've put my hand in his and let me him lead me inside.

Rob

Someone, somewhere clearly loves me. Either that, or it's just my lucky day. I only went outside for a breath of fresh air, and I caught sight of Petra, struggling along the street with an enormous box. I wasn't gonna let that opportunity pass. Okay, so she was mad at me, and she dismissed me, and it looked like she was gonna leave… but then she let me kiss her. She didn't fight me. In fact, she responded – she *really* responded. That's one of the things I love most about her. She's real receptive, and open, and physically demonstrative. She doesn't hold back. And yeah… I did just say 'love' then. Because I realized during the night when I was thinking about her, and my message to her, and wondering if she'd reply, that regardless of what I said to Ed the other day, I can't contemplate my life without her in it, and that I love her. I'm surprised by how simple that thought was. I realize it's quick, and I realize I know very little about her, but none of that matters, because I love her. Completely. Of course, I wasn't entirely sure what I was gonna do about it, especially when I checked my messages and found she hadn't come back to me, but now I don't have to worry about that, because she's sitting opposite me in the quietest corner of the restaurant.

"Is that gonna be okay there?" She asks nodding to her box, which I've dumped over by the bar.

"Sure."

"It won't be in anyone's way?"

"I doubt they're gonna fall over it. It's kinda big." I smirk.

"Yeah. I hadn't realized it would be quite that large."

"I noticed you were finding it a struggle." I smile over at her. "Can I get you a coffee?"

"Um… okay."

"White?" I ask.

She nods and I look up and see Jackson standing behind the bar. "Jack," I call. "Can you bring me two flat whites."

"Sure, boss."

"Are you sure you don't need to be working?" Petra asks, looking around.

"Positive. Jasmine's in charge at lunchtimes." I nod toward her at the back of the restaurant. She's tall, skinny, with straight blonde hair and pale blue eyes… the direct opposite of Petra, in fact. She's also got two really noisy kids, and a husband, Cole, who's a firefighter. He works the night shift and looks after their kids during the day – and I pity him, although Jasmine's fun, so I guess life has its compensations.

Jackson brings our coffees and puts them down in front of us.

"Thanks," I say to him and he leaves again.

Petra stirs her coffee, even though she didn't add any sugar to it, and stares down at the cup.

"Talk to me," I whisper.

"What about?" She looks up. *Oh God, she really is so beautiful.*

"Tell me about your daughter."

A smile crosses her face, lighting up her eyes and I strike that last thought; she's way beyond beautiful.

"Her name's April," she says, although I already got that from what she said outside. "She's four on Sunday – hence the enormous present." She glances over toward the box. "And she's everything to me."

"I kinda gathered that," I murmur.

She smiles. "She's really amazing. She's well behaved…"

"I noticed," I interrupt.

She looks right at me. "I'm sorry about what happened," she says quietly.

I shake my head. "I'm the one who's sorry."

"I probably should've told you about her…"

"Why? All we did was kiss, really. That doesn't entitle me to know your life story."

"Is that all it was to you, Rob? A kiss." She sounds almost tearful. "I thought…"

"Hey," I say quickly. "I was so much more than a kiss for me. I tried to tell you that at the time, but I think you were in denial, or in shock…" She smiles. "If you don't mind, I would like to know about you and April."

"Why?" she asks, staring into my eyes.

"Because I still want more than a kiss with you, Petra. A *lot* more."

Her cheeks flush, but she smiles and takes a sip of coffee.

"Her father's name was Adrian," she says, putting the cup back into its saucer. "We split up before she was born, when he decided to have an affair."

"Asshole," I mutter, unable to stop myself.

"Yeah. He was."

"Does he still see April?" I ask.

"No. He's never seen her. He wasn't interested in her." That hurts her. I can tell from the tone of her voice. Still, it also explains her reluctance to let another man into her life.

"It's his loss, Petra."

"I know," she says wistfully.

"You kept the house, though?" I ask.

"Oh, no," she says. "He kept the house. It was his, not mine, or even ours. So I moved in with my mom." It's starting to add up now. "It kinda worked out well for Mom as well as me. I needed somewhere to live and she was lonely." She looks up at me and the sadness in her eyes is heartbreaking. "My dad had been diagnosed with cancer and then died quite quickly a couple of months beforehand, and it had all happened so suddenly, she wasn't coping well. But I moved in and she helped me through the end of my pregnancy and was with me at the birth. She and April are best friends." Her voice catches as she speaks and I reach over and take her hand in mine.

"It's good that you get along so well with your mom," I say. I'm lucky, I've got a great relationship with both my parents, but Ed and Sam aren't so fortunate.

"It wasn't always like this," she admits. "I was a lot closer to my dad, but Mom and I helped each other through a horrible time and it works well… mostly."

"Mostly?" I query.

"We argue sometimes, mainly about food…" Her voice trails to a whisper.

"Food?"

"Yeah." She doesn't say any more.

"Why food?" It seems an odd thing to argue about, if you ask me.

"I'm lousy in the kitchen. I'm the only person I know who can burn water." I laugh and she smiles at me. "Oh, you can laugh," she says, "but it's true. If it wasn't for my mom, April would starve."

"Well, we can't all be good at everything," I say to her. "Stop beating yourself up over it."

"Do you wanna tell my mom that?" she suggests.

"Sure, if you like." I'm serious, and she looks at me for a moment, then drinks down the rest of her coffee.

"I should probably be going," she says. "I've got to get back and send out some emails to clients… and work out where the hell I'm gonna store this kitchen."

"What kitchen?"

"The box…" She nods toward the bar. "It's a play kitchen for April's birthday."

"Ahh… You're trying to encourage her to succeed where you've failed?" I suggest, smiling.

"No. It's nothing like that. She loves cooking. She's always in the kitchen with my mom. All I can do is watch."

Judging from the tone of her voice, I wonder if she feels left out. I also wonder why her mom didn't teach her how to cook as a child and can't make the effort to include her now… What's the use in criticizing her for not cooking, but then not encouraging her to learn?

"So you've bought her a play kitchen?" I prompt, getting her back to the topic and trying to cheer her up a little.

"Yeah. She's gonna love it." Her eyes sparkle again. "Only I didn't realize it was as big as it is. Goodness knows why though… I mean, it was never gonna fit in a matchbox, was it?"

I shake my head, smiling at her. "And you've got nowhere to hide it?"

"Not that I can think of… And as for how I'm gonna get it into the house without her seeing it…"

"I'll keep it for you."

She looks up at me. "You will?"

"Sure. I can stow it in the office until later and take it home with me tonight."

"Are you sure?"

"I'm positive. I can drop it to you on Saturday night when I finish here."

"I can't ask you to do that. But I can come and pick it up from you."

"Saturday night?" I ask. "It'll be late. I don't finish here until midnight, normally."

"I know," she smirks. "I was here at the opening, remember?"

I smile again – I feel like I have to when she's around. "How could I forget?" She smiles back. "I really don't mind dropping it at your place."

"No. I'll pick it up." She gets her phone out of her purse. "Give me your address and I'll come by when you've finished work."

I'm not about to say no to that…

Once she's typed my address into her phone, she gets up, and I stand too.

"Shall I give you my number?" she asks.

"I've already got it. Ali gave it to me, along with your address and email. That's how I tracked you down."

"You… you tracked me down?" she repeats, her eyes widening a little. "I assumed you'd just looked me up on the Internet."

"No. It wasn't that easy. But I wanted to see you again, so I contacted Ali in England."

"Oh." She seems surprised and stares at me for a moment, before blinking. "Okay. Well, um… text me when you're finished on Saturday and I'll get a cab to your place."

"Right."

"You're sure this is okay?" She looks at the box again.

"I'm positive."

"Thank you." We make our way toward the door.

"No… thank you."

She stops and turns to me. "What for?"

"For coming in here. For having coffee with me. For telling me about yourself."

"I haven't told you everything," she murmurs, looking embarrassed.

"You don't have to." I hesitate. "You're giving me a chance. That's all I'm asking for. That's all that matters."

I pull her close, and she raises her face as I lean down and kiss her. She parts her lips and welcomes my tongue, her hands coming up around my neck, holding me. Within seconds, her breathing changes and her breasts are heaving into my chest. I place a hand in the small of her back and pull her onto me so she can feel my erection. I want her to know what she does to me and her quiet moan tells me she likes what she's feeling. So do I. I break the kiss eventually and stare down at her.

"I like kissing you," I whisper.

"I like kissing you too."

I caress her cheek with my fingertip. "So, does that mean we can do it some more?"

She nods her head and, giving me a sweet, sexy smile, she leaves.

Fuck, that was hot.

I turn back into the restaurant to find all six of the wait staff are standing, staring at me.

"What? None of you ever seen two people kissing before?" I remark, trying to sound nonchalant.

"Yes, but not quite like that," Jasmine says, grinning, and she picks up a menu from the table beside her and fans her face with it.

"Oh, ha ha," I reply sarcastically. "Get back to work." I give her a wink and go through to the office, picking up April's play kitchen on the way.

"You're looking pleased with yourself," Ed says, much later on, walking into the office without knocking.

"That's because Petra's been in this morning. I think we're back together."

"*Back* together?" he queries.

"Well, together then. Whatever."

He comes around to my side of the desk and leans against it. "Good," he says. "I'm pleased for you." He means it too. "Just try not to mess it up."

"I'm gonna do my best."

He nods and smiles.

"Did you come in here for a particular reason?"

"Yeah. I've had a message from Sam," he says.

"At last." We haven't heard from him since he got to England, other than when I contacted Ali to get hold of Petra's details. "When's he coming home?"

"He hasn't said. He wants to have a Skype call with us in…" He checks his watch. "Five minutes."

I look up at him. "Why am I suddenly feeling a little nervous?"

He shrugs. "Maybe he's just missing us," he says, but I sense he's as worried as I am. Sam's the kind of guy who sends one word text messages. I'd expected to get one with his flight details and 'meet me' after it, not for him to want to chat to us about his plans.

I open my laptop and activate my Skype.

"What time is it over there?" Ed asks.

I check my watch. "Nine-thirty?"

He nods, just as my computer starts to warble. I connect the call and we wait. After a few moments, Sam's image appears on the screen.

"Hi," he says, sounding disconnected.

"Hi," I reply. Ed moves around and stands behind me.

"Hey, Ed," Sam adds.

Ed waves and says, "Hello."

"How's things?" Sam asks.

"Okay," I tell him. "How about with you?"

He pauses – noticeably. "That's why I'm calling," he says. "I need to tell you guys something."

"What?"

There's another pause. "I'm gonna be staying here until the end of the month," he says bluntly.

"The end of the month?" That's three and a half weeks away. I'm incredulous. Ed's silent, but I think it's stunned silence.

Sam holds up his hands before either of us can say anything else, although the motion is kinda juddered. "I'm sorry," he says. "I really am… and I wouldn't do this to you guys if it wasn't really necessary."

"It had better be fucking necessary, Sam," I say, raising my voice. "You said a few days… not a few weeks."

"I know. And I really am sorry."

We both wait. He's gonna have to tell us why if he wants us to go along with this.

He takes a sip from what looks like a glass of red wine, then looks back at the screen. "Ali and her sister Tess own a house on the south coast in England," he says.

"Right…"

"And they rent it out – well, they did. Only the tenants didn't pay the rent and when the agents sent them a reminder, they trashed the place." He frowns. "And I mean trashed. When Ali and I got here on Sunday night, there were broken windows – which was great considering it was pouring with rain and blowing a gale – there wasn't even a chair to sit on, and as for what they'd done on the mattresses…" He leaves the sentence unfinished, but we've both got enough imagination to work that out.

"Christ…" I reply before Ed.

"Yeah. We're staying at a local hotel at the moment, and working on the house during the day…"

"And you wanna stay there and help her fix the place up?" Ed guesses.

"Well, yeah."

"Why do I sense there's more?"

"Because there is. I've asked Ali to come back to the States with me," he says, hesitating. "But she won't come without her sister."

"And?"

"And her sister's at college at the moment, but she's due to finish at the end of the month…"

"And then you're all gonna come back here?" I ask.

"That's the plan."

I'm not sure why he doesn't just say 'yes'.

"What aren't you telling us?" I ask him.

"Ali isn't sure Tess is gonna want to come," he replies. He looks a bit deflated… even defeated by that. "She's speaking to her now."

"And if she doesn't?" Ed asks.

"I'm really hoping it won't come to that." He sighs. "Ali and I have spent a lot of the last couple of days talking. We've got everything out in the open now. I've told her about Amber—"

"You mean she didn't know?" I ask him, a little surprised that Sam hadn't told Ali about his ex-wife. I suddenly remember my text message to her and wonder if maybe that's what prompted Sam to tell her. Obviously I thought he already had done, or I'd never have sent that, but I doubt he's very pleased with me…

"No." His voice interrupts my thoughts and I notice he's still smiling, so maybe he isn't planning how to murder me just yet. "We hadn't gotten around to talking about the past… We hadn't gotten around to talking much at all."

"I don't think you need to tell us any more," Ed replies.

Sam shakes his head. "No, I don't suppose I do. Anyway, I'm in love with Ali, and well… she's told me she's in love with me too. And we want to be together, but…"

"But Ali won't come over here without her sister?" I finish his sentence for him.

"No."

That's gotta be hard for Sam to take. She loves him, but not enough to leave her sister behind. I imagine there must be something behind that…

"Like I say, we talked, and now I know they're real close," he explains. "And I mean *real* close. So, I've just gotta hope Ali can persuade Tess."

"Okay."

"And in the meantime, I need to stay here with her while we work everything out… the house, and our future."

I glance up at Ed.

"Okay," we say together.

"We'll cope… somehow," I add.

He smiles. "Thanks, guys. You can call me anytime you need to."

"I probably will," Ed says.

"I'm just a phone call away," Sam replies reassuringly.

We get through the evening's service, without either of us mentioning Sam's bombshell. I think Ed needs to mull it over for a while before we talk it through. I know he's already exhausted and was looking forward to Sam coming home soon. He sure as hell wasn't expecting this – any more than I was.

"I'm gonna go to bed," he says as soon as we walk through the door to the apartment. I put the play kitchen down in the hallway, but Ed doesn't even comment on it.

"You don't wanna talk?" I ask.

"Not yet. I just wanna work things out in my head first."

"You can handle it, you know."

"Yeah." He sounds kinda distant and wanders down the hallway toward his bedroom.

"Ed," I call after him. "If Sam didn't think you could do this, he would've come back."

He turns around and looks at me. "You really think that?"

"Yes. I do. He loves Ali, but he wouldn't just abandon us if he really thought we needed him. He knows we can do this without him. We've just gotta work out how."

He nods his head and disappears into his room.

I think, deep down, even Ed knows he can cope with the extra work, in terms of the cooking. What he's not great with is the added stress of being in charge. He never wanted that. I'll give him a couple of days to think and if he hasn't come to me, I'll make a point of checking that he's okay and can handle the pressure. If he can't, we'll work something out, although quite what that will be, I don't have a clue.

I sit down, turn on the table lamp, and open up my laptop. After Sam's call, I didn't bother to check my messages again.

I open up my mail and see straight away that there's an answer from Petra.

I smile and click on it, and my smile broadens as I read:

'Dear Rob,

I'm really grateful to you for storing April's present. It's helped me out a lot. I'll hear from you on Saturday about picking it up.

Also, thanks for paying my invoice so quickly. I didn't expect that.

I'm glad we sorted out our differences. I enjoyed talking to you. I enjoyed the coffee. But I enjoyed the kissing most of all.

See you soon.

Petra. x'

I'm grinning by the time I finish reading and, rather than replying by email, because that feels a little too formal to me, I get up and go and grab my phone from my jacket pocket, then sit back down again and program her number into my contacts, and type out a message to her.

— **Hi. Thanks for the email. I enjoyed the coffee and the talk too. But the kissing was the best of all. Ever. Hope we never have any 'differences' again. I miss your lips already and can't wait to kiss you again. Rob xx**

It's nearly twelve-thirty and I'm sure she'll be asleep by now, but I send it anyway and sit back, looking up at the ceiling. I like telling her how I feel. It's new to me, but I like it.

My phone vibrates in my hand. I always have it on silent when I'm working and forgot to turn the volume back on. I check the screen. The message is from Petra.

— **I can't wait either. Petra xx**

Still grinning, I reply:

— **It's late. Why are you still awake? R xxx**

Her response is instant.

— **Because I was hoping to hear from you. Does that make me pathetic? P xxx**

I laugh.

— No, it makes you adorable. Glad I didn't disappoint. R xxx

Her next reply makes me choke.

— I'm sure you never will. P xxx

Chapter Eight

Petra

— *What are you doing? R xxx*
— *Working. You? P xxx*
— *I've just got in. It's late. You shouldn't be working. You should be in bed – preferably with me ;) R xxx*

I smile. His texts have been like this all week. So have mine. And yes, I know he's a flirt and he probably does this all the time, but I can't help myself. His words make me feel good about myself, and I haven't done that for a long time. Believe me, after the evening I've had, I need the distraction; I need something to make me feel better.

— *Behave yourself. P xxx*
— *You know you don't mean that. I've been thinking about you all day. R xxx*
— *What have you been thinking? P xxx*
— *Do you really want to know? R xxx*
— *I don't know. Do I? P xxx*

There's a delay and I wonder if he's trying to decide how to tell me he's made a mistake. Then my phone rings and I check the display. It's Rob and, smiling to myself, I connect the call.

"I've been thinking that I can't wait to see you again tomorrow night. I need you, Petra. I need to feel your lips on mine," he murmurs, his voice soft and low, and very sexy. "I need to have you in my arms, and I need to touch you… everywhere." He whispers that last word, and my whole body shudders at the thought.

"Oh, please… yes." The words escape my lips in a slow breath.

"You want that too?"

I nod my head.

"Petra?"

"Yes," I whisper. "Yes, I do."

"Tell me what you want," he urges.

"Do I have to? I mean… can't I send you a text?" I can feel myself blushing. We did something similar to this earlier in the week – on Wednesday, I think it was – but that was by text. It was hot, and a lot less embarrassing…

"No. I want to hear you say the words this time. I thought you understood… I want us to be together. *Really* together. You said on Wednesday night, you wanted the same thing, and that means we've gotta be able to communicate with each other."

He's right, I did say that, and I meant it. The thing is, it was a lot easier to say by text than in actual words. "Texting is communicating," I reason.

There's a pause. "Okay," he says, "so if we're on your couch and I'm kissing you, and you decide you want me to do something more, what are you gonna do? Send me a text?"

"No."

"Then tell me what you want…"

"You."

I hang up and drop my phone, like it's a red hot coal. It buzzes again instantly, but I ignore it and after five rings, it stops, only to start again. It's no good…

"Why'd you hang up?" His voice is so full of concern, it takes my breath away.

Isn't it obvious? "Because I can't do what you want. I can't be what you want."

"What the hell does that mean?"

"I'm no good at this." I can feel tears pricking behind my eyes, but I'm not gonna cry, dammit.

"Stop it," he says. "Stop putting yourself down, and tell me what's really wrong."

And despite my best intentions, I burst into tears.

"Petra? Are you crying?" I can't reply. "Please don't cry. I'm sorry."

"It's… it's not you," I mutter, between sobs.

"Then what is it?"

"It's my mom. We had a big fight."

"Do you wanna talk about it? Do you want me to come over?"

"It's twelve-thirty in the morning, Rob…"

"I don't care."

"April's asleep. So's my mom."

"I can be real quiet," he says.

"No… it's okay." I manage to stop the tears and grab a Kleenex from the box on my desk to wipe my eyes.

"Tell me what happened?" His voice is even softer now, like he's whispering directly into my ear.

It's hard to know where to begin. "She went out for the evening."

"Okay…"

"And when she got back, we were talking in the kitchen and she noticed that I'd given April chicken strips for dinner. I'd left the carton on the countertop…"

"And?"

"Precisely. I didn't think it was a big deal. But listening to my mom, you'd have thought I'd fed her toxic waste…" I bite back the tears, remembering her harsh words. "That's not really the worst of it though," I continue.

"Why? What else happened?"

"In the heat of the argument, she let slip that she'd been on a date…"

"Oh." He falls silent for a minute, and then says, "Did that bother you?"

"No. Not in itself. It's over four years since dad passed, and my mom's not even fifty yet. She's an attractive woman and I never expected her to stay on her own forever…"

"But?"

"But I don't understand why she didn't tell me. She's evidently been seeing this guy for nearly six months and I only really got to find out about it by accident. When I asked her why she didn't tell me, she made a point of reminding me that this is her house, and she can do whatever she likes." I start crying again. "It hurt…"

"Oh, baby." I stop for a second. He called me 'baby'… I'm sure he did. "Please let me come over there."

"I really don't think that would be a good idea. She'd be bound to hear and then she'd treat me like I was back in high school, sneaking a boy into the house…"

"You did that a lot, did you?" I can hear his smile.

"Well, no. I never did that actually, but you get my point."

"Yeah." He sighs. "Yeah, I do. And I'm sorry."

"What for?"

"For playing silly games with you when you're feeling so down."

"It's okay. You weren't to know."

"I wish I could be with you," he says quietly. "I really wanna hold you, and do whatever it takes to make you feel better."

"You just did."

He lets out a long breath. "Are you gonna be okay?"

"Yeah, I'll be fine."

"And I'll see you tomorrow?"

"Definitely. You'll text me when you finish work?"

"Yeah." He pauses. "I really can't wait to see you."

"Neither can I."

"I guess we'd better say goodnight." I can hear his reluctance.

"Yeah. It's getting late."

"Don't worry about your mom. Things get said in the heat of the moment. I'm sure it'll all be forgotten in the morning."

"Maybe."

"Hey," he says. "Smile."

I do.

"Are you smiling?"

"Yeah."

"Good. Now, get a good night's sleep, and I'll see you tomorrow, beautiful."

"Thank you," I whisper.

"What for?"

"Listening… understanding."

"Anytime. Goodnight…"

We both hang up and I wait a moment before I start typing into my phone.

— *I want your hands, your fingers, your lips, your tongue. I want you. All of you… P xxx*

I get up and go through to my bedroom, closing my door just before my phone buzzes and I glance down and read:

— *I'm all yours. R xxx*

The cab drops me off outside Rob's apartment building at just after midnight and I ring on the bell marked with his and Ed's names.

"Come on up. Second floor." I hear his voice through the intercom, and the door buzzes and clicks open.

He's waiting for me outside the apartment door and, as I approach, he steps forward and holds out his arms. I fall into him and put my arms around his waist, hanging onto him.

"God, I've missed you," he says into my neck.

"Hmm. Me too." I lean back and he stares down into my eyes, then kisses me gently, before turning us around and leading me into his apartment.

We go straight into a big living space, which is furnished with a huge couch and a single chair, a low coffee table, a couple of bookcases and a wall-mounted TV. Beyond that is a dining area with a rectangular table and six chairs. There's a corridor off to my right, that has three doors leading off of it, and to my left, there's a doorway that leads through to what seems to be a very modern kitchen.

"Nice place," I say to him.

"Thanks. Let me take your jacket."

I shrug it off and he takes it and hangs it up on a hook on the wall behind the door.

"Come sit down," he says and leads me over to the couch, letting me sit. "Can I get you a glass of wine?"

It's late, but… "Okay. It'll have to be a quick one though. I've got to be up early tomorrow to get ready for April's party."

He goes through to the kitchen. "She's having a party?" he calls over his shoulder.

"Yes. I'm dreading it… A bunch of screaming, over-excited four year olds." I shudder. "It's not my idea of fun."

He comes back in carrying two elegant, long-stemmed glasses, half filled with white wine, and hands one to me before sitting down beside me.

"Sounds like hell," he says, smiling. "Cheers." He holds up his glass and I do the same, then take a sip.

"That's lovely." I swallow the delicious wine and look over at him.

"It's a Sicilian Chardonnay," he replies.

"Do you drink anything that isn't Italian?" I ask him.

He thinks for a moment. "I don't think so, no." He grins. "So you're not looking forward to the party?"

I shake my head. "I'm not looking forward to getting up early either."

"No. Neither am I."

"You've got an early start too?" I know the restaurant's closed on Sundays, so I've always imagined they'd take it easy on their day off.

"Yeah. Ed and I have got a few things we need to go through."

"Oh." It's none of my business, so I don't pry.

He moves a little closer. "I didn't mention it earlier in the week because it's kinda complicated, but we had a call from Sam," he explains, unprompted. "He's gonna be staying in England until the end of the month to help Ali out."

I sit forward. "Why? What's happened?"

He puts his wine glass down and runs his fingers through his hair. "It turns out she and her sister own a second property, and they rent it out, but the tenants have trashed the place and left without paying the rent."

"Oh no. How awful."

"Yeah. Evidently the damage is really bad. So Sam wants to stay and help her deal with it."

"Did he say anything about bringing her back here?" I ask, intrigued as to the persuasive powers of his brother, which I've heard so much about.

"Yeah. He's asked her to come and she wants to, but she's real close to her sister and it seems the decision's gonna lie with her. Ali won't leave without her."

"Wow. That's gotta be difficult for Sam."

He looks over at me. "That's what I thought," he says, gazing into my eyes.

"So, what is it you and Ed need to talk about?" I ask him, taking another sip of wine.

"We're a chef down," he says, sitting back and sighing. "Ed said he thought he could handle it, but after tonight's service, he's finally admitted the stress of being in charge is getting to him... he's exhausted." He nods toward the corridor. "He's already in bed and probably fast asleep, which isn't like him."

"You're worried about him, aren't you?"

He nods, and looks at me again. "Yeah... Yeah, I am."

"Can I help?"

He smirks. "Um... I hate to point out the obvious, but even you've admitted you can't cook."

"No, I can't. But you can, can't you?"

"Yeah, but I'm needed in the restaurant. I don't see how that helps..."

I smile at him. "Well, I did used to be a waitress."

He sits forward again and moves close enough that his knee touches mine. "You did?"

"Yeah. It was a while ago, when I first started out in photography. I was the junior in a studio and it didn't pay much, so I did some part-time waitressing to supplement my income. I could maybe help out during the evenings and that would free you up to work in the kitchens...?"

He stares at me. "What about April?" he says.

"I'd have to check, but I'm sure my mom would look after her for me."

"You made it up with her then?" he asks.

"Kinda. She apologized for the things she said, especially about the house being hers. She knew that had hurt me. We didn't talk about her boyfriend though. She's still being cagey about that."

"Give it time," he says, resting his hand on my leg, and I nod. "So, when was the last time you did any actual waitressing?" he asks.

"About seven… maybe eight years ago, I guess."

"And you think you could handle it?"

"Um… handle what, exactly?"

"Taking over from me."

"You mean be in charge?"

"Absolutely. I've got enough waiters. But if we're gonna do this, and I'm gonna step into the kitchen, then someone's gonna have to take over my role."

"And that couldn't be Jasmine?"

He shakes his head. "No. Her husband works shifts. She's got kids. She can't do evenings."

"Oh. I hadn't realized that."

"If you don't think you can do it…" he says.

"You'd have to train me up," I tell him. "It's been a while and I'm sure your systems are different to anything I used before."

"Our systems are still pretty new to us," he replies, smiling. "But of course I'd train you. I wouldn't just throw you in at the deep end." He leans closer. "Are you sure about this?"

I nod. "As long as I get to spend the bulk of my day with April, then I'm fine with it. I won't give that up."

"I wouldn't ask you to." He lets out a long sigh. "This is so kind of you. And we'll pay you, of course," he adds, as an afterthought.

I chuckle. "Ah… so now we get down to the real negotiations."

"Right now, I think you could pretty much name your price," he says, looking at me expectantly.

"Well, I don't even know the going rate for waitressing these days, so I'll just take whatever everyone else gets."

He shakes his head. "We'll see about that," he says, and then he takes my wine glass from my hand and puts it down on the table next to his.

"Thank you," he whispers and leans in, his eyes focused on mine.

"Wait." I put my hand on his chest and push, just gently. He stops instantly.

"What's wrong?" he says.

"I need to ask you something, and tell you something." I've been dreading this, but it's got to be done.

"Okay." He stays still, looking down at me, waiting.

Now I've got to this point, it's hard to know what to say, but it's been bothering me all week. I'll start with the easy part… well, the comparatively easy part.

"I need to know," I say tentatively. "What we've been doing this week… is that the kind of thing you do all the time?"

"Kind of thing?" he queries.

"Yes. You know… the flirty text messages, the phone calls…"

"No," he replies, leaning back a little, but still staring at me. "I've never done that before."

I still can't hide my doubt. "So you're honestly telling me you don't have a contacts list full of women's names?"

"Yeah." He pulls his phone from his pocket and, after touching the screen a few times, hands it to me. "See for yourself."

I take it from him, and look down. I scroll through the thirty or so names listed, surprised by how few there are for one thing. A lot of them are Italian names, which I guess makes them family members, Ali's name's there, as are his brothers and parents – listed as 'Mom' and 'Dad' – and there are a couple of other men. And me…

"It's mainly family," he confirms. "Except Ali, obviously – although she's pretty much family too now. And Ryan and Joe are a couple of guys I was at college with. We get together a few times a year for a beer…" His voice trails off.

"What about your business contacts?" I ask him.

"I store their details on my laptop. That's work. This is personal." He nods to the phone. "Obviously, they've got my number and they can call me if they need to, but most of them call the landline. If I need to call them, I look up their numbers."

I hand him back his phone. "I'm sorry," I murmur.

"It's okay," he says.

"Are you angry with me?"

I look up at him at last, and find he's smiling at me. "No, of course not." He leans over again. "You just need to accept that I want you… and no-one else." His lips connect with mine and a shockwave passes through my body as our tongues collide, and anything else I needed to talk to him about is forgotten. He groans and pushes me back into the corner of the couch and I reach up behind his head, holding him in place as he deepens the kiss. Within moments, he's moved us down, so we're lying together and, without breaking the kiss, he yanks my blouse from my jeans, quickly undoing the buttons with one hand, and pulling it apart. I feel a hand on my left breast, kneading gently, then his fingers and thumb tweaking my nipple, and I squeal into his mouth as the sensation jolts straight to my already drenched pussy.

"Yes…" I murmur into him.

"Tell me," he whispers back. "Tell me what you want."

"You. All of you." He smiles and sits up a little, pulling me with him, then pushes my blouse from my shoulders and throws it onto the floor behind him. He reaches behind me and undoes my bra, releasing me, then leans down and captures one nipple in his teeth, while his fingers pinch on the other. The feeling is like nothing I've ever experienced. I can barely control my breathing, let alone anything else, and I reach between us, rubbing my hand along the length of his cock, sucking in a breath as I realize how long and hard he really is. He groans loudly at the contact and flexes his hips forward. Emboldened, I pull on his belt, but I'm shaking and can't undo it, so he uses his free hand and does it for me, leaving me with the button and zipper, which are easier. I feel inside and run my fingers down the length of his rigid erection. His cock is so hard and so long, and it feels really thick as I start to stroke it from base to tip, through the thin material of his trunks. He groans again, even louder and I feel his free hand move down my body, undoing the button on my jeans and pulling down the zipper, insinuating his fingers between the denim and the thin lace of my panties.

"You're so fucking wet," he murmurs. He releases my nipple and raises his face, looking up at me. "Your panties are soaking."

I raise my hips into him a little.

"What do you want?" he asks, his voice deep and sexy.

"You," I whisper back.

"Where?"

"Everywhere."

"Be precise." He circles his fingers over my clit and, even through my panties, the sensation is electrifying.

"Do I have to?" Isn't it obvious what I want?

"I just wanna know," he replies, stilling and staring at me. "I want you to express yourself."

"I'm not very good at that."

He grins. "Yeah… I noticed."

"I'm sorry," I mutter.

"Hey, don't be sorry. We'll get there." He leans in and kisses me gently, deepening the kiss within an instant, and as my arousal heightens, I rub along the length of his erection again, savoring the feel of his hard shaft in my hand.

"I wanna see you," he murmurs suddenly, breaking the kiss, and he sits up against the back of the couch. Then he pulls me onto his lap, his erection pressing hard against my core. "God, you're beautiful," he says, resting his hands on my ass and pulling me onto him. I flex my hips, rubbing myself up against him and watch as he closes his eyes and rocks his head back. "Fuck… yeah," he mutters under his breath. He leans forward again, opening his eyes once more and stares at me. "We either stop this right now, or I'm gonna have to take you. Which do you want?" he says, urgently. "It's your choice, baby. Only, please choose quickly."

I still, my body resting against him and he gently kisses my breasts, one at a time. If that's meant to help me make a decision, it's really not working. "Both," I whisper.

He laughs. "I don't think that's possible."

"I know." I pause and he looks up at me. "I want you," I explain. "But I'm not sure I want it to be like this."

He relaxes back into the couch. "Neither do I," he says and I feel myself deflate, just as he reaches up and cups my chin, making me look at him. "And that's not because I don't want you," he adds hastily. "I think that much is blindingly fucking obvious, don't you?" I nod, leaning into him. "The thing is," he continues, "I want our first time to be a bit more special than a quickie on my couch, which is really all we've got time for." He holds onto my ass and sits up a little, bringing me with him. "I want to make love to you, real slow," he murmurs softly, "and I want to feel your pleasure. I want to hear my name on your lips while you writhe in ecstasy beneath me, and then I want to come deep inside you." He pauses, still staring into my eyes. "I think our first time should be at your place too."

"Why?" His words have got my head in a mess, but I can't work out what difference it makes where we are.

He smiles at me. "Because you need to be where April is."

"I do?"

"If we're gonna spend the night together, then yeah."

"The night?"

"I want to spend the night with you."

"You do?"

"Yeah, I do." I smile down at him and lean in to kiss him, just as he puts a finger on my lips to stop me. "I need to ask you a question though," he adds.

"Okay…"

"Will I need to bring condoms?" I lean back. "I've always been real careful about using protection," he explains, "and I know I'm clean… but…"

"I'm on birth control," I whisper. "And I'm clean too." I got tested after Adrian left, just in case, and it's been four long, lonely years since then.

A broad smile spreads across his lips. "So you'd be okay with not using them?" I nod, and his smile widens still further. "Because I really don't want to. Not with you. I want all of you."

I lean down again, when something dawns on me. "You said condoms… plural…"

He chuckles. "Yeah. Of course I did. You don't actually think once is gonna be enough, do you? I wanna make love to you all night long."

I shudder into him, as he pulls me down and kisses me with such breathtaking intensity, I almost forget we said we were going to wait.

Rob

We dragged ourselves away from each other in the end, but it was damn hard. Painfully hard actually. The temptation to take her was almost overpowering and it was only the thought of how much better it would be if we could take it slow and spend the whole night together that stopped me.

In the end, I took her home in a cab, with the play kitchen wedged into the front seat by the driver. I didn't want her to struggle by herself, but also, I wanted to spend a bit longer with her. When I leant down to kiss her goodnight, she asked me if I wanted to come to April's party. She warned me again that it would mean being around a bunch of screaming four year olds, but I was so humbled by the fact that she was prepared to introduce me to April properly, I wasn't about to decline.

I let the cab go, and walked home, thinking about our evening, how great she felt, how responsive she is, how hard she seems to find it to communicate even the most basic things, and how much of a big deal it is that she's letting me into April's life already. I really do get that.

Petra sent me a text message early this morning, thanking me for taking her home, to say her mom was okay with looking after April in the evenings until Sam gets back, and that she'll see me later on at April's party. To be honest – screaming four year-olds or not – I can't wait.

"Good night?" Ed says to me over breakfast.

"Yeah, thanks." I don't look up at him.

"Petra okay?" He's digging.

"She's fine."

He sighs. "She didn't stay then?"

"No. She didn't stay." I look up at him at last. He's smiling at me. "Nothing happened."

"Is that what all the noise was about?"

"Okay… nothing *much* happened." I smile back.

"I wouldn't say that to Petra, if I were you. She probably wouldn't like to have whatever you did described as 'nothing much'."

"You know what I mean." I drop the smile and give him a glare instead. "Besides, you owe her one."

"I do?" He takes a bite of French toast and looks at me quizzically.

"Yeah. She's solved our problem."

"Our work problem?" I nod. "How?" he asks.

"She's gonna cover for me in the restaurant, so I can help you out in the kitchen."

"She's done this before, has she?"

"She's done waitressing before. The rest of it is just turning on the charm. It's really not that hard."

"I know. You do it."

"Funny, Ed. Real funny." I pour myself some more coffee and top up his cup at the same time. "I'll still handle the business side of things during the day while Jasmine's out front, but Petra's gonna come in during the evening shifts so I can come and help you."

"It's been years since you did any real cooking," he reasons, doubtfully.

"I'll be fine. When I took her home last night, we arranged that she's gonna come in tomorrow afternoon to go through everything, then she'll stay and help out during the evening service, shadowing me. Then on Tuesday, she can work the shift by herself and I'll come into the kitchen. Are you okay with that?"

He chuckles. "Yeah. I'm looking forward to it already. I can't wait to boss you around."

"Oh, really…"

"And anyway, you're not fooling me… I know you've only got Petra coming in so you can spend more time with her."

"And?" I'm not gonna bother to deny it.

"You're hooked, aren't you?" he asks, shaking his head.
"Completely."

After a really quick shopping trip, I catch a cab to Petra's house, having left Ed at the apartment. He says he's gonna chill in front of the TV, but I think he'll probably sleep. He seems more relaxed, knowing he won't be on his own in the kitchen for much longer. He was never really on his own; we've always got at least six sous-chefs working out there too, as well as a couple of kitchen hands, but he felt the responsibility a little too heavily. With me out there, he can pass some of that off. And while I may not be the greatest chef, I can make a decision, and for Ed, that's half the battle.

I ring on the doorbell and wait for a moment, before Petra answers and looks me up and down. I don't think she's ever seen me wearing anything but the black clothes I wear at work, and she seems surprised to see me in jeans and a white button down shirt.

"Hi," she breathes, giving me a very sexy smile.

"Hello." From somewhere behind her, I can hear a God-awful racket, like someone's strangling a cat. "What's going on?" I ask.

"That's what happens when you put twelve four year olds together and get them playing Escape the Monster."

She stands back and I step inside. "What the hell is Escape the Monster?"

"A really stupid idea…" She walks down the hallway and I follow her into a huge living room, where the furniture's all been moved to one end, leaving a large area that's currently occupied by said four year olds, three of whom are in the middle of the room, while the rest are standing to one side. "The point," Petra explains, "is that the ones on the edge try to get to the other side, without the ones in the middle – the monsters – catching them. Those who get caught become monsters too. The last one not to be a monster is the winner." We stand and watch as the nine girls standing to one side make a break for it. The noise level shoots up as they squeal and scream, and four of them are caught, making seven monsters against five. With any luck this will soon be over. My eardrums can't handle much more.

I look around the room and notice an older woman, who I assume from her looks, to be Petra's mom. She's staring at me and I smile over. She pauses for a minute, and then smiles back. Whether that was genuine, or good manners, I don't know, but I guess I'll find out. At the other end of the room are three more women, standing together. Two of them are talking, but the other one is looking at me, her gaze fixed to the point where it's uncomfortable and I look away, just as the screaming starts up again. Two of the little girls are caught this time, so we're down to three.... thank God. Please let it end. Soon. Considering how pretty they all look in their party dresses, with their hair tied up in ribbons, they're damn loud.

Finally, the last two are caught and a little girl in a purple dress is declared the winner. Petra steps forward and hands her a small wrapped present, which she rips open, wide eyed, thanking Petra for the bangle contained inside.

"April?" Petra calls, pulling her away from the gaggle of giggling girls. "Just come with me a second." April, who's dressed in a yellow flowery dress, follows obediently, as Petra brings her to stand in front of me. She looks up as her mom says. "I want you to meet my… my friend, Rob." I notice the hesitation and the flush that creeps up her cheeks, but ignore them both for now and crouch down in front of April.

"Happy birthday," I say, and I hand over the present I've had tucked under my arm.

"Thank you," she says quietly. She looks up at Petra.

"Do you want me to put it with the others?" Petra asks her and April hands it over.

"Thank you, Mommy," she says. *Jeez, she's gorgeous.*

She looks up at me again and Petra releases her hand and tells her she can go back to her friends. She runs away and joins the noisy group again, quickly becoming the center of attention.

"I'll just take this into the other room," she says. "You didn't need to buy her a present though."

"Yeah I did." I follow her through the hallway and into a dining room. The table is loaded with food and, on one side is a dresser that's piled high with presents. Petra adds mine and then turns back and I grab hold of her. "Come here," I whisper and pull her into my arms, kissing her gently.

"We'd better get back," she says, breaking the kiss, although she's flushed and breathing hard already, and I can feel her reluctance.

"Okay." She takes my hand and leads me back into the living room, where her mom has got the girls all seated on the floor in a circle and they're playing pass the parcel. Although I'd have expected this to be a quieter game, every time the music stops and someone unwraps a layer of paper, the noise level shoots up again. It's unbelievable…

As the game progresses, I'm aware of the woman who was looking at me earlier moving closer. She's got blonde hair, she's around five foot seven, and she's not unattractive, but there's something kinda false about her and, as she comes to a stop beside me, I realize that parts of her are fake. Certainly her breasts are. They're too large for the rest of her body, and they just don't look natural. I've been with enough women to know what's real and what isn't, and I'd stake my share in Rosa's that this woman has been professionally 'enhanced'.

"Hello," the woman says, holding out her hand. "I'm Courtney."

I take her hand and shake it, releasing it as quickly as I can without appearing rude. "Rob," I say in return.

"Are you the dad of one of these little monkeys?" she asks.

"No. I'm a friend of Petra's." I decide not to call myself anything that she didn't, even though 'friend' feels a bit inadequate.

"Oh. Really?" Her eyes widen and she slowly looks me up and down. *Seriously? She's checking me out? At a kid's party?* "She's never mentioned you," she adds.

"Well, we haven't known each other for very long."

"I see." She moves closer.

The game concludes and I look over to where Petra is helping to supervise, to see she's staring at me – well, us. She's looking bewildered, maybe even a little scared.

"Excuse me," I say quickly and move away from Courtney, going straight to Petra. "Okay?" I ask as soon as I get to her.

She nods, but doesn't say anything and I notice tears welling in her eyes.

I lean down and whisper, "I'm with you. No-one else."

She looks up at me and just about manages a smile, and I take her hand and keep hold of it.

"What's next, Petra?" The woman I'd assumed to be her mom comes over.

"It was gonna be food, but they're way too hyped up."

A distant memory comes into my head. "Can I try something?" I say to her.

She turns to me. "Sure." Her smile widens slightly and I feel the relief deep in my chest. "As long as it doesn't involve recreational drugs."

"If my idea doesn't work, we can try that later," I say quietly and she laughs out loud.

"Okay, girls," I call out, loud enough to get their attention. "We're gonna play something called Sleeping Lions."

They all come a little closer to me, staring up, and I feel like the Pied Piper.

"I need you all to lie down the floor," I say and they obey. "Get comfortable, because you've all gotta stay real still and real quiet for as long as you can." I think quickly, remembering how this works. "April's mom's gonna walk around and she's gonna do her best to get you to move, but you've gotta try not to. Okay?" Their silence tells me they understood and they all lie still, like statues.

"You're on," I whisper to Petra. "You can talk to them, sing to them, tickle them, whatever… Your mom and I will watch them, and if they move, we'll call them out."

"Okay." She grins up at me. "I'm liking this game already," she murmurs. "It's so peaceful."

She starts to move among them and her mom comes and stands beside me.

"I'm Thea Miller," she whispers.

"Rob Moreno," I reply and offer my hand. She takes it and gives me a firm handshake.

"You own the restaurant where Petra's going to be working?" she asks.

"With my two brothers, yes," I confirm.

She nods. "Excuse me a second," she says. "Emily, you moved." How the hell did she spot that? The girl in the purple dress stands up and moves to one side.

The game continues, with Petra walking between the silent, stationary girls until there are just two left and we decide to call it a tie and they both receive a prize.

"Time to eat," Petra declares and, with April leading the way, they all rush through to the dining room.

"Thank you for that," Petra says, coming over to me. "It was a great idea."

"No problem."

We follow the girls through to the dining room, where her mom is already helping them to the food. "Why didn't you want to do the tickling, teasing bit yourself though?" she asks. "It was your game…"

I look down at her. "I don't know these kids," I explain. "And they're all girls… It didn't feel right for me to be tickling them."

She looks up and leans into me, just slightly, and I put my arm around her, and leave it there for a while. Even as we're watching over the girls, I'm aware of Courtney, standing in the corner, looking at me still.

Once the food has been cleared away, Petra tells April she can open her presents, and I help her move them onto the dining table. One by one, she opens them up, revealing dolls, coloring pencils, games, a skipping rope… but mainly dolls. As she opens each one, she makes a point of thanking the person who's given it to her, before moving on to the next. I hope Petra's proud of what she's achieved with her little girl. She should be, because she's amazing. She gets to my gift and rips off the wrapping, then stares at it, and for a moment I wonder if I've screwed up. Then she holds up the box and turns it around.

"Look, Mommy," she says. "Look." The excitement in her voice tells me everything I need to know. I got it right.

Petra pulls away from me and goes over to April, crouching down beside her. "Aren't you lucky?" She looks up at me, her eyes shining. Without any prompting at all, April jumps down from her chair and comes straight over to me. I kneel down and she blows me away by putting her arms around my neck and giving me a hug. "Thank you," she whispers. "Thank you very much."

I hug her back, just gently. "You're welcome," I say.

"It is real, isn't it? It's not pretend…"

"No, it's real," I reply, "it's just smaller, and that means you're not allowed to use it without a grown up helping you. Okay?" She nods her head, pulling away from me.

"Mommy bought me a play kitchen which I can use all by myself," she says.

"Yeah. I know. So you can brush up on your skills with your play kitchen and, one day soon, if mommy says it's okay, I'll come back and I'll teach you how to make biscotti, with chocolate chips in."

"With my own baking set?" she asks, wide-eyed.

"Of course. That's why I got it for you."

"That's okay, isn't it, Mommy?" she asks, turning to Petra, who's standing now, tears clearly visible in her eyes.

"It's just fine, baby girl," she says, managing a smile.

I let April go and stand, giving Petra a wink as April runs to her, hugging her legs.

The rest of the party goes really quickly. Petra's mom has made a cake, which is beautifully decorated and quite impressive and once they've all sung *Happy Birthday* and the cake's been cut, they have a couple more games and then it's time for everyone to go home.

As Courtney's leaving – with the little girl in the purple dress, who was called Emily, if I recall – she comes over to me. "It was lovely to meet you," she says, holding out her hand again. I shake once more, feeling a piece of paper passing between us. I let her go, not saying a word, and put it in my pocket. She smiles and turns away, taking her daughter's hand and going out the door.

April's exhausted and Petra takes her upstairs to get her ready for bed, leaving me with her mom. In coloring, she's very similar to Petra, with dark hair and olive skin, but she's thinner and smaller.

"I assume you can cook…" she says while I help her clear up the mess in the living room and re-arrange the furniture. "Based on what you said to April, that is."

"Yeah. I can cook. It kinda goes with owning the restaurant."

"Of course. I'd forgotten about that." She stops picking up loose bits of wrapping paper and turns to look at me, like she wants to ask me something, but then she changes her mind and goes back to what she was doing.

"Where do you want this?" I ask her, pointing to the sofa that's been pushed back against the wall. It clearly doesn't belong there.

"It goes in front of the fireplace," she says, pointing to the other end of the room.

"Okay." I start to shift it across the room.

"You do know that Petra can't cook to save her life, don't you?"

I stop what I'm doing and stare at her. "Yeah. But then I can't take a photograph to save my life either. We can't all be good at everything… and your daughter takes a mean photograph."

"She gets that from her father," she says. "They were inseparable when Petra was a girl." She turns away, and I wonder if I can sense a hint of resentment, if her mom's jealous of the time Petra spent with her dad and not with her.

I glance around the walls, which are filled with photographs, some clearly of Petra and her mom, and some of landscapes, taken in various parts of the world.

"Are these his?" I ask, nodding toward them.

"Yes," she replies, wistfully. "Petra has some more upstairs in her office."

"She doesn't display her own work?"

"No."

I'm still wondering why when she comes back into the room, with a very sleepy April in her arms. "She just wants to say goodnight," Petra says.

"Have you had a good day?" Petra's mom asks, moving forward and kissing April on the forehead. I can see she loves her granddaughter very much, even if I am kinda confused about her feelings toward Petra.

"Yes, thank you," April replies.

"Sleep well."

Thea steps away again.

"Goodnight." April looks over at me.

"Goodnight, April." I go over to her. "I hope you enjoyed your birthday."

"I did. And thank you again for my present."

"You're welcome. And I will come and show you how to make biscotti. Okay?"

"With chocolate chips?" she asks, yawning widely.

"Yeah, with chocolate chips."

She smiles and I feel a warmth starting to spread through my chest. *Well, I'll be…*

"I'll just take her up to bed and I'll come back down and help out," Petra says, interrupting my train of thought.

"Okay."

It took us another hour and a half to clear everything away, and then Petra's mom said she was tired and was going to her room. I think it was her subtle way of leaving us alone, but then maybe she really was tired. I'm not sure the woman really does subtle.

"I'm so sorry," Petra says, taking my hand and leading me back into the living room and over to the couch, where we sit next to each other.

"What on earth for?"

"For introducing you as my friend," she says. I'd forgotten all about that. "My mind went completely blank and I wasn't sure how you'd feel about me calling you my boyfriend in front of everyone, so I decided to err on the side of caution."

"Hey," I say, reaching over and running the backs of my fingers down her cheek. "I'm absolutely fine with you calling me your boyfriend. Anytime, anywhere, and in front of anyone you like."

She smiles. "And thank you for getting April the baking set. I think she's rather taken with it… and with you."

"It's entirely mutual, believe me," I reply, because I've realized it's true.

"You were very kind to offer to bake with her."

"It's my pleasure. I'm looking forward to it." I lean across and touch the necklace that's hanging down just above her breasts. "I'm guessing the 'A' is for April?" I ask, because I know her ex was called Adrian, and I hope this isn't some kind of keepsake from him. I noticed the necklace last night when we were making out on the couch at my place, but I didn't want to spoil the moment by mentioning it and, with all the noise of the party, I'd forgotten about it until seeing it again just now.

"Yes," she replies. "My mom bought it for me when she was born."

I smile my relief and kiss her deeply. When she finally breaks the kiss, I know there's something else I need to tell her and I reach into my pocket. "There's something I need to show you," I say. I need to be honest with her. "That woman… the one who was talking to me earlier…"

"Courtney?" she prompts.

"Yeah. She… um… she gave me this." I hand over the piece of paper. I haven't looked at it, but I know what's gonna be on it.

She opens it and looks down, then stares at me. "It's her phone number," she says.

"Yeah. I thought it might be."

"You mean… you mean you didn't look at it?"

"No. She gave it to me when she said goodbye and I put it in my pocket, rather than making a scene in front of the kids, but I really wanted to ask her what the hell she was playing at, doing something like that at a kids' party… especially when she's married."

"How do you know she's married?" she whispers.

"The wedding ring was a bit of a clue," I reply.

She nods her head. "Why are you giving this to me?" she asks.

I turn and look at her. "Because I need you to trust me. I need you to understand that it doesn't matter how many women do dumb things like that, I'm not gonna act on it… not now. I want you, Petra. No-one else." I place a finger under her chin and raise her face to mine. There are tears in her eyes.

"You're sure?" I can hear the doubt in her voice.

"I'm positive."

"Even though Courtney's more…" she hesitates. "More perfectly formed," she says eventually.

"More surgically formed I think you mean." I move a little closer. "I prefer my women natural," I whisper. "Like you."

She smiles. "Thank you," she says.

"Don't thank me. I told you, and I'll keep on telling you. I don't want anyone but you."

She swallows hard and puts the piece of paper down beside her. "I don't know what to do," she says quietly.

"How do you mean?"

"About Courtney."

"You don't have to do anything," I reply. "Just throw that away and forget about her."

"I can't."

"Yeah, you can. Nothing's gonna happen."

She looks up at me, staring straight into my eyes. "Not with you, maybe, but what about the next guy."

"Well, that's not really your problem, is it?"

"Except it is… well, it kind of is."

"I don't understand."

She pauses. "Courtney isn't just another mom," she says. "She's my cousin's wife."

"Holy shit," I whisper.

"Yeah. So, what do I do?"

"Nothing."

"Nothing?"

"Yeah." I reach over and hold her, pulling her back into the couch with me. "It's still not your problem."

"But Mateo is such a nice guy."

"Mateo being your cousin?" She nods. "I'm sure he is a nice guy," I continue, "but he won't thank you for telling him."

"And he will thank me for keeping quiet?"

I sigh. "Sometimes people just have to find things out for themselves. If you tell him, he probably won't believe you anyway. One day, she'll slip up, and he'll discover the real woman behind his wife, and then you can be there to help him. If you tell him now, he'll probably go into denial and push you away and then, when it all falls apart, he'll be on his own."

"You sound like you've been through this before," she says, leaning back and looking at me.

"With Sam, yeah."

"I'm sorry...?" She looks confused.

"He was married," I explain.

"He was?"

"Yeah. It was a couple of years ago... and she cheated."

"And you knew about this?" she asks.

"Well, not exactly. I didn't know for sure that she was cheating at the time, but I knew she was going to."

She stares at me, and tilts her head to one side. "I don't understand what you're saying," she mutters.

"I knew she'd cheat on him at some point, because not long before they got married, she came on to me." I'm not sure I want to put it any more strongly than that. And I don't think Petra can handle the details.

She pulls away and sits up. "Seriously?"

"Yeah. Nothing happened. Absolutely nothing. She came to the apartment and made it clear what she wanted... I threw her out."

"And you never told him? Not even after she cheated and they split up?"

"No. He'd have been devastated to know she'd have done that to him. It was bad enough that she was screwing her boss, but to know she'd tried it with me too..." I leave the sentence hanging. "When he found out what she was really like, it was me he came to, not Ed. He had no idea what had happened before the wedding, and he needed someone he could really open up to, no holds barred. Ed's a bit more sensitive than Sam and me, and Sam didn't need the constraints of someone else's feelings getting in the way. But I seriously doubt he'd have been able to talk to me like he did, if he'd known what had happened… Anyway, we got more drunk than I've ever been in my life, and he told me things about their relationship he probably wishes he hadn't, but at least he got it all out."

She nods her head and leans back into me again, her head resting on my chest.

"I'm not sure Mateo would turn to me like that," she says.

"Even so… You need to leave that door open for him. And besides, no-one really knows what goes on in someone else's relationship. For all you know, he might already be aware of what she's like, and have decided to stick around for the sake of their kids. But he won't appreciate someone pointing out the problems in his marriage. Let him deal with it in his own way – whatever that is – and, if he does need you later on, you'll be there for him."

She nestles into me and I run my fingers down her back.

"Thank you," she murmurs.

"I wish you'd stop thanking me."

She looks up and smiles and I lean down and kiss her gently. She opens to me and I delve inside, her tongue meeting mine. She's soft and yielding, and I want her, but even as I deepen the kiss, I can feel her yawning into me. Well… that's certainly never happened before.

I pull back and smile at her.

"Sorry," she says, sheepishly.

"It's okay. You're exhausted."

"Yeah. I am."

"I'll go. You need to rest."

She looks a little sad and dejected and I kiss her again, letting my lips rest on hers for a second, then I move down and kiss her neck, working my way very slowly up to her ear. "There's nothing I want more than to stay here, with you," I whisper, and I hear her sigh and lean back, looking down at her. "The thing is," I say a little louder, "I want our first time to be special… which means it'd be real great if you can actually stay awake for it."

She giggles and I kiss her just once more, before getting up and, once we've said a proper goodbye, walking slowly home.

Chapter Nine

Petra

I arrive at the restaurant at four on Monday afternoon. Rob called me this morning to set a time, being as we'd neglected to arrange it yesterday. To be honest, even if we had arranged it, I'd probably have forgotten by now. In between the noise of the party, the excitement of being with him again, seeing the way in which April reacted to him and the revelation that Courtney is so open to cheating on Mateo, I was struggling to remember my own name by the end of the day. Rob was really sweet though and, after we'd talked and kissed, he left me to get some sleep. The thing is, even after all of that, I know I need to tell him about Adrian – more than ever. I just need to find the right moment…

Jasmine lets me in and, before we've even reached the bar, Rob appears from the corridor that leads to the kitchen. He comes straight over to me and pulls me close, leaning down and kissing me, long and hard. As he pulls away, he looks down into my eyes.

"Hi," he whispers. "I missed you."

"I noticed." I smirk.

We turn and see Jasmine staring at us.

"You've gotta stop doing that, boss," she says to Rob, smiling. "Or I'm gonna ignore the fact that I agreed to stay on and help out this afternoon, and I'm gonna go home and ask Cole why he doesn't kiss me like that anymore."

"That'll be because your kids have worn him out," Rob tells her, grinning.

"Yeah… kids," she murmurs. "Best way to ruin a moment…"

Rob looks down at me again. "Oh, I don't know," he says. "April's real cute."

"April?" Jasmine enquires.

"My daughter," I explain. "She's four."

"And adorable," Rob adds, hugging me.

"And no doubt besotted with you," Jasmine says to him, rolling her eyes. I stifle a laugh.

"Get back to work, woman," Rob says, with mock authority.

"I didn't think Jasmine worked the evening shift," I say quietly as he moves us toward a table near the front of the restaurant, where an iPad and some menus are set up.

"She doesn't, but she agreed to stay on today to make sure we're ready for tonight, so I could run through things with you."

"Oh. That was kind of her."

"Yeah. She's like that."

We sit down and he looks over to where Jasmine's laying up the tables at the back of the restaurant, just as Ed appears from the corridor. He's wearing his chef's whites and, yet again, I'm struck by the resemblance between him and Rob.

"Hi," he says, coming over to us. "How are you?"

"I'm well, thanks. You?"

"I'm good. Looking forward to having you working here," he says, smiling.

"Yeah," Rob puts in, "but that's only because he thinks he's gonna get to boss me around in the kitchen."

"No," Ed replies, leaning on the table, "it's because I *know* I'm gonna get to boss you around."

"In your dreams," Rob says.

"No… in *your* nightmares."

I stifle another laugh. "Get back in the kitchen and let us get on," Rob says.

Ed straightens up and looks down at me. "Don't take any nonsense from him," he says, nodding toward his brother. "Everyone knows I'm the better looking twin anyway." He turns and starts walking toward the back of the restaurant again.

"Ed?" Rob calls after him and he turns back.

"Yeah?"

"Fuck off."

Ed bursts out laughing, Rob grins over at him, and I know I'm going to enjoy working here.

"I'll get us a coffee," Rob says, turning back to me, "and then we'll start going through everything."

"Okay." He gets up and goes behind the bar, returning a few minutes later with two cups of steaming hot coffee.

"I've got no idea how to use a barista machine," I tell him as he sits down again.

"Don't worry about that," he says. "Whoever's working behind the bar deals with that."

"Oh… okay." I heave a sigh of relief.

He leans forward. "None of this is that hard, baby," he says softly.

I nod and, taking my hand, he starts talking me through how the iPads work.

It only takes about an hour, and we're finished, and we've still got well over an hour until opening time. Jasmine's left, the evening shift staff haven't arrived and we've got the place to ourselves. I'm wondering if now might be a good time to tell Rob about Adrian, or whether I should wait until we're not at work. Rob goes to make us another coffee, then comes back and we sit together, while I study the menu to familiarize myself with the names of the dishes, wishing they weren't in Italian.

"Most of the customers can't pronounce them either," he says, taking my hand. "So don't worry about how you say things."

I smile over at him. "Am I that obvious?"

"It was the way you were mouthing the words that gave you away," he murmurs, leaning over and kissing me. "You look really cute when you're concentrating, though."

He takes the menu from me and puts it down on the table.

"Can I ask you something?" he says.

"Sure."

"Why don't you display your photographs at home?"

"Sorry?" That's a confusing question.

"I asked your mom about the photographs in the living room and she said they were your dad's, not yours, and that you don't display yours. I just wondered why."

"Oh, I see." I look down at my hands, my fingers entwined, just as Rob places one of his over them.

"If you don't wanna tell me…" he says.

"No, it's not that…" I look up at him. "It's just that when someone is so much better at something than you are, there's not much point…" I let my voice fade to a whisper.

He looks at me, like he's thinking, then his face clears. "Was… was your dad Peter Miller?" he asks.

I nod. "Yes. I'm named after him."

"I see." He leans forward. "Just because he was amazing at what he did doesn't mean you're not too," he says.

"I know. He used to tell me I was good."

"Well then."

"But he was so much better."

"Comparing what you do with what he did is like comparing salami with cheese. They're both great, but they're two entirely different things."

I smile at him, lean over and kiss him gently on the cheek.

"What was that for?" he asks.

"For understanding… again."

He moves his chair closer to mine. "Did you go into photography because of him?"

"Yes. He was my hero, ever since I was old enough to work it out." I tell him. "I mean, he'd never have let me do the same kind of photography he did. It was far too dangerous. But I wanted to get as close to what he did as I could. That said, I made a decision right at the beginning not to trade off of his name. I wanted to make it by myself."

"And you have done."

"In a way, yes."

He takes a sip of coffee and puts the cup down. "How did your parents meet?" he asks.

"They met in Greece, when dad was there on vacation. He was between assignments and needed a break. Mom would have been about twenty, I guess, and Dad about thirty-five."

"That's a fair age gap," he points out.

"Yeah, but it didn't seem to bother either of them."

"So, it was a holiday romance?"

"Yes." I nod. "They met at a taverna where my mom worked part-time as a waitress…"

"It runs in the family then?" He smirks.

"You could say that… Anyway, Dad always used to say it was love at first sight. He went back the next day, and the day after, but then she wasn't working that night, and he was so disappointed, he asked the guy who owned the place for her address. The guy took pity on him and told him where she lived, and he went round there and asked her to go out with him. She accepted and they spent the rest of his vacation together. According to my dad, on his last night there, he took my mom to the beach, and one thing led to another…" I leave that sentence unfinished.

"And according to your mom?" he prompts.

"That part didn't happen." I smile.

"Well, I guess you'll never know."

I smirk. "Except you're looking at the proof that it did," I tell him.

He laughs, throwing his head back. "So, it was a shotgun wedding?"

"No… no, it wasn't. Dad flew back to the US the next day, but he missed Mom so much, he went back to her a week later and asked her to marry him. She said no, because she was scared about the job he did. She was worried she'd give up her life and her family in Greece and move here, and then he'd be killed one day and she'd be left on her own. So, he told her he'd give it up." I swallow down my tears. "He told her he'd give up his career, his way of life, for her."

"And she accepted him?" Rob asks.

124

"Yes. She loved him really. She was just scared. He was asking her to leave everything behind for him."

"How did her family feel about it?"

"Her parents were reluctant to start with, but they came around and she married him in Greece a couple of weeks later. Most of the Greek relations have been over here quite a lot and I've been there too, although I've never taken April... And Mom's sister, Stephanie lives here now too – just a couple of blocks away."

"Did your dad regret it?" Rob asks. "Giving up his career, I mean, not getting married."

"No. He always said she was worth it. She needed the security of knowing he'd be safe and he gave her that." I smile over at him. "Of course, they found out within days of getting back here that Mom was pregnant with me."

"So how exactly did your mom maintain that she wasn't pregnant when they got married?"

"Well, most people didn't really know the precise dates of everything and, because dad was out of the US for most of the time, and they married in Greece, they could always get away with fudging the issue." I smile at the memories. "But, dad used to bring it up on purpose sometimes, in private. It was a kind of personal joke between them."

"It sounds like they were happy," Rob says.

"Yeah, they were."

"Is that why it's hard for you to think of your mom with another man?" he asks me.

"No. I get that she needs to have someone in her life. I'm okay with it. I just wish she'd talk to me about it, rather than sneaking around."

He gets up, bends over me and kisses me gently. "Tell her, baby," he whispers. "Tell her how you feel. She's probably scared you're gonna be upset."

"You think?"

He shrugs and pulls me to my feet and into his arms. "Yeah. I'd say she knows how you feel about your dad, and how much you worshipped him, and she's worried about your reaction to her seeing another guy." He kisses me again. "Just talk to her."

He leans over and kisses me again and I know the moment to tell him about Adrian is lost – again.

The last half hour passes really quickly and five minutes before we're due to open, I come out of the ladies' room and back into the restaurant to find Rob waiting for me.

"Okay?" he says.

"Just nervous."

"Don't be."

"I meant to ask… Am I wearing the right clothes?" I purposely chose black pants and a white blouse, because I'd noticed that was what the other waiting staff wore at the opening.

"No," he says softly.

"Oh." *Shit.*

"Ideally, you wouldn't be wearing anything, and we'd be in your bedroom right now." He smirks.

I slap him on the arm. "Don't do that. I'm worried enough already." I look down at what I'm wearing. "Seriously, am I alright in this?"

"You're perfect." He leans down and kisses me. "You can wear a black top, if you prefer. It's up to you."

"Everyone else is wearing an apron," I say. "Should I be?"

He takes a step back. "See me wearing one?"

"No."

"Right." He takes my hand and leads me back toward the bar. He already introduced me to everyone earlier, when they all arrived, but I'm grateful they all wear name tags, because there's no way I'd remember who they all are.

He checks his watch and goes to the front door, unlocking it and coming back to me. "Just follow me for tonight," he whispers. "And stop looking so nervous. You're beautiful."

The evening's going really quickly. It's already nine-thirty and I feel like I've only been working for about an hour.

I've been shadowing Rob all the time, but just a few minutes ago, he was busy dealing with a problem at the back of the restaurant, and a table of six people arrived, so I went forward and helped them by myself, showing them to their table, giving out their menus and introducing Jackson as their waiter. He gave me an encouraging smile as I walked away, which I thought was nice of him. Then, before I could get back to Rob, the couple on what I think is table four queried their check. Their waitress was Abi. She seems quite young, and she'd gotten kinda flustered because the guy at the table was being difficult. I went over and dealt with it, showing him on the iPad that the check was correct. He apologized and left Abi a big tip. When I looked up, Rob was standing by the bar, smiling at me. I was on my way over to him, when another customer asked me for clarification of something on the menu. I was aware of Rob taking a step forward, but I managed to explain what the guy wanted to know, and get back to the bar before anyone else could interrupt me. Rob's moved away now though and is talking to a group of men on one of the back tables.

"You couldn't get me a glass of water, could you?" I say to Greg, behind the bar. "I'm dying of thirst."

"Sure," he replies, filling a glass with ice and pouring San Pellegrino over it, before handing it to me. "How's it going?"

"Okay, I think." I shrug, taking a long drink of water.

"It's going a lot better than okay." I feel Rob come up behind me, his hands on my waist. "You're doing really well," he says. "I'm so proud of you."

No-one's said that to me since my dad died and I have to swallow down the lump in my throat and blink back my tears before I can turn to him and smile.

Rob

Last night went so well, I'm not even vaguely worried about leaving Petra on her own this evening. I'm more concerned about how I'm gonna handle working in the kitchen. It's been years since I've done any professional cooking and I've got a horrible feeling it's gonna show.

Despite his threats to boss me around, Ed's actually being great. He's encouraging, rather than anything else and I've wondered during the course of the evening whether it would have gone as well if it had been me and Sam working together. Somehow, I doubt it.

I haven't had time to look at the clock, but I guess we're about half way through service when Abi comes in to collect the appetizers for table twelve, followed by Melissa.

"She's lovely, don't you think?" Abi says.

"Yeah. She's really friendly to the guests, but she's not worried about pulling her weight. She handled my drinks order on table seven because I was held up."

"I know. She did the same for me, too…"

They wander off again and I know they're talking about Petra.

"Your girlfriend's made a hit." Ed's standing right behind me, his voice barely a whisper.

"So it would seem." I turn to face him, smiling.

"Who'd have thought you'd have such good taste…" He smirks, walking away, but I'm too wrapped up in not screwing up the sauce I'm trying to make to answer him back.

The last customers leave at eleven fifteen, by which time, we're almost cleaned down in the kitchen and I go out front to see how things are going – well, to check on Petra, really.

She's helping clear tables, and talking with Greg and Abi.

"Hi," I say, going over to her.

"Hello." She looks up.

I glance around. "Need any help?" I ask, although she seems to have everything under control.

"No, I think we're okay," she replies.

"I'll get cleaned up, and let you finish, and I'll take you home."

"I can get a cab." She did last night, because I decided to let her go before closing time – she was so tired and I thought she needed some sleep. That would've worked fine, but we then spent an hour texting each other, so it was gone one before either of us got to bed.

I shake my head and gaze at her. "I'll take you."

She nods. "Okay… if you're sure."

"I'm sure." I lean down and kiss her, then go back into the kitchen, letting Ed know that I'm gonna take Petra home.

"Should I wait up?" he says, mockingly.

Three of the sous-chefs are still there and they all stop and look at me. *Thanks, Ed…*

"You wouldn't anyway," I say as evasively as possible, unbuttoning my white jacket and shrugging it off.

"See you tomorrow," he replies, grinning. *Asshole.*

"Maybe…" I reply.

I head for the door, but he calls me back. "Thanks for tonight," he says, sincerely for once. "It really helped having you out here."

"Yeah, I know. I made you look good…"

He laughs and I head out the door, grab my jacket from the office and go into the restaurant again, where Petra's waiting for me.

"Do you want to come in for a drink?" she asks me when we get to her front door. We walked home, rather than taking a cab. It's a nice night and we both felt like walking.

"I'd love to. I'm not really that tired yet."

"No. Neither am I." She unlocks the door and lets us in. "It's weird," she says, lowering her voice to a whisper now we're inside. "I thought I'd be exhausted, but I feel… I don't know… wired."

"It can be like that, after a really good service."

"I guess that means it went well then."

"From what I heard, it went really well."

Petra takes off her coat and I shrug off my jacket and she hangs them up in a closet by the front door before we go through to the kitchen.

"Wine? Or coffee?"

"Oh… wine, definitely," I say.

"I'm so glad you said that." Her smile is infectious.

She pours us both a glass of something red and brings it over. "It's not Italian, I'm afraid."

"I'm sure I'll live." She takes my hand and we go through to the living room, where she flicks on the lights and we sit together on the couch.

"Did you get around to speaking with your mom yet?" I ask her.

"No. She works on Tuesdays and Thursdays at the hospital."

"Really?"

"Yeah. She does volunteer work."

"Oh, I see."

"So, I haven't really seen her for long enough to be able to talk to her."

"Maybe tomorrow then…" I suggest.

"Yeah, maybe." She looks at me, her eyes burning into mine.

"You don't really wanna talk about this, do you?"

She shakes her head.

"Is there something else you wanna talk about instead?" I ask.

"Yes, but I'm not sure now is the best time."

"In that case…" I take her wine glass and put it with mine on the coffee table, before leaning over and kissing her. As usual, she opens up to me and our tongues dance, while I unbutton her blouse and reach inside for her breasts. They're irresistibly full, and fit my hands perfectly and, I've gotta be honest, I'm kinda addicted to them already. I feel her fingers fumbling with my belt again and – just like the other day – I reach down and give her a hand, undoing it, and the button of my chinos, leaving her to do the rest. I deepen the kiss, then bite on her bottom lip, while she makes light work of my zipper and I feel her fingers touching my cock through the thin material of my trunks. I'm already hard as nails, but that sweet torture is enough to drive me insane, and I try and distract her by undoing her pants and feeling my way inside. Her panties are drenched, her pussy juices soaking through them.

"Do you want more?" I ask her breaking the kiss.

She nods and pulls away.

"Not here," I murmur.

"No." And she gets up, her pants falling down around her ankles. I lean down and hold onto them.

"Step out," I tell her and she does, kicking off her shoes at the same time. I pick up them and her pants and she grabs the wine, while I stand and re-do the top button of my chinos, so they don't fall down.

"Follow me," she murmurs, and leads the way back out of the living room and into the hallway, flicking off the lights as she passes. I follow her up the stairs, watching her perfect ass before me and resisting the urge to reach out and touch. At the top of the stairs, there are four doors, two on the left, and two on the right; we turn to the right, go past a closed door and she opens the next one, waiting for me to enter, before closing it again. Inside, from what I can see in the moonlight, there's a king-size bed against the far wall, with an ottoman at the end, a dresser, closet and two nightstands, and a door in the corner, which I guess leads through to a bathroom. She goes over to the nightstand on one side of the bed, puts down the wine and turns back to me. I put down her pants and shoes on the ottoman and move across to her, placing my hands on her cheeks and leaning down to kiss her again. She responds immediately, reaching up behind my head and holding me in place, while her breasts heave into my chest. I turn her and walk her back to the bed until she hits it. Then, without breaking the kiss, I lower us both down.

Her breathing changes almost immediately, becoming even more ragged and pronounced, and I reach down, inserting my fingers beneath the lace of her panties and feel along her soft, swollen folds. Fuck, she's wet. She parts easily for me and I gently caress her clit. The contact makes her gasp and she raises her hips off the bed, in evident desperation for my touch. She told me she hadn't dated since April's dad left her, which was before April was born… so I guess it's probably been a while.

I break the kiss and look down at her.

"I want you naked," I say softly.

She nods just once and, kneeling up, I pull her into a sitting position, and push her blouse from her shoulders, then undo her bra, releasing those perfect breasts. I lean down and kiss each one in turn, but I don't delay for too long. I want to see all of her, and I move off of the bed, standing before her.

"Lift," I say, not taking my eyes from hers, and as she raises her hips, I pull down her panties, dropping them onto the floor, and sucking in a breath. "You're so beautiful," I murmur, taking her in, at last. Her hair is spread out, dark and curly on the white comforter, her eyes gazing into mine, although after just a moment, I drag mine away and lower them to her large, firm breasts, with dark, rigid nipples. Further down still, she has rounded hips and at the top of those perfect, shapely thighs, a shaved, glistening pussy, her lips swollen with arousal.

I go to climb back onto the bed, but she sits up, tugging at my t-shirt.

"You want me naked too?" I ask her. She nods, smiling and I chuckle and stand up again, pulling my top over my head as she lies down and watches. Without even seeming to realize what she's doing, her right hand moves to her breast and she lets it rest there. I quickly kick off my shoes and I undo the button of my chinos, lowering them, together with my trunks, and bend to peel off my socks, before standing again. Her eyes widen and she gives her breast a gentle squeeze. That's fucking hot.

I climb back onto the bed and lie beside her, raised up on one elbow, and lean down to kiss her. She moans softly into my mouth as my tongue finds hers with ease. Then I reach back down between her legs, to her soft folds and, parting them, I gently rub her clit, with a slow circling motion. She shudders, spreading her legs wide and arching her back off the bed and then, breaking the kiss for a moment, I watch her tweaking at her nipple with her fingers and thumb and I hear her deep, long sigh. Just as our lips touch again, I feel her hand moving between us, her fingers gripping my cock, which twitches and flexes against her as she starts to stroke it gently. Her touch is magical and I slowly insert a finger into her entrance, pushing deep and rubbing against that sweet spot on the front wall of her vagina. She bucks against me and starts to pump me harder. She's close – but so am I and this is not what I had in mind…

"Stop," I say, pulling my finger from her and grabbing her hand. "Why?"

"Because you're gonna make me come," I say.

"Well, you're gonna make me come too," she replies.

"Which is fine…" I smile down at her. She's still holding her breast, caressing it gently. I guess during four years on her own, she's gotten used to pleasuring herself, and that idea has me more than turned on, especially as she's so responsive. Still, I want her first time with me to be special… really special. "Do you have towels?" I ask her.

"Towels?" She looks up at me.

"Yeah. Bath towels."

"Oh. Yeah. In the box at the end of the bed."

I nod and get up, going to the ottoman and fetching two large bath towels. I come back and, folding them into four, I place them on the bed right by her ass. "Lift," I say to her again and she releases her breast and raises her hips up off the bed, letting me slip the towels in beneath her.

"What are those for?" she asks.

"You'll see." I kneel by her side again, looking down at her. "I don't know if you've ever done this before," I say.

"Well, I've never done anything that needed towels," she replies, "so probably not."

I smile. "Okay. In that case, I should probably warn you, it's gonna be intense." Her eyes widen. "You're almost certainly gonna want to scream," I add. "But you can't because your mom and your daughter are here. So try and hold it in." I reach behind me and hand her a pillow. "Bite down on that, if you have to," I add, smirking.

I lean over her and, placing my hands on her knees, I push her legs wide apart, exposing her pussy.

"You're gonna watch?" she says, noting my position.

"I'm gonna do *and* watch," I reply. "Just relax."

She nods her head slowly and I keep my eyes focused on her, feeling my way back up her leg with my right hand then gently rubbing her clit with my thumb until she's moaning and writhing again.

"You need to stay still," I whisper.

"Then you're gonna have to stop doing that."

I chuckle. "We both know you don't mean that."

"No, I don't."

I move my left hand and rest it just above her mound. "I guess I'll just have to hold you in place then," I tell her. Her eyes widen and she sucks in a breath as I push down on her, my thumb still circling over her hard nub. She tries to buck against me, but I hold her firm, and keeping up the motions with my thumb, I gently insert two fingers inside her, using my fingertips to rub against the front wall of her vagina again. Once more, she arches off the bed, but my hand keeps her steady as I rub harder and then start to pump my hand up and down inside her – hard. She stares at me, confused, maybe even scared.

"Go with it, baby," I murmur.

"What's happening to me?"

She starts to shake.

"Just go with it. I won't hurt you."

She clamps a hand on each of her breasts, squeezing them hard, tugging on her nipples as I increase the pace and intensity.

"Oh, God…" she whispers, through clenched teeth. "Oh… Oh my God."

She lets go of her right breast and grabs the pillow thrusting it to her mouth as her orgasm claims her and she squirts streams of hot liquid in a high arc, all over the towels. She thrashes against me, but I hold her still, keeping up the movement, driving her wild as she continues to gush repeatedly, soaking through the layers beneath her.

After what feels like minutes, she starts to calm, and I slowly remove my fingers from her, the last of her juices drenching my hand as I pull away and move up the bed toward her head. She's still holding the pillow tightly in her hand and I gently pull on it, but she's stiff and won't let go.

"Hey," I whisper. "You okay?" She doesn't move and, in a moment of panic, I straddle her and push the pillow away from her face. "Petra," I say urgently. "Speak to me…"

She shakes her head. Thank fuck for that. For one awful moment…

"I thought you'd smothered yourself," I say, heaving out my relief.

"No. I've just humiliated myself," she whispers and tries to turn away, even though I'm on top of her. Her eyes are still closed.

"What are you talking about? That was incredible." She can't mean that, surely…

I can feel her moving beneath me. "Oh God, I'm so wet," she says.

"Yeah, I know."

She covers her face with her hands.

"Stop it," I say, pulling them away again and pinning them beside her head. "Look at me."

"No." She keeps her eyes closed and shakes her head, just in case I didn't understand the simple word.

I sigh. "What do you think just happened?" I ask her.

"I—I just pee'd in the bed," she says and I hear the tears in her voice, even if I can't see them in her eyes.

I lean right down, so my lips are almost touching hers and I know she'll be able to feel my breath on her. "No, you didn't," I whisper.

"Well it damn well feels like it to me."

"Did it feel like you were peeing when you came?" I ask.

She thinks for a moment. "Well… no, not really."

"Exactly."

She slowly opens her eyes and looks at me.

"Then what happened?" she asks, gazing up at me.

"You ejaculated, baby."

"I what? Isn't that what men do?"

I chuckle. "Yeah. But some women can do it too." Although if I'm being honest, I've never seen anyone do it as spectacularly as that.

She stares at me. "It really isn't pee?"

I shake my head. "No, it's not. It's you… being amazing." She still seems uncertain. "Want me to prove it to you?" I ask her.

"How?"

I move down the bed, still straddling her, then shift my legs and kneel between hers, pushing them further apart with my hands and, raising her ass off the bed, I pull out the towels and throw them on the floor.

"We won't be needing those anymore." I lie down between her legs and, using my fingers to part her silky, wet lips, I run my tongue, just once, across her still swollen clit. She sucks in a breath and I feel her relax beneath me. I plant soft kisses over her mound, licking her clean, before turning my attention to her clit again, circling it with the very tip of my tongue and flicking it softly until she's moaning and writhing. It only takes a few minutes before she comes apart, and I feel her hand on the back of my head, holding me against her as she bucks and twists against me, whispering my name into the moonlit room.

As her breathing returns to normal, I look up at her and slowly lick my lips, tasting her sweet juices.

"Now," I say softly. "I've gotta be honest. If you'd pee'd, I probably wouldn't have been quite so keen to do that."

She giggles and I raise myself up above her.

"Okay now?" I ask and she nods, resting her hands on my biceps. "Taste yourself, baby… you're mighty sweet." I lean down and kiss her and she opens her mouth willingly, licking my lips with breathtaking need, and relishing the taste of her divine nectar. Without breaking the kiss, I balance on one arm and reach down, guiding my cock to her entrance, before pushing forward. She gasps into me, clutching my arms and deepening the kiss, and I thrust again, giving her my whole length and hearing her groan deep in my mouth.

She breaks the kiss. "Oh… Oh my God, Rob…"

I still and she looks up at me. "You okay?" I ask.

She nods. "Yes," she murmurs. "You feel so good."

I smile. "Nowhere near as good as you do. You're really tight."

"That's because you're really big."

I lean down, my lips poised above hers. "Then we're a perfect match," I say to her, and I start to move.

"More," she whispers. "Give me more."

I'm happy to oblige and I pick up the pace, going deeper with every stroke and taking her harder. She raises her legs, and I take it up another notch, grinding into her pussy, giving her everything I've got, until I know I can't hold out much longer.

"I'm gonna come," I warn her.

"Me too," she says, looking up into my eyes, and right at that moment, she clamps around my dick and I hear my name leave her lips in a long slow whisper. That's as much as I can take and, with one last thrust, I explode deep inside her, my whole body shuddering into hers as I murmur her name over and over.

I've never had a longer orgasm than that, or a more fulfilling one and, when it's finally over, I look down at her to see she's staring at me.

"Thank you," she whispers.

I shake my head. "Don't thank me."

"It was perfect."

"Yeah. It was."

I turn us both onto our sides, so we're facing each other.

"Are you okay?" I say quietly, kissing her soft lips.

"Hmm…" she murmurs, evidently overcome with tiredness.

We're lying on top of the comforter, but there's a blanket at the end of the bed and, unwilling to pull out of her yet, I reach down and grab it, pulling it over us.

"Sleep, baby," I say softly.

She nestles into me, bringing her arms around me and holding me tight.

Sleep is claiming me too – which isn't surprising after what we've just done – and the fact that it's probably around two in the morning by now. But, before I drift off, there's something I've gotta say to her – even if she's too far gone to hear me.

I pull her closer. "I love you," I whisper in her ear, and I feel her tense in my arms, and hope I haven't just fucked everything up.

She relaxes again almost immediately, nuzzling into my neck. "I love you," she mumbles.

And I know I'm right where I belong… and I'm staying. Forever.

I wake the next morning at six.

I can do that, when I have to. I told myself I'd needed to wake early today and I did.

Unfortunately, I've also gotta wake Petra, because I need to ask her a question and I need to do it right now, before it's too late.

She's still in my arms, although we're no longer joined, more's the pity.

"Hey," I whisper, kissing her softly.

She squirms and fidgets but doesn't open her eyes.

"Petra, baby…" I try again.

This time, she opens up very slowly.

"It can't be morning already," she says.

"It is. But it's very early."

"How early?"

"Six…"

"Why on earth are you waking me at six?" she asks.

"Because I need to ask you something…"

"And it couldn't wait until a more civilized hour?" I'm gonna take a guess that she's not great at mornings.

"Not really, no."

She huffs. "Okay… having woken me, what's so damn important?"

I smile at her. "God, you're beautiful when you're angry."

"Stop trying to sweet-talk me and spit it out. Why have you woken me up so early?"

"Because I need to know if you want me to leave…" I whisper. She stares at me, clearly confused. "I can get dressed and go home now, before April and your mom see me," I explain. "I get that this is a big deal for you and, if you're not ready to have them see me here first thing in the morning, then I'm okay with that."

She looks a little sheepish now. "I'm sorry," she says, leaning up and kissing my stubbled chin. "You're being really thoughtful, and I just bit your head off."

"It's okay," I reply. "So, what do you want me to do?"

She leans back a little in my arms, staring right into my eyes. "You said you loved me last night," she says.

"Yeah."

"Did you mean it?"

"Of course I did." I kiss her gently. "I intentionally didn't say it before we made love, in case you thought it was a ruse to get into your panties, and I didn't say it while we made love, in case you thought it was just a heat of the moment thing. I've never said that before to anyone, baby. I wanted to say it when it meant the most."

"So you're serious… about us, I mean?"

"Yeah. I'm very serious." I let out a sigh. "I may have fooled around a bit." She frowns at me. "Okay… a lot… I know people thought of me as a player, and maybe I was, but that's all in the past as far as I'm concerned. That's how I know this is different. That's how I know it's real. Love might be new to me, but I know what it means."

She smiles a really sweet smile.

"You said it too though. Did you mean it?" I ask.

"Yes," she says simply and, to be honest, that's all I need.

"Tell me what you want me to do." Time's moving on and I need an answer.

"Can you stay and have breakfast with us?"

I smile. "Sure. When's breakfast?" I ask.

"Usually around eight."

My smile widens. "Then you've got a choice, baby… Either you can get another hour's sleep before we have to get up and shower…"

"Or?"

"Or, I can make you come at least…" I pause, thinking. "At least three times, and then we can shower together."

She thinks for a moment. "As much as I love my sleep… I think I'll take option two, if that's okay with you."

"Oh… it's very okay." I roll her onto her back and lean down to kiss her, just as she puts a finger against my lips. "What's wrong?" I ask.

"It's just…"

"What?"

"If you're gonna stay for breakfast…"

"What?"

"Can you cook it?"

I laugh, right before I lean down and kiss her. Hard.

Chapter Ten

Petra

Rob was as good as his word and made me come three times… twice in bed, and once more in the shower, where he exploded deep inside me.

I keep thinking I should tell him about Adrian, but talking about him when we're in bed feels wrong. I need to find a time when we're together, but fully clothed, and in private to explain about my past…

We're dressed and downstairs before everyone else, and I put the coffee on while he goes over to the refrigerator.

"Will everyone eat pancakes?" he asks.

"Everyone will love pancakes."

Normally we just have cereal, or toast on weekdays and luxuries like pancakes are reserved for weekends, when mom's got time to make them.

"Okay," he replies, getting out some eggs and milk. "Where do you keep your flour?" he asks.

"Um…"

"Don't tell me you don't know." He grins over at me.

"I told you. I'm a useless cook. I rarely use flour."

He laughs, and starts going through the cabinets, finding it at the second attempt.

He's just put it down on the countertop, when my mom appears in the doorway, announcing her arrival with an unsubtle cough.

I turn and notice that she's staring at Rob, her arms folded, and her eyes dark and suspicious.

"Mom, this is Rob Moreno," I say quickly, making the introductions. "Rob, this is my mom, Thea."

He comes over, holding out his hand, although for a moment, she hesitates and I wonder if she's actually going to refuse to shake hands with him. At the last second, she relents and offers her own.

"We met at April's party. Good morning, Mrs Miller," Rob says, very respectfully.

Their handshake is brief and my mom doesn't say a word. Rob pulls back, looks over at me, raises his eyebrows and goes back to where he was standing.

"What are you doing?" my mom asks.

I'm not sure if she's asking what Rob's doing in her kitchen, or why I have a man in the house this early on a Wednesday morning, and I decide she has a right to know the answer to the first question, but not the second.

"Rob's just gonna make us some pancakes for breakfast."

"Is he?"

"Yes." *Please don't be rude, Mom. Don't embarrass me.*

"Do you want me to leave?" Rob asks, clearly picking up on the awkward atmosphere my mom's creating.

"No," I reply quickly. "Let me find you a bowl."

"You have no idea where the bowls are kept, Petra," my mom comments, sarcastically, and comes into the room, going over to the far side of the kitchen, opening one of the cabinets and pulling out a large mixing bowl, which she hands to Rob.

"Thank you," he says, giving her the benefit of one of his best smiles. She's unmoved, and leans back on the countertop, staring at me.

I can't handle this. "I'm gonna go and get April," I announce. At least if she's in the room, my mom will be behave herself better.

"Okay," Rob replies, and I realize that means I'll be leaving him on his own with my mom. He gives me a smile though, to let me know he's okay with it, and I leave, relieved to be away from the strained situation.

April's clearly only just woken up. She's sleepy and yawning as I go into her room.

"Hello, sleepyhead," I say to her.

"Hello, Mommy."

I go over and lift her into my arms, loving that soft, cozy feeling of her next to my body. "Did you sleep okay?" I ask.

She nods her head.

"Wanna come downstairs for some breakfast?"

"Hmm, I'm hungry."

I smile. "Well, that's good, because I've got a surprise for you." I decide it's best to forewarn her. "Do you remember the man who bought you the baking set for your birthday?"

"Rob, you mean?" She remembered his name, and that makes my smile even wider.

"Yes." I nod my head. "Well, he's here."

"Has he come to bake those special cookies with me?" she asks.

"Not today, baby. But he is making us breakfast."

"Oooh." She grins, her eyes lighting up. "What's he making us?"

"Pancakes."

"Yummy." She licks her lips and rubs her tummy at the same time, and I laugh, as we start down the stairs.

We get into the hallway and I stop as I hear voices coming from the kitchen.

"I thought I brought her up better than that," my mom's saying. Well, that only hurts a little bit.

"What exactly is it you think Petra's done, Mrs Miller?" Rob asks, his voice calm and soft.

There's a moment's silence and I'm aware of April studying my face.

"Spent the night with a man she barely knows." Great. I needed my daughter to hear that.

"She knows me enough to know I'm here to stay," Rob says. "She also knows I'm in love with her."

"Oh, really?" My mom's sarcasm is obvious, even from here and I take a couple of steps toward the kitchen to tell her to butt out of my life.

"Yeah, really." Rob's voice has taken on a harsher tone. "You don't know me, Mrs Miller. You don't have the right to judge me, but I love Petra."

"I have the right to judge, if you're spending the night in my house." *We're back to that again?*

"If I'm not welcome here, Mrs Miller, then I'll leave," Rob replies, "but I won't stop seeing your daughter. Not for you – or anyone."

I enter the room just as he finishes speaking and I smile over at him.

He returns my smile before looking back to my mom and lowering his voice. "I don't want to argue with you," he says. "Family matters to me, and I'd really like for us to all get along. I appreciate that this is your house, and if you really don't want me here, I'll respect that, but like I say, nothing you say or do is gonna stop me from seeing Petra, or from loving her."

My mom stares at him for a moment. Then she moves forward. "I didn't mean you weren't welcome," she says, calming down. "I—It was just a shock. That's all."

"Okay." Rob nods, then looks back to me again. "Good morning," he says to April, a broad smile on his lips, his demeanor changing instantly. "Would you like to help me make some pancakes?"

"Yes please." April jumps down out of my arms and runs over to him, and he gives me a quick wink just as he pulls out a chair from the kitchen table, lifts April onto it, and sets out the mixing bowl in front of her.

Rob has to leave by nine-thirty. He needs to go home and change and get into the restaurant by ten. Breakfast was great, in terms of what Rob cooked, but the atmosphere was awkward, to put it mildly. Rob tried to make conversation, but my mom wouldn't relent and gave him one word answers at best.

Fortunately April is so besotted with him, she won't give us a moment's peace and, even as we stand on the doorstep, saying goodbye, she's still clasping his hand firmly, evidently unwilling to let go.

"I'll see you later," he whispers to me.

"I'll be there at five." He smiles.

"Looking forward to it already." He gives me a wink. "Will you be okay?" He nods back toward the kitchen, where we left my mom a few minutes ago.

"I'll be fine."

"Will you be here for breakfast again tomorrow?" April asks him, and Rob looks at me.

I stare into his hope-filled eyes. "Yes, baby girl," I reply. "He'll be here for breakfast again."

"Oh, great!" April's enthusiasm makes us both chuckle, and Rob leans down and lifts her into his arms. My breath catches in my throat at the sight of him holding her.

"I'll only come to breakfast if you agree to help me," he says to her.

"I'll help," she replies, so eagerly, we both have to laugh again.

"Okay," Rob says. "It's a deal." He lowers her back down to the ground, placing her beside me, his hand resting on her head. "See you tomorrow," he murmurs.

"See you tomorrow," she replies.

"And see you later," he adds, leaning into me and giving me a quick kiss on my cheek.

He walks away and we go back inside, closing the door. April leads me down the hallway to the kitchen, even though I'd rather avoid my mom, and head straight upstairs to get April dressed.

Mom's scrubbing the countertop like her life depends on it, and I know what that means. She's mulling over something – and today, that something is Rob. Well, it's Rob and me.

"Do you not like him?" I ask her outright, because I can't be bothered to pussy-foot around.

"I don't know him well enough to decide," she replies, without looking up. "And that's the problem. Neither do you."

"That's rich," I say. "You were very quick to judge both of us. But you got together with dad after just a few days. I've known Rob longer than that. And besides, at least we're being open."

She turns and faces me. "What does that mean?"

"We're not sneaking around, Mom." I fold my arms across my chest. "We're not lying about our relationship, or keeping it secret. I'd have thought you were old enough not to have to do that."

I notice her cheeks flush. "We're not talking about me," she replies.

"We're not talking about me either. Not right now." I bend down and lift April into my arms. "If we're gonna have this discussion, I think it's best if we have it later, in private, don't you?"

I go to leave, but she calls out, "Have you told him about Adrian?" and I stop in my tracks, turning back to face her.

"Yes. I've told him." It's kind of true.

"And he's okay with that?"

I nod, because what I can't tell her is that I haven't told him everything – and that if I did, he probably wouldn't be okay with it, especially not now I've let things go as far as they have. I don't wait for her to say anymore though, but I head upstairs, take April into her room, and start to get her dressed. My hands are shaking and I have to stop, and go over to the window, taking deep breaths to try and calm down.

"Are you okay, Mommy?" April asks, coming over and tugging on my sleeve.

I crouch down beside her. "I'm fine, baby." I run my fingers through her hair. "Let's finish getting you dressed."

April's playing quietly in the corner of my office, but I can't concentrate and around twelve, I send Rob a text message:

— **Hi. Sorry to bother you. Miss you so much already. P xxx**

It's not what I want to say, but I'm not sure how to put that in a text.

I put my phone down and try to focus on my computer screen, but it's not working. Nothing can take my mind off of the argument I had with my mom. She's judging me for something she did with my dad when they first met, and for something she's doing herself now, and the injustice of it is making me angrier by the minute. And if I'm being honest, I feel guilty for not telling Rob everything, and that my mom, unknowingly, caught me out in that lie. I wish he and I had a little more time alone together… I let my head fall into my hands and sigh, just as my phone rings. I check the screen and am surprised to see that it's Rob.

"Hello?" I pick up straight away.

"What's wrong?" he asks.

"Nothing."

"Bullshit, Petra."

"Am I not allowed to send you a text telling you I miss you?"

"Yeah. But that's not what you meant, is it?" How does he know?

"No," I whisper.

"Then tell me what's wrong."

"I had another fight with my mom," I say quietly, leaning back in my chair and looking over at April. She's playing with her dolls' house, and is seemingly in a world of her own. Lucky her.

"About me?" Rob asks.

"Kind of. It was also about her double standards, about her seeing this man, and not telling me about it."

"Oh."

"It feels like she's saying it's okay for her to sneak around, but not for me."

"We're not sneaking around," Rob replies. "That would have been a fair comment if I'd left before your mom and April woke up. As it is, we're being open about seeing each other. That was the whole point of this morning, wasn't it?"

"Yeah. Which just makes it so much worse."

There's a short pause. "Do you want me to come back? I can talk it through with your mom, if you think it would help. I can explain to her – again – that I'm serious about this; about you… about us."

I consider his suggestion, but I know this is something Mom and I have to work out between ourselves. "No," I reply. "I need to do this by myself. But thanks."

"Sure?"

"Sure. I'm grateful for the offer, though."

"I'm here if you need me, baby," he says, softly.

"I know. Thank you."

"Can you stop thanking me?"

I smile. "No."

I hear him chuckle. "In that case, I'm gonna have to really give you something to be grateful for."

My pussy tingles. "Yes, please," I breathe.

"Shit," he whispers. "I really wish I hadn't said that."

"Why not?" What does he mean? What's wrong?

"I'm hard now," he murmurs quietly into my ear. "Bone hard. And we're booked solid, which means I've gotta wait tables."

I laugh, and reply, "Well, we all have our problems…" And I hang up on him.

Just a few seconds later, my phone beeps.

— *It'll be your problem later. R xxx*

I reply straight away.

— *I don't regard that as a problem. P xxx*

His response makes me laugh.

— *That kinda depends what I do with it ;) R xxx*

— *As long as you're doing it with me, it's still not a problem. P xxx*

His next reply brings a tear to my eye.

— *Always and only with you, baby. R xxx*

I manage to spend an hour doing paperwork. Anything even vaguely creative is beyond me, but admin is boring enough to fill the time, without taking up too much brain power.

I've just finished the last of the invoices when my mom knocks on the door frame. The door itself is always left open when I'm working, but I guess she feels the need to announce herself – or maybe to ask permission to come in. I turn my chair toward her and see that she's been crying, and I get up and go over, giving her a hug.

"I'm sorry," she murmurs into my shoulder.

"I'm sorry too," I reply and we go back into the room. I sit down at my desk again, and she takes the chair beside it, leaning forward. She's clutching a Kleenex in her hand, rubbing it between her thumb and fingers, like she's nervous. "I do love him, Mom," I whisper, "and he loves me."

"I know." She sniffs.

"Do you have a problem with him staying here?" I ask outright. I'm twenty-seven years old; I didn't think I needed to ask permission anymore, but I guess I could be wrong.

"No. It's not that."

"Then what is it?"

She leans closer. "It genuinely was just a shock to see him in the kitchen."

"Then why have you been crying?" The sight of Rob in her kitchen didn't make her cry earlier, so why now?

"Because… because I called David earlier."

"Who's David?" I ask. "Is that the man you're seeing?"

She nods. "I was feeling out of sorts after we argued, and I called him to talk it through. And… and he told me he thought you were right. He said he didn't like the fact that I hadn't told you about him; he said it made him feel like I'm ashamed of him, and our relationship, which I'm not. And then he said he felt it was unfair to you that he was here last night while I was minding April, and I hadn't told you, and yet I objected to you having your young man here."

"He was here?" I'm surprised. "Last night?"

"Not all night," she clarifies. "Just for part of the evening."

"Has he met April?" I ask, fearing her answer. I don't think I like the idea of April meeting him before I have.

"No, of course not. I wouldn't introduce her to him without you meeting him first." I heave a sigh of relief. "He came over after April had gone to bed." She pauses for a moment. "But in a way I think that made it worse. He felt like we were sneaking around – which is exactly what you said we were doing. He felt very uncomfortable about that. But he wanted to see me, and that was the only way, being as I had to be here for April."

"I see." I put my hand over hers. "Did you fight – just now on the phone? Is that why you're upset?" I ask.

"No. We didn't really fight. But he said he doesn't like seeing me behind your back. He's told his kids about us, and he felt the secrecy meant I either was ashamed of him, or that I wasn't serious about him.

He was upset about the whole thing, and that's why I started crying. He wanted to come over, but I said you and I needed to talk first."

She sniffles and wipes her nose. "Why didn't you tell me, Mom?"

"I was worried you wouldn't approve. I know you worshipped your father. I thought you'd hate me even more…"

"Hate you even more? What are you talking about, Mom?"

She stares at me. "Oh come on, Petra. We both know I always came a poor second to your father."

"You didn't."

"Yes, I did."

"It wasn't a competition, Mom. He just did things that interested me more. You could've joined in, you know."

"I didn't want to join in with you. Photography never interested me in the slightest. I wanted you to enjoy spending time with me, like you did with your dad."

"I did like spending time with you, but I never liked cooking or sewing, or all the other things you did. And I thought taking pictures was magical."

She lowers her eyes, then raises them again, and I see they're filled with tears. "Imagine how you'd feel if April preferred Rob to you," she whispers.

I half chuckle. "I think she already does." Then I reach over and take her hand. "Rob is fun for April. He does the things she enjoys doing, but that doesn't mean she loves me any less." I take a breath. "I loved the things I did with Dad, but I always loved you, Mom. I always needed you. I still do. And if I haven't shown that very well, then I'm sorry."

She looks up at me. "I'm being silly," she murmurs.

"No. But I wish you'd told me how you felt a little sooner. Then maybe I could've set your mind at rest. I could've explained that I love you and dad just the same."

"David isn't a replacement for your father, you know," she says quietly.

"I know," I tell her. "I do understand, Mom. And I do approve. Well, I'm sure I will, if I can meet him."

"You want to meet him?" She looks at me, a smile forming on her lips.

"Of course I want to meet him. Do you think he could maybe come over on Sunday, for lunch?"

"This coming Sunday?"

"Why not? And, if it's okay with you, I'll invite Rob too. If we ask him nicely, he might even do the cooking."

Her smile broadens. "Doesn't he have enough of cooking during the week?"

"He won't mind. As long as you don't."

"I don't," she says. "Like he said this morning, I just want us all to get along. Including David."

"Then call him back and invite him."

She leans over and kisses me gently on the cheek. "Thank you," she whispers, then gets up and leaves the room. I'd like to say I feel relieved – and in a way I do – but now I also feel nervous about meeting this man, who evidently means a lot to my mom.

What if we don't get along?

Rob

It's been a busy day, with a full lunch service, followed by a long meeting with a new supplier, but if I'm being honest, all I've done is worry about Petra and how she's getting on with her mom. I've never been in this situation before, mainly because I've never stayed the night with anyone, and all the women I've slept with have had their own place – so running into parents, has never been an issue. I guess when we decided that I was gonna stay for breakfast, I knew I'd meet Petra's mom again, and we'd gotten along okay at April's party, so I didn't think it would be a problem, but I never anticipated her being quite so negative about our relationship, or me. I just hope that Petra's managed to have a better afternoon than the morning was.

My supplier leaves at just before five, and Petra arrives a few minutes later, coming over to me at the bar and hugging me.

I hug her back and look down into her eyes. "You okay?" I ask her.

She nods, but doesn't reply and I know it's because she can't. I don't say anything else either, but take her hand and lead her back into the office, closing the door behind us.

"We've got a few minutes," I say quietly, pulling her into my arms again. "Tell me what's happened."

She rests her head on my chest, her arms around my waist and sighs deeply. "Mom came and saw me at lunchtime," she whispers. "I asked her why she didn't tell me about David…"

"Who's David?" I ask.

"The man she's seeing."

"Oh. I see. What did she say?"

"That she thought I wouldn't approve, that I'd hate her…"

"Hate her? That's a bit strong, isn't it?"

"Yeah." She nestles into me, but looks up, so I can see her. She looks kinda sad. "It was all to do with my childhood. She said she felt like I didn't love her, because I did everything with my dad. But it really didn't feel like that at the time. I loved them both, but what he did fascinated me then, just as much as it does now. What Mom did seemed dull by comparison. Evidently, she felt left out. It was like she was jealous of my relationship with my dad. It's kinda sad really. It was so long ago, but I guess she's never forgotten." She smiles just slightly. "I suppose it explains her attitude about me not cooking, or feeding April the right things. I guess she feels that if I'd spent time with her when I was younger, and learned the skills she wanted to teach me, I wouldn't be so helpless in the kitchen now."

"You're not helpless," I say, kissing her forehead.

"Yeah, I am."

"Well, even if you are, being able to cook isn't everything… especially now you've got me." She smiles properly this time. "The point is, did you resolve anything?" I ask her, holding her close.

"Yeah. She told me she'd spoken to David about the situation."

"And?"

"And he told her he agreed with me."

"I'll bet your mom didn't like that too much."

I feel her chuckle, even though it's silent. "Not a lot, no," she says. "She got upset. But David told her he felt she was ashamed of him, because she wouldn't let me meet him, even though he's been to the house, when April's there."

"He's met April?" I'm astounded her mom would do that, especially without asking.

"No," she replies quickly. "He only comes over when April's asleep, but he doesn't like sneaking around."

"I don't blame him."

"So… we've agreed that he's going to come over for lunch on Sunday. Mom called him back after she and I had spoken, and he's really enthusiastic about it."

"Well, that's good. You'll get to meet him at last."

She leans back and looks up at me properly. "So will you."

"I will?"

"Yeah. I want you to be there too. That's why I suggested making it Sunday."

I can't help the broad grin that spreads across my face. "Thank you," I murmur, and bend to kiss her. She leans away from me and shakes her head.

"You might not thank me," she says, and I notice the mischievous glint in her eyes.

"Why not?"

"Because I've volunteered you for cooking the lunch." She's trying so hard not to laugh.

"You want me to cook for your mom… and her boyfriend?"

"Do you mind? I know it's your day off…"

"I don't mind at all. As long as your mom doesn't object to me taking over her kitchen."

"I think she's gonna want to check up on what you're doing, but I know she's also worried about how David and I are going to get along, so if she was doing the cooking, I imagine she'd probably ruin it in some way or another."

"I'm gonna be fairly on edge myself, so I'm offering no guarantees, but I'll do my best."

She brings her arms up around my neck and leans into me. "I know you will," she whispers and kisses me deeply. It takes a while before either of us is willing to break the kiss, but eventually she pulls away and looks up at me. "I've got something else I want to talk to you about," she says, looking a little shy.

"Okay." I try to sound reassuring, although I've got no idea what's coming.

"Do you have time to go back to your place before we open tonight?" she asks.

I check my watch. "Um… I guess so. Why?"

She hesitates, then whispers, "Because I wondered if you wanted to bring some clothes over tonight, and maybe a toothbrush?"

I smile down at her. "To keep at your place, you mean?"

She nods. "That way, you could stay for an extra half hour in the mornings, rather than having to go home to change, and it would be more like… more like…"

"More like we're a couple?" I suggest. She nods again and I lean down and kiss her. "I'd love to," I say. "But if I'm gonna go, I've gotta go now. I've only got about twenty minutes before I have to be in the kitchen."

"Then stop kissing me, and go," she says, and pushes me toward the door.

The evening shift is, if anything, even busier than it was at lunchtime, and by the time we've finished, we're all exhausted. Once we've cleaned everything down, I say goodnight to Ed, grab a small box of fresh fruit from the refrigerator, pick up my bag, which I left in the office, and head out into the restaurant, where Petra's just finishing off.

"What's all that for?" she asks me, looking at the box I'm holding under my arm.

"Breakfast," I reply. "I wanna get in your mom's good books. So, I thought we'd have something healthy tomorrow."

"Creep," she mutters, and leans up to give me a kiss.

She finishes up quickly and we head out the front door, which I lock behind us. The walk back to Petra's place is quick – thank goodness – and when we get there, I put the fruit away and we go straight up to Petra's bedroom.

I dump my bag on the ottoman at the end of the bed and, without saying a word to each other, she sits down on the bed to take off her boots as I start to undress, undoing the buttons on my shirt and taking it off, before I look up and see she's struggling.

"Let me help," I say, going over, kneeling down in front of her, and pulling her boots off one at a time.

"That's such a relief," she mutters, curling her toes and twisting her feet around.

I stand and she leans forward, her hand resting on the buckle of my belt, her eyes capturing mine. The air seems to crackle with unspoken need and she releases the buckle, and the button behind it, and lowers my zipper, before reaching inside and running her fingers along the length of my cock. I suck in a deep breath at her touch, and she slowly lowers my jeans, then still looking in my eyes, pulls down my trunks, releasing my dick into her waiting hand. I don't even think she's aware that she's just licked her lips, but the sight of that makes my cock twitch and she smiles up at me, then leans further forward, opening her mouth. I shift slightly closer toward her, stepping out of my clothes as I do so, and standing between her parted legs. She dips her head a little and starts to suck me, taking my cock in her mouth, tentatively to begin with, but within moments, gaining in enthusiasm, her tongue flicking over me. I reach around behind her head, holding her in place and, keeping eye contact, I very gently start to move back and forth, fucking her mouth. She groans and moves her hand up and down my shaft, as she takes me deeper, my cock hitting the back of her throat. Fuck, this is hot, and it's not gonna be long before I come. I release her head and place my hands on her cheeks, then gently pull out of her mouth. She lets go of me, and sits back, her eyes filled with sadness, and something else… disappointment, I think.

"What's wrong?" I ask her.

"Nothing."

"Bullshit, Petra." I hate it when she does that.

She raises her feet up onto the bed, pushes herself back and then turns over, so she's kneeling, before she starts to crawl to the other side. *What the fuck?*

"Hey, come back here." I grab her legs, pulling her back over, so she's lying before me on her front, then I sit beside her. "Tell me what's wrong."

She shakes her head, which is buried in the comforter.

"Petra," I whisper, lying down next to her. "I wanna make love to you, but I'm not going to, until you tell me what's wrong."

She turns to face me and I see the tears in her eyes.

"Why are you crying?" I pull her close, even though she's stiff in my arms.

"Because you stopped."

"I stopped. I stopped what?"

"What we were doing."

The penny finally drops. "You mean I stopped you sucking me?"

She nods and goes to turn away again, but I grab her chin with my hand and keep a hold of it, forcing her to look at me.

"I'm sorry," I whisper.

She swallows hard and blinks, and a single tear falls from her eye. "I—I've never done that before," she murmurs.

"Never?"

She shakes her head. "No." She sniffles. "I'm sorry if I wasn't as good as—"

"Jesus, Petra," I interrupt. "You were the best. That was the problem, baby. You were too good." I contemplate telling her that no-one's ever made me want to come that fast, but I guess now's not the time for comparisons. "I only stopped you because I was gonna come."

"And?" she says.

"And I didn't want to come in your mouth."

"You didn't?"

"Not tonight, no. I want to make love to you tonight, and after the shift we've just had, I don't think I can go more than once before I fall asleep, but next time, if you want, we can take it further."

"And you'll… you know… in my mouth?" Her eagerness is disarming, even if she still won't say exactly what she means.

"Yeah. I'll come in your mouth." I've already got an idea in mind for that. "But for tonight, I want to make love. Well, to be more precise, I want you to make love to me."

Her brow furrows. "You want…?"

"I want you to go on top. I've been thinking about it all day…" She tenses. "What's wrong?" I ask again.

"I can't do that."

"Why not?"

"Because…" she hesitates. "Because I'm not thin and beautiful… not like all the other women you've been with."

I lean back sharply. "What do you mean?" I realize too late that I raised my voice.

She puts her finger to her lips. "Shh," she admonishes. "April's asleep just across the hall, and my mom's only upstairs."

"Sorry." I take a deep breath. "But what the fuck are you talking about?"

"Exactly what I just said." She's looking at a place just below my chin, rather than making eye contact with me now. "I've seen the type of women who chase after you. And I'm nothing like them. I'm not thin, or beautiful, or sexy. I don't want you to be able to see me when we're… you know…not all open and… exposed, like that."

I hold her closer. "Okay. To start off with, the type of women who chase after me – as you put it – don't interest me—"

"You slept with them," she interrupts.

"Yeah, some of them, but I didn't spend the night with them. I didn't meet their families. I didn't fall in love with them." I sigh. "Baby, I haven't been able to take my eyes off of you since the first time I saw you, because you're my idea of perfect. I've seen your body – all of it – and, whatever you think, I *know* that you're beautiful. You're more than beautiful. You're exactly what I want. I love your body, and right now, there's nothing I want more than to watch you take me. I want to be able to touch you, and kiss you while you ride my cock. I want to see you come." She closes her eyes and sucks in a breath. "Please. Please, will you take me?"

She raises her eyes to mine and leans up, kissing me gently on the lips, before rolling me onto my back. Then she kneels and undoes her blouse, shrugging it off and throwing it to the floor. Her bra follows and I reach over and squeeze her nipple between my thumb and forefinger, making her moan and throw her head back. Next, she stands and I watch her undo her black jeans, lowering them and her panties to the floor, before crawling up my body until she's straddling me, raised above my erect cock.

"Take me, baby," I whisper to her, and she slowly lowers herself down my length, taking me deep inside her wet pussy.

I suck in a deep breath as I feel her tight walls surround me, and then she starts to move. At first, she takes it fairly slow, but then she picks up the pace, riding me harder and harder, slamming down onto me. I capture her large, firm breasts in my hands and she leans forward, resting her palms on my chest and changing the angle, so my cock's buried deeper inside her. By raising my head just slightly, I can lick and suck on her nipples, which makes her moan and grind into me, my name a whispered plea on her lips. She stares down at me and, just when I think she's going to come, she sits up again, leaning right back, and placing one hand behind her, on my thigh. At this angle the tip of my cock strokes the front wall of her vagina with every movement and I know that's gonna make her come real soon. Sure enough, within a few minutes, she starts to pant and moan, whispering my name a little louder and begging me for more. I raise my hips to hers, taking her deep, matching her rhythm and, just when I know she's about to go over the edge, I use my thumb to caress her clit. That's all it takes, and she loses it. Her inner walls clamp around my cock, she throws back her head, and lets go, just as I explode deep inside her.

Only once I know she's calm and capable of understanding do I speak.

"You're incredible," I whisper. "You're beautiful. You're sexy, erotic, intense. You're passionate and exciting. You turn me on all the time. You give me everything I could ever want – and more. And I never – ever – want to hear you say, or think, that you're anything but perfect. Because you are. You're perfect for me – and that's all that matters."

She stares down at me, tears welling in her eyes. "God, I love you so much," she murmurs.

"And I love you." I pull her down into my arms and turn us onto our sides, holding her close until I hear her breathing change and I know she's asleep.

When we get downstairs for breakfast, the kitchen is empty, which surprises me, being as we're quite late down today, but that's entirely my fault. I had to make love to Petra this morning. It wasn't optional.

Her mom appears just a few minutes after us, and I wonder for a moment whether she was waiting until she heard us before coming down. I don't say anything though, other than a polite 'good morning' to her.

Today, she's a lot more accommodating. When I greet her as 'Mrs Miller', she insists that I should call her Thea, and then sits at the table drinking coffee, while Petra goes to fetch April.

"Petra told me about Sunday," I say to break the ice.

"Are you sure you're okay with cooking lunch?" she asks.

"Absolutely. Although it won't be Greek," I warn her. "It'll be Italian. It's about all I know."

"I'm sure it'll be fine." She sounds like she needs a little convincing, but I've already decided what I'm gonna cook. I talked it through with Ed last night during the evening service. He gave me a couple of ideas and I've reached a decision. Although a thought has just occurred… "Is there anything that you or David don't like?" I ask her.

She thinks for a moment. "No. To be honest, I haven't really cooked much for him. Because we've spent a lot of time at his house, he's done most of the cooking, or we've eaten out, but he's never mentioned not liking any particular foods."

I think that's the longest speech she's ever made to me and, for a moment, I'm a little taken aback by the detail.

"Okay," I manage to say, just as Petra and April come into the room.

"Good morning," I say to April and she rewards me with the cutest smile, before letting go of Petra's hand and coming straight over to me.

"Hello, Rob," she replies. "What's for breakfast?"

"French toast and fruit," I tell her.

"Fruit?" She pulls a face.

"April's not the greatest fan of fruit," Thea says. "We try, but she's yet to be convinced."

"Well, we'll have to see what we can do about that, won't we?"

I pull out a chair at the kitchen table and lift April onto it, pushing it in again slightly, while Petra goes and pours herself a coffee.

"I've been thinking, Mom," she says over her shoulder. "Do you think David's kids would like to come on Sunday too?" She glances over at me. "You wouldn't mind cooking for everyone, would you?"

"No," I reply, "I'm fine with it." I'll go along with whatever she wants. And, let's face it, at the moment, I'm cooking for around a hundred and fifty people a night in the restaurant. Sunday lunch for a dozen or so is a comparative walk in the park.

"I think we should maybe leave the arrangements as they are for now," Thea says quietly.

"Oh. Okay." Petra sits down opposite her mom. "Have… have you met David's kids?" she asks, and I know almost at once that she's gonna regret asking that question.

"Yes." Thea's answer is almost inaudible. Petra doesn't reply. "I've spent a fair amount of time at his house. They came over one day, unannounced." She shrugs.

I glance at Petra and notice the tears in her eyes, just before she pushes back her chair, gets up, and leaves the room.

Thea looks at the space her daughter just vacated, then turns to me, looking confused. "You need to explain it to her," I tell her.

"I did. We talked yesterday. I thought we'd cleared the air."

"Well, obviously not. You need to make it clear to her why you've left her out."

"I haven't. Not deliberately. David's kids really did arrive unannounced, and I didn't know how to tell Petra about him. She was so attached to her father, you see…"

"I know. But I think she explained to you yesterday that her spending time with her dad didn't mean she loved you any less—"

"She told you about that?" she interrupts.

"Yes. Look, one of us needs to go and make sure she's okay. If I go, you'll lose her trust, Thea. She's hurting, and she needs reassurance, but she needs it from you, not me." She blinks quickly, like she's trying not to cry in front of me. "I'll watch April," I add, making it clear she should go, and she gets up and follows Petra from the room.

Once she's gone, April turns to me, looking a little doubtful. I'm worried about Petra, but I'm now also concerned that her little girl has been left with me and that maybe she's also confused, because the two people she knows best in the world have just abandoned her to a relative stranger.

"Wanna help with the breakfast again?" I ask her, and she nods enthusiastically, a perfect smile forming on her lips. *Clearly not that worried about me, then.*

I go over to the refrigerator and grab a few ingredients, including the box of fruit I brought with me last night, then grab two knives from the drawer before coming back and sitting beside April.

"First we're gonna make the French toast," I explain. "And then I'm gonna show you how to cut the fruit." I show her the bluntest knife I could find. "And I'm gonna teach you how to do it safely, without hurting yourself."

Her eyes light up and she looks into the box of fruit. "That's a lot of fruit," she says.

I pick out a strawberry. "Do you know what this is?"

She nods. "Stawby." *Fuck, that's so cute.*

I smile. "Yeah… it's a stawby." I hand it to her and take another for myself. "Take a bite."

By the time Petra and her mom come back into the kitchen, I've made the French toast and it's keeping warm in the oven, and we've cut up all the fruit we need, although April's got a fair amount of it over herself and around her mouth. Still, despite the mess, my ploy worked... I remembered that Mom got the three of us to eat fruit and vegetables by letting us help prepare things with her, and getting us to taste them. April didn't like everything, but she tried it all.

"Sorry," I mutter, and I get up and go over to the sink, wetting the edge of a towel and bringing it back to wipe her down. "We got a bit carried away while we were cutting the fruit." April grins up at me as I dab the corners of her mouth, which are stained red from the strawberries she was stealing. They were definitely her favorite.

"You... you let her use a knife?" Thea stares at the the knives, laid down on the table, and the resulting chopped fruit.

"Yeah. But it was the bluntest one I could find." I hold it up to her. "And I showed her how not to cut herself. I also explained to her that she must never ever use a knife without asking you or her mom first."

"He did, Yaya," April confirms, although I have no idea what a yaya is.

Thea nods her head slowly and sits down, while Petra comes around the table. I can see she's been crying, but she's smiling right now.

"You got my daughter to eat fruit?"

"Yeah. I'm incredibly persuasive, you know."

"That's a family trait, is it?" Her expression is playful.

"Hmm, evidently." I kiss her gently, then turn to April. "You particularly liked the stawbies, didn't you?" I say to her and she nods.

"Stawbies?" Petra smirks.

"Yeah. These." I hold up a strawberry, and roll my eyes at April. "How can your mom not even know the name of your favorite fruit?" I say and she giggles, and I wonder if there's a sound on this earth more adorable than that.

Once we've finished breakfast, it's time for me to leave. I say goodbye to Thea, who thanks me for cooking and Petra sees me to the door, accompanied by April, who's got a firm grip on my hand.

Standing on the doorstep, I lift April into my arms, like I did yesterday, only this time, she holds on, her tiny arms clinging to my neck, and I notice tears forming in Petra's eyes again.

"You okay?" I ask her.

She nods her head. "It's just…" She doesn't finish her sentence, but runs her hand gently over April's hair.

"Are you alright with this?" I wonder if she has a problem with me holding April. She didn't seem to mind yesterday, but should I have asked first?

Petra moves closer and I put my free arm around her, so I'm holding both of them. "Oh, I'm more than alright with it," she whispers into me and I gently sigh out my relief. I don't really have a clue what I'm doing, but I do like having them both in my arms.

"How did it go with your mom?" I ask and Petra leans back.

"She said she's sorry for leaving me out, and then we just talked some more about how I used to be with my dad. She remembered a few times when Dad and I went off doing things together and she wasn't included. She told me how that made her feel left out, and I asked her if she was punishing me now for what happened then, leaving me out, like she felt she was."

"What did she say?" I ask, holding her closer. It sounds like it got fairly heavy.

"She said 'no', of course, but it feels a bit like she is, if I'm being honest." She pauses and, once again, she runs her hand down the back of April's head. "I remember him holding me like this," she whispers. I kiss her forehead and give her time. "I told Mom that excluding me from David's family was hurtful, because that meant she was excluding me from her life, just because I loved – I still do love – my dad. It's fine now. We've made up and she says she won't leave me out any more." I feel her shrug, almost like she doesn't believe it. She still needs reassurance, only this time it's gotta come from me.

"Hey," I say quietly. "I'm sure she won't. Maybe she was just feeling uncertain… not just about the past, but about the future too."

"How do you mean?"

"It's a bit like you letting me into April's life. You had to be sure. So does your mom."

"About me?" She looks into my eyes, hers filled with doubt.

"No, not just about you. About David, about *his* kids, about their relationship, about everything. She doesn't want to introduce David to you, or April, if you're gonna get upset about him being in her life, or if there's a chance everyone won't get along."

"And yet, she met his family."

"Well, she did say it wasn't planned. And maybe their mom isn't held in quite such high esteem by them as your dad is by you."

She thinks for a moment and then nods her head slowly. "I'm being unreasonable, aren't I?" she murmurs.

"No, you're not. But neither is your mom. Not really." I hold her tighter. "Just wait until Sunday. Meet the guy. I'm sure it'll be fine."

She hugs me. "And you'll be here?"

"Of course I'll be here." Was that in doubt? "I won't let you down, Petra. Ever."

She rests her head on my chest and, in a touching role reversal, April pats her hair, just gently.

"Don't cry, Mommy," she says. "Rob will make it okay."

I feel Petra's silent sob, at the exact same moment that I become aware of April crawling into my heart and staking a claim there.

Chapter Eleven

Petra

The rest of the week has been unbelievably busy; so busy that Rob and I have literally fallen into bed at the end of each day, and gone straight to sleep. We've made love in the mornings – quickly, quietly, and spectacularly. When I got into work on Thursday, he was in a meeting, and on Friday, there was a problem with a wine order, which held him up, so we've had no time alone at all, apart from in bed – and I'm not going to discuss Adrian with him when we're in bed, so he's still blissfully unaware of the true circumstances of my marriage. The thing is, the longer it goes on, the harder it's becoming. When I was getting ready for work this evening, I was looking in the mirror while putting on my lipstick, and I wondered whether it matters that Rob doesn't know the full story. We're happy, and Adrian's in the past. Who benefits now from the truth coming out? Even as I thought that though, I felt awful. I *have* to find the time to tell him.

Given that I can't find a spare half hour to sit down and speak to Rob, I'm really not surprised that it's taken me until late on Saturday night to come up with a valid reason to raise the word 'strawberry' in front of him – and the whole kitchen – but I'm pleased that the opportunity has finally arisen. The man on table seven has an allergy to strawberries and has asked whether they're included in the red fruit coulis that's served with the basil and black pepper panna cotta. I'm almost certain they are, and I know that one of the other members of staff could tell me, but this is too good a chance to pass up, and I've waited so long, so I tell him that I'll go into the kitchen and check.

Rob is plating up a couple of main courses and looks up, giving me a smile as I go through to Ed's section, where he's preparing an Affogato for table three, which has to be done at the last minute. He stops working while I ask my question about the ingredients.

"Yeah, the coulis contains strawberries, redcurrants and raspberries," he replies. "I guess we should've listed that on the menu really."

I try hard to stop myself from smiling. "I'm sorry, did you say 'strawberries'?" I ask.

"Yeah, why?"

"Strawberries?" I repeat.

He frowns. "Yeah. Strawberries."

"Not stawbies."

He raises an eyebrow at me, then shakes his head. "No, definitely strawberries," he replies.

I turn and look at Rob, who's finished what he was doing and is now standing at the other end of the kitchen, leaning back on the countertop and watching us. I'm not sure if he can hear us, but judging from the smile on his face, I doubt it. "Well, that's odd, because your brother told me – and my daughter – that they're called stawbies."

Ed smirks. "Oh, he did, did he?" He looks over my shoulder. "Hey, Roberto," he calls. "What's all this about you not knowing how to pronounce the word strawberry?"

Rob looks from me, to Ed, and back again, then slowly pushes himself off of the countertop and starts walking over. "I suppose my girlfriend has been telling you that it's pronounced 'strawberry'," he says, his lips twisting up into a perfect smile. "When we all know that they're called 'stawbies'."

"We do?" Ed queries.

"Yeah. We do." He looks at Ed. "Or is it just me and four year old girls who know how to say things right?"

Ed shakes his head, smiling. "I guess it must be just you and the four year old girls."

"I thought as much."

He comes over to me and puts his arms around me. "You're no fun," I tell him.

"Oh, really?" he murmurs, kissing my neck.

"I was trying to embarrass you, and you just took it in your stride."

I hear Ed chuckle behind me. "If you're trying to embarrass him, you've gotta go a lot further than that," he says.

"A hell of a lot further," Rob confirms, and kisses me again. "And I'll show you how much fun I can be later," he murmurs, loud enough for just about everyone in the kitchen to hear, and I blush to the roots of my hair, while his lips curve up into a broad grin. "Anything else we can help you with?" he asks.

"No, I think I've humiliated myself enough," I reply and pull away from him. He grabs me and pulls me back, holding me close.

"I'm looking forward to later already," he whispers.

I gaze up into his eyes. "Hmm, me too."

Although he's brought home a fair few ingredients for tomorrow's lunch, we quickly stow those into the refrigerator and almost run up the stairs, in breathless anticipation. The scene in the kitchen earlier clearly gave us both something to think about.

"I'm sorry," he murmurs, pulling my blouse from my shoulders and undoing my bra, letting it fall to the floor.

"What for?" I suck in a breath as he captures one of my nipples between his teeth.

"For that scene in the kitchen." He releases my nipple to speak. "I didn't mean to humiliate you."

"I brought it all upon myself." I grab the back of his head and hold him in place as he moves to the other breast.

"I love how responsive your nipples are," he whispers, kneeling in front of me and undoing my jeans, lowering them and my panties to the floor and helping me to step out of them. "But right now, I need us both naked."

"I already am," I tell him.

"Yeah." He stands and looks me up and down, his eyes devouring my body. "And mighty fine you look too." He quickly tugs his t-shirt over his head, undoes his jeans and lowers them and his trunks to the floor, stepping out of them, and standing before me, gloriously naked and aroused.

"You look so good."

"Good enough to eat?" he asks, mischievously.

I nod my head quickly. I want to taste him again. He kisses me, his tongue delving deeply into my mouth, and walks us back towards the bed, turning so it's behind him and, just when I think he's going to lay us down, he breaks the kiss and stares down at me. "Ready?" he asks.

"Yes," I breathe. I'm more than ready.

He nods, just once, then bends and grabs hold of me. I have no idea quite how, but he flips me over, so I'm upside down in his arms, one thigh over each of his shoulders, his arms tight around my hips, his hands on my ass, holding me up and in place, his cock directly in front of my face. Without waiting to be asked, I rest my hands on the sides of his legs, take him in my mouth, and start to suck him. Just like the last time I did this, it's a struggle to take very much of him, but I manage and start to build a rhythm. He moans and then I feel his tongue on me, flicking across my exposed clitoris. The sensation is incredible and I move faster, taking him deeper and bringing one hand up to hold the base of his cock, squeezing and pumping him at the same time. He groans louder and then I feel like the world flips over again, as he falls down on the bed, on his back, his tongue never leaving my aroused nub, my mouth still clasped tight around his erection, as he raises his hips in time with my movements. I can feel his hands coming further around, and then he inserts a finger – maybe two – inside me and that's all it takes to push me over the edge. Unable to scream or cry out, because I have a mouth full of his cock, I buck against him, and sensing my orgasm, he tenses and I know at that moment, he's going to come too. Despite the continuing waves of pleasure washing through my whole body, as his tongue keeps flicking over me, I brace myself, not really knowing what to expect and finally, I feel the first spurt of hot liquid hit the back of my throat and I swallow it down, just as the next follows, and the next, and the next. He's writhing beneath me, as I continue to suck him, swallowing hard every few seconds until eventually, it subsides and he stills.

Breathless, I lie still for a moment, and then roll slowly off of him. I want to see his face, so I twist around and crawl up to him, my limbs heavy and barely working.

He's lying still, his eyes closed, his face expressionless.

"Rob?" I kiss his cheek, but he doesn't stir. "Are you okay?"

"No. I'm dead," he replies, his voice barely audible. "You killed me."

"Sorry."

"Don't be sorry. It was the best way to go," he says, opening his eyes, a smile forming on his lips. "There's none better." Very slowly, he turns to face me, putting his arms around me and holding me close against him. "You're amazing," he whispers.

"I think you'll find that was you." I nestle into him. "That thing you did, when we were standing up and you flipped me over… that was incredible."

He smiles. "Well, I'd have done it for longer, but I knew if I came in that position, I'd probably have collapsed, and being as your head was nearest to the floor, it could have ended badly."

"Hmm, very badly."

He leans back a little, still holding me. "Was that okay?" he asks, his voice more serious.

"Didn't we already establish that?"

He smiles. "I mean me coming in your mouth."

"Oh. Yes, it was. I liked it."

His smile widens. "Good. So did I."

David arrives at twelve-thirty precisely. I have to admit to feeling nervous, and although I'm trying not to let it show, I know Rob's noticed, because he keeps giving me reassuring hugs and telling me it'll be okay. He's been busy cooking most of the morning, and the smells he's creating are making us all hungry.

My mom brings David through to the kitchen where we're all gathered, waiting, and he leaves her side, coming over to me and offering his hand.

"It's a pleasure to meet you at last," he says. He's got a deep voice. I'd say he's probably around six feet tall, so just a little shorter than Rob. His hair is dark, with traces of gray, most noticeably at the temples, and his eyes are a deep blue. He's well-built, with a tan and is very good-looking.

I take his hand and he gives me a firm shake.

"It's good to meet you too," I manage to say, despite my nerves, and then I'm aware of Rob's arm tightening around me.

"Hi," he says. "I'm Rob."

"Ah, the chef," David replies, shaking his hand now.

"Well, the restaurateur. I'm only a stand-in chef while my brother's over in England."

David nods. "I see."

"And this is April," Rob says, performing the introduction that I should have remembered to make. April is standing between Rob and I and David crouches down and smiles at her.

"Hello, April," he says.

"Hello." She sounds a little doubtful and Rob immediately places a protective hand on her head.

"David is Yaya's friend," I explain and she looks up at me, nodding.

"Who, or what is Yaya?" David asks, standing again and looking from me to my mom.

"I'm Yaya," my mom explains. "It's Greek for grandma."

"Ah," Rob says. "I wondered about that."

"And you didn't ask?" I say, looking up at him.

"In case you haven't noticed, I'm easily distracted," he replies, giving me a wink, and I can't help but smile.

David's grinning, and he turns and goes back to my mom, taking her hand in his. "Whatever's cooking smells good," he says to her.

"I'm not responsible." She holds up her free hand. "You have Rob to thank for today's lunch."

David turns to Rob, who shrugs. "I'm doing my best," he says.

My mom steps forward. "I know it's lamb," she says, pulling out a chair and sitting down at the table, motioning for David to sit beside her, "but what have you done to it?"

Rob leans back against the countertop, while April and I join Mom and David at the table. April's got a coloring book and some crayons laid out in front of her and is soon absorbed in what she's doing – and obviously bored by the adult conversation going on around her. "I've just roasted it with garlic and rosemary, and a secret ingredient." He smiles down at us.

"And you're not going to tell us what that is?" I ask him.

"Well if he did, it wouldn't be a secret," David replies.

Rob chuckles. "That's very true. And there's also the minor point that, if I told you, you'd very probably refuse to eat it."

"Why?" Mom asks.

"Because it's kinda weird to put this particular thing with lamb."

"Now I'm really intrigued," David says, sitting forward.

Rob holds up his hands. "I can't claim any credit for this. It's my brother's recipe."

"Which brother?" I ask him.

"Sam, of course."

"Why 'of course'?" David asks.

"Well, because Ed is really the pastry expert, whereas Sam invents savory recipes."

"I see." David nods. "And you?"

"Oh, I run the front of house normally. Like I say, I'm just helping out in the kitchen at the moment, and Petra's doing my job for me, while Sam's in England for a few weeks, trying to sort out his love life."

"Which is a very long story," I add, before we get into that in front of April.

"Yeah," Rob adds, then turns to my mom. "So, if you were making roast lamb, Thea, how would you do it?"

"Probably the same way, but without the secret ingredient, I imagine," she replies. "I'd use garlic and rosemary as well."

Rob nods his head. "I guess some things are just meant to go together." He stares at me as he speaks and gives me the sweetest smile.

"How are you finding working in the restaurant?" David asks me.

"Oh… um… it's fine," I stammer out a reply, surprised by his direct question. "I enjoy working with Rob." David nods. "What do you do?" I ask him. "Or are you retired?"

He smiles. "I'm not quite that old… yet," he replies. "I work in insurance, which is just about as boring as it sounds."

"Have you always done that?" Rob asks, opening the oven door and checking on something inside.

"Yes. It may not be exciting, but the pay is fairly good. I married young, and needed a steady income, being as our son came along at the end of the first year." He smiles, like he's remembering something. "So, a well-paid job was a distinct advantage."

"You married young?" I pick up on that, recalling my own youthful marriage, and subsequent regrets.

"Yes. I was twenty-two. Marianne was nineteen."

"That is young," Rob says, turning back to face us.

"Yeah." David takes my mom's hand. "We were both at college."

"And you got married?"

He nods. "It felt like the right thing to do at the time," he explains. "And then Marianne fell pregnant just after I graduated, so I got the best paid job I could find and she dropped out." He looks up at the ceiling. "I think she resented me for that."

"It wasn't your fault," Rob says.

"No," David replies. "It wasn't anyone's fault. Sometimes these things just happen. And by the time James was born, she was fine with it. Well, she seemed fine, anyway." His voice is a little wistful and I feel sorry for him.

"You've got a daughter as well?" I ask.

"Yes." He smiles. "Clare was born two years later."

"And they have children of their own?" I keep the questions coming.

"Yes. James has two girls, Sophie and Isabel. Clare has a baby boy – Daniel – and is expecting another in about five months."

"So soon?"

He nods. "Yes. Daniel's only fourteen months old, so she's going to have her hands full."

"She sure is." I sigh. "I don't envy her." I don't. "Is Clare a full-time mom?" I ask.

"Yes. Before Daniel was born, she was a nurse, which is how she met her husband." He looks from me to Rob and back again. "He's a surgeon, called Nathan. It started off as one of those doctor-nurse romances, and then Clare fell pregnant with Daniel." He sounds a little disappointed, but tries to hide it.

"So they got married?" I ask.

"Yes. It was their choice. Nobody forced them." I wonder for a moment how happy Clare and Nathan are, but she's expecting again, so it can't be all bad.

"What does James do?" Rob asks, breaking the silence.

"He's a structural engineer." I can hear the pride in David's voice again. "His wife is Eloise. She's French by birth. They met when he was working in Paris for six months right after he graduated. They fell in love and he brought her back here and married her."

"And do your children both live in the city?" I ask.

"They do. I don't," he explains. "I have a house in West End. I grew up in an apartment and always wanted somewhere with a big garden."

"It's a lovely garden," Mom adds. "And it's enormous."

"Yeah. I do sometimes think I was over ambitious with the size of it," David says, shaking his head.

"Well, I like it." Mom leans into him, reassuringly.

I'm still unclear about what happened to his wife, and I'm not sure how to ask, although I feel it's quite important.

"Marianne never did," he replies. Then he turns and looks at me. "I'm divorced," he says simply, as though he'd been able to read my thoughts.

"Oh." I can't think what else to say.

"We drifted apart when James and Clare went to college," he explains. "Without the kids at home, we realized we had no reason to stay together any more. It was all very amicable in the end. She lives in San Francisco now, with her new husband."

"Do James and Clare see her?"

He shakes his head. "Not as much as she'd like them to, but it's a long way for them to take their children, when they're so young. Sophie and Isabel are five and three and, like I said, Daniel's still a baby. Maybe as they get older…" He leaves the sentence hanging.

"She could come here, couldn't she?" Rob asks.

"She does, for Christmas and during the summer, because all the grandchildren were born in June and July. Marianne and I see each other at birthday parties, and family gatherings, and we get along okay. Her husband's a nice guy."

We fall silent for a moment, before Rob speaks. "Sounds to me like you did a good job," he says from the corner of the kitchen, where he's stirring something on the stove. We all turn to look at him and he shrugs. "Well, despite the fact that you and your wife couldn't live together any more, you didn't let it affect your kids, or your relationships with them, or each other."

"No. I guess you could say we're a good example of how to break up a family well."

Rob nods, then folds his arms across his chest. "If I give you guys five minutes, do you think you could set the table?"

"Is lunch that imminent?" I ask him.

"Yeah," he replies, and we all get up and start setting out cutlery, plates and placemats on the table.

"You're going to have to tell us," mom says, taking another bite of lamb. "I can't guess."

"I didn't think you would," Rob replies, "but I don't think you'll thank me." He's smirking. "It's anchovies."

"Anchovies?" We all say at once, except April.

She looks at Rob, who she insisted on sitting next to, and says, "What are chovies?"

He grins at her pronunciation. "They're little tiny fish," he tells her, leaning over.

"Fish?" She pulls a face.

"Yeah."

"Yuk."

He smirks again. "But do you like how it tastes?" he asks.

She thinks for a moment, looks at her half-empty plate and nods her head.

"So, it's not yuk then, is it?" he says, and she smiles up at him.

When we've all finished eating, Rob and David clear the table and then Rob leans over April, from behind and asks if she can help him to prepare some 'stawbies'. She jumps down enthusiastically and goes across to the other side of the kitchen with him, while he looks over his shoulder and gives me a wink.

"I want to apologize to you," David says, leaning a little closer to me and lowering his voice.

"What for?" I ask.

"For you being kept out of the loop," he replies.

I want to say that it wasn't his fault, but then that will sound like I'm blaming my mom and I don't think that will be particularly helpful. Instead, I just say nothing.

"It wasn't intentional," he adds, breaking the silence. "I didn't set up the meeting between your mom and my kids. They arrived without telling me."

"I know. Mom explained."

"They knew I was seeing someone," he continues, smiling at my mom. "They'd noticed how much happier I was, and they confronted me about it a few weeks beforehand, so I told them about your mom. But I decided against introducing them to her until she'd told you about me. I wanted things to be on an equal footing... Except they all turned up one evening and kind of ambushed us," he says, smiling lightly.

"So you've met David's grandchildren as well?" I ask, turning to my mom.

"Yes." She nods her head, and bites her lip, like she's worried about my reaction.

"I'm really sorry about all of this, Petra," David says, speaking for her. "I've been wanting to meet you for a long time and I know it's not easy for you. It's not like it is for my kids. They know how things were between their mom and me; and they can still see Marianne if they want to." He grips Mom's hand a little tighter. "I understand that it's very different for you. I know how you feel about your dad, and I want to tell you that I'm not here to try and take his place – not in any capacity. I just want to make your mom happy, that's all."

I feel tears stinging behind my eyes and blink rapidly, just as Rob comes over, carrying April in his arms.

"Come sit with mommy for a moment," he says and they take a seat right next to me, and he puts his free arm around my shoulder, letting me lean into him.

I swallow hard, blinking again a few more times. "You do," I say to David, and my mom bursts into tears. He turns to her and pulls her into a close hug, kissing her cheek and stroking her hair as she sobs into his shoulder.

"Is Yaya okay?" April asks.

"Yaya is just fine," Rob replies, being as I think he's the only one capable of speech.

"Then why is she crying?"

"Believe it or not," Rob says, giving me a squeeze, "she's crying because she's happy. Grown ups do that sometimes."

Much later, when April's tucked up in bed and David's gone home, I'm lying in Rob's arms feeling safe and wanted, my head resting on his chest.

"Thank you for today," I whisper.

"Do you think everyone liked the lamb – in spite of Sam's anchovy idea?"

I smile. "Yes, but I wasn't talking about the lamb. I was talking about you, being so supportive, and so helpful with April."

He shrugs. "Anytime, baby," he murmurs and kisses the top of my head. He takes a breath and I have a feeling he wants to say something.

"What?" I ask him. "What were you going to say?"

"Just that I like David, that's all," he replies.

"Yeah, so do I."

"Was that hard to say?" he asks.

"No." I shake my head. "It wasn't. He's a nice guy." I pause, wondering how to ask my next question. "Do you think they'll end up living together – or getting married?"

"Maybe," Rob replies.

"Do you think they'll want to live here?"

"They might. Although he did make a point of telling us how much he loves his garden. So maybe they'll want to live at his place. Who knows?"

"If they want to live here, do you think they'll expect us to move out?" I ask him.

He moves, turning us both on our sides to face each other. "Does that worry you?" he asks.

"In a way, yes. I've gotten used to having my mom around. I know we argue sometimes, but I love her, and I like the way we live. It's very… Greek."

He smiles. "It's kinda Italian too," he says. "We tend to all live together too – lots of generations in one house." He kisses the tip of my nose. "Nothing's happened yet, but if it does, we'll work it out. Okay?"

"How?" I ask.

"Well, maybe we can still all live together. Or, maybe we'll get a place of our own nearby."

"We?" I query, holding my breath.

He frowns. "Sorry… I thought… I thought I was included." His voice fades.

"You are," I say quickly. "But only if you want to be." Does he? Does he really want that much with us?

He smiles again. "Of course I want to be." Would now be a good time to tell him? I know we're in bed, but… I open my mouth to speak, just as he flips me onto my back. "But right now," he whispers, "I just wanna be inside you." And the moment's lost – again.

Rob

This week has started off just as last week ended – namely busy. Ed's working mainly in the pastry section, which is good, because he's really the only one who can handle that, and I'm covering most of the main kitchen, with him stepping in when I need him. To be honest, I don't know how Sam does this day in, day out, because it's nearly killing me. I know I'm having to do my office work during the day, as well as cover the restaurant in busy lunchtimes, but Sam works a full day in the kitchen, every day. The man must be immune to fatigue… I have to admit, I'm in awe of him, now I really understand what he does, not that I'm ever gonna tell him that.

Ed moving back into the pastry section for the best part means he's a lot more relaxed than he was. He'd become real tense and nervous, but he's much more like his old self now – so just lacking in confidence, and generally a bit uneasy. Petra's definitely happier since the weekend. Meeting David has set her mind at rest and she and her mom are getting along a lot better. David's evidently been at the house each evening, because Thea's gotta be there to watch April, so he's been coming over when he finishes work to help out, and keep her company. As I said to Petra, I like the guy. I think he's good for her mom.

The only downside to life right now is that I'm so tired, I don't have the energy to make love to Petra when we get back to her place at night – well, sometimes it's the early hours of the morning by the time we actually get into bed. It's pretty much all I can do to hold her for a few minutes until I'm fast asleep. I try to make it up to her in the mornings, and make love to her before we get up, and usually again in the shower… I just hope that's enough for her, because I'd really hate for this temporary glitch at work to get in the way of our relationship. That said, this temporary glitch is kind of what brought us so close together in the first place.

We've managed to get through to Thursday again, without any major catastrophes – unlike last week, when the new wine supplier managed to send only the white wine part of our order, and no red whatsoever. It took me over an hour to sort that out. I wasn't pleased, to put it mildly. They're due to deliver again tomorrow, so I've just called them to make sure they've got it right this week. They assure me they have, but I guess I'll only find out tomorrow. If they screw up again, I'm gonna have to find someone else.

Petra arrives on time as usual and comes through to the office to find me. I get up, go around the desk, and give her a hug. I miss her so much during the day. It's pathetic, I know, but there it is.

"You taste good," I tell her, kissing her soft lips, and biting gently on the bottom one.

"So do you," she replies, giving me the sexiest smile ever.

"This door locks, you know," I whisper.

She smirks. "Does it now?"

"Yeah." I lean down and kiss her again, more deeply, my tongue delving into her mouth and swallowing her soft moan. "Wanna try my desk for size?"

She leans back, resting her hands on my chest. "I'd love to," she says, "but can we talk first?"

"Sure." I take her hand and lead her over to the desk, sitting in my chair and bringing her down onto my lap.

"Is this the best position for us to be in, if we're going to talk?" she asks.

"Probably not, but I like it." I kiss her neck and she nestles into me. "What did you want to talk about?"

"My mom." Okay. That's not what I'd hoped for and I sit up a little, my ardor slightly dampened.

"What about your mom?" I ask.

"She wants to take April out on Sunday."

I thought that was normal for Thea and April. "But I thought that's what she usually did. She told me she had to cancel taking her out last Sunday, because of David coming over."

"It is what they usually do," Petra explains. "But they normally go to Aunt Stephanie's."

"And she wants to do something different?"

"She wants to take April to David's."

"And you don't want her to?" The doubt in Petra's voice is a bit of a giveaway.

"It's not that," she says. Except I think it is. "It's just that his grandchildren are gonna be there too."

"Ah, I see."

"You do?"

"I think so." I hold her a little closer. "Your mom and David have arranged for all the grandchildren to come over, without their parents… is that right?"

"Yes. How did you know?"

I smile. "Because you said his grandchildren would be there, but you didn't mention James and Clare, or Nathan and Eloise – just the grandkids."

"Is it wrong of me to be worried?"

"No. But you don't need to be."

"You don't think this means my mom is still trying to keep me at arm's length?"

"No, baby." I kiss her neck again. "Try not to take it personally. I think they're just worried that there might be an atmosphere if they try and get everyone together at the same time. If you ask me, it's a good idea to have the grandkids over to get them together first. At least that way, when you and David's kids meet up, you won't be worrying about how all of your own children are getting along."

"I suppose…" I can hear the doubt in her voice.

"You're not being left out, Petra. Besides, I got the feeling there was something David didn't like about Clare's husband, so maybe he's worried about having him there too."

She turns to look at me. "I got that feeling too." She nestles into me again. "So you think it'll be okay?"

"I'm sure it'll be fine. Your mom will look after April and we'll have the house to ourselves for the whole afternoon – so it has its compensations."

She turns and smiles up at me. "I hadn't thought about that," she says.

"I had." I trace kisses up her neck to her ear. "It's pretty much all I think about."

She smirks. "Really? I hadn't noticed," she whispers.

"Then I'm clearly doing something wrong." I check my watch quickly. "We've still got time," I murmur, "unless there was anything else you needed to talk about?"

She hesitates for a moment. "No. There's nothing that won't keep." She leans up and kisses me, her tongue flicking against mine and I groan into her. She breaks the kiss eventually and looks into my eyes. "What did you have in mind?" she asks, breathless.

"Right now, my mind is full of ideas," I murmur, standing her up and getting to my feet, before I lean down and kiss her again. "But first I'm gonna lock the door."

She nods and I go over and turn the key in the lock, coming back to her and pulling her jacket from her shoulders, letting it fall to the floor. Her blouse soon follows and then I undo her bra and release her breasts, taking one in each hand and giving them a light squeeze. She lets her head roll back and moans gently. We don't have that long, so I tell her to kick off her shoes before I sit down on my chair, undoing her jeans, then inserting my thumbs into the waistband and pulling them down, together with her panties, which she steps out of, so she's naked in front of me.

I stand and move my laptop to one side of the desk, clearing a space in the middle.

"Lie back," I tell her, supporting her while she lies back on my desk, which isn't that wide. Even though her ass is right on the edge, her head is almost tipped off the other side. Admiring the view of her spread in front of me, I lean over and gently lick along her already wet, swollen folds. Instinctively, she arches her back off the desk and raises her legs, exposing her beautiful pussy.

I stand again, yanking my shirt over my head and undoing my jeans, lowering them and my trunks. My cock springs free and I grab Petra by the hips and pull her closer, so her ass is almost off the desk.

"I'll fall," she whispers.

"No you won't," I tell her. "I won't let you." I take hold of her ankles, pulling them wide apart and edge forward, the head of my cock finding her entrance first time. "Ready?" I say, looking deep into her eyes. She nods and I push hard inside her, giving her my whole length.

"Oh, God yeah. That's good," she murmurs, and I start to move, keeping hold of her ankles as I pound into her, deep and hard. With every stroke, I'm pushing her further onto the desk and I know I'm gonna have to try something…

I pull out of her and, despite her moan of disappointment, I kick off my jeans and trunks, and move quickly around to the other side of the desk, pulling her toward me again, so her head is tipped upside down, her body still laid out before me. "Open up, baby," I say softly and she does just that, and I slowly insert my cock into her welcoming mouth. "Taste how sweet you are." She moans even more loudly and starts to suck ravenously, while I give her more, stroking my dick in and out of her. I can't keep this up for too long, and I really want to come in her pussy, so I pull out of her.

"Will you stop teasing me," she scolds.

"No." I smirk, going back around the table and slamming my cock deep inside her once more.

"Oh… yes," she hisses, as I lean forward and grab her hands, pulling her up, so she's sitting, facing me, right on the edge of my desk. "Fuck me," she murmurs, staring into my eyes, and I smile to myself because, for once, she's actually said what she wants. "Please," she begs.

"With pleasure." I place my hands behind her, firmly on her ass and, with my cock still embedded deep inside her, I lift her off the desk. "Wrap your legs around me," I tell her. "And hold my shoulders."

"I'm too heavy," she whispers.

"Bullshit." I start to move her on my cock, taking her deeper with every stroke and she clings to me, rocking against me.

"That's so good," she murmurs.

"You're so good." I can feel a trembling deep inside her and I know she's gonna come. "Let me feel you come, baby," I whisper in her ear.

"Yes, Rob, yes." A whispered hiss escapes her lips and she comes apart around me, clamping tight around my cock as I thrust into her harder and harder, and finally erupt, holding her close to me, filling her deeply.

As we calm, I lean down and kiss her. "You taste of you," I sigh into her.

"Hmm," is all she can reply and I sit her back down on the edge of the desk, pulling out of her.

"Did you like that?" I ask her, looking down into her contented face.

"Which bit?" she asks, smiling up at me.

"All of it."

"Yes, thank you."

"Hey, don't thank me." I lean down and kiss her gently.

"Why not? I'm grateful."

I hold her face in my hands. "I don't want you to be grateful," I say, seriously.

"But you just did something I never thought possible," she replies, still kinda dazed.

"What's that?"

"Holding me up like that. I never thought I'd get to experience that."

"Why ever not?"

She tries to look away, but I don't let her. "Because… because I'm not exactly light," she whispers.

I kiss her again, to make sure I've got her attention. "Stop putting yourself down like that," I say quietly. "I love you exactly – and I mean *exactly* – as you are. And I'd do that all over again, if we had time."

"Hmm… I wish we could." She smiles up at me again and it's all I can do to remember that I really should be in the kitchen by now.

"So do I, but duty calls, I'm afraid, babe."

I've barely finished my sentence before I hear a knock on the door, and someone tries the handle. Petra startles and grabs my arms.

"Rob?" It's Ed.

"Yeah?" I call out, trying to sound normal.

"Why is the door locked?"

"I'll be there in a minute." What else can I say?

"Quick, get dressed," I whisper to Petra and she giggles, which is kinda contagious, and I laugh with her. "Stop it."

"Why?" She pulls her panties back on, followed by her black jeans, as I button up my shirt.

"Because it's me who's gonna have to explain this to him."

"Have fun with that," she replies. "Where's my bra?"

"Stop enjoying this so much, or I won't tell you."

"Then I'll just go without one."

"Like hell you will." I bend down and pick up my jeans, finding her bra and blouse underneath, and hand them both to her. "You do not go without a bra unless I'm with you – understood?"

"Yes, sir," she quips.

"I mean it."

She leans up and kisses me. "I know you do."

I'm serious for a moment, even though I'm struggling to get my trunks back on. "You're wearing a thin white blouse, Petra."

"I know," she says quietly, her own voice more serious now. "I was only kidding."

"Good. I know what guys are like." I zip up my jeans.

"So do I." She's struggling with her bra now and I turn her around and re-fasten it for her, then hold out her blouse, helping her into it.

We're soon dressed again, although I think we both look a little disheveled. I hand Petra her jacket and she shrugs it back on before I pull her into my arms. "I love you," I whisper.

"I love you too," she replies.

"And you're mine."

She nods her head and I kiss her. Quick and hard.

I put everything straight on my desk again, and then take Petra's hand and lead her over to the door, which I unlock and open. Ed's standing on the other side, leaning up against the wall.

"Oh… I get it now," he says, looking at both of us and rolling his eyes.

"And?" I challenge.

"And nothing," he replies. "It's just that we open in…" He checks his watch. "Ten minutes. I was wondering if you'd care to grace us with your company."

"God, is that the time already?" Petra says. "I should be helping out in the restaurant."

She goes to move away, but I grab her and pull her back.

"You okay?" I ask her. She nods and gives me a quick kiss on the cheek, before going down the corridor and into the restaurant.

I look at Ed and he smirks. "Don't say a fucking word," I murmur, going past him and into the kitchen.

Chapter Twelve

Petra

As I fall asleep late on Saturday night – well, Sunday morning, really – all I can say is, thank goodness tomorrow is Sunday. It's been another exhausting week. It's had its highlights, of course – the best of which was, without a doubt, sex in Rob's office. That was something very special – very special indeed. He was deeper inside me than I think he's ever been, and being held up like that, in his arms, was erotic, fulfilling, and intense, like nothing else I've ever experienced. He's made love to me since – a lot – but I hope he does that again soon, because I need it. We've got the house to ourselves this afternoon, and I've got my fingers crossed. What am I saying? I'm almost breathless with anticipation. The thing is, I also know that we need to take this chance of a little peace and quiet away from work and April and my mom, to talk about Adrian. And that, I'm dreading…

I'm awake before Rob, but he's not far behind me and he turns over and pulls me into his arms, holding me tight.

"Good morning, beautiful," he murmurs.

"Good morning." He kisses me gently.

"Feel like showering with me?" he asks.

"That depends," I tease, because I know what I want from him. "On what?"

"On what you're going to do while we're in the shower."

He smiles. "What would you like me to do?"

I've boxed myself into a corner now. The thing is, I'm not sure I can say it. "That thing," I whisper.

"That thing?" He looks perplexed. "I'm afraid you're gonna have to be a little more specific than that, babe."

"The thing we did in your office."

His eyes glint and his lips twitch upward. "I really don't think my desk is gonna fit in your shower," he says.

I lean back and glower at him, as best I can. "You know that's not what I mean."

"Then tell me what you mean. Remember? You've gotta communicate with me. You managed it when we were in my office…"

"I did?" I don't remember much about that, other than how good it felt, and Ed nearly catching us out.

"Yeah, you did. You told me to fuck you."

I think back. He's probably right. But that was different. "That was when we were in the middle of something," I explain. "This is just us…"

"That was just us too, baby. There wasn't anyone else there."

"I know, but… it's different. I don't want to say it. Not like this." I can feel myself blushing.

He sighs. "Okay. You want me to take you standing up… while I'm holding you. Is that it?" I nod my head eagerly and he chuckles. "You know, for someone who likes sex as much as you do, you're truly awful at communicating what you want."

"Then it's just as well you're so good at working it out."

"Yeah, isn't it." He pulls away from me, and takes my hand, pulling me out of bed and into the adjoining bathroom, where he makes my dreams come true – again.

Over brunch, Mom tells us about the plans she and David have made for the afternoon. She's gonna take April at two, which means she'll get to David's around two-fifteen. They're gonna go to a park near where he lives and let the kids play there, and she'll be back around four-thirty or five. Rob says he'll cook us a lamb casserole, which he's prepared already and which he'll put on after we've finished eating brunch, and we can eat whenever we want this evening. Mom thinks this is a great plan, being as April might be quite tired when she gets back.

"I bet I won't be tired," April counters, even though we all know she will be. "And I want Rob to make those special biscuits with me when we get back."

Rob looks at me, but I don't know what to say. "I don't think we can today," he replies and her face falls. "But I promise we'll do them next Sunday. We can do them in the morning, before you go and visit Aunt Stephanie, okay?"

"Promise?" April pushes.

"I promise." Rob puts his hand over his heart and she smiles up at him. The smile he gives her back melts my heart and I wonder just how far inside him my baby girl has already gotten.

"Is there anything you need me to get for these biscotti?" Mom asks Rob. "In the way of ingredients, I mean."

"No, it's fine," Rob replies, turning to her. "I'll bring everything we need."

"Are you sure? You keep bringing us food. It feels unfair…"

"It's fine." He starts to clear away and April gets down to help him. They make a good team and, again I'm struck by how quickly he's integrated into our lives – or is it that we've integrated into his? I'm not sure anymore. We just seem to have become one.

Rob and I stand on the doorstep and wave goodbye as my mom drives off, with April sat in her car seat in the back.

"Stop worrying," he says, the smile still firmly planted on his lips as they round the corner.

"I can't help it."

We go back inside and he closes the door behind us.

"Yeah, you can. It'll be fine. Your mom won't do anything that isn't in April's best interests, and David's a good guy. She's gonna be okay." He moves closer. "Do you think I'd have let her go if I didn't believe that?"

"No." I know he wouldn't.

"Well then." He leans down and kisses me, deepening the kiss in an instant, and only breaking it when we're both breathless. "We've got a couple of hours, and the whole house to ourselves. What do you wanna do first?"

"First?" I tease.

"Yeah… first." He kisses me again.

I'm nervous now, because I know I've got to talk to him before we do anything else.

"Well, first I need the bathroom…" I don't, but I'm buying time.

He smirks. "Okay." He releases me and I go upstairs and into the main bathroom, which is next to April's bedroom, and opposite mine, flicking on the light as I enter. There's the loudest bang as I hit the switch and I scream, instinctively putting my hands over my ears.

Within moments, Rob's beside me. "What happened?" he says, holding me.

"The bulb," I murmur. "I turned on the light and it blew."

He chuckles. "You screamed like that because a bulb blew?"

"It made a really loud bang."

He hugs me tighter and kisses my forehead. "Oh dear," he says with mock sympathy, and I push him away.

"If you can't be sympathetic, the least you can do is change the bulb."

He shakes his head. "Whatever happened to equality? Don't tell me you can't change a lightbulb by yourself…"

"Of course I can. But I'm in shock."

He chuckles again. "Okay. I'll let you off. Where do you keep the spare bulbs?"

"I don't know if mom's got any," I reply. "I know one blew in the kitchen a few days ago and she said she needed to get some more." I think for a minute. "But I've got some in my nightstand."

"In your nightstand?"

"I know it sounds odd, but the one in my lamp blew a couple of weeks ago, and I bought a pack. I changed the bulb – because I can – and I put the rest of the pack in the nightstand."

"Okay," he says quietly, turning and heading across the hallway toward my bedroom. "You stay there and I'll go and find them. Which drawer?"

"I can't remember now…" I call after him.

"I'm sure I'll find them."

He's been gone all of thirty seconds when I remember what else I keep in my nightstand and I run after him. I'm too late…

Rob's standing beside the bed and has just opened the middle drawer, staring inside it as I enter my room. He looks up at me, his smile widening, and then he reaches down and pulls out my wand, holding it up. I can feel the blush spreading from my neck to my hairline and I know I've never been so embarrassed in my life.

"Come here," he murmurs.

"Do I have to?"

He nods his head. "Yeah, you do. You really do." His voice is deep and so sexy, and I walk over to him, his eyes fixed on mine. "Is this something you use a lot?" he asks, glancing down at the enormous vibrator in his hand.

"Not a lot, no. And I haven't used it at all since I met you."

He smiles widely. "Not at all?"

"No."

He takes a step closer to me. "Well, I think we need to do something about that, don't you?"

Rob

I've used toys on women before quite a few times, but they've usually been small vibrators, anal beads, or the occasional butt plug, if that's what they've wanted. The toys have always belonged to the women and I can take it or leave it, if I'm honest. If they like it, that's fine, but I'm kind of ambivalent. This thing is different. For a start, it's huge and if its size is anything to go by, it's gonna be powerful, and I'm already hard and turned on as fuck just thinking about what it's gonna do to Petra. There are three buttons on the side. One is obviously for the power, while the other two are 'plus' and 'minus', which I guess adjust the setting. It seems fairly self-explanatory, and without taking my eyes from Petra's I hit the power button, letting my hand rest against the wand's bulbous head.

"Fucking hell," I say out loud, above the deep pulsating noise.

"What?" she whispers.

"It's powerful." It is. There's no subtlety with this thing. Even on the palm of my hand, the vibrations are intense.

"Yeah, it is." Her eyes sparkle. She's as turned on as I am.

I turn the wand off again and throw it on the bed, grabbing Petra and pulling her to me. "I want you… naked… now."

She moans but doesn't reply and I yank her t-shirt over her head, then pull her bra straps down, revealing her breasts, sucking on one and then the other, before I undo the clasp as the back and throw it to the floor. She's breathing hard already and I make light work of her jeans and panties, then I lift her and drop her on the bed, letting her bounce just once before I drag her back to the edge and place my hand just above her mound, leaning over her. "I'm gonna make you come so fucking hard," I growl, my voice low.

"Oh… please," she whispers and parts her legs.

I straighten again, and smile, using my hands on her knees to spread them still further, exposing her glistening pussy. She's wet already – really wet.

I pick up the wand in my right hand and flick it on again, feeling the vibrations through the black shiny handle, then I part her lips with my fingers, and place the throbbing head directly on her clit. She bucks off the bed and squeals loudly, but I hold it still and steady, even as she writhes and thrashes against me.

She's not even coming yet, but she will soon. "Ride it out, baby," I tell her, applying a little more pressure.

"Yes," she screams. "Please, Rob… Oh fuck… yes." She opens her eyes for a moment, making contact with mine, and then she's gone. Her head rocks back and she loses control, screaming my name over and over, yelling out her pleasure, her arms and legs flailing. I keep up the pressure and she goes on, and on, until eventually she screams at me to stop. I pull the wand away, turning it off, and she stills, breathing hard, her body twitching still. The comforter and the floor are both soaked with her juices and she's spent – for now.

"What… what did you just do to me?" she asks, catching her breath.

"I made you ejaculate again," I tell her. "We're gonna need to change your sheets, and mop up the floor." I'm grateful she's got a wooden floor and not carpet.

"I don't think I care. That was…" She's lost for words.

"The best orgasm I've ever seen." I help her out.

"The best orgasm I've ever had." She looks up at me. "Ever."

"Want another one?" I smile down.

"I'm not sure I can."

I shake my head. "You know you should never say that to me." I quickly strip off my clothes, leaving them in a pile on the floor, then get onto the bed, turning her around and pulling her up so her head's resting on the pillows. I kneel up between her legs, parting hers wide, and insert my cock deep inside her.

"You feel good," she whispers as I start to move. Then I grab the wand, turn it on again and, keeping up a steady rhythm, I part her lips wide and apply it to her clit.

"Oh God… yes!" She bucks into me and comes straight away, writhing and thrashing on the bed as I fuck her harder, pushing the vibrator against her and letting her scream out her pleasure again. She's clamped so hard around my dick it's almost painful, but I manage not to come and I wait for her to tell me to stop, and then pull the wand away, although I don't withdraw my cock. I keep moving slowly inside her.

It takes a while before she can speak. "It's even better with you inside me," she murmurs.

"It sure is," I reply. "You felt amazing."

I keep moving until I know she's calmed, and then I put the wand back on her. She takes a little longer this time, but manages a third screaming orgasm.

"I can't," she breathes as she calms. "I can't do anymore."

"Yeah, you can." I don't give her time to recover, and put the wand back straight away.

"No, Rob. I can't."

"You can." I press harder and she comes apart yet again.

"No more," she urges when I finally take the wand away for the fourth time. "Please, Rob."

"You sure?" I lean over her and kiss her. She's covered in sweat and her pussy's drenched.

"I'm positive."

I turn off the wand and pull out of her real slow.

"Don't you want to come?" She looks up at me, surprised.

"No. I've had a great time. I can wait until later."

"Later?" Her eyes widen. "You think I can do that again?"

I chuckle. "Not with the wand, obviously. But yeah, I think you'll be able to go again in a few hours." I lean down and kiss her gently. "You forget how well I know you."

"Better than anyone." Her hands come around behind my head and she deepens the kiss.

"Sure you don't wanna go again?" I ask her eventually.

"Well, I need to be able to walk when April gets home," she murmurs.

"So that's not a no?"

She smiles up at me and I pick up the wand again, grinning down at her. "Maybe one more then."

"Did you have a good time, baby?" Petra crouches down and greets April, giving her a hug as she comes into the kitchen. I'm putting the finishing touches to the dinner, even though it's only five. I know Petra's famished after her exertions this afternoon and I'm sure Thea's right – April's gonna be tired. We can eat early, go to bed at a reasonable hour – for once – and I can hopefully have a little more fun with my beautiful girlfriend.

"I had a great time," April replies. "Daniel's too little to play properly, but Yaya read us all a story, and then we played with his building bricks for a while. And then Jessca, Sophie and me played dress-up, and after that David took us all to the park and we went on the swings, and had ice cream, and then we went home."

"Sounds like a great day," I say, going over to them. Petra releases April and struggles to stand again.

"Have you hurt your back?" Thea asks.

"No, it's just my legs. They're… um… stiff." Petra looks up at me.

"You must've slept awkwardly," I suggest, trying not to laugh.

"You seemed fine this morning." Thea looks puzzled.

"Jessca and Sophie have a great playhouse at David's," April chimes in, saving the moment, and I pour three glasses of wine, handing them out to Petra and Thea, and a glass of juice for April, which I leave on the table.

"And you can play with it too, whenever you're there," Thea adds quickly.

"I know," April replies. "They keep lots of toys over there." She looks up at Petra. "Can I keep some toys at David's house too, Mommy?" she asks.

"I'm sure you can," Petra replies, looking at Thea, who nods quickly, smiling. "I'll have to speak to David, or to Jessica's mom and see what toys they've got, so we don't duplicate things." She takes a sip of wine

"Yeah, I'm sure Jessica's mom won't mind comparing toys with you," I murmur, keeping my voice low. Petra chokes, and I go over to her, giving her a pat on the back. "You okay, honey?" I say, smiling.

She recovers quickly and glares at me. "I'm fine, darling," she says, but her lips are curving up at the sides and I know I'm on fairly safe ground.

After such a spectacular Sunday, I didn't want to go back to work yesterday, but needs must, and I had meetings all day, which took my mind off how great Sunday afternoon had been, not to mention Sunday evening, which Petra and I spent in bed, once April had almost fallen asleep in her dinner. Last night was another late one, but today has been a little easier and, for once, we make it home before midnight.

"I'm gonna take a quick shower," I tell Petra as we get into her room.

"Oh, okay."

"I won't be long." I go over to her and give her a kiss. "And then I think I've got the energy to give you at least a couple of orgasms."

"Oh, do you?" She smirks.

"Yeah." I know we've gotten out of the habit of having sex at night on workdays, but it's still not midnight yet; it's early by our standards and I want her. "You can join me in the shower if you want?"

"No, I'm fine out here," she says quietly, smiling up at me.

"Okay, well I won't be long."

I go into the bathroom, undress and have a quick shower, washing my hair to get rid of the kitchen smell that tends to linger, before I come back out and wrap a towel low around my hips. I've got to admit, I'm looking forward to making love to Petra before going to sleep for once. Don't get me wrong, I love what we do in the mornings – and I especially loved what we did on Sunday – but I miss going to sleep feeling satisfied and comfortable, with her in my arms, all soft and contented.

I open the bathroom door and I'm fairly sure my jaw hits the floor. Petra's lying naked across the bed, her legs spread wide, the fingers of her right hand gently caressing her clit, while she tweaks her left nipple between the thumb and forefinger of the other hand. She looks real hot and my cock, which was already stiff at the thought of making love to her, is instantly bone hard.

"You decided to start without me, then?" I murmur, going over to her and standing between her parted legs, looking down at her fine display.

She smiles, her fingers working just a little faster. "Hmm," she whispers. "I decided I needed to teach you a lesson."

"Oh? Why?"

"For making that joke in front of my mom… about toys."

"Um… that was on Sunday. Today's Tuesday. You've waited a while."

She changes positions slightly and dips her middle finger into her soaking entrance. "Yes well we got into something else on Sunday

194

night, and yesterday we were late back, but I thought I'd remind you that I don't need toys."

"I didn't say you did," I reason, watching her avidly. "I was just kidding, baby." I drop the towel, and palm my cock, stroking the length of it right above her. Her eyes widen. "And two can play at that game…"

She licks her lips and pinches her nipple, fingering her clit once more. "Oh, really?" she teases, bringing her legs up and rubbing herself much harder. She's close – real close – and I can't resist. I reach down and insert my middle finger inside her, and that's all it takes to push her over the edge. I let her reach the peak of her orgasm and then I quickly withdraw my finger and flip her over onto her front.

"No, Rob… Please—" she grumbles, her moment lost – or so she thinks, as I pull her up onto her knees and straight back onto my cock. "Oh God, Yes…" she hisses and comes again straight away, bucking against me as I plunge deep inside her, her juices running down her leg. She starts to recover, dragging deep breaths into her lungs, but I don't relent. I keep up the rhythm, pounding her, real hard. "I can't," she murmurs. "No more…"

"Yeah, more," I say and raise one foot up onto the bed, holding her hips and leaning over her to take her deeper still.

"Oh… fuck, that's good," she murmurs, and I have to smile.

But I'm not done yet… I plunge into her a couple more times, before I pull out, trying not to laugh at her groan of disappointment. Then I flip her over once more, push her back up onto the bed, crawl up to kneel between her legs and grab her ankles, holding them wide apart, just as I enter her again.

"Rub your clit," I tell her.

"While you're…?" She nods down to where we're joined.

"While I'm what?" I still inside her. "Say the words Petra. I'm just gonna stay here until you do."

"While you're fucking me." The last two words are a barely audible whisper.

"Yeah, while I'm fucking you." I lock my eyes with hers as I start to move again. "Rub your clit," I repeat.

She brings her hand down and I feel her touch herself, just gently to begin with, but then with more and more intensity. "I'm gonna come… again," she mutters, her back arching off the bed. "Please, Rob… Please."

I know what she wants and I grind into her, flexing my hips, taking her deep and hard and, just as she grips my cock and shatters around me, I let go and fill her, my whole body convulsing into hers.

It feels like hours before I can breathe properly again – although I know it isn't – and I slowly pull my cock out of her, release her legs and lower them to the bed, lying down beside her.

"I was supposed to be teaching you a lesson," she whispers, turning toward me and resting her head on my chest.

I put my arms around her and hold her close. "Rule number one, baby… Never kid a kidder. And I'm a kidder. Always have been."

"I noticed."

"Didn't you learn anything with the strawberries incident?" I ask her.

"Evidently not." She leans back and looks up at me, the sweetest smile on her lips. "But if you're going to keep doing things like that to me, I don't care."

Chapter Thirteen

Petra

He laughs. "While we're on the subject of toys," he murmurs, leaning down and kissing me.

"I didn't realize we were."

"We were when all this started," he qualifies.

"Oh yeah. I suppose we were. Well, what about them?"

"Do you have any others?" he asks.

"No." I snuggle into him.

"None?" He seems surprised.

"No. Why?"

"It's just that your wand is kinda powerful. I guess I just assumed you'd worked your way up to it."

I giggle. "No. I decided to start with the best."

"Based on the way you reacted to it, I guess you did."

"I got it a few months after April was born. I was photographing a hen party and one of the bridesmaids bought the bride a vibrator as a joke present. I'd been feeling frustrated, and it gave me an idea. So, I went online the next day and had a look at what was available."

"And you decided to buy a wand?" Again, he seems surprised.

"There was a lot more choice than I thought there would be. It turned out to be a difficult decision. So I read the reviews and that got the best ones. I didn't realize it would be quite as loud as it is."

"They should supply ear defenders with it."

I chuckle. "Yeah, they probably should. That's the only downside to it, really. I can't use it unless I've got the house to myself."

"Which must be a bit limiting."

I shrug. "Well, it was."

"It was?" he queries.

"Until I met you." I lean up and look down at him. "It's not like I need it anymore, is it?"

"No." He smiles up at me. "But it gives you pleasure, and fun, so it would be nice if you could use it whenever you want, rather than having to wait for the house to be empty."

"You don't mind me using it then?"

He rolls me onto my back and raises himself above me. "Of course not. I love your pleasure, and I love your reactions." He seems to think for a moment. "I know I've promised to make biscotti with April on Sunday, but how about if we put aside a little time in the afternoon for ourselves?"

"To play with my wand again?" I ask, and I can't hide my enthusiasm.

"Of course, we can do that, if you want." He hesitates. "And maybe we can go online and find some toys of our own."

I feel the smile forming on my lips. "Really?"

"Yeah, really." He leans down and kisses me tenderly. "I'm sure we can find something a lot quieter that you can enjoy whenever you feel the need."

"Even though I've got you?"

He nods. "Oh yeah. There are all kinds of toys out there."

"Toys we can use together?" Using the wand on myself has always been intense, but it's nothing compared to when Rob used it on me, and I'm not sure I want to give that up. I hope he doesn't…

"If you want to. I don't have a problem if you feel the need to entertain yourself from time to time, Petra, but I love what we do together. I love all of it."

I reach up, putting my hands behind his head and pull him down into a deep kiss. "I love it too," I whisper.

I wander the dark and deserted streets, searching for him. The little girl holds my hand, calling out his name, but he's nowhere to be seen.

"Rob, come back!" I call, but there's no reply. No sound, no sight of him. We're completely alone.

"Where is he, Mommy?"

"I don't know."

"Why did he leave us?"

"I don't know."

"I don't understand why he'd leave us. Doesn't he love us anymore?"

"Petra… Petra, baby… Wake up." I can hear my name being called.

"I'm here," I call back.

"Petra?" It's a man's voice. I struggle to open my eyes, but when I do, all I find is darkness.

"He's gone," I whisper.

"Who's gone?" the voice says.

"Rob."

"No, I'm here, baby. I'm right here."

I feel his lips on mine, his arms coming around me, holding me.

"You're here," I murmur, between kisses.

"Of course I'm here. Where else would I be?"

"You left."

"No. I didn't go anywhere. You were having a dream."

I shake my head. "I was having a nightmare."

He tightens his hold on me. "Well, you're safe now, baby. Whatever you dreamt, it's not real. I'm here and nothing's gonna hurt you. I promise."

His words soothe me, but even as I drift off to sleep again, that feeling of dreaded isolation washes over me once more.

Saying goodbye to Rob this morning is the hardest it's ever been. I know it's because of the dream I had last night, but no matter how hard I try, I can't seem to shift this sense that it wasn't just a dream, that this is all too good to be true, and this kind of happiness can't last.

April's with us at the door, and Rob holds her for a few minutes while we talk, but just at the last minute as he's waving to us from the sidewalk,

I choke up and struggle not to cry, and I think he knows it, because he sends me a text message within a few minutes of leaving.

— *Call me if you need me. Anytime. I'll pick up. I love you.* **R xxx**

It's so sweet of him, and so perceptive. I call him.

"I need you," I say as soon as he answers, which is after the first ring.

"What's wrong?" he asks. "You seemed upset at the door."

"I was."

"Tell me."

"I don't know. I just didn't want you to leave."

"You'll see me later this afternoon."

"I know." I can feel the tears stinging behind my eyes again already.

"Petra," he murmurs. "Are you okay?"

"No."

"Do you need me to come back?"

Yes. "No. I'm fine. You have to get to work."

"I can come back," he reiterates.

"I'm being pathetic. I'll see you later."

"Sure?" he asks.

"Yes, I'm sure." I'm not, but I need to pull myself together. I don't even know why I'm feeling like this. I just need to get on with the day.

"Okay," he says. "I love you, baby."

"I love you too." I struggle to get the words out, before the tears start to fall, but I bite them back so he won't hear.

We say goodbye and hang up, and I go through to the kitchen to clear away the breakfast things. I still can't stop crying and April hands me a Kleenex, and gives me a hug, which just makes it worse. Then we get on with the chores and start loading the dishwasher, just as the doorbell rings. Mom's expecting a delivery today, although she said it wouldn't be arriving until this afternoon, but I guess they've probably brought it early and I go through to the front door and open it, wiping my eyes again as I do so.

"I knew it," Rob says, and comes right in, pulling me into his arms. "I knew you were crying." He kicks the door shut and walks me further back into the hallway. "What's wrong?" he asks.

I shake my head, because I can't speak, and he just holds me and lets me weep.

"You're scaring me, baby," he whispers after a few minutes. "Please, tell me what's wrong."

"I don't even know."

He leans back, still holding me, and places a finger under my chin, raising my face to his. "You don't know?" he queries. I shake my head. "You're crying like this, and you don't know why?"

"I think I'm scared."

"Of what?" He moves a little closer.

"Losing you?" I say it like a question, because I'm so unsure of myself.

"Losing me? How's that gonna happen?"

"I don't know." I sigh.

"Is this anything to do with your dream?" he asks. "The one you had last night?"

I nod my head.

"Wanna tell me about it?" He doesn't wait, but takes my hand and leads me back into the kitchen, sitting me down at the table. He quickly finds April a coloring book and some crayons, and sets them out in front of her. "Mommy and I are just gonna talk for a while," he says to her.

"Okay," she replies and opens up the book.

Rob comes and sits beside me, taking my hands in his. "Tell me," he says quietly.

"It's nothing," I reply.

"I can't say what I want to say to that, Petra, because April's here. But we both know that's not true. It's not nothing, because whatever it is, it's making you cry. So, tell me."

I look up into his eyes, which are filled with love, and concern.

I sigh. "I just dreamt that you left me, that's all."

"And why exactly would I do that?"

"I don't know. But I couldn't find you. April and I were searching everywhere, but you'd gone. I felt so alone, and she was asking me why you'd left us…" I hesitate. "She wanted to know if it meant you didn't love us anymore." I blink back the tears.

He releases my hands, and clasps my face instead, leaning forward so our noses are almost touching.

"It was a dream, baby," he whispers.

"It felt so real."

"Dreams usually do." He closes his eyes for a moment. "I will never leave you," he says really slowly. "Never. No matter what happens, no matter what you say or do, I'm here to stay. I love you both far too much to ever walk away from you, or give this up. Do you hear me?"

"You love us both?" I can't believe he just said that.

He nods his head. "Yeah. I do."

"You love my baby girl?"

"Yeah. She kinda found her way into my heart, and made a home there, right next to you."

I start crying again, but this time, I'm smiling too.

"Is Mommy okay?" April asks from the other end of the table.

"Mommy's just fine," Rob tells her. "Do you wanna come and sit with me?" he offers. She jumps down and runs along the length of the table, then Rob lifts her onto his lap and sits her between us.

"Why is Mommy crying then?" April asks.

"Do you remember I told you that sometimes grown-ups cry when they're happy?" Rob says.

April nods. "Is Mommy happy?"

"Mommy's never been happier." I reply through my tears. "In fact, Mommy's wondering what she did to get so lucky." I can't help smiling at the two people I love most in the world, sitting in front of me – one holding the other.

"With you two beautiful girls in my life," Rob replies, winking at me over April's head. "I think you'll find that I'm the one who got lucky."

I know now that I have to tell him. "I need to talk to you," I manage to say, wiping my tears and swallowing hard. This isn't going to be easy, but it's got to be done.

"I'm here, baby."

"I've been meaning to tell you this since the beginning," I begin.

"Sounds serious." He smiles over at me and nods at April, who's curled into him on his lap, and I wonder for a moment if I should wait until we're alone. The thing is, now seems like a really good time, bearing in mind he's just told me he loves April – it makes me feel like we really are a family, and that means he needs to know…

Rob's staring at me, waiting, but just as I'm about to open my mouth again, his phone rings. He pulls it from his jacket pocket and glances at the screen.

"It's Ed," he says. "Sorry, babe, I'd better take it."

I nod and I know already the moment's lost.

"Hi," Rob says into the phone. He listens, then closes his eyes, lets out a long sigh and says, "What's wrong with her?" There's another pause and he sighs again. "Oh God. Really?" He looks over at me. "Is she okay—?" He stops talking. "That was a dumb question. Of course she isn't okay…" He waits again while Ed speaks. "Stop panicking. I didn't have much planned for today anyway. I'll leave now and I'll be there in ten minutes," he adds, mouthing 'sorry' to me as he finishes speaking. I nod my head and get up from the table, going over to the sink while he finishes the call.

I feel him come up beside me, April still held in his arms.

"I'm really sorry, Petra," he says, leaning down and kissing my cheek. "Jasmine's called in. Her daughter's sick and she's had to take her to the hospital."

"What's wrong?" I ask, turning to face him, my own problems forgotten.

"They're not sure. At the moment, they're thinking it could be meningitis."

"Oh my God."

"Yeah. She and Cole are with her, and her mom's looking after Eli."

"Is that her son?"

"Yeah. He's six."

"And how old is her daughter?"

"Scarlett's three."

"Jasmine must be worried sick."

"Yeah. She is." He lowers April to the floor. "I'm sorry. I know you needed to talk—"

"It can wait." I take April's hand and we make our way toward the front door.

"Ed's panicking…" Rob explains.

"Why? Jasmine not being in doesn't affect him, does it?"

"Well, it wouldn't normally, but one of the sous chefs booked to have today off a couple of weeks ago, so Ed was hoping I'd be able to help out in the kitchen."

"Oh. And now you won't be able to?"

"No."

"My mom's working this morning, but she'll be back at twelve. I can come in, if that helps."

He turns to look at me.

"Could you?"

"Just for a couple of hours. I'll need to come back between the shifts to see April."

"Of course." He leans down and kisses me. "You're a lifesaver."

"Hardly. But I can sympathize with Jasmine. She must be in hell right now." I lean down and lift April into my arms. I can't even imagine what Jasmine is going through, and as I hold my own baby girl, I don't want to.

Rob puts his arms around both of us. "Call me if you need me," he murmurs in my ear. "And we'll talk later."

He kisses me, tweaks April's nose playfully, and walks away, and as I think about Jasmine and Cole, and all of their problems, my own suddenly seem really insignificant.

The lunch service wasn't as busy as the evenings usually are and Rob's able to come out and take over from me at two, which means I can get home and see April. I decide there's nothing I need to do that's really urgent this afternoon, and April's in the mood for Elsa, so we sit down and watch *Frozen*, for probably the hundredth time. Mom watches it with us and the two of them get into singing 'Let it Go' with gusto, which makes me laugh – especially considering my mom is completely tone deaf.

Just after the song's finished, she goes out to make us a cup of coffee each, when the doorbell rings. To be honest, I'm kind of hoping it's Rob – which is possible, considering it's only just after four – and I get up to answer it. I'm more than a little surprised to find David standing on the doorstep, looking pale and tired.

"Hello, Petra," he says, sounding weary.

"Hi." I stand to one side to let him in. "Is something wrong?" I ask him.

"Yeah. You could say that."

I sense it's something serious and lead him through to the kitchen, leaving April to finish watching her movie.

"David?" Mom's clearly surprised to see him too. "Why aren't you at work?"

"I took the day off," he explains. "Something happened at home this morning, and… well, I wouldn't have been able to concentrate anyway, so it seemed a little pointless going in today."

"Sit down." She pulls out a chair for him. "I'll make you a coffee." She gets an extra cup from the cabinet and David sits down heavily at the table. He really does look like he's got the weight of the world on his shoulders. Mom brings the French press over to the table and sits down too. I'm not sure whether what David has to say is private – between the two of them – and am undecided as to whether to stay with them, or go back to April, but my mom passes my cup over to me, like she expects me to sit, so I do, opposite them.

"What's wrong?" she asks David, once all the coffees are poured and she's pushed the French press into the middle of the table.

"It's Clare," he says, looking down at his hands.

"She's not ill, is she?" Mom asks.

He shakes his head. "No."

"And the baby's okay?"

"Yeah, the baby's fine."

"Then what?" Mom turns to face him. "Tell me, David. You've obviously come here because you need to talk – so talk."

He sighs and takes a sip of coffee, then looks up at her. "I was just leaving for work this morning when she arrived on the doorstep, with Daniel. She says she's left Nathan."

My mom's mouth drops open. Mine doesn't, but then I'm not as easily shocked as she is.

"Why?" she asks.

"He came home really late last night," David starts and already I know what's coming. But then I would…

"And?" my mom prompts.

"He… he'd been with another woman," he says quietly.

"Oh my God." I did say my mom was easily shocked.

"How did Clare know?" I ask – because to me that's the obvious question.

He turns to me. "He told her."

Nice. It probably made him feel better, but it will have destroyed her. "Is it a long-standing thing?"

He shakes his head. "No. Well, he says it isn't. He says it was a one-off – a mistake. He promised her it'll never happen again."

They all say that.

"She must be devastated. She's four months pregnant." My mom clearly thinks we'd forgotten that part of it.

"Yes," is all he seems to be able to say. He looks up again. "The thing is, I don't believe him."

"What do you mean?" My mom moves a little closer to him. "You don't believe he was with another woman? Or you don't believe it was a one-off?"

"Oh, I'm absolutely certain he was with another woman. But I really don't think it was the first time he's done it."

"Why?" I ask.

He shrugs. "Instinct." He sighs deeply. "I never liked him. When he and Clare first started seeing each other, I got the impression he was a player…"

"A player?" my mom queries, and I'm struck by the fact that Rob once described himself in exactly the same way. The thought sends a shiver right down my spine.

"Yeah," David continues, "I thought she was one in a long line of nurses he'd had relationships with. But then, when she fell pregnant…" He pauses. "Let's just say that getting married wasn't his first suggestion."

"What was?" my mom asks.

"He asked how she felt about having an abortion – he even recommended one of his friends, who he said would be willing to help out."

"No." My mom's really bad at hiding her emotions.

"They broke up for a while and she moved back in with me and I thought she'd be a single mom," he continues. "I was fully prepared to help her out, but Nathan came over about three weeks after they split, he apologized and talked her into getting back together with him, and then he proposed." He shakes his head. "And she accepted."

"Was it a nurse he was with last night?" I ask him.

"No." A dark shadow crosses his eyes. "That almost makes it worse… It was a patient."

"A patient?" Now even I'm shocked.

He nods his head. "Well, a former patient. He's a cosmetic surgeon. She'd gone to him for treatment of some kind – although I don't know what – about a year ago, or so Clare says. Nathan's adamant that nothing happened between them until last night. He bumped into her as he was leaving his office, she invited him for a drink and one thing led to another."

"Like it does…" I murmur.

April comes into the kitchen. "*Frozen's* finished, Mommy," she says. "Can I have some juice now?"

"Sure, baby." I get up and pour her a glass of chilled juice, putting it on the table while she clambers onto a chair.

"Shouldn't you be with Clare?" my mom asks David.

"At the moment, Eloise is with her," he replies. "I called her earlier, when Clare arrived. They've always gotten along well, and I thought it might help for her to have another woman to talk to." He shrugs. "I didn't really know what to say to her that didn't involve threatening her husband." He turns to face my mom, taking hold of her hand. "I won't be able to come over tonight, I'm afraid. Eloise will have to get home to put the girls to bed, so I'll need to stay with Clare."

"That's fine," my mom replies. "I understand."

"I'm sorry," he says. "This is going to change things for us… at least until Clare decides what she wants to do. I have to be there for her."

"I know," Mom says, patting his hand. "What do you think she'll do?"

He looks her in the eye. "I'm afraid I think she'll go back to him." He seems to deflate. "She'll rant and rave for a while, and then he'll sweet talk her into forgiving him – it'll be just like it was before they got married. I can see it happening…"

"This is different though, surely," I suggest.

He looks across the table at me, and whispers, "If she can forgive him for suggesting she aborts their child, I think she can forgive him anything," and he looks away again.

Rob looks up from where he's standing by the bar as I go into the restaurant.

"Sorry I'm late," I say, quickly taking off my jacket.

He comes over and pulls me into a hug, kissing me deeply. "I was starting to get worried," he says softly. "I was gonna call."

"I'm sorry."

"Don't be. Is everything okay?"

"With me, yes."

He tilts his head to one side. "What does that mean?"

"David's been round this afternoon," I tell him, lowering my voice. "Clare's left Nathan."

His eyes widen. "Really?"

"Yeah. He came home late last night and admitted to sleeping with one of his patients… well, former patients, but who's counting."

"Jeez. What an asshole."

I nod my head. "And David told us that, when Clare got pregnant with Daniel, Nathan's first reaction wasn't to propose, or even to say he'd stand by her…"

"He suggested an abortion?" he guesses, moving closer. I nod my head and his eyes darken. "And she married this son-of-a-bitch?"

"Yes."

"I'm almost inclined to say 'it serves her right', but I guess it's like I told you when we were talking about Mateo and Courtney, you can't tell what goes on in someone else's relationship."

"Evidently not."

"So, is Clare at David's?" he asks.

"Yeah, although he's fairly convinced she'll go back to Nathan."

"Seriously?"

"That's what he seems to think."

He shakes his head. "Guys like that don't change," he murmurs and I suddenly feel really cold and sick.

"What's wrong?" he asks me.

"Nothing."

"I really wish you wouldn't bullshit me like that, Petra," he says, seriously. "You've gone as white as a sheet. Something's wrong."

I look around at the waiting staff preparing the tables for the evening.

"Can we go into the office?" I ask him. "Have we got time?"

He checks his watch.

"Sure," he replies and takes my hand, leading me to the back of the restaurant and down the corridor to the office, closing the door softly behind us. "What is it?" He looks down at me, holding both of my hands in his. "Is this to do with what we were going to talk about this morning?"

"No." I look up at him. "That can wait for now." This suddenly seems so much more important. He nods his head, waiting, and I lower my eyes, looking at the top button of his shirt. "It's something David said," I murmur.

"Okay… What did he say?"

"He said that Nathan's a player."

"I'm not gonna disagree with that assessment," he replies and I feel my skin prickle.

"But I remember you once said you were a player too." I raise my eyes to his. He's just staring at me. "And you just said that guys like that don't change…" I leave my sentence hanging, hoping he'll understand my fear.

He nods his head slowly. "And you think I haven't changed either?" he whispers, moving a little closer to me.

"Surely, if it applies to Nathan, then…"

"Then it applies to me too?" He finishes my sentence for me, then lets out a long breath. "How can you still not get it, after everything I've said?" His voice is soft, concerned, caring, and I focus on his lips as he speaks. "I may have been a player. I may have slept around – and I have no doubt Nathan's the same, based on what David's said, anyway – but there's one big difference between me and him. I've never been a cheat. What I meant was that cheaters don't change, not that players can't change. He may have married Clare, but he clearly wasn't ready to give up his previous life. I am. I have. I don't want that life anymore. I never want that again. I just want you."

He leans down and brushes his lips against mine. I hear my own soft moan filling the room and he steps closer, his feet either side of mine, so I can feel his erection pressing into me as his tongue sweeps deep inside my mouth, claiming me. He clasps my cheeks in his hands, his fingers twisting into my hair and he swivels his hips, letting me feel him.

"I want you," he whispers, breaking the kiss and resting his forehead against mine. "But we don't have time."

I can feel the disappointment washing over me.

"Tonight," he says, with certainty. "After we finish here, I'm gonna take you home and – I don't care how late it is, or how tired we are – I'm gonna make love to you." He leans back just a fraction and looks into my eyes. "If I can't convince you that I'm serious about us with my words, then I'll see if I can convince you with my body instead."

"I am convinced," I tell him quickly, resting my hand against his hard chest.

He smiles. "Are you saying you don't want me to prove the point?"

"No. I'm not saying that at all. I'm saying you don't have anything to prove. I'm sorry for doubting you, Rob. I believe everything you're saying… but if you want to show me too, then I'm absolutely fine with that."

His smile widens. "I'm almost disappointed," he says, caressing my cheek with his fingertips.

"You are?"

"Yeah. I'd just thought of something really persuasive, but if you're already convinced…"

I lean up and kiss him. "I can always take a little more persuading…" I whisper, and he laughs.

"Yeah. I know you can."

Rob

Petra's almost breathless with anticipation by the time we get back to her place, which is good, because that's just how I want her.

Within seconds of closing the front door, I bend down, pick her up and throw her over my shoulder, grateful that April and Thea are both in bed already. Petra squeals in excitement and I slap her ass to quieten her. It doesn't work, and she moans her pleasure at my touch.

"You're not very good at being quiet, are you?" I carry her up the stairs.

"You'll have to stop turning me on, if you want me to be quiet," she whispers.

"That's not what I had in mind." I open the door to her room, go through and close it behind us, taking her over to the bed and lowering her down my body to stand on the floor. She's wearing her leather jacket, with a white blouse, and black wide-leg pants, with her black high-heeled boots underneath. Those are staying on. But as for the rest of it…

I pull her jacket from her shoulders and drop it down by her ankles, then look into her eyes.

"You're not overly fond of this blouse, are you?" I murmur, but don't wait for an answer before I rip the buttons open. She gasps, as I pull down the flimsy lace of her bra and suck hard on her left nipple, pinching her right one between my finger and thumb. With my other hand, I undo the button and zipper of her pants and, because they're wide-legged and loose, they fall to the floor. I release her breasts, step back and admire her.

"You look fucking amazing," I tell her. She does, standing, with her legs slightly parted, her knee-high boots screaming 'fuck me'… and I intend to. Hard.

I step forward again and move my hand between her legs, feeling her clit through her soaking lace panties.

"You're wet, baby," I whisper. "Real wet."

She leans into me as I circle her hardened nub, clutching my shoulders, clinging to me already, her breathing becoming harsh and ragged. Can she be that close, this soon? I stop my movements.

"Do you want my cock?" I ask her.

"Yes," she murmurs. "Yes, please."

"Then take it. It's all yours, baby." She smiles up at me and, without any prompting, kneels down on the floor, making light work of my belt, button and zipper, lowering my pants and trunks and freeing my straining cock. She doesn't hesitate, but takes me straight into her mouth, sucking hard. I grab a handful of her hair and use it to pull her a little closer, taking her deeper, stopping just short of making her gag on me. The harder I force her onto me, the more she moans, her hand coming up and clasping the base of my dick.

"Rub your clit," I tell her, and she looks up at me, her eyebrows raised, her mouth beautifully full of my cock. "Spread your legs a little, move your other hand down, use your fingers, and rub your clit," I instruct her. She moans again, and I feel her shifting slightly, as she parts her legs. And then her breathing changes and I know she's fingering herself. "Feels good, doesn't it, baby?" I murmur, holding her head still while I fuck her mouth. She nods, her tongue flicking over me. "Don't come," I instruct and she looks up at me again. "I've got a point to prove, remember?"

I feel her lean back, pulling away, and I let her, releasing my cock from her full lips.

"You don't," she says softly, still holding me with her hand. "You really don't, Rob."

"Yeah, I do." I pull her to her feet and we stand, facing each other.

"I believe you when you say you're serious about me," she says, sounding worried.

"I know," I tell her, soothingly. "But I still wanna show you what you mean to me." She nods, and swallows, the expression in her eyes a mixture of excitement and apprehension. "I won't hurt you."

"I know you won't."

"Then don't look so scared."

"I just don't know what you're going to do."

"Good." I smile at her. "That's the point. I wanna show you that you can trust me… entirely." I reach down and push my fingers inside her panties, finding her swollen clit with ease and rubbing it with the gentlest touch. "I know I said I don't mind you pleasuring yourself," I explain, "but for tonight, I own your orgasms. All of them."

"All?"

"Yeah. All." I kick off my jeans and trunks, then lean down, kissing her, biting her bottom lip and walking her back to the bed. As she hits it, I let her fall, then pull my shirt off over my head.

I put my fingers inside the top of her panties and pull her toward me. "These are pretty," I tell her. "Where did you get them? Can you remember the store?"

She looks confused. "It's on the label."

"Good." I tug hard and rip through the seam.

"Rob!" She stares at me. "I thought you liked them."

"I do. And as long as I can replace them, that's fine."

I kneel between her legs and insert two fingers inside her, using my thumb to rub her clit, real hard and fast. She's shaking and breathless within seconds.

"You can come now," I tell her and she looks up at me, as I rub the front wall of her vagina, flicking my fingers over her sensitive spot, just as she comes apart, thrashing out her pleasure.

I wait until her orgasm is just starting to subside, and I change position, lying down and getting closer to her. I keep my fingers where they are, but use my tongue on her instead of my thumb. She groans and I feel her hand come around behind my head as she rocks her hips up into me.

"You... you're gonna make me come again... already," she whispers, and she's gone. I hadn't expected that, but I ride it out with her, flicking my tongue across her until she's starting to regain her composure, and just as before, I don't give her time to recover. I kneel up again and turn her onto her side, breathless and panting still. Then I raise her top leg and place it on my shoulder, the soft leather of her boot resting against my skin. I straddle the other leg, my cock poised by her entrance and, with one easy move, I push deep inside her.

"Oh, fuck... that's deep," she mutters and I still, waiting.

"It's meant to be. Remember? You've gotta trust me to pleasure you, not hurt you." Once I'm sure she's ready, I start to move, holding her leg in place with one hand, while the other grips her shoulder, pulling her onto me with every stroke. I change the angle just slightly, so the tip of my cock hits the front wall of her vagina each time I slide into her and, within a few minutes, she's on the brink again.

"Rob," she whispers, looking up at me. "I'm gonna..."

"I know. Go with it, baby,"

She detonates around me, gripping my cock like a vise as I pound into her, over and over.

Yet again, she takes a while to come back down to earth and I slow the pace, gently teasing her with my cock while I wait for her.

"You're still not done?" she asks, breathless.

"Nope. Not yet."

"Oh my God."

I pull out of her and roll her onto her back, quickly unzipping her boots, pulling them off and throwing them onto the floor. Then I kneel up close between her legs, spreading mine wide, so hers are forced apart, and I lean over her, my hands either side of her head as I enter her again, slow and deep. She sucks in a breath, looking up into my eyes. The contact is something else – like the purest connection there is.

I lean down and kiss her gently. "I haven't been communicating with you very well, have I?" I murmur into her, kissing her again.

"Yes, you have." She runs her hands up my arms, across my shoulders and around my neck. "It was about my insecurity, Rob, not about anything you're doing wrong."

I keep up a steady rhythm, and kiss her once more. "If you're feeling insecure, then I'm doing something wrong." I take her a little deeper. "I don't ever want you to feel insecure about me – or about us. I know I'm not great at some of the emotional stuff that goes with being in a relationship, but I need you to understand… I. Will. Never. Leave. You." I emphasize my point, pushing my cock deep inside her with every word. "Ever. There's nothing on this earth that could make me leave you." Tears have gathered at the corners of her eyes and are waiting to fall. I lean down, kissing each eye and tasting her salty tears. "Please, please believe me Petra, I love you. You mean everything to me." The words that are forming on my lips aren't ones I thought I'd ever say – or ask, to be more precise – but I know now it's what I want. I'm just about to open my mouth again when she starts to cry. And I mean really cry. She's sobbing so hard, I can't keep making love to her, and I pull out of her and lower myself down, holding her and letting her weep into me. It takes about five minutes before she's capable of speech.

"I do believe you," she mumbles.

I raise myself up again and smile down at her. "Any particular reason why you're crying?" I ask her.

"Just that I never thought anyone would love me like that… let alone someone like you."

"Hey, there's nothing so great about me, babe."

"Yeah, there is." She leans up and kisses me and I return and deepen the kiss, although the moment's lost. My proposal will have to wait for now.

Today's Friday, which means Sam's due back tomorrow… in theory. I say 'in theory' because he still hasn't confirmed that and I know Ed's worried. I am too, if I'm being honest. As much as I love having Petra working here, the extra work is killing me, especially as

Jasmine isn't back yet. Her daughter's still in the hospital, and while the doctors don't think it's meningitis, which is good news, they don't know what's wrong. She's still real sick, and according to Cole, the not knowing is what's making it worse. Petra's going to cover lunchtime for me again, which is really good of her. We've got a full compliment in the kitchen today, but I've got a meeting booked for one-thirty, which I could cancel if I had to, but I'd rather not. Right now – as much as I hate to admit it – we need Sam.

We're due to open in about thirty minutes and Petra's got everything under control, as usual. I can't stop thinking about last night. Everything kind of ground to a halt after Petra started crying, so we just hugged, which was fine with me. I still wish I'd been able to propose to her, but I'm thinking that Sunday might be a better day for that now. I've promised to make biscotti with April, and Petra and I have said we're gonna go online and buy some toys, but I'm sure we can find some quiet time to sit down and I'll ask her then. In the meantime, I need to buy a ring… because I've realized there's not much point in me proposing without one.

"Rob?" Ed comes into the office, holding his phone.

"Yeah?" I look up from my laptop.

"It's Sam. He wants to talk to both of us." Ed looks nervous.

"Is it on speaker?" I ask.

"Yeah, it is." Sam's voice rings out. It's been a while since I've spoken to him, although I know he and Ed have been in touch fairly regularly, and it's almost odd to hear his voice again.

"How's things?" I ask him.

"That's why I've called you," he replies.

I look at Ed, but he's not saying much. "Should we be scared?" I ask Sam.

"That kinda depends on whether you need me to come back, or not," he says, and I can hear his smile. *Asshole.*

"I think 'need' might be overstating it," I reply.

"Yeah… that's not what I've heard." I glance at Ed and he shrugs. If he's been telling Sam that we're struggling without him, I'll never live it down.

"Stop dragging it out and tell us what you're doing," I say impatiently.

Sam's sigh is audible, even from three thousand miles away. "The house is finished," he replies. "Ali's put it up for sale, and we drove back to London this morning." I check the time on my computer. It's just after eleven-thirty here, so it's four-thirty there. "I've booked the flight home," he adds.

"When for?" Ed asks, clearly dying to know.

"Tuesday. The flight lands at Logan at twelve, or just before, so I guess we'll be with you around four-thirty."

"Four-thirty? It doesn't normally take that long."

"It does when you have to clear immigration."

I look at Ed and we both smile. "You're bringing her home?" I say.

"I'm bringing *them* home."

Ed smiles and shakes his head. "How the hell have you managed that?" he asks.

There's a moment's silence before Sam replies, "I can be real persuasive."

Neither of us really has a reply for that and, after he's given us the flight details and asked me to arrange a surprise for Ali's return, we end the call, with Ed telling him that we're looking forward to seeing him on Tuesday. We don't tell him about Jasmine, because there's no point. There's nothing he can do from where he is, and he'll be back soon enough.

I go out into the restaurant and find Petra leaning up against the bar, talking to Greg.

"Hey," I say, coming up behind her, my hands resting on her waist.

"Hey yourself." She turns in my arms and I lean down and kiss her. Everyone's gotten kind of used to this now and they don't seem to even notice anymore.

"Ed and I just spoke to Sam," I tell her, bringing her over to one of the tables and sitting her down.

"And?" She looks almost as nervous as Ed did.

"He's coming back on Tuesday."

"Tuesday?" she repeats.

"Yeah." I take her hand in mine. "Is that a problem?"

"No. Of course not." Her voice is monotone and she's clearly lying.

I lean closer. "Bullshit, Petra," I whisper. "What's wrong?"

"Nothing."

"You need me to repeat myself?" I say, tilting my head to one side.

She stares at me for a moment, then sighs, her shoulders dropping. "Can we talk about this later?" she asks.

"No. We can talk about it now."

"We're due to open in ten minutes."

"I don't give a fuck. If we have to sit here while people eat their lunch around us, we will. Tell me what's wrong."

She sighs again. "You won't need me anymore," she blurts out and pulls her hand away from mine, running to the back of the restaurant and into the ladies' room.

I don't go after her, because I can't – it's the ladies' room – but I get up and go over, standing outside the door. Jackson comes up to me after a few minutes.

"It's opening time, boss," he says.

I hand him my keys. "Open the door then," I tell him.

"Um…" He stands there, looking at me.

"It's a key, Jackson. Put it in the lock and turn. It's fairly simple."

"I know," he replies. "But what about the customers?"

"We have tables, numbered one through thirty-two. Seat people at them. I'll get there."

He looks at me for a moment, then turns and leaves, just as Petra appears through the door.

"Gonna talk to me now?" I say to her.

"No. It's work time now."

"Like hell it is." I grab her hand and pull her over toward the corridor that leads to the office. "Jackson," I call over my shoulder. "You're in charge for ten minutes. Don't destroy the joint."

"Rob!" Petra pleads, trying to pull away from me.

"Wait," I tell her and push her through the open office door, slamming it closed behind me, and backing her up against the wall beside it. "Now, what the fuck was that about?" I whisper, breathing hard. "Who says I won't need you anymore?"

"Me," she murmurs. "I'm only here because Sam's away. Once he comes back, you won't need me."

"You're here because I love you," I correct her. "And I needed you before I even knew you."

Her mouth opens slightly and I lean down and kiss her really hard. She groans into me and I step closer, using my body against hers, holding her where I want her.

"Everything's gonna change," she whispers when I eventually break the kiss, and I hear her voice cracking.

"Not everything, baby." I run the backs of my fingers down her cheeks.

"I won't see you so much though, will I?"

"I don't know." It's the truth. I don't know. I haven't worked out yet what we're going to do once Sam gets back. To be honest, I haven't even had time to think it through. "But whatever happens, we're not over. Okay?"

She stares at me. "Can we talk about it later?" she asks, her voice still cracking with emotion.

"Only if you agree first that this doesn't mean we're over. Otherwise, we're just gonna stand here… all fucking day, if necessary."

"I—I don't know what it means, Rob," she whispers.

"Then believe me when I say that it doesn't mean we're over."

She looks into my eyes and gives me the slightest nod of her head. "Can we talk about it later?"

"Yes. And I'm sorry if I was rough with you."

"It's okay."

"No, it's not." I kiss her gently. "Don't run from me, Petra. I'll always listen to you, and I'll always talk to you. Just never run from me – it scares me."

"It *scares* you? *You?*"

"Yeah. I am capable of feeling fear, you know. Well, I am when it comes to you, anyway."

"What did I do to deserve you, Rob?" She puts her hand on my chest and leans into me.

"You walked into my life." I hold her close for a few moments, then pull back and look down at her. "I guess we should get back out there," I murmur, reluctantly. "Jackson's a bag of nerves. I dread to think what he's done by now."

"Okay." She looks up at me and I'm sorely tempted to ignore my responsibilities and lay her out on my desk again.

"Can you go out first?" I ask her. "I'll follow in a couple of minutes."

"Um… sure. Why?"

I lean closer, my mouth next to her ear, and whisper, "Because I'm really hard right now. My pants are tight enough, without a hard-on, and I don't think the customers need to see that, do you?"

She chuckles. "No, especially as it's mine."

I bend and kiss her again, just quickly. "It's all yours, baby."

We get home at just after midnight and we're both exhausted. It's been a busy and emotional day. Petra's been quiet for most of it, and I know she's worried about Sam coming back and what that means for us, although she hasn't let her concerns affect her work.

We go straight to bed and I lie on my back, pulling her into my arms, where she nestles into me, her head resting on my chest. I know she wants to talk and if that's what she needs, that's fine with me. Exhausted or not, she needs to know nothing's gonna change.

She traces small circles across my abs with her fingertip and I sense she's building up to something.

"Whatever you wanna ask, just ask it, baby," I tell her.

She twists, looking up at me. "Is Sam coming back alone?"

I didn't expect that. "No," I reply.

She smiles. "He's bringing Ali back?" I know they got along really well, and I guess she'll be as pleased to see Ali as Ed and I will.

"He's bringing Ali *and* her sister."

She sits up a little, leaning on me. "*And* her sister?"

I nod. "He didn't explain how he persuaded her, but he said they're both coming with him, so I guess we'll find out what happened when they get back here."

She bites her bottom lip, which is real sexy and I fight down the urge to bite it myself. "What are you thinking?" I ask her instead.

"Is he always so bossy and overbearing?"

"Who, Sam?"

She nods. "I haven't actually met him yet," she points out. I think about it for a moment and realize she's right. She hasn't. "He looked kinda scary when I saw him at the opening," she continues. "A bit dark and brooding."

"Dark and brooding?" I repeat. "Yeah, I guess you could say Sam was like that… before he met Ali, that is. She's changed him – for the better." I pull her back down into a hug and she rests against me again. "Don't get me wrong," I add, "Sam's always gonna be controlling and domineering – in all kinds of ways – and maybe he is a little dark too, but he's a lot calmer than he used to be."

"And Ed gets on okay with him? Working in the kitchen all the time?" She seems surprised.

"Yeah. If it was me and Sam, that would be a whole other thing. We'd probably fight all the time, but Ed's so placid…"

"He lets Sam walk all over him?" she suggests.

"No. It's not like that."

She looks up at me again. "How is it then?"

I turn over, so we're facing each other. "Sam's always looked out for Ed," I explain.

"In what way?"

"In lots of ways." I reach around behind her and pull her closer, letting her feel my seemingly ever-present erection. She smiles and squirms into me, clearly liking what she feels. "For example, Ed's had a few unsuitable girlfriends over the years," I tell her. "And Sam's helped him out."

"Unsuitable? How?"

"They've wanted him to give up too much."

"Such as?"

"Such as his career. They didn't like his hours, his devotion to what he did…"

"And Sam's persuaded him to give up the women, rather than anything else?" Her brow furrows.

"Yeah, but it's not how it sounds. You've gotta remember that Sam knows Ed – maybe even better than I do. They share the same passion for their work."

"To the exclusion of everything else?"

"No. I'm sure there'll be a woman out there who's just perfect for Ed."

"What? Because she's willing to sacrifice her own needs and passions for his?" She pulls away from me a little.

"That's not what I said, and it's not what I meant. What I meant was that one day, Ed will find someone who's right for him and, if he really feels the need to, I'm sure he'll be willing to give up whatever he has to for her. He just hasn't met her yet."

"It seems to me he's very easily led," she replies, still evidently a little mad at Sam, even though she's never even met him.

"He isn't. He's not weak. But he does look up to Sam – a lot."

"Is that because Sam's the chef he always wanted to be?"

I laugh. "No. If you sat down with Sam on his own, he'd be the first to tell you that Ed's the better chef. He always was. He just doesn't have Sam's confidence."

"Does anyone?" she asks, half joking.

"Maybe not. Sam can be an arrogant asshole at times. But that's because he's damn good at what he does. And he does a lot more than cooking." I take a deep breath. "Ed's confidence problems go back a long way," I explain. "Our dad did that to him."

She stiffens in my arms. "How?" she asks.

"He didn't like the idea of Ed becoming a pastry chef, so he… he kinda shunned him, I guess. And he gave all his time and attention to Sam instead. If Dad hadn't done that, Ed would probably be an even better chef than he is now, but he took a backward step and turned in on himself. The guy you see now is a hundred times more confident than he was a few years ago, and that's mainly down to Sam. He and Dad fought about it… and they were epic battles, I can tell you. Sam's got one hell of a temper, but so's our dad, and they went head-to-head over it."

"Sam defended Ed?"

"Yeah, of course. To the hilt. Since Mom and Dad moved to Florida, it's been easier on Ed – but he still defers to Sam, even though Sam admits to knowing damn all about pastry."

"Why do you keep calling it 'pastry', when Ed makes desserts?" she asks, and I smile.

"Because pastry refers to anything sweet."

"Oh, I see. But are the two things really so different?" she asks. Then she adds, "Surely cooking is cooking," and I remember she knows damn all about what goes on in a kitchen. Period.

"Yeah. They're completely different. As an example, when they were reinventing the menu while Ali was here, I can guarantee you that Sam would have been in his apartment throwing things into pans and messing around with ingredients."

"Like anchovies with lamb?" she suggests.

"No, that's something he came up with years ago."

"It was?"

"Yeah. It wasn't on the menu, but Sam's always taken our mom's recipes and played around with them a little."

She nods her head. "You were telling me about the differences between what Sam and Ed were doing…" she prompts.

"Hmm… well, while Sam would have been doing things by trial and error, I know Ed was at our place, jotting things down in notebooks, working out ingredients, adding things up, and generally being a lot more scientific in his procedures. In pastry cookery, certain ingredients can interact with each other and completely ruin a recipe. That doesn't happen so much in the main kitchen, so where Sam can get away with mixing it up, Ed has to be real precise. Sam knows all the rules, obviously. He just doesn't have to apply them like Ed does. And then Ed has to make it taste and look as good as Sam does too." I pause for a moment, thinking. "I think he's learned a lot during the last few weeks."

"Like what?"

"Oh, just little things. It's nothing to do with his cooking, but I've noticed he's a little more self-assured than he was. He doesn't shy away from telling someone if they've screwed up, whereas before he'd have let Sam handle that."

"So he's taken responsibility?" she suggests.

"Yeah." I pull her up my body so we're facing each other, and I kiss her. "I think Sam knew he'd do that – and I think that's why he trusted him to get on with it. He could've put me into the kitchen himself – above Ed – not because I'm that great a chef, but because I'm assertive enough to run a kitchen. But he didn't do that. He left it to Ed, and made it very clear that Ed was in charge, to show him he could do it."

"But then Ed had to bring you in anyway. Hasn't that dented his confidence?"

"No. We both know he only did that because he was exhausted, not because he couldn't handle the work itself. I think we've both come to appreciate how much Sam actually does… and that we'd be kinda lost without him."

She looks into my eyes. "You speak very highly of them both."

"Yeah. Just don't repeat any of this to them, will you? If they knew what I really think, they'd never let me live it down – especially Sam."

"I'm sure he'd value your good opinion of him."

I laugh. "No. That's not how we operate, babe."

"So, you never actually tell your brothers how you feel about them?"

"Hell, no."

She shakes her head and whispers, "Maybe you should."

She yawns deeply. "Am I boring you?" I ask, pulling her closer.

"No. But I am bone tired."

"I know. I'm sorry this is such hard work for you."

"I don't mind."

"We'll try and make some time at the weekend," I tell her. "We'll do some stuff with April, and we'll sit down and buy the toys you wanna get, and we'll talk."

"Talk?" She looks up at me.

"Yeah. You were gonna tell me something the other morning, before Ed called. Assuming it can wait a little longer, we can talk it through on Sunday, if that's okay with you…"

She nods her head, smiling. "That's fine. Sunday would be great." She looks kinda relieved.

I lean in and kiss her really gently. I don't mention that I've got something I need to ask her. I think that's way to much of a clue, and I don't want her to guess. Besides, I've still got to get the ring yet, but I'm gonna do it in the morning on my way into work… If I'm a half hour late, Ed will understand. Well, he will when he knows the reason.

I wake up before Petra and watch her sleeping for a while – a long while. She doesn't even stir until nearly eight, by which time I can already hear someone moving around downstairs. I'm just wondering if I should wake her, when she stretches her arms above her head and opens her eyes, looking straight into mine.

"Good morning," I say to her and lean down to kiss her.

"Good morning."

"You've been asleep for hours."

She startles. "Why? What's the time?"

"Just before eight."

"Oh, God." She throws back the covers and goes to get up, but I pull her back into my arms.

"Not so fast."

"We don't have time, Rob," she giggles, and doesn't try to get away from me in the slightest.

"We don't have to make love. But we do have to kiss." I put my words into actions and kiss her again, more deeply this time, enjoying the feel of her lips on mine. "And hug." I hold her against me, her breasts crushed against my chest.

She pulls back a little, looking up at me. "It's late," she murmurs.

"I know."

"Why didn't you wake me? Then we'd have had time to…" she leaves the sentence hanging, as usual.

"Time to what?"

"Make love," she whispers and I smile. At least she said it without too much prompting.

"We can do that later… or tomorrow. We've got all day tomorrow. You needed to sleep."

"Yeah. I did." She stretches again. "And right now, I need to pee… and shower."

I chuckle and let her go, and she heads off to the bathroom.

"I won't be long," she calls over her shoulder.

I lie back, my arms behind my head, and stare at the ceiling. Our talk last night has got me thinking… I know Petra's worried about what's going to happen when Sam comes home next week. It's probably going to change things a little bit, but it doesn't have to change us, not if we don't let it. And besides, I've already decided I want her to stay on working in the restaurant, if it's possible. I haven't mentioned it to her yet, because I have to speak to Sam and Ed first. I'd hate to ask her and for her to get enthusiastic about the idea, only to have Sam or Ed veto it. So, I have to make sure they agree first, and I have to check that we can afford to hire her on a more permanent basis. She wouldn't be there full-time, of course. She's got her own work to think about, and I'm aware she's put that to one side for the last couple of weeks to help us out. We also can't expect her mom to mind April every single night of the week. That's not fair on either of them. But I'm wondering if we could come up with some kind of rota, so that Petra could maybe work a couple of evenings a week with me in the restaurant, and I'm gonna see if I can take some time out during the day – even if it's just an hour between the shifts – so I can come back here and be with Petra and April.

I'm fairly sure Petra's worried about me going back to being in the restaurant again. I imagine she's thinking about the women who'll flirt with me, like they did before. So, I'll need to reassure her that it's just work, as far as I'm concerned, and that nothing's gonna happen. They don't mean anything to me – not anymore. I won't be flirting with anyone except her. I love her way too much to screw this up, but I think I need to find a way – a way of my own – to show her that my life is all about her now. I know we've got Sunday coming up, which I'm gonna try and make as special as I can, but…

I smile to myself. Of course. I'm being an idiot. I grab my phone from the nightstand and go online… It doesn't take more than a few minutes to find what I'm looking for and as I place the order, with express delivery, I settle back on the pillows again. I just *know* she's gonna love this…

Chapter Fourteen

Petra

I stand under the shower and try to concentrate on anything other than next Tuesday. But I can't. Ever since Rob told me that Sam's coming back, all I can think of is that everything is going to change between us. Even with Jasmine being off work, I'm sure that Rob will be able to handle the restaurant by himself, and I won't be required anymore. So, I'll only see him when he finishes his evening shift – which is really late – and I know how tired he is then. We'll get a couple of hours in the morning, but April's around then too, so we don't have much of a chance to be alone. And when we're not together, he'll be with other women, flirting with them, just like he used to. I can feel tears forming already and I hate myself for being so jealous, even though he's told me over and over that he loves me and he doesn't care about other women anymore. I can't help it. I feel so insecure and these changes are going to make everything so different. I don't want that. I like things – no, I *love* things – exactly the way they are…

After our conversation last night I'm also concerned about Sam. He persuaded Ed to give up all of his previous relationships because the women he was seeing weren't 'suitable'. While I don't necessarily think they did the right thing, expecting him to sacrifice his career like that, I do believe Sam's controlling nature has a huge impact on his brothers' lives. What scares me most is that, when he gets to find out about me, he'll do his best to split us up, on the basis that I'm just as unsuitable for

Rob as those other women were for Ed. Obviously, I'm not asking him to give up his business, but I am thinking about how much it's going intrude on our personal lives, how little time we'll get to spend together, how little 'us' time we'll get, especially when we're not working together anymore. Add in all the baggage that I bring with me, some of which Rob doesn't even know about yet, and I can already see Sam sitting Rob down and giving him a good long talking to, pointing out all my flaws…

I finish rinsing off and climb out of the shower, wrapping a towel around my hair and drying myself quickly. Then I go back into the bedroom, where Rob's lying back on the bed, looking very pleased with himself.

"What's happened?" I ask him.

He looks over at me, his smile widening.

"What makes you think anything's happened?" he replies.

"Just that look on your face."

"I was just lying here thinking what a lucky son-of-a-bitch I am," he says, getting up off the bed and slowly coming over to me, his eyes roaming up and down my naked body. "I get to look at your perfect body every single day. That alone makes me the luckiest guy on the planet."

I can feel myself blushing.

"I'm not perfect," I whisper.

"I keep telling you. You're perfect for me." He grabs hold of me and pulls me close, his erection pressing into my hip. I wish we had more time…

I bring my hand down between us and grasp his cock, gently stroking along his length. He sucks in a breath. "I thought we didn't have time," he murmurs, looking deep into my eyes.

"We don't. But a girl can dream, can't she?"

He smiles. "She sure can." He pulls back just slightly and looks down, watching my hand caressing his long shaft. "That looks good," he whispers.

My gaze follows his and, for a moment, we're both mesmerized.

"Can we carry this on later?" he asks. "April's gonna be up soon, if she isn't already."

I pull away sharply. We're both completely naked in my unlocked bedroom, and Rob's aroused. She could walk in at any moment. Just because she hasn't done it since he's been staying here doesn't mean she won't. "Yes. Sorry."

He takes my hand and pulls me into the bathroom. "Don't be sorry," he whispers, kissing me gently. "I just don't wanna be caught out by your daughter."

"Neither do I." My problem is that I don't know why I didn't think of it first. Well, I do know why. I'm distracted by Sam coming back, and what that's going to mean for us. But April's my daughter. I should be responsible, rather than relying on Rob to think about her.

"I'll shower," he says. "I won't be long."

"Okay. I'll get dressed." He kisses me, and gets into the shower cubicle.

Back in the bedroom, I grab some underwear from the drawer and pull it on, adding a long blouse and jeans. I'm not sure if Rob needs me at work this lunchtime, but if he does, I'll change into something more appropriate later. This will do for now.

By the time I've dried my hair, Rob's out of the shower and dressed, in his usual black shirt and pants. He comes up behind me, his hands on my waist and moves my hair to one side, kissing my neck.

"You have to stop that, or we won't have time for breakfast."

"I know. I just wanted to kiss you," he murmurs, doing it again.

I lean back into him and he puts his arms around me.

"Time to face the day?" he says.

"I guess." I don't feel at all enthusiastic and it must show.

He turns me around in his arms. "Everything will be okay," he whispers, kissing my lips, his tongue flicking against them. I don't reply, but I open my mouth to his and let him reassure me that way instead.

Downstairs, Mom's already in the kitchen. She's not making breakfast though, she's cleaning. This isn't a good sign. My mom likes a tidy house, but when she cleans this early in the day – and this ferociously – it means something's wrong.

I glance up at Rob and raise my eyebrows. "What's wrong?" I say, turning to my mom.

She flips around. "Oh. I didn't see you," she says.

"No. You're too busy trying to take the pattern off the tiles."

She looks down at the cloth in her hand, then puts it down on the countertop and lowers her head. "It's that obvious then."

"It is to me."

"Shall I go get April?" Rob suggests. "We can take our time…"

I lean up and kiss him, for being so thoughtful.

"Thanks."

"No problem."

He leaves and I go over to my mom. "Tell me what's happened."

She looks up at me and her shoulders drop. "I called David early this morning to see how things are," she begins.

"And?"

"And he said that Nathan called Clare last night."

"Oh. How did that go?"

"Well, they talked for a long time. Nearly two hours, evidently." That *is* a long time.

"They did?"

"Yes. David's not very happy. Clare's arranged for Nathan to go over there this afternoon."

"Is she going to take him back?"

Mom shrugs. "I don't know. She says it's so he can see Daniel, but David's not convinced. He'd already offered to take Daniel over to see Nathan, so she wouldn't have to see him herself, but when she came off the phone, she announced she'd made this arrangement." She sighs. "But that's not the worst of it."

"There's more?"

She nods. "Clare's said she doesn't want David to be there."

"Seriously? It's his house…"

"I know."

"What did David say?" I ask.

"What could he say? He told her he didn't think it would be wise for them to be by themselves, but she was adamant. She was evidently not very nice about it. She said David's too negative."

"He's only trying to look out for her."

"She clearly doesn't see it that way."

"So, what's he going to do?"

"He's going to come here, if that's okay with you."

"Why wouldn't it be? It's your house, mom."

"No. It's *our* house." She smiles at me and I move closer and give her a hug.

"Thank you for saying that," I murmur.

"Well, it's the truth." She pulls away. "We all live here. Including Rob." She looks into my eyes. "I was wrong about him, wasn't I? He's a good man."

"Yeah. He is." I smile, and she cups my face with her hand.

"It's good to see you so happy, Petra."

"It's good to feel this happy."

We move away from each other and Mom leans back against the countertop, while I sit at the table. "Are you working today?" she asks.

"I don't know yet. I'll ask Rob when he comes down." I look up at her. "Are you still planning on taking April to Aunty Stephanie's tomorrow?" I ask her. I'm not sure if David's problems will interfere with Mom's plans.

"Yes. I didn't see her last week, so I feel that I should. Why? Is that going to be a problem for you and Rob? Did you have plans?"

I shake my head. "No. That's just fine." It's perfect, in fact. It'll give Rob and I some time to ourselves. We can do all the things we talked about…

"Look who I found," Rob says from behind me and I turn around to see him holding April in his arms. She's nestled into him, her head resting on his chest and I feel my heart swell at the sight of them together. This is exactly what I want for her, but even as I'm thinking that, the dark cloud of doubt starts to descend. What if Sam's return messes everything up? What if we find we can't make it work if we're not seeing so much of each other as we do now? What if Sam decides to try and separate us? Did I do the wrong thing letting Rob into April's life? What'll happen to her if he decides to leave us? I'll be broken-hearted, but what about my baby girl? She'll be devastated…

"Do you wanna go to Mommy?" Rob asks her, and she shakes her head, clinging on to him.

"Oh, I see how it is," I say to her, getting up and going over to them. "Now you've got Rob, you don't need me anymore…" I fake a pout and April leans over toward me, giving me a slightly sloppy kiss.

"Of course need you, Mommy," she says. "But I like Rob's cuddles."

I look up at him and notice he seems to be having trouble swallowing, and his eyes are glistening. "Hmm, so do I, baby girl," I say, giving her a kiss on her cheek and letting him pull me into a hug with his free arm, enfolding us both. I glance over at my mom. She's just smiling at us and, for a moment, all my worries are forgotten, because this is perfect. It's just perfect.

April finally lets Rob put her down, but only because he says she can help him cook the breakfast. We're having bacon and eggs today and he lets her break the eggs for him, showing her how to do it with one hand, which ends messily. They have so much fun together and it's very satisfying to sit and watch them laughing as April gets egg all over the place and Rob clears up behind her, with breathtaking patience.

Mom sits beside me, drinking coffee. "Petra was supposed to ask you if you need her today?" she asks him as he dishes up the breakfast, because I'm so distracted, I've forgotten.

"I need her every day," he replies, winking at me and smiling.

Mom chuckles – which is a good sound to hear – and says, "You know what I mean… Is she needed at work?"

"Well, Jasmine's still not back yet," he explains, bringing the plates over and helping April into her chair. "Cole sent a text earlier, while I was up with April. They've got all Scarlett's tests back and they've confirmed she's got Lyme disease."

"That's quite serious, isn't it?" Mom asks him.

"I don't know, I think it depends on how early it's diagnosed, but he's said she's gonna be in the hospital for a while, having treatment, and then she's gonna need some care at home."

"So Jasmine's gonna be off for some time."

He shrugs and sits down beside me. "I guess."

"Is that why you need me to come in today?"

"I can cover for her, but if you can come in, it'd really help out. If you can't, I'm sure we'll manage…"

"What are your plans, Mom?" I ask her, because I don't want her to think I'm taking her for granted.

"Well, David's coming over this afternoon, around two, I think. And, to be honest, I don't know when he'll be going home… But apart from that, I was just gonna do some laundry and cleaning."

"What time would you need me?" I ask Rob, taking a bite of perfectly cooked bacon.

"You can cut it fine, if you need to, and get in for just before we open."

I nod. "It's only that I want to spend as much of the day with April as I can…"

"I get that," he says and takes my hand in his. "We could both come back here between shifts, if you want?"

"Both of us?"

"Yeah. Why not? Then the three of us can do something together…"

I can't help smiling. It sounds like such a 'family' thing to do. "I'd like that," I tell him.

Rob turns to April. "Would you like us to come back here this afternoon for a little while?" he asks.

She nods enthusiastically, helping herself to a forkful of eggs. "Can we bake the special biscuit things?"

"We're doing that tomorrow," Rob explains. She nods, but a frown settles on her face. "How about if we make some cookies today though," he offers, and she nods, grinning.

"You'll have been working, and you're going to be cooking all evening," I reason with him.

"It's fine," he says. "We'll just make some chocolate chip cookies." He looks over at my mom. "Do you have chocolate chips?"

"I don't think so…"

"Don't worry. I'm sure Ed will have something I can use."

"Are you sure about this?" I ask him. "You're gonna be so tired."

"No, I'm not." He turns back to April. "Would you like to make chocolate chip cookies?" he asks. I love that he asks her, rather than just assuming she'll go along with everything.

"Yes, please."

"And do you think we can get Mommy to help us?"

She looks up at him, her face so serious. "Mommy?" she queries. "You want Mommy to make cookies?"

"Yeah. What do you say?"

She gives a comical, over-emphasized shrug and holds her hands up. "I guess so, but I'm not eating them," she says, shaking her head and going back to her breakfast. Rob and my mom both laugh loudly.

"You cheeky monkey," I say, doing my best to ignore their amusement at my expense and I get up from the table and go around to April, leaning over her and tickling her until she's giggling beyond control.

"Rob! Help me," she calls, and he gets up and comes around behind me, and starts tickling me too.

"Stop it!" I giggle, trying to pull away, but he keeps a firm grip and April escapes, jumping down from her chair.

"I'm free," she yells, waving her arms in celebration, and Rob finally lets me go too, just as April comes up beside him. "You saved me," she says, looking up at him, her eyes filled with unbridled adoration.

He leans down and picks her up, holding her in one arm and placing the other around me. "I'll always save you, baby girl," he says, kissing her forehead. Then he turns to me and smiles.

"And me?" I ask him, my voice catching, because he just used my pet name for April… and I really liked hearing him say that.

"You know I'll always save you," he murmurs.

"Unless she's tickling me," April puts in, resting her head against him.

"Absolutely," Rob agrees, and winks at me.

"Thank you for this morning," I say to Rob. We're holding hands, walking back to my mom's after a good lunchtime shift. It was busy, but not crazy, which is how I've come to like it. Crazy shifts are a little too much to handle, and based on the number of reservations we've got for tonight, I think we're due to have a hard time later on. So I'm glad the lunchtime slot wasn't too difficult.

"Why are you thanking me?" he asks. We haven't really had time to talk. He's been in the kitchen or the office most of the time.

"For being so amazing with April."

He shrugs. "I'm not really aware of doing anything," he says. "It just seems to come naturally when I'm around her."

I lean into him. "And that's what's so amazing."

"I think you'll find she's the amazing one," he murmurs, looking down at me. "And whatever she is, is one hundred percent down to you." He lets go of my hand and puts his arm around me. "She's a beautiful baby girl," he adds.

"We're gonna have to stop calling her that one day," I say quietly.

"Why? She'll always be your baby girl, won't she?"

I smile up at him. "Yeah, she will."

We get to my mom's and I let us in. April comes running out of the living room to greet us.

"You're back!" she cries, like we've been gone for at least a week, rather than a couple of hours.

"We said we would be." I reply, taking her hand and leading her back into the living room again. Mom and David are sitting together on the couch and, much to our surprise, Mateo and Courtney are in the chairs opposite.

"Hi," I say, looking at them, but struggling to hide my confusion. I can't even remember the last time they came round to visit.

Mateo gets up and comes over, kissing me on both cheeks, then he looks at Rob.

"This is my boyfriend, Rob," I say, giving him his proper title this time around.

They shake hands. "Hello," Mateo says to Rob, and I wonder for a moment if Courtney's mentioned him and Mateo's come over to check him out.

"Mateo and Courtney have come over to ask a favor," my mom explains as he sits down again.

"Oh?" I look from her to Mateo.

"We need to ask your mom if she'll look after the kids for a few hours next week," he clarifies. "Just on Thursday afternoon."

"I'm going into hospital," Courtney adds, smiling just slightly.

"You are? I didn't realize you were unwell."

"I'm not," she says. "I'm having another procedure."

I nod my head. I think this will be her fourth – maybe her fifth – cosmetic surgery. I've lost count, and interest, in what she has done. "Courtney's going in on Wednesday and will be out Thursday evening," Mateo continues, "but Mom's having her roof fixed next week and doesn't want the kids running around while there are workmen everywhere."

"It's fine," Mom says. "I don't mind them coming here." She turns to me. "You won't be working will you? It's just with three little ones running around, I might need an extra pair of hands…"

I look at Rob. "I doubt it. Sam and Ali will be back by then, so I imagine you'll be able to manage without me, won't you?"

Rob pulls me close. "Sam and Ali coming back is irrelevant. If your mom needs you here to help out, then you should be here."

I lean into him.

"That's great!" Courtney chimes. "I was booked in to have some work done on my chin, but I've had to change surgeons…" Her voice fades for a moment. "I've been really lucky to get a cancellation with this new guy, so I don't want to turn him down."

I glance at Mateo and notice his face has darkened, before he looks away and all of a sudden, a thought occurs to me. I glance up at Rob and I know he's thinking exactly the same thing.

"So you're sure it's alright?" Mateo asks my mom.

"Yes, it's fine." She nods her head while speaking, and Mateo and Courtney both get up.

"We'll leave you to enjoy your afternoon," he says and my mom and David both stand too, and accompany them to the front door. The moment we're alone, I turn to Rob.

"Are you thinking what I'm thinking?" I whisper.

"Yeah. Courtney's previous cosmetic surgeon is suddenly off limits… and Nathan admits to sleeping with a former patient. It's gotta be, hasn't it?"

I nod. "And it looked like Mateo knew all about it. Did you see the look on his face?"

"Yeah. I guess he's decided to accept the situation."

"Why would he do that?" I ask.

"Maybe for the kids. Or maybe she's convinced him it's a one-off too… just like Nathan told Clare."

"And he believed her?"

"Sometimes people believe what they want to."

We hear laughter from the front door and I hold Rob a little tighter, grateful to have him in my life.

"Sorry about that," my mom says as she and David come back into the room. "How are you both?"

"We're fine," I reply for both of us.

"I hear cookies are being baked this afternoon," David says, smiling. "April insisted on telling everyone about it."

"I can imagine."

He chuckles, turning to Rob. "I've heard of hero-worship…" he mutters, shaking his head and smiling.

"What can I say? I guess some of us have it…" Rob joins in the banter, shrugs off his jacket and then looks at his watch. "If we're gonna get these cookies baked," he says, "we'd better get started." I'm as aware as he is that we're on the clock, and we've just wasted the first fifteen minutes of our break.

April doesn't need telling twice and, taking his hand, they go through to the kitchen.

"Are we allowed to watch?" Mom asks.

"Of course," Rob calls over his shoulder. "I can't guarantee to be very entertaining though. Or very professional, for that matter. I should've brought Ed, shouldn't I?" He turns and looks at me. "He'd probably have invented something spectacular… and knocked me off my pedestal in April's eyes."

"Unless Ed can not only make sparkling chocolate chip cookies, sing 'Let it Go' in tune while dressed exactly like Elsa, and knows the names of all the Disney princesses, I really don't think that's possible," my mom replies, following us.

We reach the kitchen and Rob puts down the bags he's brought with him from work, before helping April to sit at the table. Then he leans back on the countertop behind her and folds his arms across his broad chest. "He can definitely manage sparkling chocolate chip cookies. He's enough of a genius to work out how to make them sparkle, that's for sure. I'm not gonna vouch for whether or not he'd be willing to wear a dress, but he's got a damn good singing voice. The high notes might be a problem for him, but I guess he'd give it a try… and as for the Disney princesses… well, that's a family secret and we try not to talk about it…" Everyone laughs, except April, who turns and looks at him.

"Who's Ed?" she asks.

Rob leans over her. "He's my twin brother."

"What's a *twin* brother?" She's fascinated.

"It means we were born at the same time. Sometimes twins look the same, and other times, they don't."

She stares at Rob for a moment. "And do you look the same as your twin?" she asks.

"No. He's a lot uglier than me."

She nods her head and Rob chuckles, then turns to my mom. "I forgot to double check this morning if you had all the ingredients we're gonna need, so I brought everything from work for the cookies and tomorrow's biscotti." He nods over toward the bags he just deposited on the countertop.

"Shall I make coffee?" I suggest as Mom and David sit down at the table.

"You can," Rob replies, "but don't think for one second that making coffee is gonna get you out of helping with the cookies."

"I tried," I fake my disappointment. For the first time in my life, I'm actually looking forward to cooking something.

"I'll make the coffee," David offers, getting up again.

"Is that so you can all watch me get this wrong?" I suggest.

"Yes." He smiles at me.

"At least you're honest."

"Always." He glances at my mom and I wonder what that look means.

Rob opens the bag and pulls out a blue apron and a white jacket, handing the apron to me, and going over to April with the jacket. Her face lights up, and she clambers down from her chair to let him help her put it on.

"Is this for me?" she asks, wide-eyed.

"Yeah," he replies, smiling. "It's even got your name on it."

He points out her name, embroidered above the tiny breast pocket and she gasps and tries to twist it around so she can see it better.

"For me?" she mouths, clearly taken aback by his gesture.

"For you," he says and kisses her forehead.

She reaches up and throws her arms around his neck. "I'm a proper chef," she says.

"You sure are," he replies, and holds her for a while, before getting to his feet.

"Where did you get that?" I ask him, going over to them, my apron in my hand.

"I had to speak with the guy who supplies all our whites and aprons about something else. It turns out they do a kids' range too. So I ordered this for April. I hope it's okay?"

"Of course it is." How could it not be when it makes her so happy. "When did you do this?" I ask him. I've been with him most of the time and haven't been aware of it.

"Yesterday, after I spoke with Sam. He needed me to arrange something as a surprise for Ali, and the guy agreed to get this to me for today, as a special favor. I was gonna save it for tomorrow, for when we make the biscotti, but being as we're cooking now…"

I lean up to kiss him. "Thank you," I murmur.

"You don't have to thank me," he replies.

"Why didn't you get a white jacket for Petra?" my mom asks.

"Oh, Yaya, I thought you'd understand," April says trying to cross her arms, "Mommy isn't a chef yet, she's still practising. When she's good enough, Rob will get her a jacket too, won't you, Rob?"

"Sure," Rob replies, trying not to laugh.

He turns and nods down at the apron I'm still holding. "Speaking of practising, do you need help with that?"

"I think I can manage an apron." I look at him, in his black clothes. "Are you not going to wear one? Surely we're going to be using flour, aren't we?"

"Yes, we are. And no I don't need one."

"Is that wise?"

"I wasn't planning on having a flour fight," he says.

"You might not be…"

He smiles down at me. "Well, I'll be working in the kitchen later, so it won't matter if I'm covered in flour beneath my whites. You're the one who's gonna need to change if you get covered." He pauses. "And if you take me on in a flour fight, trust me, you're gonna get covered."

I hold up my hands. "I've learned my lesson already," I tell him, and although I can feel both my mom and David looking at me, there's no way I'm explaining that.

The cookies turn out beautifully, and I think I even helped a little bit, although Rob let April do most of it. It was meant to be about her enjoying it, anyway. He certainly makes cooking fun, which is something I never thought I'd say. That said, I think Rob makes everything more enjoyable. I can't think of a single thing in my life that hasn't been made better by having him in it

"Time to go, baby," he whispers to me, as I'm finishing my second cookie.

"Already?"

"Well, I have to. You can stay here a little longer, if you want."

I check the time and realize that, if I'm going to get everything set up before we open again, I'm probably going to have to leave now too. I was in such a hurry to get back to April, I didn't lay up all the tables for tonight, and being as we're fully booked, there's a lot to do.

"I'd better come with you," I tell him.

"Sure?" He looks into my eyes.

I nod. "Yeah, I'm sure." He takes my hand and pulls me to my feet. April looks crestfallen.

"You're going already?" she says.

"I'm sorry," I say, letting go of Rob and going around to her. She's sitting between my mom and David, still wearing her white jacket, which I have a feeling she's gonna insist on wearing to bed tonight. Rob follows me.

"We'll bake biscotti tomorrow," he says, coming to stand beside me.

"You're not working tomorrow?" she asks.

"No. Tomorrow's Sunday."

"Oh yes." She smiles. "Does that mean you're here all day?" She's looking at Rob, not me.

"Yes," he replies.

April turns to me and beckons me closer with her forefinger. I lean down and she whispers in my ear, "Can Rob read me my bedtime story tomorrow?"

I lean back a little. "Yes, I'm sure he can."

"He won't mind?" she asks.

"No. He won't mind."

I turn to Rob and he looks at me inquisitively, but I say nothing. April's obviously embarrassed at asking, or she'd have said it out loud. I'll tell him once we're outside.

He raises an eyebrow but I give him a slight shake of my head and he nods. "C'mon then," he says and takes my hand again. Everyone gets up and we all go through to the front door.

"Where's your jacket?" Rob asks, grabbing his from the living room, where he threw it over the back of the chair earlier.

"I left it at work. I was too hot, remember?"

He looks out through the window. "It looks like it's cooled off now. It even looks like it might rain. Do you want to go upstairs and get something else?"

I shake my head. "No, I'll be fine. It's only a short walk."

"Okay."

I give my mom a hug and, whisper, "Is everything okay?" to her.

"Yes," she murmurs back, letting me go. "David and Clare had a fight, that's all."

"Another one?" We keep our voices low. Rob and David are talking and I don't think they can hear us, but even so…

"Yes. I don't know all the details yet, because we haven't had a chance to talk, what with Courtney and Mateo arriving like they did, but I got the feeling he told Clare a few home truths and she didn't like it."

That makes sense of his comment about always being honest, I guess.

"Oh dear." I can't think what else to say.

"I'm kind of pleased he's here today," she continues. "We can talk it all through later, once April's gone to bed, and it'll give him some time away from Clare. I think he's finding her attitude a little hard to take right now."

"I guess that's understandable. He wants what's best for her and he doesn't think Nathan is." Who would? Except Clare, evidently.

Silence has descended behind us and I can sense Rob's waiting for me. "We'd better be going."

"Yes. I think we'll have eaten all those cookies by the time you get back," Mom says, raising her voice so everyone can hear. "They're delicious."

"That they are," David adds in, as we wander over to them.

I lift April into my arms and give her a kiss. She hugs me tight and then turns to Rob, twisting away and leaning toward him. She wants him to take her, but doesn't want to ask… and she doesn't need to. He holds out his arms and takes her from me, holding her close and, as she puts her arms around his neck, he closes his eyes for a moment. When he opens them, they're shining and filled with emotion. She really has made a home in his heart.

Outside, he puts his arm around me and leans in close.

"Thank you," he whispers.

"What for?"

"Letting me into your lives."

I turn to him and he holds me close, his arms coming around behind me. "Thank you for making our lives so much better," I say and he kisses me.

"What did April say to you?" he asks, breaking the kiss and looking down at me.

"Oh. She just asked if you'll read her a bedtime story tomorrow night."

He stares at me for a moment. "She did?"

"Yeah."

He seems lost for words and takes my hand, leading me out onto the sidewalk. "Have you missed that?" he asks.

"Missed what?"

"Reading to her. Putting her to bed…"

"Yes, I have."

He stops and pulls me back. "I'm sorry," he says. "If you wanna stay here, I can manage. I'll—"

I put my index finger up to his lips to stop him talking. "You can't manage," I say. "Tonight's gonna be the busiest yet, and you know Ed won't be able to handle it by himself."

"I know, but—"

"But nothing, Rob. It's fine."

"No, it's not. I've been so selfish."

"No, you haven't."

"Yeah, I have. I've just realized what a big deal it is for you to be with April. You don't get much time with her as it is, and I've stolen some of that away from you."

"It was my choice," I tell him. "I offered, remember?"

"I know." He sounds really sad.

"Don't, Rob."

"Don't what?"

"Don't feel guilty. Don't give yourself a hard time. I've enjoyed every moment of being with you at the restaurant. I've loved what you've given us, and I wouldn't change a second of it." He looks at me, like he doesn't believe me, and I don't know how to convince him, so I lean up and brush my lips against his. In the blink of an eye, he pulls me into him, one hand behind my head, the other in the small of my back, and his tongue delves deeply inside my mouth. He groans as I respond, my tongue flicking over his, my breasts crushed against his chest.

"Stop," he pleads, breaking the kiss, and I lean back in his arms, looking up at his dark eyes. "We have to stop."

"We do?"

"Yeah, we do." He moves his mouth right next to my ear. "I wanna fuck you," he whispers, and my pussy tingles. "But I'll get arrested if I do that here." I chuckle. "And we can't go back to your place."

"No."

"Which means we've gotta stop."

I deflate. "I guess so."

"At least until tonight," he adds, his eyes sparkling now.

I nod my head and he takes my hand, pulling his jacket down, I presume to hide his erection.

We start walking again, our hands clasped together. "Do you think I should tell David that we've worked out that it was Courtney who Nathan slept with?" I ask him, just to take our minds off of what we want to do to each other, if nothing else.

"No."

"Why not?"

"Because, when you think about how both of the couples concerned are behaving, they both seem kinda resigned to the situation, maybe even settled about it, don't they? I mean, it's pretty obvious that Mateo knows about Courtney and Nathan, but he's choosing to say nothing and we have to respect that. I also think that Clare will go back to Nathan before too long, and the last thing she needs is to find out that your cousin's wife is the woman her husband slept with. I'm sorry baby, but some things are best kept quiet."

I look up at him. "I guess it might cause problems between Mom and David too," I murmur. "And I'd hate that."

He grins. "The guy's grown on you then, has he?"

I nod. "I like him. He's good for her."

"Exactly."

He squeezes my hand just as I feel the first raindrop fall on my arm. Another follows quickly; then another. To start off with, it looks like being just a very light shower, but within moments, the heavens open and it pours torrentially.

Before I've even had time to think, I feel Rob place his jacket over my head and shoulders, shielding me from the worst of it. "Run." His voice is urgent and I obey, keeping a firm hold of his hand with one of mine, and using the other to keep his jacket in place, as we dart along the sidewalk, trying to dodge the worst of the quick-forming puddles.

By the time we reach the restaurant, Rob is drowned. I'm a lot better off. It's really just my jeans and boots that are wet and, being leather, they'll soon dry. He pulls his keys from his pocket and lets us inside.

"Fucking hell," he mutters, and I look at him, a smile forming on my lips. His shirt is sticking to him, as are his jeans and his hair's matted to his head. "Don't you dare laugh," he says. "Or I'll never lend you my jacket again." I pass it back to him, sheepishly and he looks at it, the water dropping from it onto the floor. "Still, it worked. You're fairly dry."

"I think the word you're looking for is 'comparatively'," I remark, still trying not to laugh.

"Probably."

"What happened to you two?" Ed's standing by the entrance to the back corridor.

"The rain," Rob replies.

"Your brother lent me his jacket… and drowned in the process."

"Ever the gentleman." Ed rolls his eyes. "Why don't you go upstairs and get dry, rather than dripping all over the floor," he suggests. "I'll clean up the mess you've left in here." I look down at the pool of water we've created on the floor.

"Good idea," Rob replies.

"Upstairs?" I query.

"Sam's apartment," Rob explains.

"But he's not here." Rob takes my hand and leads me through the restaurant, thrusting his jacket at Ed as we pass him.

"Put that in the office for me?" he says, and we continue down the corridor, without waiting for an answer.

He stops in front of the door right at the back of the corridor and opens it with one of his keys, revealing a narrow staircase, which we go up, to another door at the top, which is open. Inside, there's a small kind of hallway for hanging coats and things, which opens onto an enormous living space, in the middle of which is a big black L-shaped couch, with a low coffee table set in front of it. On the far side, over by the window is a long, rectangular dining table, with eight high-backed chairs around it and, over to the right there's an opening which leads into the kitchen. I might not cook, but even I know this is an impressive kitchen – it's like something out of a magazine. Rob moves behind me, and goes down a long corridor to my left, disappearing through one of the doors, and returning a few moments later with a couple of towels.

He hands me one. "Do you want to take your jeans off?" he suggests.

"Here?"

"We're alone," he points out. "And there's a dryer."

"Oh. Okay." I unzip my boots and bend down to pull them off. I don't want to sit anywhere because I'm wet.

"Let me help." Rob kneels in front of me and I raise my leg, so he can remove my boots. "They're dry on the inside," he says, standing them to one side, before reaching up and undoing my jeans, pulling them down over my hips and thighs, lowering them to my ankles. "Step out," he says, holding his hand up for me to take, so I can keep my balance. I do as he says and he pushes my jeans to one side, keeping hold of my hand and looking up at me. "This is real tempting," he murmurs. "But I'm soaked." He stands, bringing my wet jeans with him. "I'm just gonna get dry, and see if I can find something of Sam's to wear." He turns. "Make yourself at home."

I go across to the couch and sit down, feeling a little uncomfortable, being half naked in Sam's apartment, without Rob for company. I grab a cushion and hold it across my lap, although how I think that helps, I don't know.

Rob

I'm absolutely drowned. There's no way my shirt's gonna dry off any time soon, but I can borrow something of Sam's. My pants are pretty wet too, but I think they'll dry, or at least be wearable, so I take them off and put them and Petra's jeans into the dryer and turn it on for thirty minutes, and leave my dripping shirt in the sink for now. Then, dressed in only my trunks, I go across the hallway and into Sam's bedroom. Unusually for him, it's a mess in here, but I guess he packed in a hurry. A lot of the drawers are open and there are a couple of sweaters on the bed. He probably couldn't decide whether to take them or not and decided against it, but didn't bother to put them away again. I wonder if I should close the drawers for him and go over to his nightstand, where he's taken out the top drawer completely and emptied it onto the bed, looking for his passport, I presume. I pick up everything, dump it back inside and replace the drawer, catching a glimpse of a black silk rope and what looks like a pair of leather cuffs in the drawer below. I smile to myself… Sam doesn't change.

I decide to leave the rest of his bedroom as it is, not because I'm worried about what else I'll find, but because I want to get back out to Petra. She didn't seem very comfortable being here.

I think Sam keeps his t-shirts in the dresser, so I go over to it and start looking, finding one easily and taking it with me back down the hallway and into the living room. She's sitting in the corner of the couch, looking a little scared, biting on her bottom lip, playing with her fingers, with a cushioned clamped to her lap.

"It doesn't hide much, baby," I say to her. I presume she was trying to disguise the fact that she's hardly wearing anything.

"I know." She looks up at me, smiling, a lot less fidgety, and clearly happier now that I'm back. That makes me feel good.

She moves the cushion to one side and, as I take in the sight of her shapely legs and her lacy white panties, my cock stiffens in an instant, and I recall our public kiss just a few minutes ago, out in the street. That was hot… and I really did want to fuck her, right there on the sidewalk. I've never wanted anyone like that before – not with such a beyond control need. And as I look at her now, that feeling is back. I've gotta have her.

"Come here," I murmur.

Without question, or hesitation, she unfurls her long legs and gets up, walking slowly over in just her thin blouse and her lace panties, her eyes fixed on mine. Fuck, that's so sexy.

"Yes?" she says softly, when she gets to me.

"Nothing's changed."

She tilts her head to one side. "What does that mean?"

"I still wanna fuck you."

She smiles, her eyes widen and her mouth opens, just a fraction. I can see the tip of her tongue and all I can think about are all the things I want to do to her divine pussy. I reach out, grabbing her arms and pulling her close, covering her mouth with mine and claiming her. She moans into me, opening up and finding my tongue with hers, and I undo her blouse, resisting the urge to rip it off of her, but only because I know she needs to wear it later. Once the buttons are undone, I push it from her shoulders and let it fall, adding her bra within seconds, and palming her breasts, feeling her nipples harden to my touch.

She reaches between us, her fingers finding their way into the top of my trunks.

"Why are you shaking?" I ask her, pulling back from the kiss and looking down at her.

"Because I want you," she breathes, panting slightly.

"That's all? There's nothing wrong?"

She shakes her head. "No. I just want you."

"You've got me, babe."

She smiles and crouches down to lower my trunks. As my cock springs free, she licks the tip, then captures it in her mouth, sucking me and I watch her as she builds the tempo, raising her eyes to mine, almost like she wants confirmation.

"That feels so good," I tell her, and she takes me just a little deeper, but as much as I'm loving what she's doing, this isn't what I had in mind… and time's limited. I put my hands either side of her face and, holding her still, I step back, forcing her to release my cock. She looks up at me.

"Don't look like that," I whisper. "We don't have long, and I want you."

"I want you too." She lowers her gaze to my dick and I put my arms under hers, pulling her to her feet, and kissing her again, then pushing her backwards over the end of Sam's couch, so her back is on the seat and her ass is raised up, on the arm. I pull her panties off, dropping them on the floor, then part her legs with my hands and lean down, using my fingers to spread her pussy lips wide and flick my tongue across her clit.

"Yes," she hisses through clenched teeth. "Please, yes."

I circle around and across her clit, then insert two fingers inside her soaking entrance. She arches off the couch and detonates around me, as I pull my fingers from her, then stand and replace them with my cock, my thumb taking the place of my tongue. Her orgasm intensifies and I lean over slightly to take her deeper. I need this. I wanna fuck her so damn hard. She pinches her nipples, pulling on them, as she rides out her pleasure and that sight is too much for me. Without warning, I shatter, pouring myself into her. *Shit… that wasn't meant to happen. Not yet.*

"Sorry that was so quick," I whisper as she finally calms and focuses on me again.

"Don't apologize," she replies, smiling. "That was incredible. As always."

Nothing like that has ever happened to me before, and just the thought that she could ever be dissatisfied with me fills me with fear. I take her hands, pulling her up to her feet and holding her close to me.

"What's wrong?" she murmurs, caressing my neck.

"Just promise you'll tell me if you're ever anything but happy with me, and give me a chance to put it right."

She pulls away sharply. "How on earth could you think I'd ever be anything but happy with you?"

"Just promise me." I look into her eyes. I need to hear it from her.

"I promise," she says quietly. "But it's never gonna happen."

I lean down and kiss her, really hard, not breaking the kiss until I really have to.

"Are you okay?" she asks.

"No."

"What happened?"

I rest my forehead against hers. "I don't ever want you to feel unhappy, or disappointed, or dissatisfied with me, and not tell me, that's all. This relationship thing is still new to me, and if I'm getting it wrong, in any way, I need you to tell me, so I can try and put it right." I kiss her gently. "I can't lose you."

"You're not going to. And I don't think you could get it wrong, Rob. Everything you do is perfect."

"No it isn't."

"As you keep saying, you're perfect for me."

"I hope so."

I kiss her quickly again, and pull away. If I'm being honest with myself, although I can't tell Petra this in so many words, I'm feeling a little embarrassed about having come so quickly, and about that moment of self-doubt as well. It's not like me, but then none of this is like me, really. I'd never have thought myself capable of falling in love, let alone within hours of meeting someone, or of accepting that they've got a daughter, or of loving that daughter myself, like my life depends on it. I don't really know what's going on, nor do I claim to understand it, but the idea of it ending, or of losing Petra and April fills me with a greater fear than anything I've ever known in my life.

"Do you think our clothes will be dry yet?" Petra asks, as though she's sensed my discomfort.

"Dry might be overstating it. I think the best we can hope for is dryer than they were."

"In the case of your pants, that wouldn't be hard."

"No. I'll go check." I go back along the corridor, into the laundry room and open the dryer. Petra's jeans are damp on the seams, but otherwise, they're fairly dry. My pants are actually okay. I get them out and go back to the living room.

"They're not bad," I tell her. "Mine are dryer than yours."

She looks up at me, smiling. "Yeah, but then you do have a habit of making me wet."

I chuckle. "So it would seem."

I gather up our clothes and put them on the couch, handing Petra her panties. We dress quickly and quietly, with me putting on Sam's t-shirt, rather than my own soaking top.

"That's tight," Petra observes as I pull it down.

"That's Sam. He likes tight t-shirts. What can I say?"

"Is he as muscular as you?"

"Probably more so." I smile.

She comes over to me, resting her hand on my chest, her body burning into mine. "Well, you're more than enough for me," she whispers.

"Good."

I take my shirt with me when we go downstairs and it's only when I'm locking the door again that I realize I left it open, and that Ed could've come up at any time. Still, he didn't, so it's okay.

"I'm gonna put this in the office," I tell Petra.

"Okay. I'd better get on with some work," she replies. I'm holding her hand and, as she goes to move away, I pull her back and kiss her.

"I still want you," I murmur into her.

"Mom's taking April out tomorrow," she says, leaning back and looking up at me. "I know we've got things to talk about..." She pauses and I notice a shadow cross her face. "But maybe we'll still have time to have some fun?"

"I can guarantee it," I reply. No matter what she's got to tell me, I'm taking her to bed at some point tomorrow afternoon.

We share one more brief kiss and then she goes back down the corridor and into the restaurant. I take a moment to admire her ass, and then I go into the office, depositing my wet shirt on my desk, and opening the top drawer. I put my purchases in here this morning when I got to work, because I couldn't really carry them around all day, but because I don't want to forget later, I take them out now and put them into my jacket, which Ed's hung up on the back of the door.

I still intend to propose tomorrow, but I think it's gonna have to be in the evening, because I found something today that makes the whole thing just that little bit more perfect. I really hope Petra's okay with what I've done… well, with what I'm gonna do. But I guess there's only one way to find out. I'm nervous, but I also can't wait for tomorrow. I just hope I've got it right.

"You took your time," Ed says, as I go into the kitchen. There's still no-one else in here and he's smirking. He knows exactly why we've been upstairs for so long.

"Well, you know how it is," I remark, smiling over at him as I pull on my whites.

"I think I can just about remember, yeah."

I know it's been a while for him, but he's way too nice a guy to be on his own for long. The back door opens and three of the junior chefs come in, dripping wet.

"It's still raining then?" I turn to them.

"Just a little bit," Jane says. They traipse through the kitchen, leaving a trail of water in their wake.

"We'd better get some mats down," Ed says from the back the kitchen. "Or someone's gonna slip over."

"I'll deal with it,"

"It's okay," he says, coming over to me. "I'm already prepped for this evening, I'll handle it."

He's just about to turn away, when he stops and faces me again. "You're really serious about her, aren't you?"

"Petra?" I clarify, although I don't really know why. Who else would he be talking about? "Yeah I am."

"How serious?" he asks.

"Very." I look him in the eye. "Let's just say it doesn't get any more serious than this."

I can almost see the penny drop.

"Really?"

"Yeah. Really…"

"You've asked her?"

"Not yet."

"But you're going to?"

I nod.

He pats me on the arm. "Good luck, man."

"Do I need luck?" My nerves resurface in an instant.

"No. Of course you don't. She so obviously loves you…" His sentence fades as the guys come back into the kitchen. He gives me a smile and goes over to the storage closet where we keep the cleaning supplies and the mats.

In a way I wish we'd had a little longer. He was saying that Petra obviously loves me and I'd have liked to ask him how he knows that, what it is that gives it away. But what does it matter? The point is, she does. And I love her. And tomorrow, I'm going to ask her to marry me, and be mine forever.

Chapter Fifteen

Petra

Of all the evenings that I've worked, this has been the most hectic yet…
and the worst. I don't think the weather's helped, but it's just been
crazy. Horribly crazy. People had booked tables and didn't arrive, so
I had to go and check with Rob what the policy was, because I had
people who hadn't booked standing at the door, hoping to get a table.
He told me that if the no-shows were more than fifteen minutes late, I
could let the table go. The policy is stated on the website and people are
warned when they book by phone, so they're aware… except evidently
for the guy and his wife, who arrive over thirty minutes late for their
seven-thirty booking, and who immediately start to yell and swear at
me for giving their table to another couple. I try reasoning with him –
and with her, because she's just as rude as her husband – but they're not
listening. I tell them, quite calmly that they're welcome to sit at the bar
and wait for another table to become available, but that just seems to
make the guy even madder still. He goes red in the face and accuses me
of trying to make money out of them by selling them overpriced drinks
while they wait for a table that might never become free. While he's
ranting, I quickly check their reservation and discover that they booked
online, so I go to the website, and show them the restaurant's policy on
late arrivals, which is clearly stated in red, on the reservations page. He
huffs and puffs and dismisses that – and calls me an 'incompetent bitch',
into the bargain. Meanwhile, a queue of people who had booked, and

arrived on time, is now forming and I know I'm just getting more and more flustered.

"Can I help?" The familiar voice behind me is like a soothing balm, and I turn to see Rob striding toward me, and notice Greg going back behind the bar. I guess he must've gone to tell Rob what was going on. Rob's removed his whites and is wearing Sam's tight black t-shirt and his own black pants. He looks like sex on legs to me, and judging from the expression on the guy's wife's face, I think she agrees with me.

"Who are you?" the guy asks Rob.

"I own the restaurant," he replies. "Is there a problem?" He comes and stands beside me, showing his support.

"We made a reservation," the guy explains, and I let him, because I know I'm right. "And when we arrived, this stupid bitch told us she'd given our table to someone else, and now she expects us to wait at the bar until another table's free. Why the fuck am I gonna do that, just because she's too fucking dumb to do her own job?"

I feel Rob's anger, even though I'm not looking at him, focusing instead on the couple in front of us.

"We could stay, couldn't we, Grant?" the wife says, eyeing Rob.

"Shut up," the husband says to her and then turns back to Rob.

"Please don't refer to my staff in that way," Rob says stiffly, ignoring their spat and the guy's 'problem'.

"I'll refer to them however I fucking well want," the guy says. "I made a reservation here. I expect you to honor that."

Rob leans forward, and lowers his voice. "I don't give a flying fuck what you expect," he whispers.

He leans back again and waits.

"You can't talk to me——" the guy blusters.

"I can," Rob interrupts. "Remember me? I own the joint."

"And so do I." I turn and see Ed standing behind us. He's still wearing his whites, and I didn't even notice him coming in.

"And we're asking you to leave," Rob concludes.

"Asking?" The guy smirks at them.

"Politely." Ed adds.

Rob leans forward again. "But if you're still here in thirty seconds, we won't be so polite. Please. Leave. Now."

"I think we should go, Grant," the wife says, tugging on his arm.

"You wanted to stay a minute ago." He turns on her.

"I changed my mind."

"For fuck's sake." He looks back at me. "I don't wanna eat here anyway." His eyes roam down my body and back up again, like he's mentally undressing me, but his expression is pure disdain, and I feel like a piece of rejected meat. Rob takes a half step forward and the guy moves back, as his wife pulls him toward the door, through the crowd of waiting diners, who grumble at them for causing the trouble in the first place.

Ed's got his hand on Rob's shoulder and only lets go once the guy and his wife are outside. Then he turns to me. "Are you okay, Petra?" he asks.

"Yes, thanks." Even though I'm talking to Ed, I'm staring at Rob. His dark eyes are fixed on mine.

"Okay. I'll leave you with Rob." He nudges his brother. "We're slammed back there. Don't be long."

Rob nods as Ed departs, although he's still staring at me. "Sure you're okay?" His voice is soft and caring.

"I'm fine – thanks to you."

"Thanks to Greg."

"I'll remember to thank him later."

"Not too much though, okay?" he murmurs.

"I won't."

He steps back. "And now, you're gonna hate me," he says.

"I am?"

"Yeah." He smiles.

"Why?"

He looks around. "Because I'm about to give you a whole load more work."

"How? I don't think we could get any busier."

He chuckles. "Yeah, you could." He pauses, then sucks in a breath and raises his voice above the background noise and music that plays constantly. "Greg?" he calls out and the barman looks over. "A round of drinks for everyone… on the house."

A cheer goes up around the restaurant. Rob takes my hand in his and raises it to his lips, kissing my fingers and looking me in the eye, then leans forward and whispers in my ear, "Sorry, but it had to be done."

On his way back through the restaurant, most of the diners grab hold of him and thank him, and he stops and has a quick word. I overhear a couple of them congratulating him on his handling of the situation and I know the damage is limited, both by his generous gesture, and just by him… being him. He takes a quick detour via the bar, and then disappears into the kitchen again, and it's only then that I realize why he said I might hate him, because suddenly every person in here wants to order a fresh round of drinks, knowing they won't have to pay for them, and we have to make sure they're not logged on the iPads, but that everything else still is. It's complicated, and coupled with the fact that I've got to seat all the customers who were kept waiting while the argument went on, the next twenty minutes are ludicrously busy.

It's just starting to calm down to routine chaos when Greg catches my eye and calls me over. I make my way to the bar and he pushes a highball toward me. It's filled with ice, a few slices of lemon and enticing clear bubbly liquid. I'm really thirsty and a glass of iced sparkling water is just perfect.

"Thank you," I say to him, smiling. "This is exactly what I need."

I down three huge gulps before I realize I'm not drinking water.

"Greg, what the hell is that?" I slam the drink back down on the bar and take a deep breath.

He smirks. "It's a vodka-tonic," he replies.

"And you gave me that because…?"

"The boss told me to."

"Rob told you to give me a vodka-tonic?"

"Yeah. He said it would help to calm your nerves." He chuckles. "I don't think he quite expected you to drink half of it down in one go."

"No. Because I thought it was water."

He nods. "Yeah, I gathered that."

"And you didn't warn me?"

"No." He shakes his head. "Rob's really gonna enjoy this…"

"And neither of you is worried about me being drunk while I'm working?"

"It's one vodka-tonic, Petra. I think you can handle it."

He has a point and I slowly take another couple of sips. Rob was quite right, I do feel calmer already.

"Thanks," I say to him.

"You're welcome."

"And thank you for getting Rob."

"Once again, you're welcome." He picks up a glass and polishes it with his cloth. "That guy was being an asshole."

"He still made me feel useless."

"You're far from useless, Petra. Rob wouldn't leave you in charge if he had any doubt about you."

I give him another smile, take another sip of vodka and go back to work.

Even though it's nearly nine-thirty, things still haven't calmed down and, as I look around the restaurant, we're as busy as we've been all evening. We've got one table free – table ten – but that's reserved for a couple, who should be here any minute, I hope. I'm feeling a lot better, probably because of the vodka, and also because the rest of the shift has gone so smoothly. I've just finished answering a question for the group on table two, when the door opens and I turn to greet the new customers… and my heart stops.

It's Adrian.

I stand for a moment, with my mouth open, staring at him. He hasn't changed at all, even though I haven't set eyes on him in over four years. He's still tall, dark and handsome. He always was. He's also still got that arrogant air, and he looks me up and down, a smug smile forming on his lips.

"Petra?" He's obviously surprised to see me, but then why wouldn't he be?

I take a deep breath and go into 'work' mode, taking in the leggy blonde who's hanging off his arm. She's beautiful and looks about twenty, or maybe a couple of years older, but definitely no more than that. And as for her body… well, let's just say she clearly works out.

"Good evening," I reply politely. "Do you have a reservation?"

The blonde steps forward. "Yes," she says quietly. "It's in the name of Sadie Brown."

I nod my head and check the iPad, even though I know these two are destined for table ten. I need a few moments to calm down and gather my thoughts.

"Oh, yes," I say, as though their reservation is a complete surprise to me. Then I grab a couple of menus. "If you'd like to follow me?"

Unfortunately, table ten is right at the back of the restaurant, which gives Sadie the opportunity to keep talking. It's not that there's anything unpleasant about her. It's just that I'd rather not have to listen to her, or pretend I'm interested.

"I booked the table as a surprise for Adie," she says and I cringe at the shortening of Adrian's name. I can't imagine he likes it that much either, and the thought of them calling themselves 'Sadie and Adie' is laughable. But as I turn to reveal their table, he's smiling at her, and she simpers, and leans in and kisses him on the cheek. I think I'd quite like to vomit now…

"This is your table," I tell them, stating the obvious. "And your waiter for the evening will be Jackson."

I wait for them to sit, and then hand them their menus. Just as I'm about to leave, Adrian grabs my arm. Every instinct in my body is screaming at me to yank it away from him, but I know he'll only make a scene and, after what happened earlier, that's the last thing I need.

"Can I help you?" I say, staring at his hand, rather than making eye contact.

"I didn't realize you were a waitress here," he replies, that smug grin returning to his lips.

"It's a temporary thing," I tell him, even though I don't owe him any kind of explanation. "I'm just helping out the owners."

I pull away from him and he lets me go, thank God, and then I check around to make sure everything seems okay in the restaurant before heading straight for the ladies' room, where I make for the first stall, and empty the contents of my stomach.

Once I know I have nothing left inside me, I come back out and splash cool water onto my face, in the vain hope it'll make me feel a little better. It doesn't work, quite simply because I know I've ruined everything. I just needed to get to tomorrow, that's all. I was going to tell Rob tomorrow and then everything would have been fine. So why did this have to happen now? Why did Adrian have to come in here tonight. It's all his fault… Well, that isn't strictly true. It's my fault. I should've told Rob before. I've had plenty of chances, and if I'd taken just one of them, then none of this would matter. As it is, he's bound to discover who Adrian is, and then everything will come out, and then he'll blame me for not telling him…

As I step back and look at my reflection in the mirror, I wonder whether Rob needs to find out about Adrian being here; whether I can somehow keep it from him. I stare into my own eyes… Dear God, what am I thinking? It's bad enough that I didn't tell him the truth in the first place, but now I'm thinking about actually lying?

I shut my eyes to stop the tears from falling and wonder if there's any difference.

Rob

We don't often get people behaving like that jerk who was in here earlier – maybe because it's usually me who's out the front, and they don't try to start a fight with me in the first place – but I've gotta say, that's the first time I've ever wanted to punch a customer. I'd have done it too, if he'd gone much further. Luckily, his wife seemed just as keen to get him out of here as I was, even though she'd wanted to stay to start with. I know why that was – she'd lit up like Christmas the moment I appeared, which I'm sure Petra noticed too. I can't see how she can have missed it, the woman was almost drooling. What was worse though, was the way the guy looked at Petra just before they left. It was a cross between an eye-fuck and total contempt, and I guess between those two, it probably made her feel like shit. An eye-fuck can be great in the right circumstances. I've given and received a few in my time, but the contemptuous element would have just made her feel inadequate, and even as I walked back to the kitchen, I resolved to do everything I can later on to make her feel better about herself. And, of course, I remembered my plans for tomorrow... I really hope I've got it right.

I can't imagine for five seconds that any of the waiting staff appreciated me giving everyone a drink on the house. I've done it several times over the years, and I know how much work it makes for them, but it was necessary to lighten the mood. I also spoke to Greg and asked him to give Petra a vodka-tonic. I'd have suggested a brandy, but I didn't want the customers to think she *needed* a drink, even though she probably did, and the vodka-tonic looks just like iced water in the glass, so no-one but Greg, Petra and I will ever know about it.

Hopefully it's done the trick and she's a little calmer than she was. Whenever I've had a few minutes to spare during the evening, I've taken the chance to check up on her through the kitchen door. There are round windows set into the wooden doors, at roughly head-height, and I've just peeked through, whenever I can, to make sure she's okay. So far, she seems to be fine.

"You're gonna check on her again?" Ed asks, coming over to me and ambushing me, just as I'm making my way to the doors for about the fourth or fifth time. He checks his watch. "It's only a half hour until we close."

"I know."

"And you're still worried?"

"Yeah. I'm still worried." I look at him. "One day, you'll get it."

He chuckles. "This bad? I doubt it."

I pat him on the shoulder. "Don't you believe it, man. I think when you fall, you're gonna fall harder than any of us."

He shakes his head and wanders back to the dessert section, and I continue over to the door and peek out. Petra's clearly visible. She's just seeing a couple to the door. They're quite a striking couple too. The guy is probably around thirty-five – quite tall, with dark hair, very muscular, and *very* good looking. The woman is blonde and thin, and quite scantily dressed, and when she turns to speak to Petra, I can see she's pretty, but quite young – probably only in her early twenties. They stop and talk for a moment, and the guy says something to the blonde and she wanders on her own to the front door, leaving her date alone with Petra. That seems odd and I open the kitchen door to get a better view, just as he moves a little closer to her and places his hand on her shoulder. Then, as I watch, he strokes his fingers up and down her arm a few times, still talking to her, before moving slightly and bringing his hand around behind her to the small of her back and then further down, to her ass, letting it rest there. Their heads are closer together now, and they seem to be whispering. There's something really intimate about it, and as I watch them, a pain starts deep in my chest. I've never felt anything like it before. It's hard to breathe, hard to even catch a breath and I lean against the wall for support. Petra nods a couple of times, then the guy speaks again and leaves. Petra doesn't go to the door with him, but stands, watching him, and then she turns. She doesn't look up – thank God, because if she did, she'd see me. Instead, she's staring into space, mesmerized, her hand on her mouth. What really captures my attention though is her expression. She looks happy… sublimely happy, like those few moments with this guy have made all her dreams come true.

I don't want her to see me. I don't want to talk to her – not yet, not until I've worked out what's going on, and how I feel about it. I have no idea how, but I manage to push myself off the wall and quickly duck back inside the kitchen.

Even as I look around the now familiar space, I feel as though the world as I know it has just come to an end. Everything I thought was right and perfect is wrong and confused – including me. Chefs are milling around, getting on with their jobs, the kitchen hands are clearing up, cleaning down, keeping up with emptying the dishwashers, Ed's in his section, preparing something; the noise level is fairly high, as usual. It's all exactly as it was just a few minutes ago, before I saw my girlfriend being felt up by another man – and letting him do it. And seeming very, very happy about it too.

I can't be here. I need to think…

Without speaking to anyone, I go straight through and out the back door, slamming it behind me. The alleyway is quiet and a little damp from the earlier rain, which has thankfully stopped, not that I'd care if it hadn't.

"Rob?" Ed's voice rings out in the darkness.

"What?" I turn gruffly, facing him.

"What's wrong?"

"Everything." I'm not generally one of those people who says that nothing's wrong, when something clearly is.

He comes and stands in front of me, the light from the kitchen window showing his concern. "What's happened?" he asks.

I stare at him for a moment, gathering my thoughts, then take a breath. "I just saw Petra with another guy," I say as calmly as I can. Hearing the words makes it sound so much worse than it already felt, and that pain in my chest intensifies, to the point where my breath hitches in my throat.

I feel Ed's hand on my arm. "You okay?" he asks.

"No, I'm not fucking okay."

"Sorry. That was probably a stupid question."

I don't want to say that it was; but it was.

We stand, looking at each other for a long moment. I hope he's gonna say something soon, because I don't even know where to start.

"What exactly did you see?" he asks, putting me out of my misery.

"Petra, with another guy."

"You've already said that. Elucidate."

"It was with a customer. They were talking."

"And?"

"And he was touching her."

He sighs, then swallows. "Define touching. Where did he touch her?"

"Her shoulder, her arm, her back… her ass."

"Anything else? They didn't kiss, or anything like that?"

I shake my head.

"He may just be a friend," he reasons.

"You have many friends who touch your ass, Ed? No. They were… I mean, it was like they knew each other really well. At least as well as she and I know each other – maybe better. There was something deeply personal and sexual about it."

"And you have no idea who the guy was?"

"No. It was no-one she's told me about, that's for sure."

"You could check the reservations," he suggests. "You can access them from your laptop."

"I'd rather she'd just told me about the guy," I tell him, but I can see he's got a point and, after just a few seconds' hesitation, I go back inside. He follows, but stays in the kitchen, while I go through to the office, sit at my desk, open my laptop and check the evening's reservation list.

Sadie Brown. Well that's really fucking unhelpful. The blonde obviously booked the table in her name. I wonder for a moment how she'd feel if she knew her date was feeling up the waitress – having dismissed her first. But that's not my problem.

My problem is that Petra let that guy touch her, and I can't get away from the idea that they know each other really intimately, which suggests there's something fairly major that she hasn't told me.

My other problem is that I love her. I know I'll always love her. And right now, loving her fucking hurts.

Chapter Sixteen

❦

Petra

A couple of hours ago, I thought my life was over – or at least my life with Rob. And if it wasn't over, it was certainly at great risk of being so. But now, I almost feel relieved. Obviously, I've still got to tell him everything, but now I can sweeten it with the best news I've had in ages.

I can't believe Adrian thought it was okay to touch me like that, and if he hadn't been telling me the only words I ever want to hear from his lips, I'd have slapped him and told him to take his stick-insect girlfriend and go to hell. But in the circumstances, I decided it was better to let him have his last moment of perceived ownership, and get what I want, rather than risk ruining everything for the sake of a little female pride. My future with Rob is much more important than that. And besides, if I had kicked up a fuss, he'd only have laughed, found it amusing, and probably done something far worse, far more embarrassing. I know Adrian. I knew he had something in mind the moment he dismissed the blonde and asked her to wait outside. She was remarkably docile and went without question. But I guess that's the miracle of youth for you. She's too young to question his motives. She's still in that fresh, innocent phase, believing in everything he tells her. She'll learn, just like I did, that Adrian is not all he seems.

The last group – a table of six – finally pay their check, and leave. They were quite drunk and rowdy, and I'm not surprised they're here so late, but they've left a big tip, which kind of makes up for it. We've been clearing up around them, so there's not much left to do, and I've already let most of the waiting staff go. There's only me, Jackson and Greg left. I check my watch and am surprised to find it's already gone midnight. I'm even more surprised that Rob hasn't come out yet. Every night so far, he's finished up in the kitchen and come out to see me, to check up on things, and make sure the evening's gone okay. Then we've headed off home together. Tonight though, there's no sign of him. Still, I guess the fact that it was a particular busy shift means there's a lot to do in the kitchen too.

We make quick work of the rest of the clearing up, Greg leaves first, followed by Jackson and then I'm on my own. I don't want to wait for Rob, so I lock the front door, using his keys, which he always leaves me with when we open in the evenings, and go through to the kitchen, putting the keys down on the countertop by the door. Even before I've looked up, I'm aware of the awkward atmosphere out here. Rob and Ed are standing talking – well, whispering – and as soon as they become aware of me, Ed says something quietly, then turns and walks toward me, ducking around me and out through the swing doors, without saying a word, or making eye contact. That was damn strange. If I see him at the end of a shift, he normally asks how the evening went, or just asks if I'm okay, and after what happened with that customer earlier, I'm surprised he didn't make a comment, considering he was quick enough to come to my defence.

I look over at Rob, but he's staring at the floor now and doesn't look up. Something's obviously happened out here during the course of the service and I go over to him.

"Is everything okay?" I ask, putting my hands on his arms. He looks up now, but his eyes are dark, like he doesn't recognize who I am. "What's wrong? You didn't come out into the restaurant once the shift was over…"

"No," he replies, his voice quiet and a little aloof. "I—I'm not sure I should come home with you tonight."

That felt like a slap to the face and I take a step back. "Why not?"

His eyes are fixed on mine, like he's trying to read me. "I don't claim to know a lot about relationships, Petra, but I do know they're supposed to be honest, and it's meant to be a two-way street. You said when we first got together that you needed to be sure about me. Well, now I need to be sure about you."

I'm suddenly ice cold. "And you're not?"

"No."

"Am I allowed to know why?"

"Sure." He could be talking to me from Mars, his voice is so distant. "I saw you with that guy earlier. I saw him touching you, saw you letting him, saw you whispering to each other. I didn't like it. I didn't like how it made me feel – how it's making me feel."

"You… you saw us?"

"Yeah, Petra. I fucking saw you." He raises his voice and I flinch at his anger. "Why? Were you just gonna let the guy feel you up and not tell me? For fuck's sake… after everything you said to *me* about flirting—"

"I wasn't flirting." I raise my voice too, interrupting him. "I was talking to Adrian."

His face pales, quite noticeably. He opens his mouth, then closes it again, then he swallows and finally says, "That was Adrian? Your ex?"

And I know I have to come clean. "Yes. Except he's not my ex."

His brow furrows. "I'm sorry. I don't understand."

"He's not my ex. He's my husband."

He seems to stumble and grabs the countertop for support. I move toward him, but he holds up his hand to stop me. "Your husband?" he whispers. "You're still married?"

"Yes. But only on paper," I say quickly. He needs to know this. Now. "We're not even married in name… not really. I went back to using my dad's name as soon as Adrian left. I have no feelings for him, Rob. None."

He nods, like he's trying to understand what I'm saying. Then he runs his hands down his face. I want to hold him. More to the point, I want him to hold me, and I take a step toward him again, just as he moves away and takes a step back.

"When were you gonna tell me?" he asks.

"Tomorrow."

"Tomorrow? Well, that's fucking convenient, isn't it?"

"It's the truth."

"You expect me to believe a fucking thing you say, when our whole relationship is built on a lie?"

"It isn't." I try to swallow down my tears, but I can't, and they start to fall. Even though everything's a blur, I notice Rob's expression soften, and he moves closer, before he stops himself and steps back again.

"I told you," he says. "I told you right from the start that I was serious about you. You knew all about my background, about how I used to live my life, and how I was putting that behind me for you… for us. I've never kept anything from you, not one thing. I've been straight with you from the moment we met. You've had so many chances to tell me, Petra. Why didn't you?"

"I tried," I sob. "I really did. I tried so many times, but the moment was never right, or we got interrupted."

"You mean you haven't been able to find a few minutes in the whole time since we got together to tell me you're still fucking married?" he shouts.

I startle again at the sound of his raised voice. "No," I whisper. "I'm sorry."

He turns away for a moment, and the sight of his back fills me with fear.

"Please," I beg. "Please don't turn away from me. D—don't leave me." His shoulders heave. "I—I'm sorry," I whimper. "I didn't mean for this to happen."

He flips around. "You didn't mean for this to happen?" he repeats. "You didn't mean to lie to me about your marriage? Or you didn't mean to get caught in the lie? Which is it?" He glares at me. "Or is it that you didn't mean for me to fall in love with you, to commit to you, to think about a future with you?"

"A future?" I whisper, looking up into his dark eyes.

"Yes. A future we can't have now, Petra, because you're still married," he yells, breathing hard. "I've reassured you so many times that you're it for me… I've put my heart out there for you, but you're not even free to be mine." He pauses. "And what about April?" he shouts, and I sob even louder. "Have you even thought about what happens to her in all of this?"

"Of course I have."

"Right… you worried about introducing me to her, about letting me into her life, because you were scared about letting her get attached and then what it might do to her, how it might hurt her, if I left you. I knew that. That's why I've been completely honest with you from day one. But what about the consequences of *your* lies, Petra? How's she meant to understand this?" He pauses and runs his fingers through his hair. "You can't play games with people's emotions like this, Petra. For Christ's sake, you let me fall in love with her too," he shouts, although I can hear a crack in his voice, and he takes a moment to calm down. "What did you think would happen when you came back here just now? Did you think you'd tell me that the guy who was feeling up your ass is still married to you, and we'd just carry on as before like nothing had changed? Or were you planning on lying still?"

We stare at each other for a moment and then, as the thought of my nightmare, of my life without him becomes a reality right in front of me, I turn and run, clattering through the swing doors and out into the restaurant. I'm vaguely aware of Ed, taking a step toward me as I run through, knocking over chairs as I pass, but I ignore everything except the need to be somewhere else. Anywhere else but here – with the results of my own actions, my own mistakes, my own lies, staring me in the face.

I reach the door and grab the handle, giving it a firm tug. But it won't budge, because it's locked. I locked it earlier, and left the keys in the kitchen. I'm trapped. I start to breathe fast, to panic, and I tug the door again, over and over.

"Stop." Rob's voice is quiet and gentle beside me. His hand rests over mine. "Calm down," he murmurs, soothingly.

"Open the door."

"No. Not until you've calmed down."

"I am calm."

"Bullshit, Petra."

I turn to face him. He looks worried. "Let me out," I plead.

He sighs and pulls the keys from his pocket, unlocking the door. I go to open it, but he holds it closed, his hand still resting firmly on mine.

"I'll take you home," he says.

"No! Just let me go."

I wrestle away from him and pull the door open, bolting out into the street. I can't bear to see him. I can't bear to see his hurt and know I'm the cause of it. I've ruined everything. I've hurt him, I've hurt myself and I've hurt April, and after everything I've said to him, I know I'll never forgive myself.

Rob

"I'll be back," I call over my shoulder to Ed, and I follow Petra out into the street. There's no way I'm letting her go home by herself and I run behind her, keeping a reasonable distance, but making sure I'm close enough to help her if she needs me. There's a kind of blind desperation to the way she's moving – like she's got no idea where she's going, and she doesn't care much either, and part of me expects her to carry straight on past her own house, and just keep going. I know she won't though, because despite everything I just said to her, April's her world. She'd never leave her baby girl. She'd never do anything to hurt her either, and I feel terrible for accusing her of that. I was hurting – I still am – but saying that to her was wrong.

She reaches the house and fumbles in her jacket pocket for her keys. I'm half tempted to go and help her, but I don't. I stand on the sidewalk at a discreet distance and wait until she's fallen through the door, before I turn and walk away, taking a slow stroll back to the restaurant.

How the fuck can she still be married? And, more importantly, why didn't she tell me? How could she let me get this deep into her life – and April's – and still not tell me such a fundamentally important thing –

that she and April's dad aren't divorced. I stop and shake my head, looking up at the dark night sky. Despite everything I just said to her, I don't really care that she's still married. I mean, obviously that is an issue, but what I'm really struggling with, if I'm honest, is the deceit.

When I get back to the restaurant, Ed's still sitting at table four, where I left him a few minutes ago. I ignore him for a moment, go around behind the bar, grab a bottle of vodka and two glasses and come back over, sitting down opposite him.

He looks from me to the vodka bottle and back again, before grabbing hold of it.

"Before you get started on that," he says calmly, "we need to talk."

"I can talk and drink."

"Not sensibly, you can't."

"Then I'm not sure I wanna talk." I try and get the bottle from him, but he pulls it further away, closer to his body. "Ed, give me the fucking bottle."

"No." His voice is firm. "I heard what you said to Petra in the kitchen."

"And? Are you gonna try and tell me I was wrong?"

"No, I'm not. With something like that, she should've told you." He puts the bottle down on the floor, then leans forward, looking directly at me. "She certainly should've told you before letting you get involved in April's life…"

"My thoughts exactly," I interrupt.

"But she did say she tried to tell you about it," he reasons. "Can you remember her trying? Think about it." He stares at me.

I try to think back, try to blot out all the good things, all the times I've been inside her, all the times I've touched her, and I've tasted her. I feel tears welling in my eyes and shake my head.

"Think, Rob," Ed urges.

"I am."

"Not about the right things, you're not."

I take a deep breath. "I guess there have been a few times where she's started to say something and either April's come in, or her mom has, or we've been here and someone's interrupted." I lean back and stare at the ceiling, the down-lighter, shining in my eyes. "And she said she needed to speak to me the other morning, but you called and told me about Scarlett going into hospital. We agreed we'd set some time aside…" I pause, feeling like a fucking idiot. "Tomorrow," I finish.

"Tomorrow?"

"Yeah. She just said she planned to tell me about Adrian tomorrow. I basically told her I didn't believe her – I said it was a bit convenient, her saying that. But we did agree earlier that we'd find some time tomorrow to talk."

"So she was probably telling the truth?"

I nod slowly, and look back at him. "The thing is though, she's had so many chances to tell me."

"Like when?"

"I don't know."

He shakes his head. "You're forgetting how crazy it gets around here. But you guys have also been dealing with her problems at home, then Jasmine's been off, which has meant more work for everyone… but especially for you, and a lot of the time, April's around. I can't imagine Petra wants to have this conversation in front of her daughter."

"No, I get that. But what about at night? She could have told me when we got home, one evening."

He stares at me for a moment. "At night?" he queries. "What do you guys do when you get home at night?" he asks.

"We… we go straight to bed."

"Right. To sleep?"

"Sometimes. I've been pretty tired."

"I'm not asking you to justify anything," he says quietly. "I'm just saying that, at the end of each day, you go home and you get into bed together. And you're now suggesting that you think that would have been a good time for her to start talking about the fact that she's not divorced from April's father? You really wanna hear that when you're in bed with her?"

I let my head fall into my hands. "No. Probably not."

"Probably?" he queries. "I'm not you, Rob, but I know I wouldn't wanna talk about that when I was in bed with the woman I loved."

"Can I have that drink now?" I ask him.

"Drink. Singular. Yes." He picks up the bottle, opens it and pours us both a shot, which I swallow down in one go, putting the glass back on the table. "I'm not giving you another one," he says.

"I don't want another one."

"Good." He smiles over at me. "So, what are you gonna do now?" he asks.

I sigh and lean back again. "I feel like I need some time to myself, to think it all through. Just a few days, maybe…"

"Why?" he asks.

I tilt my head forward again, and stare at him. "Because the woman I love has just told me she's still married to her daughter's father, which makes my plan to propose tomorrow kinda redundant."

"You do get that her marriage is ancient history, right?" he says.

"Yeah, I guess." I can't hide the self-doubt from him. "But how am I supposed to propose now?"

"Petra loves you, Rob. She wants to be with you. The rest is just paperwork."

"Paperwork and honesty."

"Did she ever actually tell you she was divorced?" he asks.

"No. She just failed to tell me she wasn't."

"Which you've just kind of admitted was a timing issue, not a deliberate omission on her part," he points out.

I shrug my shoulders. I know what he's saying is right, but the shock of hearing she's not free is still kinda hard to accept.

"Did you mean to sound like you were breaking up with her?" Ed's voice jerks me out of my thoughts.

"What? No, of course not."

"Really?"

"No. I was angry. I was fucking angry. I still am to a certain extent, because I really don't see that it's that hard to find five minutes to tell me something as important as this… but I didn't break up with her."

"Well that's how it sounded from where I was. You just told her you don't have a future anymore. That seemed kinda final to me. And I think that's why she ran. I think to her it sounded like you were ending it, or like you were about to, and I think she blames herself. But that probably just makes it so much worse, because she's gonna be feeling responsible for all the hurt – not just to the two of you, but to April as well."

I stare at him.

"What should I do?" I ask him.

He sighs. "First, you answer two questions," he says.

"What two questions?"

He looks at me, leaning forward. "Can you imagine your life without her?"

I don't reply. He waits for a moment and I raise my eyebrows. "Next question."

"What would you give up for her?"

I get to my feet.

He smiles, stands and picks up the vodka bottle and the two glasses, taking them over to the bar. "I guess you know what you've gotta do," he says over his shoulder, but I'm already on my way out the door.

Chapter Seventeen

Petra

I run along the sidewalk, not really aware of where I'm going, just needing to go. These last few weeks have been the happiest, the most fulfilling of my life, and I've blown all of that to pieces, because I didn't tell Rob the truth. I know if things were the other way around, I'd find it hard to forgive him, or to trust him ever again, so I can't expect him to feel any different. And from the way he was talking, he doesn't. And I know that in the morning, I'm going to have to find a way to tell April that Rob won't be there to make biscotti with her, because Rob won't be seeing us anymore. I gulp down a sob. How am I going to do that? She's going to hate me too…

I get back to the house and manage to get my key out, although my hands are shaking so much, I struggle to get it into the lock, and when I do, I literally fall through the door, stumbling into the hallway, and closing the door behind me.

"What's going on?"

David appears from the living room, looking concerned, followed closely by my mom.

"You're still up?" I say the first thing that comes into my head.

"Yes." Mom looks at me. It must be obvious I've been crying, but she doesn't comment… yet.

"Why?" Surely they weren't waiting up for me – Mom hasn't done that before, although this is the first time David's been here when I've got back home.

"We've spent most of the evening discussing Clare's situation," Mom explains, coming a little closer. "We needed to unwind, so we started watching a movie."

"I see."

"And now you can tell us what's wrong, why you've been crying…" She pauses. "And where Rob is."

At the mention of his name, I burst into noisy tears.

"Come and sit down," she says, putting her arm around me and leading me into the living room. "You'll wake April."

We sit together on the couch, and David takes the chair opposite, trying not to look embarrassed.

"Shall I leave you to it?" he offers.

"No, it's fine. Stay," I murmur through my tears. He's gonna find out soon enough what a fool I've been. And I'd rather just go through this once.

"So what's happened?" Mom asks, handing me a Kleenex from the box on the coffee table.

I take it from her, holding it in my hands. "Adrian came into the restaurant this evening," I mumble.

"Did you say Adrian?" she asks, clearly surprised.

I nod.

"He came into the restaurant?"

I nod again.

"And?"

"And he was as rude and obnoxious as usual."

"Excuse me," David interrupts, "but who's Adrian?"

Mom and I both look at him. "He's Petra's ex-husband… Well, husband, I suppose…" and as she says that, I burst into tears again. "What's is it?" she says, turning back to me once more.

"It's just that," I manage to say, between sobs.

"Just what?"

"Him being my husband."

"Well, he is, Petra. You married him."

"I know."

"I'm sorry if I'm being dense, but am I missing something?" David asks from the other side of the coffee table.

I look over at him.

"It's the fact that I'm still married to him," I try to explain.

"Yes?"

"And… and that I didn't tell Rob," I blurt out, weeping into the tissue.

A momentary silence descends, but is broken almost immediately by my mom. "Excuse me?" She raises her voice.

"Keep your voice down, Thea," David whispers. "April's just upstairs."

"I know that." She turns on him, then looks back at me. "How could you?" she says, with a more chilling calm to her voice. "How could you be such a hypocrite?"

"Mom?" I stare at her. I don't know why, but I'd hoped she'd be supportive.

"How could you lie to the man you claim to love?" she demands, standing and looking down at me, disappointment and anger etched on her face.

"I don't claim to love him. I do love him."

"Really? You've got a funny way of showing it, young lady." She hasn't called me that for years, and suddenly I feel like I'm sixteen, and being told off, and I wish my dad was here. He always knew how to handle every situation, and when he was around, I never felt unsafe. Ever. Right now, I feel like my whole world is falling apart, and I have no-one to turn to.

"I made a mistake," I murmur.

"Yes you did." She's not gonna let up. "Why didn't you tell him the truth about yourself? I asked you… didn't I? I asked you if you'd told him about Adrian and you said yes. You lied to him, you lied to me, and you had the nerve to judge me for seeing David behind your back, when you were lying to Rob the whole time." She pauses again, staring at me. "I notice he's not with you… I'm assuming now he knows, he doesn't want anything to do with you." She shakes her head. "And what about April? How do you think she's going to feel?" I start crying again. "I can't even look at you," she says and turns around, storming out of the room.

I guess a few minutes go by, but I'm not really sure, because all I can do is cry, and cry. I should've known she'd react like that, I suppose, but deep down, I hoped she'd understand.

"Do you need another one of these?" I look up and see David standing above me, offering the box of Kleenex. I take another one and wipe my eyes and nose.

"Thank you."

He sits beside me, putting the box between us.

"I suppose you're going to tell me I've got it all wrong too," I mutter, not looking at him.

"No," he replies, and I turn to face him. He looks concerned more than anything else, his eyes kind and sympathetic. "You don't need me to tell you that. You already know it for yourself, so me saying it isn't going to help."

He's right. Nothing anyone says could possibly make me feel any worse than I already do.

"I'm sorry I judged you and Mom. I've done so much wrong myself, I had no right to judge anyone else."

"You haven't done that much wrong," he replies softly. "And your mom will see that when she calms down. I'll talk to her later." For a moment, I'm reminded of my dad, of all the times Mom and I would fight when I was a teenager and he'd keep the peace between us, and for the first time in ages, I manage a smile. "Divorce isn't always as easy as people think it is," he continues quietly. "I don't often talk about mine, and it was comparatively straightforward."

"I'd agree with you, except Adrian and I aren't divorced."

"Is there a reason for that?" he asks.

"We're not still in love, if that's what you're wondering."

"I didn't think you were. But you've been separated for some time, haven't you?"

"Yes. He left a few months before April was born."

"So why have you never made it official?"

"Neither of us could afford it."

279

He stares at me, and then nods his head. "I know it's expensive. I paid for mine and Marianne's costs, and it shocked me how much the lawyers wanted to charge. And we were completely amicable."

"Well, at the time, because Adrian was having an affair, and had accused me of sleeping around to justify that, and was querying April's parentage, I seriously doubted our divorce would be anything but acrimonious and drawn-out… so it could have been even more expensive. And I had April to think about. I had little enough money as it was; I didn't want to spend what I did have on legal fees, when I could be spending it on her."

He nods. "So what happened with Rob? When he found out, I mean."

"He got really mad with me."

"Can you blame him?" he asks, reasonably.

"No."

"What did he say?"

I shrug. "I think he broke up with me."

"You *think*?"

"He said we don't have a future, and reminded me that my lies will affect April too." I look across at him and start crying again.

"He's hurting, Petra. But that doesn't necessarily mean he wants it to end. You've got to understand that guys hurt too, you know. We're not immune."

"He—he told me that too once."

"Well, he was right."

"Do you think he might forgive me?" I ask him.

"I don't know." His honesty is chilling, and just as I feel yet more tears start to fall, there's a soft knocking on the door. "But I think he might," he murmurs, and gets to his feet, going out into the hallway.

Rob

I run all the way back to Petra's house again, relieved that I didn't insist on drinking that bottle of vodka. If I'd been drunk, I doubt I'd have been able to make sense of what Ed was saying to me – and he was making more sense than I have in a long while.

I get to the door and am about to bang on it, when I realize how late it is, and that April will be asleep, as will Thea. I can only knock quietly, and just hope to God that Petra hears me. If she doesn't, I'll have to text her and get her to come down and speak to me. I tap on the door, just gently, and wait.

Within a minute, the door opens and David greets me, smiling sympathetically.

"Come in," he says.

"Thanks." It's late for him to be here, but I don't comment. It's none of my business, and I've got more important things to worry about.

"Petra's in the living room," he says, standing to one side and letting me pass.

I go through and see her sitting on the couch, crying her eyes out. She doesn't look up, and David comes and stands at my side, just a little in front of me.

"Petra," he says and now she turns, sees me and starts to really sob. "Do you want me to stay?" he asks.

She doesn't reply. She doesn't do anything except weep into a tissue she's got screwed up in her hand.

"She'll be fine with me," I tell him.

He nods his head, turning to me. "Go easy on her," he whispers. "She's scared."

"That makes two of us." He looks at me for a moment, then moves away.

"David?" Petra calls, looking up again, and focusing on him, not me.

"Yes?" He stops and turns back.

"Thank you for listening," she says, sucking in a breath.

He smiles over at her. "You're welcome. And don't worry about your mom. I'll talk to her. It'll all be fine in the morning."

Petra nods and looks down at her hands, clasped in her lap. David leaves, and I hear him walking slowly up the stairs.

Now I'm here, I don't really know what to say, or where to start, but I know I need to be closer to her than this, so I go over and sit beside her, leaving maybe a foot or so between us. There's a box of Kleenex on the couch, and I move them onto the coffee table. Petra stills, but doesn't look up.

"What was that about your mom?" I ask, because I'm not sure either of us is ready yet to talk about the enormous Adrian-shaped elephant in the room.

"We had a fight," she whispers.

"What? Tonight?"

She nods. "When I got back here, just now," she confirms.

"What about?"

"Us."

"Us, as in you and me?"

"Yes."

"Tell me," I say quietly.

"It's not your problem, Rob."

"Yeah, it is."

I move just a little closer.

"She was mad at me. So, I guess that makes two of you."

"Why was she mad at you?" I ask. I'm not gonna deny that I was mad at her – that would be ridiculous, given what I said to her earlier, and how I said it.

"Because I'd lied to you, and I'd judged her and David. She was really angry with me."

I reach over and take her hands in one of mine. "You didn't lie to me," I murmur softly.

"Yes I did." I hear the crack in her voice. "I lied to you about Adrian."

"No you didn't. You didn't tell me the truth about being married to him still, but that's not the same as lying. It's not like you ever actually told me you were divorced, is it?"

"That's not what you said earlier," she whispers. "You said our whole relationship was built on a lie."

"I know. I was mad at you earlier. I'm sorry."

"Are you mad at me now?" she asks, sounding scared.

"A little."

She finally turns to look at me and my heart actually hurts at what I see. Her eyes are puffy and filled with tears, but also with so much pain, and holding her hand isn't enough. I reach over and pull her into my arms. She's stiff, but she lets me, and I hold onto her.

"Why did you run?" I ask her.

"Because you were mad," she replies, sniffling. "And because it sounded like you were breaking up with me. I was scared. I didn't want to hear that. I couldn't bear it. I couldn't bear knowing I'd done that to us... to you, and to April. It was all too much."

"So you ran, rather than stay and talk?"

She nods, but doesn't respond.

I lean back but keep hold of her, looking down into her face. She's staring at my chest.

"Look at me," I say quietly. She doesn't. "Look at me, baby." Her eyes dart up to mine and I know it's because I just called her 'baby'. "You have *got* to learn to communicate better. You've been crap at it since the first day I met you, but you really need to start trying."

"Why?"

"Why? How can you ask that?" I cup her cheek with my hand. "If you could communicate better, you'd almost certainly have found a way of telling me about Adrian, then we wouldn't be in this situation. But if we were, for some reasons, you could tell me how you're feeling, and we could talk it through, rather than me having to drag your thoughts and emotions out of you every damn time. I wouldn't have to keep guessing what you want, or what you need, or how you feel, because you could tell me."

She stares up at me. "I'm sorry."

"What for?"

"All of it."

"I don't want you to be sorry."

"Do you want me at all?" She stares into my eyes.

"Yes. Of course I want you."

Tears fall from her eyes and I wipe them away with my thumbs. "Then why… why were you gonna break up with me?"

"I wasn't. If it sounded like I was, then I apologize. That's not what I intended. I was disappointed, and I was mad at you. But I wasn't breaking up with you."

"Disappointed?"

"Yeah."

"Why?"

"Because things aren't what I thought they were."

She nods her head slowly.

"And now?" she asks. "How do you feel now?"

"I'm still disappointed, and a little mad, and I'm hurt," I say honestly. "But none of that means I want to break up with you. It just means I wanted to yell a bit, try and get some answers from you, maybe spend some time by myself, thinking things through. That's all."

"And do you still want that?"

"What?"

"What you just said; to yell, and get answers, and spend time by yourself… away from us." Her voice cracks on those last three words.

"Well, I'm done yelling," I admit. "But we do need to talk, and there are things I want to know, and questions I need answers to."

"And the time by yourself…?" she asks, doubtfully.

"I can live without that, if us being apart hurts you."

"But…"

"Petra," I interrupt. "I told you that I would never leave you, no matter what happened. You had a dream about me leaving and I told you it would never happen. I meant it. I will never leave you. And if being away from me hurts you this much, then we'll work out our problems together."

"Our problems?"

"Yeah."

"You mean my lies."

I sigh. "No. I've already said. I don't feel like you lied. And I've apologized for saying that – I was wrong."

"Do you mean the fact that I'm still married then?"

"No, although that's a bit of an issue." She tilts her head to one side, but I don't want to explain what I mean by that, so I continue, "What I'm talking about is the fact that you didn't trust me enough to tell me."

She sobs out a heartfelt cry. "I did trust you. I do trust you, Rob."

"If you trust me, I don't really understand why you couldn't have just come out and said it. You told me it's just a marriage on paper, so why was it so hard to tell me?"

"I was scared, and nervous. I wasn't sure how you'd react."

"Exactly. You didn't trust me enough to stay with you, to love you and want you, no matter what. Did you honestly think I'd break up with you over this?"

She stares at me. "I didn't know. I couldn't be sure what you'd do. And anyway, you kinda did break up with me, just now."

"No. I. Didn't. I've explained. I didn't mean it to sound like that. I'm sorry if it did. But even if I had, it wouldn't have been because you're still married, but because you didn't tell me about it. Did you really think I wouldn't have stuck around for you, just because things are a little bit complicated?"

She shrugs and I sigh, long and deep.

"Do you really think that little of me? Of yourself? Of us?" I ask her.

She doesn't reply and I turn her to face me, holding her at arm's length and looking into her eyes. She clearly has no idea what she means to me… but I think I know of something that might convince her.

"Do you remember me telling you about the women in Ed's past?" I say. She looks puzzled.

"Yes, but what's that got to do with this?"

"Humor me. Do you remember me telling you that Sam helped him out of those relationships because they weren't suitable?"

"Yes." She nods her head, looking fearful. "W—What are you trying to tell me?"

I put my index finger on her lips to quieten her.

"What I didn't explain properly was how Sam went about it. He didn't actively persuade Ed into or out of anything. All Sam did was to ask him two simple questions. Ed would answer him. Those answers would tell Ed everything he needed to know, and he'd be able to make his own decision."

"What were the questions?" she asks, and I smile to myself. At least she's interested enough to want to know.

"The first one was, 'Can you imagine your life without her in it?', and the second was, 'What would you give up for her?'." I move just fractionally closer to her. "It's kinda like when your dad met your mom. He got back to the States, and realized he couldn't live without her, and when it came down to it, and she asked him to, he gave up his career to be with her. Ed asked me those questions when I first met you, the first time you ran out on me after we'd been kissing behind the bar. I couldn't find you, or any way to contact you, but Ed had an idea for how I could go about it. Before he revealed that to me, he asked me those two questions. He wanted to make sure I was serious about you; that I wasn't gonna mess you around."

"What did you answer?" she asks.

"I told him that I *could* imagine my life without you in it, but I didn't want to, and that I would give up everything for you."

More tears stream from her eyes.

"I'm sorry," she sobs. "I'm so sorry. I spoiled everything."

I move closer still. "You didn't. That's what I'm trying to tell you. Ed asked me those same two questions again, about twenty minutes ago, when I got back to the restaurant—"

"*Back* to the restaurant? When did you leave it?"

"When I followed you home. I came after you to make sure you got back here safely."

She bursts into noisy tears and I wait, grabbing a Kleenex from the box and wiping her eyes.

"I couldn't answer him," I explain. "Not this time." And that's it. She wails and covers her face with her hands, her shoulders heaving.

"How am I going to tell April?" she cries. "I've got so much wrong. It's all my fault. She's going to hate me…"

"Petra," I interrupt. "Will you stop crying and let me finish? Please?"

She takes a moment to calm down, but after a few deep breaths, she looks up at me. Her eyes are tear-filled, and sad.

"Sorry," she murmurs.

"Don't be." I pause for a moment, then continue, "The only reason I didn't tell Ed my answers, is because I realized I needed to tell you, not him. I want you to ask me those two questions, Petra."

She hesitates, and swallows hard, then wipes her eyes. "Okay," she whispers. "Um…"

"Can you remember them?" I ask.

"Yes." I wait, and she takes a deep breath. I think she's scared. "C —can you imagine your life without me in it?" she asks, her voice a barely audible whisper.

"No," I reply immediately, leaning a little closer to her. "I'm having a hard time picturing the next hour without you in it. That's why I had to come and see you tonight… right now. Ed told me it sounded to him like I was breaking up with you. I didn't realize, and I had to come and make sure you understood that I wasn't, that I'm not leaving you; I never will."

Her mouth is slightly open and she's staring at me.

"Can you remember the second question?" I prompt.

"Um… What would you be willing to give up for me?" she murmurs. I pull her close, and whisper into her ear, "My life."

Chapter Eighteen

Petra

"Did you just say…?"

"I'd give my life for you." He leans back and looks down into my eyes, his so full of love it takes my breath away. "You're my whole world, baby. When Ed said he thought I was breaking up with you, I was so damn scared… scared at the thought of being without you; scared of never seeing you, holding you, touching you, making love with you. I was scared of no longer being a part of your life – and April's. You both mean so much to me, Petra, and just the thought of not having you with me is terrifying."

Tears start falling yet again.

"Do you think there's any chance you're gonna stop crying any time soon?" he asks, smiling down at me for the first time in hours, and handing me another Kleenex.

"No." I shake my head.

"Why are you crying now?" he asks.

"Because I can't believe how lucky I am. I can't believe we're back together…" I pause, looking at him. "We are, aren't we?"

"As far as I'm concerned, we were never apart."

I smile through my tears and lean my forehead against his.

"And because I don't have to break April's heart."

He places his finger beneath my chin, raising my face and looking into my eyes. "I will never do anything that hurts your baby girl," he whispers. "Never."

And that's enough to set me off again.

"What do I have to do to stop you crying?" He pulls me close and holds me.

"You could take me to bed," I murmur into him.

He pulls away and looks down at me, his face alarmingly serious. "Not right now," he whispers.

"But I thought…" I'm suddenly very scared.

"Don't," he says quietly. "Don't look so worried. I'm not saying we won't go to bed, but first there are some things we need to talk through."

"There are?" What more can we need to discuss at this time of the morning?

"Of course there are. Remember? I said I needed answers?" He looks away for a moment, then turns back to me. "And I've just realized that one of the reasons you found it so hard to tell me about Adrian, was me."

"What do you mean? This isn't your fault, Rob. It's mine."

"What I mean is, I know you've tried to tell me. I've been aware of you saying you had something to discuss with me, and I've let other things get in the way."

"They weren't always your fault," I reason.

"Sometimes they were. Sometimes I just wanted to get you into bed, to get inside you, so much, that I didn't want wait, or listen, or do anything sensible. But I'm gonna listen now."

"To what?" I ask.

"To you. I—I want you to tell me about him."

"You do?" I'm surprised. "You want to know about my marriage?"

"Yeah. Not in too much detail, if that's okay." He smiles, but it doesn't touch his eyes, and I know what he means. "I just want to try and understand a bit better."

"Okay. So, what do you want to know?"

He pauses, then sighs. "When did you meet?" he asks.

"Seven years ago," I reply. "I was twenty, and working in a small photographic studio, learning the trade."

"Taking what kind of photographs?" he asks, holding me in his arms, and pulling us both down onto the couch, so we're lying together.

"Fashion. It was what I always wanted to do." I look up at him. "This feels nice, by the way."

"Yeah it does." He kisses my forehead. "So, you were learning the fashion photography business and he… he walked in the door?"

"Yes. He was a personal trainer – well, he still is."

"That explains the physique," Rob murmurs.

"He's not that impressive," I tell him.

"He looked it to me."

"Well, trust me. He's not." I place my hand on his firm chest and let it rest there, hoping he'll understand, but then I remember, he asked me to communicate better. "There is such as thing as being too muscle-bound," I explain. "I much prefer the way you look. I love everything about you." He smiles again and although I'm not being very articulate, it's an improvement on nothing. "Besides," I add, "he had to spend eight hours a day in the gym to look like that."

"Eight hours?"

I nod.

"Didn't he get bored?"

"He had a low attention span."

Rob smirks. "So, he came into the studio?" he prompts, getting back to the story.

"Yes. He also did some part-time modelling work."

He huffs. "Somehow, I'm not surprised."

I decide to ignore his comment and continue, "After the first day's shooting had finished, he asked me if I'd like to go out for a drink with him."

"And you said 'yes'?"

I nod. "Yes. Then the next day, he asked me out for dinner. After that, we went back to his place—"

"And you can stop right there," he interrupts. "I can work out the next part for myself."

"We got married six months later."

"Six months?"

"I know it was quick, but my parents had married within weeks of meeting, and they'd been so happy together. I wasn't at all worried, even though I knew everything wasn't perhaps as it should have been."

He leans up on one elbow, looking down at me.

"What do you mean?" he asks.

"The sex was disappointing," I explain.

"In what way?"

"You said you didn't want details."

He smiles. "I didn't want details of him giving you a good time. But if it wasn't great, I don't mind so much." I shake my head at him. "So?" he prompts.

"I was… I was a virgin when I met him," I explain, with a little hesitancy. "I knew vaguely what to expect, and I'd had a few orgasms myself beforehand…"

"With toys?" he asks.

"No. Just by myself." He nods. "But with Adrian…"

"What?"

"It wasn't the same."

"In what way."

"It just didn't work the same."

He looks at me. "I'll get you to communicate one day," he says, shaking his head. "What you're trying to say is he couldn't make you come. Is that right?"

I nod. "Yes. Thank you for saying it."

"You're welcome." He smiles.

"Did you talk to him?"

"I tried once we were married, but he told me it was my fault."

"Asshole," Rob hisses.

"I didn't see how that could be right, not when it had worked fine before I met him."

"So, what did you do?"

"Well, after a while, I started… um…"

"Masturbating?" he offers.

"Yes. Thank you again. He used to keep irregular hours, so I'd wait for him to leave, and then I'd amuse myself for a while."

"Okay. I don't see a problem with that."

"He did. He came back one evening, because he'd forgotten his wallet, and caught me…"

"Playing with yourself?" he suggests. I nod and just smile my thanks this time. "What happened?"

"He was angry."

"He was? Why?" Rob seems genuinely confused.

"Because I was doing that."

"He didn't want to join in?"

"No."

"I would've."

"Hmm… I noticed." I can't help remembering what happened when Rob came out of the shower the other night and discovered me with my hand between my legs.

"Well, seeing you like that, it's kinda hard to resist."

"The thing is, I knew you wouldn't mind…"

"Of course not. I love your pleasure, however you get it."

"Well, he felt differently. He stood and yelled at me. He wanted to know what I was thinking about – or to be more precise, who I was thinking about. I tried to tell him that I was thinking about him, but he wouldn't believe me. He kept saying I must be thinking about someone else, that I must have a lover. He went on and on, and then he stormed out, calling me a slut. He didn't come back until the next day. I was fairly sure he'd spent the night with someone else, but when I asked him, he told me it was none of my business what he did."

"How long had you been married by this stage?" he asks.

"About a year. After that, things just got worse."

"How?"

"He started to question everywhere I went, everyone I met, every phone call I took, every text I received. He'd check my phone for messages. He'd always been a little bit possessive, but I'd taken it as a kind of love. This was something else. It was overbearing and suffocating. When we went out, to restaurants, like Rosa's, he'd insist on choosing my food for me, and then he'd order the most fattening dishes on the menu. Before long, I'd gained around fifty pounds, and I felt so ugly. I wasn't really surprised when he started calling me names, and telling me that I didn't turn him on anymore. What did surprise me, was that he kept accusing me of sleeping around. I had to change jobs in the end, because a lot of the models were male, and he came into work and accused one of them of having an affair with me. It wasn't true, but Adrian made such a scene, I couldn't face going back there. We even stopped going out, because if a guy in a restaurant looked at me, he'd start yelling at me as soon as we got home, asking me what was going on, how I knew the man, what he was like in bed… It was humiliating."

I stop, and take a breath, and Rob holds me really close. "Did you still sleep with Adrian?" he asks.

"No, not really. Like I said, he told me I didn't turn him on, but he came home quite drunk one evening and we ended up in bed. The next day, he apologized. I think that just made it worse, really."

"And after that?"

"Well, that was the night I got pregnant with April," I explain. "I wasn't on the pill at the time, and it was just one of those things. It wasn't planned…"

"But you wouldn't change it?"

"In terms of having April, no."

"What did Adrian do when you found out you were pregnant?"

"He accused me of having an affair – again. Although God knows who with. He was adamant he couldn't be the father, even though I reminded him of his drunken fumble with me. He went out that night and didn't come back for a couple of days."

"And then?"

"The accusations kept coming, as did the prolonged absences. And then, when I was five months pregnant, not long after my dad died, Adrian finally admitted he'd been having an affair. It had been going on since the night he'd caught me in bed with myself. I wasn't at all surprised. I wasn't sure what to do to start with, so I just carried on as usual, but then a couple of days later, I was out doing the grocery shopping and I had to drive back past his gym, and I saw him coming out with a brunette on his arm. They were all over each other. She was tall, slim, beautiful…"

"Stop right there," Rob interrupts. "*You're* beautiful. If he was too dumb to see that, that's his loss."

I smile up at him. "I didn't see the point in pretending anymore, so I went home, packed my bags and left."

"And moved back in with your mom?"

"Yeah."

"Did he contact you again?"

"Yes, just the once. When April was born, I got in touch with him to let him know he had a daughter. He sent me a text message, telling me she was nothing to do with him, and he didn't want to see either of us, or hear from me ever again. That hurt – more for April than for me. I wanted her to know her father."

"He doesn't deserve the name," Rob says, with a hint of anger in his voice.

"No, he doesn't. You've already been more of a father to her than he ever was."

He smiles. "Did he ask about her tonight, when you saw him?"

"No."

"Then she's better off without him," he says.

"I know."

"Can I ask you something?" His voice is quiet.

"Yes."

"Why did he touch your ass like that?"

"Because he felt it was his right." I look up into his eyes and the anger I see there frightens me so much, I pull away from him.

Rob

"Where are you going?"

"You're mad again," she whimpers, trying to pull away a little more forcefully.

"Not with you. Your ex – well, your husband – doesn't wanna come near me any time soon though. You're not a piece of meat, Petra. He doesn't get to manhandle you."

"But you do?" she asks.

"No!" How can she think like that? I guess because he's made her doubt herself, and so have I. I calm my voice before speaking again. "No. I don't have that right either, not unless you say it's okay. And he sure as fuck doesn't. Not after what he did to you."

I pull her back into my arms and hold her close.

"What did he say to make you smile the way you did tonight?" I ask her, remembering her expression.

"He told me he wants a divorce. He's a partner at the gym now and he can afford to pay for it – for both of us – and he told me he wants to marry the woman he was with tonight."

"The blonde?" I clarify.

"Yes."

"So was money the only reason you didn't get a divorce before now?"

"Yes."

I let out a long sigh. "I wish you'd told me. I'd have paid for it myself, if I'd known."

"It's not your problem, Rob."

"Like hell it isn't. It's to do with you – that makes it my problem."

I hold her for a long while, just savoring the feel of her.

"I don't envy that poor blonde," Petra says at last.

"Why?"

"Because Adrian hasn't changed, and she'll find that out to her cost."

"How do you mean?" I ask her, feeling intrigued.

"He was just the same arrogant, chauvinist, rude son-of-a-bitch that he always was—"

"What did he say to you?" I interrupt, sitting up and pulling her with me.

"Nothing I couldn't handle."

"Tell me." I'm not taking no for an answer.

"He just made a snide remark about me being a waitress now, and then later, when he was telling me he wanted to marry his date, and that he wanted a divorce, he made a comment about it not really affecting me, because no-one would wanna be with me anyway."

"Did you tell him about us?"

"No," she replies. "It didn't seem worth it. He wouldn't have believed me anyway."

"I wish you'd come and found me. I'd have come and put him straight."

She smiles. "I wish I had too. I'd have loved to see the look on his face when he saw you."

I take a moment, then lay us back down again. "The thing is, Petra… I don't want him paying for your divorce. Will you let me handle it?"

"I can't, Rob."

"Yeah. You can. One of my many cousins is a divorce lawyer. I'm sure he'd deal with it for you. And if Antonio is representing you, then I know he'll look out for you, and he'll make sure you don't have to see Adrian by yourself, because I'm damned if I'm letting that asshole anywhere near you ever again."

"Can we talk it through tomorrow?" she asks.

"Sure. But at least speak with Antonio before you decide anything?"

"Okay."

"And let me help you. I don't want Adrian thinking he still has any power over you, or that he can call the shots."

"Neither do I."

I hold her for a moment. "I'm sorry," I say, finally.

She leans up, resting her hand on my chest and looking down at me. "Why are you sorry?" she asks. "I'm the one who's got it all wrong. I'm the one who's sorry."

I put my fingers across her lips. "No, baby. I got jealous… I saw you with him, saw him touching you, and talking to you like that, and got jealous. I got angry too, and I took it out on you, without thinking it through first. Then when you told me he was Adrian, all I could think about was that you'd been with him, that you'd been married to him, made love with him… made April with him. And then, discovering that you still were married to him, and that he'd been touching you like that, making you smile in that way… Christ, I was so jealous." I hesitate for a moment, slightly scared of saying what I'm thinking, but knowing that I held something back from her this afternoon, and I have to be honest… now, more than ever. "This afternoon, upstairs, when we made love," I begin quietly. "It was so quick – much quicker than I wanted it to be – and I was worried I'd disappointed you. I was scared."

"Is that why you were saying all those things about letting you know if I was ever unhappy with you?"

"Yes." I nod my head. "I don't ever want to let you down, or leave you feeling frustrated, or—"

"How could you even begin to think that?" she asks. "This afternoon was amazing, just like it always is. And it was just what I needed."

"Even though it was over so quickly?"

"We didn't have very long."

"I know. But…"

"Rob, we can't always make love for hours on end. There's nothing wrong with a quickie."

"Did you really just say that?" I ask, feeling a little amazed she communicated herself so clearly.

"Yes, I did. And I meant it." She moves a little closer. "But even if I had felt a little disappointed, even if things had ended faster than I'd wanted, I wouldn't leave you because of that. You give me so much pleasure and I do understand that sometimes things… don't quite work out."

"But that's never happened before," I whisper.

"Rob, you're exhausted at the moment,"

"So?"

"So cut yourself some slack. And anyway, it was perfect as far as I was concerned."

"I was so scared of disappointing you, of losing you," I murmur, pulling her down on top of me, her body along the length of mine. I hold her for a while, our breathing matched.

"You know you've got nothing to be jealous of, with Adrian, don't you?" she says eventually.

"No."

"Well, you haven't."

"Petra… You were – sorry, you *are* – married to him. He's April's biological father. You loved him once upon a time, even if you don't love him now."

"And?"

"And that's a lot more than I've ever had with anyone." She looks up at me. "I know you don't like talking about – or thinking about – my past, but what you had with him is so much more, and seeing you with him made me feel really insecure."

"What have you got to feel insecure about? You're gorgeous, Rob. Women fall over themselves to be with you."

"So? You're gorgeous too, in case you haven't noticed. And the women who fall over themselves don't mean a damn thing to me. They never did, even before I met you. They just wanted me for sex. I'm not gonna lie to you and tell you it wasn't entirely mutual, but do you honestly think that women who give out their phone number to the waiter in a restaurant are looking for anything other than a meaningless one night stand? Do you actually think they would even remember my name a few days later – if they bothered to find it out in the first place. Nothing about what I did had anything to do with love. Don't you see? What you and Adrian had was so much more."

She stares at me for a moment. "What about now?" she whispers. "When women talk to you, and make suggestions, or give you their numbers…" I can still hear her insecurity, even though I've told her nothing could tempt me away from her.

"I've told you over and over, Petra, I love you. Please don't doubt that. I don't want anyone else, anymore than you want Adrian back. I know he ground down your self confidence, but you're with me now and I think you're perfect. I'm not just saying that, baby. You're absolutely perfect for me. And I really wish you'd stop feeling so negative about yourself still. I wish you could see yourself through my eyes, so you could see how beautiful you really are, and then you'd stop doubting yourself, and learn to love yourself, like I do."

Chapter Nineteen

Petra

I'm still staring at him, still trying to take in his words, and the fact that he's here, that I'm in his arms, and that he still wants me, still loves me, when he shifts, turns us on our sides, with me at the back of the couch, and clambers to his feet.

"Please don't go." I can't help the words, or the note of panic behind them.

"Hey…" He crouches down, and cups my cheek with his hand. "I'm not going anywhere. I told you, I'll never leave you."

"Then where are you going?"

"Nowhere. It's late, baby. I just wanna take you to bed, that's all."

I smile up at him and he takes my hand and pulls me to my feet. I'm bone tired – I'm beyond bone tired.

"Come here," he whispers and leans down, lifting me into his arms.

"What are you doing?"

"Carrying you upstairs." He starts to walk toward the hallway.

"I'm too heavy to carry that far."

He stops. "Enough, Petra." He looks down at me. "You're not heavy."

"I think you'll find I am compared with a lot of women. I may have lost some of the weight I put on when I was with Adrian, but I'm by no means as thin as I used to be."

"Firstly, I'm don't make comparisons, so who cares about other women. And secondly, I've never been overly keen on skinny women anyway. I love your curves."

"Well, there are a lot of curves on me to love."

"Stop it." He's serious. "I mean it, Petra. I love you as you are."

"Thank you," I murmur, because I can't think of anything else to say.

"You don't have to thank me. Loving you is easy."

He starts to walk again, flicking off all the lights as he goes, then climbs the stairs easily, and takes me into my bedroom, closing the door behind us. He doesn't bother with the lights; the drapes are open and there's enough moonlight to see by. He puts me down on the floor and, without a word, starts to undo the buttons on my blouse, letting it drop to the floor by my feet. My bra follows, and then he kneels and unfastens my jeans, pulling them and my panties down to my ankles and helping me step out.

"Get into bed," he whispers. I do as he says, climbing under the comforter and turning to face him. He's already pulled Sam's t-shirt off, exposing his perfect chest, and makes short work of removing his pants and trunks, before joining me. He moves closer, our bodies touching, and brings his arms around me, his erection pressing into me.

"Thank you for coming back to me," I murmur into him.

"I never left you, baby. I never will. Please don't ever forget that. No matter what happens; no matter what you say or do, I will never leave you."

I snuggle down further and he brings his legs around me, enveloping me in him. He's warm, and comforting and my exhaustion gets the better of me, and I yawn into his chest.

"Sleep, baby," he whispers.

"Don't you want to…?" I leave the sentence hanging and he leans back.

"Want to what?" He's smiling.

"You know…"

He sighs. "If you're asking if I want to make love to you, then the answer is yes, I do. But you're tired, and I'm tired. It'll wait until the morning."

"Sure?"

"Yes. I'm sure." He pulls me close again. "And one day, I *will* get you to communicate what you want… even if it kills me."

When I wake, he's staring down at me, leaning up on his elbow. "Hello."

"How long have you been awake?" I ask, stretching my arms above my head.

"I don't know. An hour, maybe."

"What time is it?"

"Seven-thirty."

"And you didn't wake me?" This feels like déjà vu. Was it really only yesterday morning that he let me sleep in? I guess it must've been, although I feel like I've lived a couple of lifetimes since then.

"No. You looked too beautiful to wake. And besides, it's Sunday. We don't do breakfast on Sundays, we do brunch… so…" He leans over and kisses me, his tongue delving deep inside my mouth.

"What about April?" I murmur, breaking the kiss as he turns us onto our sides, facing each other. "She could come in."

"She never has yet," he reasons. "But we can keep this subtle, if you like."

"Subtle?" What does that mean?

"Unobtrusive."

I'm raise my eyebrows, still not getting his meaning.

He smiles at me, and moves closer. Then I feel his hand behind my knee, lifting my leg and wrapping it around him. "Just lie still," he whispers, and moves down just a little, the tip of his erection finding my entrance with ease, as he pushes into me. I let out a moan.

"If we're gonna be subtle, you've gotta be quiet," he murmurs, grinning at me.

"While you're doing that?"

"Yeah." He starts to move very gently back and forth, his arms around me, holding me close. It's comfortable, and comforting, and I'm reasonably sure that if April came in and Rob stopped moving, it would just look like we were having a hug. He starts to flex his hips, going a little deeper and the sensations are amazing. It's intimate, romantic and, for us, it's the perfect fresh start, because he's thought about everything – including April.

"I love you so much," I whisper, looking up into his eyes.

"Nowhere near as much as I love you." He leans in and kisses me and I feel that familiar tingle deep inside. "Are you gonna come?" he asks, like he can feel it too.

"Soon, yes." I start to move against him.

"Try and be quiet, babe," he whispers, smirking.

That's easier said than done, with the feelings he's creating inside me. As I tip over the edge, he captures my mouth again, swallowing my cries and adding his own as he fills me.

He breaks the kiss eventually, although we're still both breathless.

"That was amazing," he whispers, sucking air into his lungs. "But later on, I'm gonna fuck you so damn hard."

"Hmm… please."

"And now," he adds, pulling slowly out of me, "I'd better go shower, just in case your daughter comes in here." He jumps out of bed and walks quickly into the bathroom, giving me a moment to admire his perfect ass, before closing the door behind him. Within seconds, he's back, crossing to the bed and leaning over. "I forgot to say… thank you for that. It was perfect." He grins down at me and, before I can reply, he's gone again.

When I come out of the shower, Rob's sitting on the bed, waiting for me.

"You can go down without me, you know," I tell him, towel drying my hair.

"I know. But I figured you might need me with you today." I look at him for a moment. "Your mom?" he adds, by way of explanation.

I'd forgotten all about that, swept away on a tide of relief and happiness that Rob and I are still together.

"Shit," I mumble, under my breath.

"I'm sure it'll be fine," Rob says, getting up from the bed and coming over to me, putting his arms around me and holding me close to him.

"David said he'd talk to her. And I can speak to her too, if it helps."

"She was so mad at me, Rob."

"Madder than me?" he asks.

"No, probably not…"

"Well, I've forgiven you – if there was ever anything to forgive. I'm sure your mom will too, when she calms down and thinks about it."

"You don't know my mom." I rest my head on his chest and let him hold me a little longer. "She's quite likely to tell me to move out."

"I doubt that. She made a point of saying this was your home too, just yesterday, didn't she?"

"You heard that?"

"Yeah."

"But that was before last night. Before she called me a liar and a hypocrite."

"We all say things we don't mean when we're upset, or mad… or both." He smiles down at me. "I know I do."

"But what if she does tell me we've gotta move out?"

"Then we'll deal with it."

"How?"

"We'll work it out, baby. But I don't think it'll come to that." I wish I had his confidence. "Dry your hair and get dressed," he adds eventually. "We can't put it off forever. And I'll be right there with you. You won't be alone. I promise."

He leans down and kisses me gently, then steps back so I can blow-dry my hair and find some clothes.

Rob holds my hand all the way from the bedroom to the kitchen, where we find April sitting at the table, with David on one side and my mom on the other. David obviously stayed the night, which I don't think he's done before, but right now that doesn't feel very important, compared to what might happen in the next few minutes.

My mom looks up and gets to her feet. She doesn't say anything, but comes around the table and stands in front of me, looking up into my eyes, then she puts her arms around me and hugs me, and Rob lets go of my hand and moves away.

"I'm sorry," she whispers.

"No. I'm sorry. I should never have judged you. I was wrong."

"So was I." She leans back and looks at me again. "I didn't understand. Why didn't you tell me it was about money?" she asks. "We'd have found it from somewhere."

"It was my problem, Mom. Not yours."

She shakes her head. "When are you going to learn? Your problems are my problems."

She pulls me into a hug again, and I look over her shoulder at David, who's still seated at the table. He gives me a wink and a smile, and I smile back.

Then Rob goes around the other side of the table and stands beside April, before bending and lifting her up into his arms. "What do you want for brunch?" he asks her.

"Pancakes," she replies, throwing her arms around his neck.

"Pancakes, with fruit?" he suggests.

"Stawbies?"

"Okay. Pancakes and stawbies it is." He kisses her forehead and looks over at me, smiling, and I know that everything is going to be just fine.

Rob

I serve up the pancakes, with April's help, while David makes more coffee, which means Petra and her mom can sit and talk. It feels important that they should have some time together. As we all sit down, they're smiling and happy again, and I feel like we've really turned a corner.

"Thea?" I say, looking over at her. She's cutting up April's pancakes for her, and turns to face me.

"Yes?"

"I was wondering… I know you planned to take April to see your sister this afternoon, but do you think you could leave her with us instead?" I haven't even discussed this with Petra, but I hope she'll be okay with it.

"Of course," Thea replies. "David and I can go by ourselves."

I can feel Petra's eyes on me and I turn to look at her. She's got her head tilted to one side, like she doesn't understand, and I'm not that surprised. We promised ourselves some time alone today, and I've just kinda ruined that.

"I thought we could make the biscotti right after brunch," I start to explain, "and then go for a walk, maybe?"

"All of us?" she queries.

"Yeah. You, me and April. And then I thought we could come back and watch a movie together, and I'll cook us all dinner tonight."

"Yes, please," April pipes up, clearly liking the sound of my plan.

"I know we said we'd talk today, but the thing we were gonna talk about is already out there, isn't it?" Petra nods, lowering her eyes. "And there was nothing else you were gonna tell me?"

"No. There's nothing else."

Everyone starts eating, although I notice that Petra's a little subdued. I also know why. We'd agreed we'd go online today and look at toys, but we'll still have this evening to do that, if she wants to. I know we also agreed to play with her wand while we had the house to ourselves, but it feels like there are more important things to think about right now…

Once we've all finished, Thea and David start to clear away and April says she's going to the bathroom and then she's going to find her white jacket, which she evidently took to bed with her last night. She wanted to wear it, but Thea wouldn't let her, in case she got too hot.

I take the chance and grab Petra, pulling her into the living room.

"If you still want to, we can go online this evening," I tell her. "I promise. I hadn't forgotten."

She looks up into my eyes. "You hadn't?"

"No, of course not."

"Thank you." She seems relieved.

"And I know we said we'd play some more today, but…" I hesitate for a moment.

"But you don't want to?" She sounds all scared again now.

I move closer and hold her in my arms. "Of course I want to. I just said we could buy more toys, so playing with the one you've got is fine. It's just, after yesterday – well, last night really – I want us to do something together… as… as a family."

I whisper out the last word, feeling a little presumptuous and unsure about myself, given that we're not a family, not in any real sense of the word.

Petra smiles up at me. "I think that sounds lovely," she says, her eyes glistening with tears. "You and I can… well, you know, anytime."

"If you mean we can play with your wand, and I can make you come till you're screaming, and begging me to stop, then yes, we can," I tease.

"Oh, please… yes," she whispers, and she leans up and kisses me, just as April bursts into the room.

"I'm ready," she announces.

"You're also impatient," Petra replies, smiling, and takes her hand, looking back at me.

I know I was going to propose today as well, but I've decided to delay that. I'm not gonna wait for Petra to get divorced. I don't need to. But the timing doesn't feel quite right – it feels insensitive to do it right on top of what's happened – and besides, I've left my jacket at work, with my purchases in the pocket. Because of what I've got planned, I need to have them with me. Okay, so I could go back to work and pick them up, but it'll wait.

It won't wait for long, but it'll wait.

The biscotti turned out really well, our walk was fun, and when we got back, April chose to watch *Frozen*. I understood from Petra that she watches it a couple of times a week at least, but I've never seen it, so I was perfectly okay with that. We sat on the couch together, with me in the corner, Petra leaning against me and April on my lap. I don't think I'd have cared what the movie was, to be honest, being here like that, with both of them, was perfect.

Thea and David arrived home just as the movie finished and Thea seemed relieved to have missed it, but I guess she's probably seen it more times than she wants to think about. We ate dinner together, and then once I'd read April a story – as requested – and she'd gone to bed, we sat up with David and Thea talking until nearly midnight. That wasn't what we'd intended, but it was a good evening, nonetheless. I think it did Petra good to spend some time with her mom, and with David. When we finally realized how late it was, Petra and I headed up to bed and I gave her a choice: we could go online and look at toys, or I could make love to her. She chose the latter, without hesitation.

Today, is unfortunately, another work day and leaving Petra and April this morning was torture. Petra can't come in at lunchtime, as she's got a job of her own to do – photographing a kid's birthday party – so I'm gonna have to run the front of house myself, and Ed will have to manage the kitchen. He's okay with that though, because he knows Sam is back tomorrow. I'll see Petra this evening when she comes in, but I'm gonna miss her today.

"I didn't get to thank you properly," I say to Ed, going straight into the kitchen when I arrive.

"What for?" He looks up. We're not alone. There are a couple of the sous chefs preparing for the lunchtime service, but Ed comes over so we can talk more privately.

"For talking everything through with me on Saturday."

He smiles. "I guessed it worked out okay when you didn't come home."

I nod. "Sorry. I probably should have sent you a text."

"Well, I assume you had your hands full."

"You could say that, yeah."

"And it's all okay?"

"Yeah. It is." He gives me a long look, and a smile and then I turn and am about to leave.

"Oh, Rob…" he calls. "I meant to say. A parcel was delivered for you, just before you came in. I left it on your desk."

I nod. "Thanks, man." I know exactly what that is and go through into the office, checking first that the two boxes I left in my jacket are still there, before I sit at my desk. The parcel in front of me is wrapped in plain brown paper and I smile to myself. *Very discreet.* Then I move it to one side and open my laptop to check my emails.

It takes me about an hour and a half to complete the necessary admin for the morning, and update the orders, and then I go out in the restaurant. We're due to open in half an hour, and Greg's behind the bar already. I go over to him and he looks up.

"Good morning, boss," he says.

"Morning." I turn and check the tables are all laid, before looking back to him. "Thanks for helping out on Saturday night – with that idiot customer."

"No problem." He smiles.

"What?" I ask.

"Did Petra tell you about the drink?"

"No." I don't tell him that we've had more important things to think about.

He nods. "I didn't think she would."

"What about it?" I ask him.

"I made her that vodka-tonic, just like you asked, and I gave it to her…"

"Yeah?"

"And she drank about half of it in one go, before she realized it wasn't water."

I laugh. "Oh, I wish I'd seen the expression on her face."

"It was a picture, I can tell you."

He goes back to polishing glasses and I make my way to the front of the restaurant, checking that everything's as it should be. It is. But then I'm not surprised. Petra left it this way on Saturday night, and she's good at what she does. She's good at everything she does…

"I missed you today," I whisper in her ear.

She's standing in front of me, in her bedroom, naked, her fingers fumbling with the buttons of my shirt.

"I missed you too." There's a crack of emotion in her voice. I think I know why that's there too. It's been a difficult few days, and I remember how worried she was about Sam coming back, which he will be… tomorrow.

"Are you okay?"

She nods, but doesn't reply.

"Would you like a surprise?" I ask her. I don't want to dwell on what's making her sad, because I don't have any answers for her yet, but I'm determined to cheer her up.

"What kind of surprise?"

"A good surprise." She stares at me for a moment. "Yes, or no?"

"Yes." She smiles.

I leave her standing where she is and go over to the bag I brought back with me from work. I told Petra I was bringing back some more fruit for breakfast – which I was – but underneath that I'd stashed the parcel that was delivered this morning. I pull it out and go over to her.

"Unwrap it," I tell her, handing it over. She sits down on the edge of the bed, pulling the wrapping away, while I finish undressing.

Inside there are two smaller packages. She pulls out the first one and looks at me.

"You bought me a lipstick?" she says, surprised.

"No."

"Well, it looks like a lipstick to me."

"Open it up," I tell her and she does, pulling the plastic tube from the plain black box.

"It is a lipstick," she says.

"Undo it."

She takes the top off to reveal a red tip and a curious expression appears on her face. "Take the bottom off," I instruct, and she does. "Now press that button." She complies and the device starts to vibrate very quietly in her hand.

"It's a vibrator?"

"Yeah. Not very originally called a lipstick vibrator. The idea being that you can keep it in your purse and use it whenever you feel the need, and no-one will be any the wiser."

She smiles. "I like that idea."

"I'll be honest," I confess. "That wasn't what I actually bought you. That was a free gift, but it looks like fun anyway."

"So what did you buy?" she asks, wide-eyed.

"That's in the other box."

The plain white container gives nothing away, and she looks up at me.

"Open it," I murmur, sitting down beside her.

She pulls the tight fitting lid from the box and puts it down on the bed, looking inside, then turning and gazing at me, her eyes filled with confusion.

"What is it?" she asks.

"What do you think it is?"

She shrugs. "I have no idea."

"You've never seen anything like this before?"

"No."

"Okay." I take the box from her. "So, when you bought your wand, you didn't see anything like this?"

"No."

"Well, it's called an egg, because of it's shape."

"An egg?"

"It's another kind of vibrator."

She licks her lips, although I'm not even sure she's aware of that, and stares at me.

"What's the tail thing for?" she asks.

"Do you wanna find out?"

"Yes." She didn't even hesitate, not for a second, and I smile.

"Lie down," I tell her, and she does, lowering herself onto her back beside me.

I remove the weird shaped object from its packaging, which I drop to the floor. "Spread your legs, baby," I murmur, and she obliges, her breathing altering as she does.

Then I hold the egg in my right hand and use the fingers of my left to part her pussy lips and, having first switched it on, very slowly insert the device all the way into her, positioning it carefully so the tail is resting against her clit. Once I'm sure it's in the right place, I sit back.

"Stand up," I say, my voice a little more commanding than usual. She sucks in a breath. "Stand up?"

"Yes." I stare down at her, and she raises herself off the bed, and gets to her feet. "How does it feel," I ask her.

She wiggles her ass and then tilts her head from side to side. "It feels fine, but… well, it's not doing much."

I laugh gently. "That's because it's not activated yet."

"Oh." She looks a little embarrassed. "How do I activate it?"

I reach behind me for the remote, and as I flick the 'on' switch, I say, "You don't." She squeals and I laugh out loud. "How does it feel now?" I ask.

She doesn't reply, but stares at me for a few seconds before she starts to tremble and moan, her head rocking back. Fuck… she's coming already. I stand quickly and hold onto her as she rides out her orgasm. It goes on and on, but eventually she calms and sags into me, and I lower her down onto the bed, lying her on the mattress and taking my place beside her.

"What the hell was that?" she says, her voice quavering.

"It's remote controlled," I explain. "And I've got the remote." I hold it up to show her, just as I press the 'plus' button and she groans loudly, and reaches down, grabbing my cock firmly in her hand.

"Oh, God…" she whimpers and then flips around so she's facing the other way, and takes me in her mouth, while I get a perfect view of her pussy. Fuck, that's good… unexpected, but good. She starts to suck me real hard and I press the 'plus' button once more, increasing the speed of the vibrations, as she grips the base of my dick with her hand, stroking me fast. Her breathing is intense, and I know she's gonna come soon, but that's okay, because so am I.

"I'm gonna come, Petra," I warn her, in case she doesn't want it in her mouth, but she sucks me deeper and, just as I shoot hot semen down her throat, her orgasm takes control of her and she thrashes beside me, until she's spent and breathless.

"Turn it off," she pleads. I oblige and slowly pull the soaking egg from her pussy, then turn around so we're facing each other once more.

"It's really powerful," she whispers, smiling. "And very quiet."

"I know."

"And you bought it… for me? This and the lipstick one?"

"Well, as I said the lipstick one was a free gift, but yeah."

"When?" she asks.

"On Saturday morning, while you were in the shower." She nods, lowering her eyes to my chest. "What's wrong?" I ask her.

"Nothing."

"Bullshit, Petra. Don't do that. Don't say there's nothing wrong when there is." She looks up at me, with tears in her eyes. "I'm sorry," I say quickly. "I'm not mad at you. I just want to know why you're upset. Didn't you like the surprise?"

"Yes, I loved the surprise."

"Then what…?"

"It's just I thought we were going to buy toys together," she mumbles.

I chuckle and pull her close, holding her and stroking her hair. "We are. I know we said we'd do that yesterday, but to be honest, spending time with your mom and David seemed more important. But me getting this doesn't stop us from buying more things together."

She looks up at me. "Why did you buy it?"

"Because I wanted to find a way of showing you that my life revolves around you, and your pleasure. Making you happy means everything to me. But there are plenty of toys out there and I'm sure we can find lots of ways to enjoy them – and each other." I kiss her gently. "I love exploring your boundaries… pushing your limits."

She squirms in my arms, like she finds that idea exciting. "You do?" she breathes.

"Oh yeah, baby. And we're gonna have so much fun doing it… because I'm never gonna stop playing with you."

Epilogue

Petra

I can smell bacon cooking. It's making me hungry. What's making me hungrier is that I know who's cooking the bacon. And after what he did to me last night with that egg thing, it's not bacon that I'm wanting… it's Rob.

Last night was spectacular, and waking up beside him again was amazing. I feel so lucky, so blessed that he's a part of my life – especially as I know how close I came to losing him.

He made love to me this morning, very slowly and tenderly, and when he came deep inside me, he whispered that he loves me, his voice cracking with emotion, and then he held me afterwards until it was time to get up.

Now, as I dry my hair and look at myself in the mirror, still trying to understand why he's with me – even though he tells me over and over that he loves me, and that I'm perfect for him – I'm struck by the fact that, in spite of how promising everything seems right at this minute, today marks an ending for us, rather than a beginning. Sam and Ali, and her sister, are due back here this afternoon and I know everything is going to change. Obviously it might take a day or two for Sam to settle back into work after the flight, but then Rob will go back to working front of house every evening. And despite everything he's said to me over the last few days, I'm haunted again by the memory of that woman handing him her phone number, and him pushing it into his pocket. I try so hard to wipe the thought, but it's there. It's always there…

I turn off the hairdryer and dig around in my drawers to find some underwear and clothes, before going over to the bed and sitting down.

"He came back for you," I whisper to myself, trying to be reasonable. "He didn't have to, not after what you did to him… but he did. That has to count for something." It does. And since then, he's been even more attentive than he was before – if that were possible. He's told me so many times that he loves me – and April. He deserves better than my jealousy, than my suspicious nature. I sit up straight and take a deep breath. I'm probably always going to feel insecure about myself, but the least I can do for Rob, after everything he's done for me, is to trust him.

"Breakfast, Petra." I hear him call up the stairs and quickly pull on my underwear, jeans and t-shirt, before running downstairs.

I pull up short when I get to the kitchen. David's sitting beside my mom, wearing jeans and a casual shirt. Yesterday morning, he wasn't here and mom explained he'd gone to work already and would be going back to his place afterwards. I didn't ask, but concluded that him staying over would be a weekends only thing.

"Good morning," David says, looking up at me.

"Hi." I look over at Rob, but he just raises his eyebrows, not saying a word, and then goes back to serving the breakfast – which April's helping with. So I sit opposite my mom and wait to see if she's gonna say anything. She doesn't, but she and David are holding hands, so I guess whatever it is, can't be bad news.

Rob brings over the plates of bacon and scrambled eggs, laying them out, and then helps April to sit in her chair, before coming and sitting beside me.

"You okay?" he asks, looking at me.

"Hmm… fine."

"You were ages coming down," he remarks, picking up his fork.

"I was thinking."

"About?"

"Nothing in particular."

He sets his fork down again and turns to face me. I know he's dying to say 'bullshit' to me, but can't because April's there. He sighs. "Tell me later," he murmurs, shaking his head. He's not angry with me. I

314

think he understands that I can't talk in front of everyone else, even if my general lack of communication is clearly still driving him crazy.

Mom picks up her coffee cup, takes a sip, then puts it down again, and coughs. "David and I… well, David really… that's to say… we've got something to tell you."

"I hope you're gonna be more coherent than that," David says, smirking, "or we'll be here all day."

"Be quiet." Mom slaps him gently on the arm, but smiles up at him, and I lean into Rob. I like seeing my mom happy like this. "As I was saying," she continues, turning back to us. "We've got something to tell you."

"Right…" I prompt.

"Clare and Nathan have decided to get back together," she blurts out.

I'm surprised. Not that they've got back together – I think that was inevitable from what David had said. But I'm surprised that this is their news. They seem nervous and this news doesn't really warrant that.

"Oh," I say, because I can't think of anything more suitable.

"I think she's insane," David says, shaking his head from side to side. "But it's not my place to tell her how to live her life. I just have to accept that she's doing whatever she thinks is best for her and her children."

"Has she gone back home?" I ask.

He nods. "Yes. She moved back home yesterday evening." He pauses, looking at me in an odd way. "And that's when I sat down and made a decision, and then I called your mom, and I came over here and we talked it through… and I decided we needed to tell you before I discuss it with my kids."

Now I'm really intrigued. So Clare and Nathan getting back together wasn't 'the news'.

"Okay…"

"David's decided he's going to sell his house," Mom says. "And he's going to move in here."

I don't know why I'm surprised, but I am.

"Does… does this mean we have to move out? Me, and Rob, and April?" I glance up and Rob and he smiles at me so lovingly I almost don't care what my mom says… except I do. I like our lives just as they are. I don't want anything to change; that's why I'm so scared of Sam coming back…

"No." David's quick to respond, and snap me out of my thoughts. "No, it doesn't mean anything of the kind."

"That's the last thing we want, Petra," Mom adds. "I mean, obviously if you want to get a place of your own, then that's fine, but… well, you know what Greek families are like." She looks at Rob, seemingly doubtful for a moment.

"The same as Italian ones?" he offers, filling in the gap for her, letting her know, I think, that he's not going anywhere.

"Exactly. We all like living together. Lots of generations together in the same house."

"And how do you feel about that?" I ask David. He's neither Italian, nor Greek.

"I love the idea," he says, smiling. "Your mom and I thought we could convert that big guest room next to her bedroom into a sitting room for us, so we can have the whole of the top floor to ourselves, and it can be our own space if we want to be quiet, and that'll give the three of you some privacy too."

"But obviously, we can all still cook and eat together down here," Mom puts in quickly.

"You can do anything you want to down here," I say to both of them. "We'd hate you to feel confined to the top floor."

Mom looks at me. "We won't, but you need some space and time to yourselves, and so do we," she says softly. "This is a good compromise."

"And you don't mind giving up your house? Or your garden?" I ask David.

He shakes his head. "No. I'd rather be nearer to my grandchildren. Just in case they need me…" He doesn't say any more and Mom moves her chair closer to his and rests her head on his shoulder. He looks across at me. "Obviously, if you have other plans then that's fine, but I really don't want you to feel like you have to move out because of what we've decided. This is your home and I think we all get along well enough to live here together, don't you?"

"Yes, I do." I smile at him and feel Rob's arm come around me, holding me tight.

Once we've finished breakfast, David and Mom clear the table, looking very domesticated together, which makes me smile, and April comes to the front door with me, to see Rob off to work.

On the doorstep, she lets go of my hand and lifts her arms up to him, waiting to be picked up.

"What do you want, April?" he asks.

She blushes but says nothing, keeping her hands raised.

Rob rolls his eyes. "You're as bad as your mother," he murmurs, leaning down and lifting her into his arms. "If you want me to pick you up, you've gotta tell me," he whispers to her. "I'll always try and do whatever you need me to do, but you've gotta tell me what it is you want. Deal?"

She nods her head, then rests it on his shoulder.

He looks down at me. "I hope she learns quicker than you," he murmurs.

"Learns what?"

"The art of communication." He takes a step closer. "Gonna tell me what you were thinking about earlier?" he asks.

"I can't." I nod at April.

"Okay. Later then."

I realize then that I don't know if he needs me to come into work tonight. I can't do the lunchtime shift because I have to edit the photographs from yesterday's party, which was my idea of hell, but at least the photographs are quiet, compared to the kids themselves.

"Do… do you need me tonight?" I ask him.

"Of course." He smiles. "Sam's gonna be jet-lagged. He's certainly not gonna want to pull a long shift in the kitchen."

"Will just before six be okay? I've got a lot of editing to do, and I'd like to spend some time with April, rather than having to cut and run."

"Just before six is fine, baby; I'll make sure everything's set up for you." He leans in and kisses me, just briefly, then plants a kiss on April's cheek and hands her back to me, before turning and leaving.

We go back in, and I take April through to the kitchen.

"What are your plans today?" I ask mom and David.

"Your mother's working until two," he replies. "I've got an appointment with a realtor at the house later this morning. Why?"

"Did you need us to mind April?" Mom asks.

"No. It's fine. I'm just editing today."

I pour myself another coffee from the pot and take it with me upstairs, April tagging along with me. She settles into the corner, with her dolls and I fire up my computer, and then wait for the programs to load.

I watch her playing and suddenly feel restless and ill-at-ease. I should've spoken to Rob earlier when I had the chance, because now I know I'm just going to spend the whole day worrying… and worrying and, being as I know he'll be seeing Sam this afternoon, before I even get to work, by the time I see him next, the damage might already be irreparably done.

I pick up my phone and go to the message app, and quickly type out a text to him.

— *Sorry. I can't wait until later. P xx*

His reply is immediate.

— *Okay. Tell me now. R xxx*

— *I'm scared. P xxx*

— *What are you scared of? R xxx*

I take a deep breath.

— *I'm scared if I'm not working in the restaurant in the evenings, you might not come back here every night and that you'll go back to your place instead, and then mornings like we've just had might not happen in the future. Will I fall asleep in your arms every night? Will you be here to cook breakfast with April? Will anything ever be the same again? P xxx*

It sounds pathetic, but it's how I feel and I press send.

I wait for a couple of minutes, then hear a knock on the front door. Either Mom or David answer it and then I hear footsteps running up the stairs.

"Come here." I turn in my chair and see Rob standing in the doorway, looking at me, panting.

"Did you run here?"

"Yes." He's staring at me. "Now, come here." I get up and go over to him and he pulls me into his arms, looking down at me. "You have nothing to be scared of," he whispers.

"But what if…?"

"None of that's gonna happen.," he murmurs. "I will still come back here every night. I'll still hold you while you fall asleep, and I'll still cook breakfast with your baby girl. Everything will be just as it is now. I promise."

"And what if Sam doesn't like me?"

He leans back even further, his brow furrowing.

"Sam? What has he got to do with this?"

"What if he decides I'm not… suitable for you?"

"He won't." Rob sighs. "I know what you're thinking… You're thinking about Ed and his girlfriends and, you're assuming that Sam will get in our way." I lower my eyes, feeling ashamed that he's seen through me so easily. "He won't," Rob repeats. "I told you. That's not how it worked out. And besides, he'd never do anything to make either me or Ed unhappy – and being without you would make me very unhappy." He smiles. "Wait until you meet him. You'll see you're worrying about nothing."

"I'm going to miss working with you… after tonight."

He kisses me gently on my lips. "Don't think about that just yet," he whispers. "And stop worrying. I love you."

"I love you."

He pulls back, letting me go.

"I'd better be going," he says, checking his watch.

"I didn't expect you to come back."

"You said you were scared. Of course I was gonna come back. And maybe one day you'll learn to be as eloquent face-to-face as you are by text."

"Maybe…"

He smiles and looks over my shoulder to where April's playing. "You okay, April?" he calls to her.

"Yes, thank you." I turn and see her look up from dressing her dolls. She smiles at him sweetly.

"Good. I'll see you tomorrow."

"Okay." She goes back to playing.

"You do know how cute she is, don't you?" he whispers to me.

"Yes."

He leans down and kisses me, hard and fast. "Better now?" he asks. I nod, trying to look more confident than I feel. "It *will* be okay. I promise." I guess I wasn't as convincing as I'd planned. There's a twinkle in his eye, but I have no idea what that means and, as he goes back down the stairs, I try to let myself hope that he can make everything okay, and make all my wishes come true.

Rob

Sam gets back just before four-thirty. I'd thought about going back to see Petra and April during the break, but decided I really should be here to greet Sam and Ali, and her sister. Because everyone knows they're coming back, they've all stayed on between the two shifts, so when they walk into the kitchen, accompanied by Jackson, who volunteered to drive to the airport to meet them, they're greeted by jeers and cheers, backslapping for Sam, and kisses for Ali. I've been working front of house all day, and then in the office, but I've come into the kitchen to talk to Ed. I'm sowing seeds already, pointing out how tough it is for me at the moment, having to work front of house at lunchtimes in Jasmine's absence, when Petra can't, then fit in the admin and paperwork, and my meetings and then work the evening shift too. We've only just started our conversation, which we're having away from everyone else, in the dessert area, when Sam and Ali arrive, so we're among the last the greet them.

Of course, I'm not even vaguely affectionate to Sam, and I just pat him on the back and remind him that he owes us for being away for so long. But he pulls me into an unexpected hug.

"Thought you were in the clear, didn't you?" he whispers, moving us away from the crowd just a little.

"What are you talking about?"

"Your stupid text message. What else?" he growls.

"Sam, we've spoken since then. I thought…"

"You thought I'd forgiven you already? Not a chance."

I let out a sigh. "I'm gonna guess that Ali wasn't too impressed to find out that you'd already been married, and hadn't told her?"

"Too fucking right she wasn't," he replies.

"And I don't blame her." I know how it feels to be kept in the dark, but I'm not telling him that. "But then, if you'd been honest with her in the first place…"

"It's not a question of honesty," he says.

"Really?"

"Yeah, really. We just didn't have time…"

Christ, where have I heard that before? "It doesn't take long to say 'I've been married before,' Sam. Sometimes it's better to make the time and take the time, than to hurt the person you love."

He lets me go and looks down at me. "You sound like you're speaking from personal experience," he says, his voice softening suddenly.

"Yeah well… maybe I am, but we're not talking about me."

"Something's happened, hasn't it?" he adds.

"Yes. But like I said, we're not talking about me."

"And we're not talking about me either… not anymore. Just forget it ever happened." He's dropped the attitude and is being much kinder – I guess I don't need to explain. Not yet, anyway.

"Is Ali okay?" I ask him.

"She is now," he says, smiling.

Ed comes over and they hug, and say something I can't hear, and we leave Sam to chat with some of the others and go over to Ali. She's standing among a crowd of the kitchen staff, but moves toward us.

"I'm sorry," I say to her.

"Why?"

"That dumb text message. I didn't realize Sam hadn't told you about Amber."

"It's not your fault," she replies. "He hasn't been threatening you, has he?"

I shrug. "Not with anything I can't handle."

Ed's looking at us. "Is anyone gonna enlighten me?" he asks.

"I might do, one day," I tell him and he rolls his eyes, before we both hug Ali.

Eventually, she pulls back and then she turns us around and we see Ali's sister for the first time. I notice almost straight away that Tess is really different to Ali. She's smaller, for one thing, with darker blonde hair and the most beautiful big eyes. And right now, she looks absolutely terrified.

The noise level is quite loud, until Ed turns around and tells everyone to give it a rest and take a break, and be back here by five-thirty, which is probably the best idea he's had in ages. Sam, Ali and Tess all look exhausted, and I need to talk to my brothers. Preferably alone.

Once everyone else has gone, Ali introduces us to her sister. I reach her before Ed, holding out my hand, which she takes. Hers is tiny by comparison, and she seems kinda fragile.

"I'm Rob." I keep my voice quiet, then joke, "People say it's hard to tell us apart, but it's not. I'm the good looking one."

She smiles and says, "Do you say that to everyone?" And I'm struck by how quiet her voice is.

"Yes, he does," Ali chips in, stepping closer.

"Hey," I defend myself, "I'm a reformed character."

"Doesn't look like it to me," Sam replies.

As they all laugh, I make way for Ed, who shakes Tess's hand.

I can't fail to spot that, as they're talking – well whispering – Ed is staring at Tess, like she's the only person in the room and he still hasn't let go of her hand. I don't think I've ever seen him react to anyone quite like that. I glance at Sam and it seems he's noticed too. Oh Lord… He's watching Ed like a dark hawk and seems *very* protective of Tess. Well, this gets even more curious by the minute.

"How's it been?" Sam asks, trying to distract Ed from Tess, I think.

"We've coped," Ed tells him after a moment's pause.

"You told me Rob's been working in here. So, how's it been out front?" He turns to me. "Has Jasmine been helping out?"

"No. In fact, Jasmine's not been here for the last few days. Scarlett got sick. She's in the hospital."

He pushes himself off the countertop he'd been leaning against and comes over to me. "What's wrong with her?" he asks, clearly concerned.

"They think it's Lyme disease."

"Isn't that the thing you get from ticks?" Ali asks.

"Yeah." Sam turns to her.

I explain about what happened and, while I do, Sam moves back to lean on the countertop, a little closer to Tess than he was, and Ali goes over and stands beside him, her head on his shoulder. He brings his arm around her and holds her, then bends and then raises her face to his and kisses her, very briefly. It's probably the most intimate thing I've ever seen Sam do and I can't help smiling. The moment he looks up, he focuses on me and raises his eyebrows, but neither of us says anything.

"Is she okay?" Tess asks. "The little girl, I mean?"

"She's getting better," Ed replies before I can say a word. "They're hoping she'll be out of the hospital in a couple of days."

"And Jasmine?" Sam asks.

"I've told her to take all the time she needs," I explain. "And I've told her we'll still pay her…" I look up at him. "She was worried."

He nods. "Good." He pauses for a moment, then says, "If Jasmine hasn't been here, how have you managed out front?"

Ed looks at me. "It's been fine," he says quickly. Maybe too quickly and Sam glances at me, and then back at Ed again.

He opens his mouth to speak, or maybe shout, but I get in first. "I need to speak to you," I say. "You and Ed."

I hope that isn't too abrupt a way of saying I need Ali and Tess to leave, but I don't really want Sam yelling at me in front of them, and there's a chance he might.

"I'll take Tess upstairs," Ali says immediately. "We're both really tired. We could do with having a coffee and putting our feet up for half an hour."

"Okay," Sam replies, reaching into his pocket and handing her his keys. "Let yourself in. You know where everything is."

I think quickly. I'm sure Petra and I cleared up after ourselves on Saturday afternoon… I'm sure we did.

Sam pulls Ali into his arms and whispers something in her ear, before he leans back and looks at her.

"That's fine with me," she says, smiling. "I think I'd prefer it that way."

"Sure?" he asks.

"Yes." She leans up and kisses his cheek, then turns to her sister, holding out her hand. "Come on," she says. "Let's leave them to it."

"Do you need any help with your bags?" Ed offers.

"It's fine," Sam says quickly, taking a step forward. "I'll take them up later."

Ali and Tess go out through the kitchen door and we hear the key turn in the lock and then their footsteps on the stairs.

"Okay…" Sam turns to me. "What aren't you telling me?"

"It's nothing bad," I say.

"It honestly isn't," Ed adds.

"Now I'm really worried," Sam replies.

I take a deep breath. "Petra's been helping out," I tell him.

"Petra? The photographer?"

"Yeah. She'd done some waitressing before and she offered to lend a hand."

"But who's been running the restaurant?" he asks.

"Petra."

"And she's been doing a really good job of it," Ed adds. "She's a real hit with the customers, and all the other staff really like her."

Sam nods. "Okay."

"There's something else…" I say and he looks at me. "Petra and I are together."

"I'm not entirely surprised by that," he replies, smirking.

"Yeah… but what might surprise you is, she's got a four year old daughter, called April, and… she's married."

"Petra's married?" He's shocked.

"Only on paper," I add quickly and he gives me a nod of understanding, like our earlier conversation makes a little more sense now.

"Her husband didn't treat her very well…" Ed takes a step forward and I realize I haven't had time to tell him about this yet. "And he left her before April was born," I continue. "They didn't divorce at the time, because they couldn't afford it. But they're getting divorced now…"

"Because of you?" Sam asks.

"Because her husband wants to re-marry."

Sam nods his head, staring at me. "Sounds like you've had an interesting couple of weeks," he says slowly.

"You could put it that way…" I pause. "The thing is, I have a favor to ask of both of you."

Sam folds his arms across his chest, waiting. Ed's staring at me, expectantly.

"I doubt you're gonna like this, but please just hear me out… What Ed said is completely true. Petra's really good at running this place, and she is a hit with the customers… So, I was wondering how you'd feel about her carrying on here, working with me, maybe a couple of evenings a week."

They turn to look at each other but I can't read their expressions. "I know we've spent a lot of money on this place in the last couple of months, but I really want this, guys. I'm in love with her, and it's gonna be real hard not seeing anything of her from breakfast until midnight. If we can just do this…"

"Oh, put him out of his misery, Sam," Ed says, smiling broadly.

"Of course she can work here," Sam replies, coming over and slapping me on the back. "And I do get the whole thing about missing her during the day. That's why Ali's gonna be working in the kitchens whenever she can. I don't wanna miss out on seeing her either." Jeez, did he really just own up to that? "I'm really happy for you…" he continues. "Although what that poor woman sees in you is beyond me. And what she's doing letting a reprobate like you near her daughter is anyone's guess, but if this is what you want, then you got it."

Ed's grinning now.

"You say that, but just wait until you meet her…"

"I've already met her… well, I've seen her, anyway. She was here at the opening," Sam says.

"No, I mean April. She'll have you eating out of her hand within minutes… And being as you'll both be her uncles—"

"Whoa… wait a second. Does this mean the divorce isn't entirely for the other guy's benefit?" Sam asks. "Are you saying marriage is on the cards? The whole ready-made family, and everything?"

"Maybe."

"Only maybe?"

"Well, I haven't actually asked her yet."

"But you're going to?"

I nod. "It's been a little busy around here the last few days…" I look over at Ed and he gives me just the slightest nod of his head, and I know he won't mention the weekend's drama. Sam knows enough already. He doesn't need to know about that.

"It doesn't take that long to propose, you know," Sam says, flipping my words from our earlier conversation back onto me, then turning away and going back over to the countertop again. He leans back against it and looks up at the ceiling. "I think it only took me a matter of seconds to propose to Ali…"

Ed's speechless, so it falls to me to fill the gap. "You… you proposed to Ali?"

Sam nods, grinning. "Yeah. And before you say anything, I know we haven't been together that long, but this is nothing like Amber."

"We know that," I tell him. "Ali is nothing like your ex."

"No. She isn't."

"I take it she accepted?" I ask, trying to suppress a laugh.

"Of course she fucking accepted," Sam replies. "It took her three weeks, but she said yes."

"Three weeks?" That's a long time to wait.

"Yeah. It was a tough decision."

"I can imagine."

He glares at me. "Asshole," he mutters. "She wasn't just accepting me, she was accepting moving here too, and that meant moving Tess." He looks at us both. "That's a long story."

It's one he's obviously not gonna tell us, as he pushes himself off the countertop once more and yawns expansively.

"I hope you're okay covering one more night in here," he says to me. "Because I have no idea what time of day it is, so I seriously doubt I should be put in charge of anything that we're expecting people to pay to eat."

I shake my head. "It's fine. We anticipated that. Petra's coming in tonight."

"She is?"

"Yeah."

"What time?" he asks.

"She's coming in a little before six. She wants to spend as much of the day as she can with April."

"Okay. I'll come down and meet her."

"Be nice to her," I warn him.

He walks over toward the doors, grabbing the bags as he passes, but as he reaches the threshold, he turns and smiles at me, saying, "I'm always nice." Then he goes out, and we hear him call. "Well, I am now."

"It's nice to meet you at last," Sam says to Petra, giving her a broad smile, and I'm almost tempted to gape. Ali smirks at me, but then steps forward and pulls Petra into a hug.

They both came down about five minutes ago, and were here when Petra arrived, looking – frankly – terrified.

As soon as Ali releases her, I step forward and put my arm around her, and she leans into me, like she needs me to hold her up.

"Rob tells me you've got a daughter," Sam says and Ali takes this information in her stride, so I guess he must've told her when he got upstairs.

"Yes," Petra replies quietly.

"And you actually let my brother anywhere near her?" he continues.

"Of course she does," I answer on Petra's behalf, because she's not used to Sam yet. "April's my breakfast helper in the mornings. She's great at flipping pancakes."

"Did she learn that from you?" Ali asks, looking at Petra.

"No," Petra replies. "I can't cook a thing."

"Oh, I don't know," I say, pulling her a little closer. "You helped out with the cookies the other day."

"You made cookies?" Ali asks.

"Yeah. It was April's birthday a couple of weeks ago," I explain. "I bought her a baking set of her own, because she likes cooking, and we made cookies… and biscotti."

Sam smiles. "Glad to hear it," he says, then turns to Petra again. "You'll have to bring her in here one day and leave her with me and Ed. We'll show her how the professionals do it."

"She'd love that," Petra replies, her eyes lighting up.

"Yeah, she probably would." I don't know why I didn't think of it.

"Well, make it a lunchtime shift," Sam says, "and maybe you can come in with her, and Rob can be around too, so she's got a few familiar faces…"

"That's really kind of you," Petra says.

"That's what uncles are for, isn't it?" He grins and winks at me and I swear to God, I'd kill him if I wasn't feeling so damn happy.

We leave it that Petra and Ali will arrange a date for April to come into work, and then Sam takes Ali back upstairs, leaving us to get on with the shift. I really need to get into the kitchen, but there's one more thing I have to do first.

"Come with me," I say to Petra and lead her into the office. I go over to my desk and open the top drawer, pulling out the now familiar white box.

"What's that doing here?" she asks.

"I brought it with me this morning," I tell her, opening it and handing her the egg, having switched it on first. "Go to the ladies' room and put it inside you."

"Why?"

"Because I'll have the remote in my pocket… all evening."

"Does it work at that distance?" she asks, her eyes sparkling.

"Yes."

She bites her bottom lip and moves closer to me, the egg clasped in her hand.

"What am I supposed to do if I come in the restaurant?" she asks.

"Do it quietly."

Petra comes to find me at the end of the shift and I can tell just from the look in her eyes that something's wrong.

"What is it?" I ask her.

"We need to go home," she says urgently, grabbing my arm.

"Why? What's happened?" I'm worried.

"Nothing. Yet. I need to… you know," she whispers. "Now."

"You know?" What's she talking about?

"Yes." She looks at me with a meaningful expression. "The egg… you know."

I get it. "Petra… why can't you just say you need to come?"

"Stop prevaricating, and take me home." She's clearly desperate, and I'm not surprised. I've been switching through the settings on the remote control all evening, changing them up and down every so often.

I laugh. "Give me five minutes."

"Are you serious?"

"Five minutes, baby," I say, and quickly finish up. She leans against the countertop, shifting from one foot to the other, occasionally letting out a sigh, and even rocking her head back once or twice. I guess this is like sweet torture for her, and I'm almost tempted to prolong it, but when I think about watching her come, I'm not *that* tempted.

"You could take it out, you know," I say as we walk home.

"I don't want to," she murmurs.

"How many times have you come so far?" I ask.

"None. I've managed not to, but it's been torture. Perfect torture." I was right then.

I look around. There's no-one in sight. So I reach into my pocket and press the 'plus' button twice and she stops in her tracks and clings onto my arms, her head falling forward onto my chest.

"You… you… oh, God…" she whispers and starts to tremble and pant. "I'm coming…"

"I know," I murmur and hold onto her until the tremors subside.

"I can't believe you just did that… in public."

"There's no-one around," I explain. "It's nearly midnight. Most sensible people are in bed."

"Which is where we need to be," she replies, and takes my hand.

"You want more?" I ask her, smiling.

"I want a lot more." I touch the 'plus' button again and she lets out a yelp of surprise.

"Don't *do* that," she breathes.

"You mean you want me to stop?" I ask.

"No."

We reach her house, she lets us in, and without even pausing, we run straight up the stairs and into her room.

Standing beside her bed, she starts to pull on my belt, but I grab her hand.

"Wait a second." I turn off the egg, and she almost sags into me. "I need to talk to you first."

"You do?"

"Yes. This is important." I smile at her. "And I know what you want to do is important too, but this needs to be said."

She takes a breath, then nods her head. "Okay."

"Did you like Sam?" I ask her.

"Um… yes." She looks surprised. "Is that what you wanted to ask me… now?"

"No. But you liked him?"

"Yes. He was nothing like I expected."

"So you think you could handle working with him?"

"Working with him?" She looks so confused now.

"Yeah." I take her hand and sit us both down on the edge of the bed, noticing how she shifts awkwardly, obviously trying to get comfortable. I need to keep this brief. "I spoke to Sam and Ed earlier," I tell her. "And I asked them if it would be okay for you to continue working in the restaurant in the evenings, a couple of nights a week."

"You did?" She turns and stares at me. "But what about you?"

I smile at her. "You'll be working with me. We'll be a team, running the front of house… I know you've got your own work to do, so you can't be in the restaurant the whole time. And we can't expect your mom and David to mind April every day, but now Sam and Ed have agreed to it, I thought we could sit down and agree a schedule that'll work for all of us. And… and I want to start coming back here in the afternoons as well, as much as I can. I want to see more of April. I know I can't come back for long, but at the moment, I'm only seeing her for an hour or so in the mornings, and I'd like a little longer. Most days I can probably come back for at least an hour, and we can maybe try and do something together, if you're around… all three of us. And if you're working, then she'll be with your mom and I'll just do something with them, or with April by herself… if you're okay with that."

"Of… of course I'm okay with that," she mumbles, tears trickling down her face.

"Sure?"

"I'm positive."

"And you like the idea of working with me a couple of nights each week?"

She nods. "It's the perfect solution."

"And on the nights when I'm working by myself, I'll finish up as quickly as I can, and come back here… and hopefully get here before you fall asleep, so I can hold you."

She smiles through her tears.

"I don't deserve you," she whispers.

"I think you'll find you do." I lean over and kiss her, flicking the egg back on at the same time. "And I think you're just about to prove it…"

This morning, I go downstairs ahead of Petra, who's gone to wake April, and I find Thea and David, sitting in the kitchen drinking coffee. David's wearing a shirt and tie today, so I guess he'll be going into work, unlike yesterday.

"Thea," I say quickly. "Do you think you could make the breakfast today?"

She looks up. "Yes, of course." She seems surprised.

"There's just something I need to do before I go to work."

"That sounds very mysterious," David replies.

I smile over at him and go out into the hall, getting the two boxes from my jacket. I'd planned to do this with Petra and April by themselves, but when I was talking to Sam and Ed yesterday, I realized that the ready-made family Sam was talking about consists of Petra's mom and David too, especially as it looks like we're all going to be living together… so I may as well do it now. Besides, I don't get a lot of time with them, so I have take my chances.

I get back into the kitchen just before Petra appears with April beside her.

"Why is Yaya making breakfast?" she asks, looking at her grandmother, who's standing by the stove, breaking eggs into a bowl.

"Because I've got something else I need to do today," I explain.

She looks a little crestfallen and I go over and take her hand, bringing her back to the table and sitting her down. Petra's standing, looking at us. "Come here," I tell her, holding out the chair beside April's and, when she's sat down, I twist both their chairs around, so they're facing me.

Picking up the two boxes from the table, I put them on the floor, as I kneel down, facing Petra and April, and I catch a glimpse of Thea, her hand covering her mouth and tears brimming in her eyes. I think she's guessed what's going on, even if her daughter and granddaughter are still none the wiser.

I turn to Petra first and hold her hands in mine.

"A couple of days ago," I say, trying to keep my voice steady, "I thought I'd lost you. I don't wanna go through that ever again. I want you by my side, where you belong, for the rest of my life. I want you to be mine forever, because I'm already yours, and I have been since the moment I first saw you. I know we have to wait for events to take their course, but as soon as you're free, will you agree to marry me?" I open the smaller of the two boxes, to reveal the white gold solitaire diamond ring inside. Petra's crying and nodding at the same time, which is kinda promising, but this one time, she's gonna damn well say the words…

"If you're accepting me," I tell her, "I need you to say it out loud. If we're getting married, you need to be able to communicate with me."

April nudges into her and whispers loudly, "Say yes, Mommy."

Everyone laughs, including Petra, and she looks at me and says, "Yes."

I remove the ring from the box and carefully put it on her finger. It fits – thank God – and I lean forward and pull her into my arms, kissing her briefly, then I whisper, "Later," into her ear, before leaning back again. Her eyes are fixed on mine, and are filled with tears, and love.

I take a deep breath and turn to April. "I realized real early on," I say to her, moving just a little closer, "that you and your mommy come as a package, and that means I can't ask your mommy to marry me, without asking you."

She tilts her head to one side. "You can't ask me to marry you," she says, her brow furrowing. "I'm only four."

We all laugh again. "I know, baby girl," I say, and I hear Petra sob and rest my hand on her leg, holding it there. "The thing is, what I've gotta ask you is, whether you'll give me your permission to marry your mommy?"

"My permission?"

"Yes. Is it okay with you if your mommy and I get married?"

She nods her head quickly. "Yes," she says.

"That's good." I pull my hand away from Petra for a moment, and grab the other box, holding it up in front of April. "The thing is, I couldn't buy you a ring because, as you've so rightly said, I can't marry you. And also, your fingers will grow, so you wouldn't be able to wear it for very long, but…" I open the box and show her the solid white gold heart pendant, with a single diamond set in one half, which hangs from a simple chain.

"Is that for me?" April asks, wide eyed.

"It sure is." I take the chain from the box and stand, fastening it around her neck.

"Why is there a diamond in the heart?" she asks, holding it and looking at it.

I kneel down again. "Well, diamonds are the birthstone for April, which is the month you were born."

"And that's why I'm called April," she adds.

"Yes. And the heart is my heart," I continue. "So… you're the diamond, and you're in my heart… because I love you. I bought you this so that, wherever you are, and whatever happens, you'll always know that I love you."

She looks at me. "I love you too," she whispers, and I hug her close. I can hear Petra crying and, without letting go of April, I reach out a hand to my future wife, which she clasps hold of tightly.

April pulls away from me after a minute or so and looks into my face, her eyes filled with tears. "What's wrong?" I ask her. "You're meant to be happy."

"I am," she says, and Petra moves closer and hugs her.

"What's wrong, baby girl?" she asks.

"This isn't fair," April murmurs quietly.

"What isn't?" I brush my fingers down the side of her face.

"You bought mommy a ring, and you got me a necklace, but you haven't got anything."

I smile and look her in the eye. "Yeah, I have. I've got everything I could ever want… I've got you two. That's all I need."

Petra leans over and lifts April onto her lap, holding her tight, but staring at me.

"Do you understand what me marrying Rob means?" she asks, clearly speaking to April, even though her eyes are locked with mine. April nods. "So you understand that in a few months' time, I'll become Petra Moreno?" April nods again, and Petra sits back slightly, so she can look down at April. "And when I do that, would you like to become April Moreno?" she asks, and I feel my heart stop beating.

I didn't expect that. Not for one second did I think Petra would offer that.

"What do you mean?" I ask her. I have to make sure I've understood what she's suggesting.

She looks up at me again. "I want you to become April's father – officially." She falters for a second. "As… as long as you're both happy with that."

A broad grin settles on April's face and she clasps her hands together. "Yes, please," she replies, excitedly.

I get to my feet and sit down beside them. "I would love to become April's father. I've got no idea how we go about it, but whatever it takes, I'll do it," I tell them both. "But I've got one condition." I turn and catch a glimpse of Thea. She's got tears streaming down her cheeks and David's holding her. She can't know what I'm about to say, but I hope she's okay with it.

"What's that?" Petra asks, sounding a little worried.

"I've known, for almost as long as we've been together, that you were named after your dad," I explain. "And I know what that means to you. I also know that, if you take my name when we get married, then his name dies. I can't ask that of you. I won't ask that of you. I want to marry you and be your husband. I want to adopt April and be her father, but I don't want you to become Petra and April Moreno."

"You don't?" Petra's staring at me, completely bewildered.

"No. If it's okay with you, and your mom, I'd like to become Roberto Miller. I'd like to take your name, so your dad's name doesn't die."

"You want…?" Petra's struggling to speak.

"I want to honor your father's memory, by taking the name he gave you."

"And you'd be okay with that?" She's found her voice now.

"I'd be more than okay with it. We'll be a family... all of us together. What more could I want?"

Thea and David come around and Petra looks up at her mom.

"I think that sounds perfect," her mom says. "Your father would have been so proud of you."

With that, Petra bursts into loud tears and I hold her close.

April looks up at me. "Is Mommy happy?" she asks.

I smile down at her. "Yeah, baby girl" I say, bringing her into the hug. "I think Mommy's very happy..."

The End

Keep reading for an excerpt from Suzie Peters' forthcoming book
Come Home With Me
Part Three in the Recipes for Romance Series.

Available to purchase from October 26th 2018

Come Home With Me

Recipes for Romance: Book Three

by

Suzie Peters

Chapter One

Tess

"It'll be okay." Ali's voice sounds reassuring, but I still feel scared. I turn and smile at her, and notice that Sam's looking at me as well. His eyes voice his unspoken concern and I try my best to look happy.

Don't get me wrong; I am happy. Well, I'm happy for them at least. Sam's good for Ali. They're good together. He makes her happy, and she hasn't felt like that for a long while, but none of that stops me from feeling worried about the step she and I have just undertaken – to sell up and move three thousand miles to begin a new life in a completely different country.

The aircraft levels out and, after a little while, we unfasten our seatbelts and an air of relaxation settles over the passengers. Well, most of the passengers. I'm anything but relaxed.

When I left the safety of our grandmother's house three years ago to start my course in History and Comparative Literature at St Mary's University in London, I didn't really know what I was going to do once I graduated. I had some vague idea of writing, perhaps, or maybe a research position. The very last thing I saw myself doing was emigrating to America, and facing a completely unknown future.

Of course, that all came about because my sister took on a job in the States at the beginning of the year, to refurbish a restaurant, and while she was there, she fell in love with Sam. And then he proposed her. She didn't accept straight away, even though I knew she wanted to. What she did was to call me, and tell me about his proposal, and then ask me to move to the States with them... because Ali and I have been pretty much inseparable since our parents were killed in a fire over thirteen years ago. The idea of living in a different country, away from the things, and customs, and people I know really frightened me. But the idea of living on a different continent to Ali terrified me more. So, when she called me a few days ago to tell me that she'd decided to accept Sam's proposal, I had to say I was okay with moving to Connecticut with them. What choice did I have?

At the time, she and Sam had been down at our house in Dorset – a beautiful seaside cottage named Waterside, that had belonged to our parents and that we'd inherited when they died. Our grandmother had arranged for it to be let out years ago, and a series of tenants have called it home since then, but the most recent ones didn't pay the rent, and when our managing agents sent them a reminder, they took off, leaving a false forwarding address, and completely trashing the place.

Ali and Sam spent a couple of weeks fixing up the house and then we took the heartbreaking decision to put it up for sale, because Ali and I both agreed that we didn't need the hassle of having bad tenants again. Parting with Waterside was never going to be easy and, in a way, I'm glad that Ali dealt with it all. I've always had a particularly soft spot for the cottage, and I'm not sure I could've faced it. That said, Ali tends to deal with pretty much everything anyway, so I don't really know why I was worried.

Once that was done, they came back to London and I had my first real chance to see them together as a couple; and I knew straight away that Ali had made the right choice.

I'd seen them together before, but only very briefly, when Sam followed Ali back from the States. It turned out they'd had a big fight over there and Ali had flown back here to help me out with the problem over the house, without even telling him. So Sam had jumped on the next flight and arrived on our doorstep just a few hours later. To say the atmosphere between them was frosty would be the understatement of the year, but even then, I could see they were meant to be together and when Ali announced she was leaving for our house in Dorset, Sam said he was going too… and I kind of helped them on their way. It was the only thing to do, especially as Ali was being a bit childish about the whole thing. She wanted to be with him; she'd even admitted that to me. And yet she was putting up roadblocks. He'd hurt her, that much was obvious, but the guy had flown three thousand miles, just to apologise. I think that warranted a little credit…

In any case, it's clear they're perfect for each other, although from what I've gathered, Sam had some persuading to do, especially when Ali found out that he'd been married before, and hadn't told her. I'm glad I wasn't there when that happened. I imagine it wasn't pretty…

Still, they worked it out eventually… And so it is that we're all on a plane to America, having also put our London flat up for sale, thus cutting all ties with home, England, the past, and our parents.

I feel a sting of tears behind my eyes and close them, pretending to be asleep.

Actually, I could do with some sleep. The last few weeks have been hectic and exhausting. I had to finish my ten thousand word dissertation, which I handed in last Friday. I don't think I've ever read so much, or made so many notes, in my life, but I got there in the end. Then Ali and Sam got back from Dorset on Saturday, and that's when the planning really kicked in. The first thing Sam did was to book us on flights for today – Tuesday – which gave us three days to pack, and arrange for the shipping of all the things we want to have with us in America, which mainly consists of books and mementos of our parents. We're not taking any furniture; we're having it moved to Waterside because the house is virtually empty after all the damage that was done and it'll probably sell much more easily if there's furniture in there. Then Ali spoke to our father's solicitor, Miles Kingston – well, I suppose he's our solicitor now – and arranged with him to put our London flat on the market. He's also going to handle the removal of the furniture to Waterside, and make sure everything gets shipped properly to America. I have no doubt he charges us for what he does, but he's an old university friend of our father's, so I imagine he helps out because he wants to, rather than because we're paying him.

Once all of that was done, all that was left was paperwork, sorting out my visa and other annoying, fiddly things that took a long time to organise, like getting my university to accept that I wouldn't be attending graduation and was leaving before the semester officially ended, even though there were no more lectures to attend, and nothing else to hand in. For some reason, it seemed to be a big deal. Almost as big a deal as arranging to have our mail forwarded overseas. That was more complicated than we'd expected too.

Now, when I look back at the whirlwind, I'm not surprised I'm feeling so tired…

Apart from being woken up for food and the occasional drink, I think I slept through most of the flight in the end, and Ali woke me about twenty minutes before we were due to land.

Now, we're on our own. Sam's not with us anymore because he doesn't have to go through immigration, which seems be taking an incredibly long time. Ali takes charge and tells me what to do, and say, and I obey. Despite sleeping on the plane, I'm still too tired to question anything.

When we come out, Sam's waiting for us and, looking at Ali's face, I can see how reassured she feels to see him. I have to admit, I am too. He seems to be very at home here, even though we're in an airport arrivals hall. Of course, he's not hard to find; at his height, he towers above most other people, and he steps towards us the moment he sees us.

"Everything okay?" he asks, taking Ali's hand.

"Yes, just fine," she replies.

Our cases are all stacked on a trolley, which Sam commandeers and he guides us towards a crowd of people who are awaiting various flights.

"Ed and Rob are both busy at the restaurant," he explains to both of us, "so they couldn't come pick us up. But Rob arranged that Jackson would meet us." He looks around while we're walking and then nods his head. "Over there," he adds, and changes direction just slightly, guiding us towards a man with short blond hair, probably just under six feet tall, who's holding up his hand.

"Hey," Sam says as we draw closer.

"Good to see you, boss," the other man replies, then looks at Ali. "And you, Ali," he says to her, leaning down and kissing her cheek.

"Hello, Jackson," Ali replies.

Then he turns to me.

"This is Ali's sister, Tess." Sam makes the introduction.

"It's a pleasure to meet you." His eyes sparkle as he smiles and moves a little closer than feels comfortable. "If you need anything, just ask for me. My name's Jackson."

Right at that moment, Sam grabs him by the sleeve of his jacket, yanking him away.

"And that'll do," he says, gruffly. "Here, if you wanna be useful, push this." He offers the trolley to Jackson, who takes it sheepishly. "Whose car did you bring?" Sam adds.

"Rob told me to bring yours."

Sam nods and smiles. "Good. I'll drive home." He turns to Ali. "See, I told you. I don't like to be driven."

She shakes her head, smiling back at him.

"Are you okay?" Ali asks me and I nod just once.

Sam and Jackson sit in the front of the car, which is a relief, being as I'd dreaded Ali wanting to sit with Sam and me being left with Jackson for the journey, which Ali's informed me will take over two hours.

"You can sleep some more, if you want to," Sam says, looking at me in the rear-view mirror.

"I've already slept for hours."

"Hmm, but you've had a very tiring few days," Ali replies. "Besides, the secret to dealing with jet lag is to try and stay up late tonight, so make the most of getting some sleep now."

I take her advice and, using her shoulder as a pillow, I settle down to sleep again.

"We're here." Ali wakes me, just as Sam switches off the engine.

"Where's here?" I look around. We appear to be in an underground car park.

"We're beneath the hotel a few doors up from the restaurant," Sam explains. "I have an arrangement to park my car here."

"Oh… okay."

Sam and Jackson get out and open the doors for Ali and I. Jackson takes my hand, helping me down from the car, which is a Toyota Land Cruiser and feels enormous on the outside, although looking around the car park, it doesn't seem so big. All the vehicles in here look much bigger than the ones at home.

"Thank you," I say to Jackson, staring down at our hands. He seems reluctant to let go, but Sam calls him to the boot of the car and he goes, releasing my hand, thank goodness. Ali comes around to me and gives me a smile, linking her arm through mine.

"Don't worry about Jackson," she whispers. "I think he's a bit smitten."

"Really?" I look up at her. She's a couple of inches taller than me… well, three, if we're being absolutely accurate.

"Yeah. Get used to it." Her smile widens and she leads me to the back of the car, where Sam and Jackson have unloaded the cases.

"Do you want some help?" Ali offers and we both step forward.

Sam gives her a look and a slight smile. "Hardly," he replies and he and Jackson pick up all the bags between them and we start towards the lifts.

"Why can't we help?" I whisper to Ali.

"Because that's how it seems to work over here. It's like opening car doors."

"Women don't open car doors?" I ask, bemused.

"They do, but men like doing it for them. Well, nice men do anyway." I nod my head. "You'll get used to it," she adds.

Will I? I wish I felt as sure as she does.

We go up to the ground level and out onto the street, where I'm struck by the height of the buildings, and the noise of the traffic. The pavement is wide – much wider than at home – but the noise feels overwhelming. Even though I'm used to London, I usually spent most of my time there in the tube, avoiding the busy streets, or in lecture halls, or in the library, or in our flat. I didn't go out much, except with Ali.

She obviously feels me flinch against the noise and tightens her grip on my arm.

"We've only got a really short walk," she says quietly, guiding me along the pavement.

She's not wrong. Within a couple of minutes, we arrive at the restaurant.

"It looks lovely," I say to her, honestly, taking in the grey paintwork and trimmed bay trees at the front door. "I mean, I don't know what it looked like before, obviously, but it looks lovely now." This is what Ali came here for originally, to make over the restaurant and, as usual, she's done a magnificent job.

"Thanks, Tess," she says, smiling at me.

Sam manages to unlock and open the door, despite the encumbrance of the bags he's carrying, and we pass through into a beautiful interior. The wall on the left is covered with small framed photographs, which are too far away for me to make out what they're of. There's one at the back though, which is easily identifiable. I'd know it anywhere. It's a huge picture that covers the whole wall, featuring a view of Positano in the evening, with the village's lights reflected in the bay below. Ali's put in spaced white vertical lines every so often, which break up the photograph, without spoiling the effect. There are several waiters and waitresses, currently laying up tables with white linen table cloths and sparkling glassware and cutlery, but they all stop and come over as soon as they see Sam.

"Hey, boss. Good to see you back."

"Where have you been?"

"We were starting to forget what you looked like."

He smiles at them and nods his acceptance of their greetings, then looks around at everyone gathered before him.

"Where's Rob?" he asks.

A dark-haired man answers. "He's in the kitchen, boss."

Sam nods. A couple of people are talking to Ali, saying hello and asking how she is, but Sam gets her attention and she goes over to him, taking me with her. "We'll make the formal introductions another time," he says, looking at me, "but this is Ali's sister, Tess."

Everyone says 'hello', or 'hi', and I nod my head, unsure how to respond.

"And now," Sam says, "I'm gonna go see if my two brothers have wrecked my kitchen."

They all laugh and make a space for us to pass through. Sam leads the way towards the back of the restaurant, going into a corridor and then through a set of double doors on our right. He holds them open until Ali and I are on the inside of a huge kitchen area, then he lets them close and turns around, dumping the cases on the floor.

"What the fuck do you call this?" Sam says loudly.

Everyone in the kitchen stops and turns, and then the noise level shoots up as they all come over and start talking at once. I feel myself tense and curl inward. There are too many people here for me and I wish I could be anywhere else. They're all greeting Ali too and she's pulled away from me, into the crowd, just as I become aware that Jackson is still with us, although I don't really know why.

"Are you okay?" he asks. I'm sure he only means to be friendly, but I don't know him.

"Yes, thank you." I move away from him slightly, even though it means getting closer to the crowd.

Just at that moment, I notice two men walking towards us from the very back of the kitchen. They look almost identical. One's wearing all black, and has short dark hair, which is spiky on top. He comes straight over to Sam and slaps him on the back, making a joke. Sam pulls him into a hug and then away from everyone else and they talk for a few minutes. Sam looks a bit angry, but then his expression clears and they seem to be okay again. The other man hangs back a little while this is going on. He's wearing chef's whites and has longer hair. It's just as dark as the first man's, and he's got brown eyes and a square, clean-shaven jaw. I guess these two must be Sam's twin brothers, Rob and Ed, although which one is which, I don't know. The one with the longer hair waits for his brother to move back and then steps forward and hugs Sam affectionately. They whisper something to each other and seem a lot closer than Sam and the other twin were.

The twins then turn to Ali, and I notice the one in black looks embarrassed, although I don't know why. He hesitates and then says he's sorry.

"Why?" Ali asks, looking at him.

"That dumb text message. I didn't realise Sam hadn't told you about Amber," he says. His accent is nice. It's soft, not as harsh as Jackson's.

"It's not your fault," Ali replies. "He hasn't been threatening you, has he?"

The man shrugs. "Not with anything I can't handle."

The man in the chef's whites is staring at them. "Is anyone gonna enlighten me?" he asks and I catch my breath. If I thought the other twin had a nice voice, this man's is breathtaking. It's beautiful and intoxicating and for a moment, I'm mesmerised, just staring at him.

"I might do, one day," the other man replies, and then they both step forward and hug Ali together.

I've got no idea what that conversation was about, but I can ask Ali later, and eventually, they break up the hug and Ali turns them around. She's about to introduce us when someone laughs loudly behind her, the noise level shoots up again, and I flinch. I wish I didn't feel so nervous all the time, but it's been like this ever since Mum and Dad died; any loud noise, and I become a nervous wreck. I try to hide it, but it's there, and it infuriates me.

The man with the longer hair, in the chef's whites turns around to face everyone else.

"Okay guys," he says, his voice deep, but still calm . "Let's give Sam and Ali a chance to catch their breath, shall we? Take some time out and be back here at five-thirty. Okay?"

They all make approving noises and slowly disperse, and then he turns back to me. And he gives me such a smouldering look, I wonder why it makes me shiver.

Ed

"I guess it depends how long Jasmine's gonna be away for," Rob says to me, and I lean back against the countertop in the dessert section of the kitchen and look across at him. He's currently propped up against the wall by the door, and I've gotta say, he looks exhausted. It's not surprising really. He's been helping me out in the kitchens for the last few weeks, while Sam's been in England, as well as doing all his usual admin and meetings, and working front of house at lunchtimes. He's had to do that, because our normal head waitress, Jasmine, hasn't been in, since her daughter got sick. Rob's girlfriend, Petra, has been helping out too, but the hours are clearly starting to get to him.

"I know. But Sam's back today. That'll help."

He shrugs. "I've still gotta cover the lunch *and* evening sessions out front," he points out.

He's right. Normally, he only works in the restaurant in the evenings; he doesn't cover the lunch session, unless we're really busy. Jasmine does that, which leaves Rob free to do all his other work in the office. I've got no idea where he's found the time to get all of that done over the last three weeks.

"Once Sam's back we can—"

"What the fuck do you call this?" Sam's voice rings out from the other end of the kitchen and we both look up to see him standing there, larger than life.

"Well, talk of the devil," Rob says.

He has some idea of how relieved I am to be handing back control of the kitchens to our big brother. I've hated these last few weeks and I can't wait to let Sam have the run of the place again. Actually 'hated' isn't really a strong enough word. I've gotten more used to it as time's gone on, but in the beginning, when he first announced how long he was gonna be away for, I was literally sick with fear at having to manage the kitchens for so long without him. I was throwing up in the bathroom at home, grateful that Rob was so preoccupied with Petra, he didn't notice. I told him fairly early on that I was struggling, but blamed it on tiredness rather than the crippling fear that was eating into me at just the thought of having to run another service. So now, just seeing Sam at the other end of the kitchen is enough to soothe my nerves.

Having Sam back is about more than that though... For the last few weeks, I've lived in even greater fear that he'd decide to stay in England, or at least move over there on a permanent basis, once he'd worked out the logistics of doing so. We know how much he loves Ali and we all know that Ali has a sister, and that moving here was always gonna be a big ask for her, and it occurred to us – well, it occurred to Petra – that Sam might decide to move to England, rather than ask them to move here. That prospect filled me with absolute dread. Obviously him moving away would leave us with a huge hole in the restaurant, but my main worry stems from the fact that Sam's been my rock, my support, my hero, if you like, for the last nine years or so, ever since our dad made clear his disapproval of my decision not to follow him into the main kitchen, but to pursue my own dream of working in pastry instead. I've come to rely on Sam and the thought of trying to work without him... well, it wasn't something I even wanted to contemplate. It still isn't. The other reason I feared him going was that we're a team. We're a family. We fight, we bicker, but we also laugh. We laugh a lot, and deep down, we love each other. Okay, we're an incomplete family, because our parents don't speak to me or Sam, but the three of us are tight. We're about as close as a family can get, and I can't think of anything worse than breaking that up, by one of us moving so far away from the others.

I haven't really had the chance to talk that through with Rob, being as he's been living at Petra's for the last couple of weeks, but he knows me well enough to gauge how I feel. We're not twins for nothing.

Rob gives me a smile and we both step out into the main kitchen area, where Sam's now been surrounded by all the other kitchen hands and chefs. Ali's there too, saying hello and smiling at everyone. God, it's good to see her again, especially looking so happy.

Rob goes straight over to Sam and slaps him hard on the back, and before I can move in to greet him, Sam's pulled Rob into a hug and taken a couple of steps away.

I can't hear what they're saying, but Sam looks madder than hell.

They talk for a few minutes and then Sam's face clears and, if I'm being honest, he looks more concerned than anything else, and finally he smiles and I heave a sigh of relief. The last thing I needed today was for Sam to start a fight with Rob.

Sam looks over at me as Rob moves away, and I just go up to him and hug him. He returns the hug, patting me on the back gently.

"You brought her home," I whisper.

"Sure did." He pulls back a little and, as far as I'm concerned, his smile makes the last three weeks of stress, fear and hard work worthwhile. "And thanks," he says.

"What for?"

"Covering for me. I really do owe you."

"You owe Rob too."

"Yeah, yeah. I know." He grins and we step away from each other, and I turn and Rob and I go over to Ali, who's still kinda surrounded. Once she sees us, she breaks away and comes over.

"I'm sorry," Rob says. I turn to look at him. I've got no idea what he's talking about.

"Why?" Ali replies, clearly as confused as me.

"That dumb text message. I didn't realize Sam hadn't told you about Amber." He hadn't? He hadn't told Ali he was married before? What an idiot… but how does that involve Rob, or a text message?

"It's not your fault," Ali says. "He hasn't been threatening you, has he?"

Rob shrugs his shoulders. "Not with anything I can't handle."

I look from Rob to Ali, and back again. "Is anyone gonna enlighten me?" I ask.

"I might do, one day," Rob replies and then rolls his eyes. I hate it when he does that, and decide to leave it for now. I'm sure I'll find out soon enough. We move forward and hug her together, before Ali pulls back and looks at us both, then turns us around. And that's when I see her sister for the first time.

My skin's tingling and my mouth's gone dry, although the rest of my body feels numb. She's beautiful… she's clearly terrified of something, but she's beautiful.

So this is Tess… I take in her long, wavy dark blonde hair, her porcelain-smooth skin and her delicate pink lips, but I'm most drawn to her eyes, which are huge, and blue, and perfect.

Ali moves away from us and takes a step toward her sister just as one of the guys behind laughs really loudly and I notice Tess flinch and pull back, her eyes widening even further. Sam might be back, and it might be his kitchen, but he's not doing anything about this, so I'm going to… I turn around and face the group behind us.

"Okay guys," I say. "Let's give Sam and Ali a chance to catch their breath, shall we? Take some time out and be back here at five-thirty. Okay?" I think it's best if we have as few people out here as possible. Tess is clearly frightened enough already. She doesn't need this.

Everyone starts moving away and Sam comes back over toward us, just as I turn back to face Ali and Tess and, as she looks up at me, our eyes meet and I actually feel myself falling into them. It's a weird sensation, but I like it. I like her too.

"Rob, Ed," Ali says. "This is my sister, Tess."

We both step forward, although Rob gets to her first.

"I'm Rob," he tells her. "People say it's hard to tell us apart, but it's not. I'm the good looking one."

She smiles, shaking his hand and her head at the same time. "Do you say that to everyone?" she asks, and I notice how soft and quiet her voice is.

"Yes, he does," Ali replies. "All the women he meets, anyway."

"Hey," Rob says. "I'm a reformed character."

"Doesn't look like it to me," Sam mocks.

Everyone laughs and Rob moves to one side as I take his place and offer her my hand. She takes it and we shake.

"Hello," she whispers. "So, if he's Rob, you must be Ed."

"Yes. It's good to meet you."

"You too."

Our eyes are locked, and now I'm this close I can see hers are a darker shade of blue than I thought, her lips are fuller too, and her skin's flawless… oh yeah, and I can't breathe.

"Did you have a good flight?" I ask, because I can't think of anything else to say.

"I slept through most of it," she replies. Her quiet voice suits her. She's shy, guarded, and based on what I've seen so far, I'd say very easily frightened. All my instincts are screaming at me to protect her – from everything and everyone.

"How's it been?" Sam's voice interrupts my thoughts and I look over and see him staring at me. At the sound of his voice, Tess pulls her hand away from mine and the feeling of loss is almost overwhelming, to the point where I have to take a moment before replying to Sam.

"We've coped," I manage to say.

"You've told me Rob's been working in here. So, how's it been out front?" He gives me a long, slow stare, then turns to Rob. "Has Jasmine been helping out?"

"No," Rob replies. "In fact, Jasmine's not been here for the last few days. Scarlett got sick. She's in the hospital."

Sam pushes himself upright and goes over to Rob, standing in front of him. He's obviously concerned. "What's wrong with her?" he asks. While they're occupied, I take the chance to look at Tess again. She's staring down at her hands, which are clasped in front of her. She looks kinda lost and I wanna take her somewhere quiet, away from everyone else, maybe hold her hands and stop them shaking so much…

"They think it's Lyme disease," Rob explains.

"Isn't that the thing you get from ticks?" Ali asks.

"Yeah," Sam replies, turning back to her and going to stand by Tess, while glaring at me once more. For some reason Sam seems to be bothered by me paying her too much attention, so I focus on him instead, while Rob explains what's been going on with Jasmine. After a few moments, Ali nestles into Sam, and rests her head on his shoulder. I guess they're all pretty tired, and he puts his arm around her, pulling her close, before he puts his finger underneath her chin and raises her face to his, kissing her, just gently. I glance at Rob and notice that he's smiling, and I'm not surprised. Sam's never been one to display his affections in public, so that was kinda nice to see.

As Rob finishes explaining about Jasmine, Tess looks up again. "Is she okay?" she asks. "The little girl, I mean?"

"She's getting better," I reply quickly. "They're hoping she'll be out of the hospital in a couple of days."

"And Jasmine?" Sam asks.

Rob looks over at him again. "I've told her to take all the time she needs," he says. "And I've told her we'll still pay her... She was worried."

Sam nods his head. "Good." He seems to hesitate, then adds, "If Jasmine hasn't been here, how have you managed out front?"

I glance over at Rob, because I don't know how much he wants to tell Sam about Petra. We haven't talked about it – again, because I've only seen him at work since he and Petra got together, so there hasn't been the time. Between running this place and his sex life, we've both been too busy. "It's been fine," I say.

Sam looks from Rob to me and back again and then opens his mouth. Knowing Sam, he's probably going to yell at Rob, or me, or both of us.

"I need to speak to you," Rob puts in, before Sam can even speak. "You and Ed."

I wasn't expecting that. And I don't think Sam was either and we exchange a quick glance.

"I'll take Tess upstairs," Ali says, taking Rob's not very subtle hint that this conversation needs to be between the three of us. "We're both really tired. We could do with having a coffee and putting our feet up for half an hour."

Sam hands her his keys. "Okay," he says, "let yourself in. You know where everything is." He pulls Ali into a hug and whispers something to her.

She leans back, looking up at him, and says, "That's fine with me. I think I'd prefer it that way. I don't want a fuss." She nods at Tess.

"Sure?" he asks.

"Yes." She kisses him on the cheek, then turns to Tess and offers her hand, which Tess accepts. "Come on," Ali says. "Let's leave them to it."

I take a step forward. "Do you need any help with your bags?" I suggest. I don't want Tess to leave – or if she has to, I want to go with her.

"It's fine." Sam's beside me in an instant. "I'll take them up later."

I hide my disappointment as well as I can, although I'm aware of Sam watching me, even as Tess and Ali go out through the kitchen door.

"Okay..." he says as soon as their footsteps have faded on the stairs up to his apartment. "What aren't you telling me?"

"It's nothing bad," Rob says quickly

"It honestly isn't," I add, defending him.

"Now I'm really worried." Sam looks down at us, his expression slightly threatening.

I don't know what to say and I feel like the ball's in Rob's court. He asked to speak to us, so he needs to start this off. He sucks in a deep breath. "Petra's been helping out," he says, looking at Sam.

"Petra? The photographer?" Sam's surprised.

"Yeah. She'd done some waitressing before and she offered to lend a hand," Rob explains.

"But who's been running the restaurant?" Sam asks.

"Petra."

"And she's been doing a really good job of it," I say quickly, because Sam seems doubtful about the whole thing. "She's a real hit with the customers, and all the other staff really like her."

Sam looks at me for a moment, then nods his head. "Okay."

"There's something else..." Rob adds and Sam focuses back on him again. "Petra and I are together."

"I'm not entirely surprised by that." Sam's smirking now, although how he had any clue about Petra, I have no idea. Unless Ali told him that Rob texted her, asking for Petra's contact details and he's put two and two together, and actually made four, for once in his life.

"Yeah..." Rob continues, "but what might surprise you is, she's got a four year old daughter, called April, and... she's married."

Sam stares at him, his face darkening. "Petra's married?"

"Only on paper," Rob replies. A look passes between them, and I wonder if it's got anything to do with their earlier conversation when Sam arrived. There's a lot going on today that I don't understand, but to be honest, the only thing that interests me right now is Tess and whether she's okay. "Her husband didn't treat her very well…" *What?* I listen up and move toward him. He didn't tell me that bit, and I wonder how long he's known… "And he left her before April was born," Rob says. "They didn't divorce at the time, because they couldn't afford it. But they're getting divorced now…"

"Because of you?" Sam asks him.

"Because her husband wants to re-marry," Rob explains.

Sam nods. "Sounds like you've had an interesting couple of weeks," he replies, his face clearing, and a smile forming on his lips.

"You could put it that way…" Rob hesitates, like he's nervous, which isn't like him at all. "The thing is, I have a favor to ask of both of you."

Sam stands up straight and crosses his arms. He's a couple of inches taller than Rob and I, and he knows this makes him look more intimidating. I'm just waiting to hear what Rob's got to say, because I don't have a clue.

"I doubt you're gonna like this," Rob begins, "but please just hear me out… What Ed said is completely true. Petra's really good at running this place, and she is a hit with the customers… So, I was wondering how you'd feel about her carrying on here, working with me, maybe a couple of evenings a week."

Sam turns to look at me and I notice there's a slight twinkle in his eye. He wants to have some fun with this, and I've got a good mind to let him, for once. This makes sense of Rob's conversation with me earlier. He was clearly trying to sound me out about Petra working here in the future – although why the hell he couldn't just ask me, I don't know. Rob sighs. "I know we've spent a lot of money on this place the in the last couple of months," he says, sounding a little desperate now, "but I really want this, guys. I'm in love with her, and it's gonna be real hard not seeing anything of her from breakfast until midnight. If we can just do this…"

I'm useless at this kind of thing. He's my brother. Even more than that, he's my twin. I can't watch him suffer, even if Sam can. "Oh, put him out of his misery, Sam." I smile across at him.

"Of course she can work here," Sam says, going over and slapping Rob quite hard on the back. "And I do get the whole thing about missing her during the day. That's why Ali's gonna be working in the kitchens whenever she can. I don't wanna miss seeing her either. I'm real happy for you... although what that poor woman sees in you is beyond me. And what she's doing letting a reprobate like you near her daughter is anyone's guess, but if this is what you want, then you got it."

I love it when Sam's like this. He can be a miserable grouch sometimes, but when he's happy, when he's being kind and generous – which is the real Sam, the one before his ex-wife messed with his head – he's a great guy to have in your corner. I should know; he's been in mine for years now...

"You say that," Rob continues, "but just wait until you meet her..."

"I've already met her..." Sam replies. "Well, I've seen her, anyway. She was here at the opening."

"No, I mean April," Rob explains. Even I haven't had that privilege yet. "She'll have you eating out of her hand within minutes... And being as you'll both be her uncles—"

Uncles. I knew he was gonna ask Petra to marry him, but I hadn't thought about being an uncle. I also didn't think he'd own up to Sam about the proposal... not yet anyway.

"Whoa... wait a second." Sam's staring at him. "Does this mean the divorce isn't entirely for the other guy's benefit? Are you saying marriage is on the cards? The whole ready-made family, and everything?"

"Maybe." Rob shrugs.

"Only maybe?"

"Well, I haven't actually asked her yet."

"But you're going to?"

Rob nods. "It's been a little busy around here the last few days..." He looks over at me and I give him just a hint of a nod. Last weekend was real dramatic for Rob, after Petra's ex – well, her husband, I guess – came into the restaurant and Rob saw them together, being a little more intimate than he felt comfortable with. He and Petra argued, and that was when Rob found out that the guy he thought was her ex is actually still her husband. I think they came close to breaking up over that, but they dealt with it and I guess he doesn't necessarily want Sam to know about it, which means he won't hear it from me. My nod to Rob is just me letting him know that.

Sam turns away from both of us and goes over to the countertop. "It doesn't take that long to propose, you know." He looks at us, smiling. "I think it took me a matter of seconds to propose to Ali…"

"You… you proposed to Ali?" Rob manages to form a sentence, because I can't.

Sam's nodding and grinning at the same time. "Yeah. And before you say anything, I know we haven't been together that long, but this is nothing like Amber."

"We know that," Rob says. "Ali is nothing like your ex."

"No. She isn't."

"I take it she accepted?" Rob's trying not to laugh now.

"Of course she fucking accepted," Sam says, glaring at him. "It took her three weeks, but she said yes."

"Three weeks?" I can't imagine Sam waiting three weeks for anything.

"Yeah. It was a tough decision," he explains.

"I can imagine," Rob jokes.

Sam stares at him and murmurs, "Asshole," under his breath, although we both hear him. "She wasn't just accepting me," he continues, speaking normally again. "She was accepting moving here too, and that meant moving Tess." He looks at us both, but focuses on me. "That's a long story." It's clearly a story that involves Tess, so I'd like to hear it, but he's obviously not going to tell us, and he stands upright again, yawning and stretching his arms above his head, before he looks down at Rob once more. "I hope you're okay covering one more night in here," he says. "Because I have no idea what time of day it is, so I seriously doubt I should be put in charge of anything that we're expecting people to pay to eat."

Rob shakes his head, smiling. "It's fine. We expected that. Petra's coming in tonight."

"She is?" Sam asks.

"Yeah."

"What time?"

Rob thinks for a second. "She's coming in a little before six. She wants to spend as much of the day as she can with April."

"Okay," Sam says. "I'll come down and meet her."

"Be nice to her." There's a warning note in Rob's voice.

Sam walks over toward the double doors, bending to pick up the bags, but then turns back and smiles. "I'm always nice," he says, then he goes out and we look at each other, just as we hear him call out, "Well, I am now."

Rob seems worried now about Sam and Petra meeting and, without even looking at me, he goes out into the restaurant to wait for her.

Left to myself, I wander back toward my own area of the kitchen, the space Ali created for me as part of the refurbishment, where I can do what Sam tells me I do best – namely make desserts. I can't help smiling to myself as I flick the convection ovens on, ready for tonight's service. The last few weeks have been hard work, and kinda lonely, if I'm being honest, and I'm looking forward to the fact that Sam's back and, after tonight, I won't be responsible for this place any longer. I'm really glad that he's brought Ali back with him too, and that they're engaged. They're right for each other, and she belongs here. On top of that, she's a damn good pastry chef. She worked with me for a while before she went back to England, and she's got talent – real talent. So I was glad to hear Sam say she'll be spending some time down here again. Not only can she cook, but she's good to bounce ideas off of.

I'm also really pleased that Rob's told Sam about Petra and that she's gonna still be working here too. Him asking us about that, rather than just doing it and telling us about it afterwards, tells me he's learned his lesson. He brought Ali over here to work on the restaurant without checking it with me and Sam first, and while that may have worked out well in the end, it was kinda ugly to start with. This time, at least he asked. We may be a team, but Rob and I have never disputed the fact that Sam is in charge. We both kinda like it that way and I know Sam will have appreciated Rob asking, rather than just doing, even more than I do. Just with that one gesture, it feels like the pieces of our jigsaw are really back together for the first time in ages. I mean, I obviously miss Rob, now that he's moved out, but we're still together at work, and he's happy; happier than I've ever seen him, so I'm okay with that.

As I get into my own section and make a start on this evening's prep, I'm still smiling. And I know why. I may be happy for my brothers and their girlfriends, and I may be happy that Sam's back, and the three of us are together again, but I've got an even better reason for smiling to myself…

Her name's Tess.

… to be continued

Printed in Great Britain
by Amazon